Through her marriage to Reggie Kray, Roberta Kray has a unique and authentic insight into London's East End. Roberta met Reggie in early 1996 and they married the following year; they were together until Reggie's death in 2000. Roberta is the author of many previous bestsellers including *No Mercy*, *Dangerous Promises, Exposed* and *Survivor.*

Also by Roberta Kray

The Debt
The Pact
The Lost
Strong Women
The Villain's Daughter
Broken Home
Nothing But Trouble
Bad Girl
Streetwise
Dangerous Promises
Exposed
Survivor

Non-fiction
Reg Kray: A Man Apart

ROBERTA KRAY

STOLEN

SPHERE

First published in Great Britain in 2019 by Sphere

1 3 5 7 9 10 8 6 4 2

All characters and events in this publication, other than those clearly in the public domain, are fictitious and any resemblance to real persons, living or dead, is purely coincidental.

A CIP catalogue record for this book is available from the British Library.

ISBN 978-0-7515-6964-3

Typeset in Garamond by M Rules
Printed and bound in Great Britain by
Clays Ltd, Elcograf S.p.A.

Papers used by Sphere are from well-managed forests
and other responsible sources.

www.littlebrown.co.uk

Introduction

In 1958 an event took place that shocked and horrified the country. A baby, Kay Fury, was snatched from the grounds of her family home and her nanny deliberately drowned in the lake. Despite a long investigation, no trace was ever found of Kay.

Two years later, Mal Fury discovered the identity of the abductor and a confrontation took place during which the man, Teddy Heath, was accidentally killed. With the death penalty still in place and fearing that he could be hanged, Mal left the scene without informing the police. The only person he did tell was his wife, Esther, a confidence he later came to regret.

Over the years, the Fury marriage fell apart but the couple stayed together. Mal, against his wife's wishes, took on the guardianship of an East End orphan called Lolly Bruce. They became close and Lolly remains fiercely loyal to him.

Seventeen years after Teddy Heath's death, Esther finally turned on her husband, revealing his secret to the police. Mal was charged and convicted of manslaughter. He's now nearing the end of his sentence and looking forward to the future.

Characters

Lolly Bruce
Originally from the East End, the orphaned Lolly was saved from being taken into care by the intervention of Mal Fury. Now, aged nineteen, she's back in Kellston in the East End of London working on the wrong side of the law. With the past kicking at her heels, she'll have to keep her wits about her. She's experienced privilege but it's street smarts she'll need in order to stay safe.

Mal Fury
Mal, Lolly's guardian, is currently serving a prison sentence for the manslaughter of the man who abducted his child. Once a successful jeweller, his life is in tatters. He's clinging to the hope, however, that Kay may still be alive, and someone's about to give him further reason to believe it.

Esther Fury
Mal's beautiful, spoiled and selfish wife is moving on, putting the past (and her husband) behind her. At least that's the plan. She's used to getting her own way but she's going to find out that there are some things she simply can't control.

Nick Trent

Nick's uncle, Stanley Parrish, was once employed to help track down Kay Fury. Now a private investigator himself, Nick knows better than to get dragged into the case that resulted in his uncle's death. But his better judgement doesn't count for much when it comes to helping Lolly. If she needs him, he'll be there.

Heather Grant

Heather, a young reporter, makes a living out of uncovering other people's secrets, but she also has secrets of her own. As she delves into the history of the Furys, examining their pain and loss, her own demons quickly rise to the surface.

Jude Rule

The handsome, talented, obsessive Jude – Lolly's first love – is now firmly attached to Esther Fury. But is the past about to catch up? Once a suspect in the murder of a teenage girl, the shadow of guilt, at least in Lolly's eyes, still hangs over him.

Vinnie Keane

Vinnie works for the boss of the East End, Terry Street. A great bear of a man, loyal and tough and built for intimidation, he appears to be indestructible. But there is one chink in his armour. Love could be the undoing of him.

1

1977

Friday 16 September. Kent

Lolly Bruce reached out from the passenger seat and angled the rear-view mirror so she could study her face, peering at her reflection with a combination of intensity and disappointment. Grey eyes, small pink mouth, brown hair swept into a topknot. She sighed. Even with all the effort she made, her make-up carefully applied, she felt she never quite pulled it off. There was something in her features that betrayed her, something more East End than West, more Kellston than Mayfair. She had learned how to imitate sophistication but not how to inhabit it.

'Do you have to do that?' Vinnie asked.

'How else am I supposed to see what I look like?'

'You look the same as the last time you checked.'

Lolly gave a snort. 'That was over an hour ago. Women of substance have to pay attention to their appearance.' She applied more lipstick and dabbed at her lips with a tissue. 'All right. I'm ready.'

Vinnie rolled his eyes and then moved the mirror back to where it belonged.

Lolly checked her fake Hermes handbag, made sure the goods were still inside and got out of the car. She took a deep breath and pushed back her shoulders. Posture was everything in this game. Well, that and confidence. She had done this same thing so often but the nerves still got to her.

As she walked towards the shop, Lolly tried to tune in to that sense of entitlement which the monied possessed. *I have every right to be here, every right to be the owner of some very classy jewellery.* The trick was to look the part – cashmere twinset, pearls, heels – and to sound it too. She could manage the latter without any difficulty. Five years at Daynor Bridge, a public school for girls, had taught her how to speak with a silver spoon in her gob. What it hadn't done, however, was to wipe away all traces of her working-class origins. Acting in a superior fashion didn't come naturally to her and nor did the art of disdain.

Today her name was Anna Carter-West and she had a driving licence to prove it. The licence was as genuine as her handbag. Sometimes they asked for ID and sometimes they didn't, but she always came prepared. Stopping outside the jeweller's, she took a moment to steady herself whilst pretending to study the window display. It didn't do to linger for too long; courage had a habit of draining away.

Inside, the shop glittered with its fancy lighting and pricey displays. Stepping up to the counter, with what she hoped would pass for blue-blooded nonchalance, she gave the man a pleasant smile. 'Good morning.'

'Good morning, miss. How can I help you?'

Lolly took one of the small velvet-lined boxes from her handbag. 'I have a ring,' she said. 'It belonged to my grandmother.

I'm not sure if I want to sell it or not but . . . Perhaps you could tell me how much it's worth.'

The man was in his forties, small and dapper with a thin face and narrow moustache. He took the box and opened it, his gaze flicking between the ring and Lolly. 'Antique,' he said, removing the ring and examining it. 'A ruby. Very nice.' He put a tiny magnifying glass to his eye and examined the hallmark. 'Eighteen carat gold.'

Lolly knew all this already but nodded anyway. 'And its value?'

The man hesitated. 'Your grandmother's, you say?'

'That's right. She passed away a few years ago. As I mentioned, I don't really want to sell it but . . .' Lolly assumed a suitably sad expression. She knew from experience that it was wise to keep things simple and not embroider the story.

'If you could just give me a couple of minutes, I'll get my colleague. He's the expert on precious gems.'

As he withdrew into the rear of the shop, ring in hand, Lolly had one of those alarm bell moments. Had he looked at her oddly? Why hadn't he left the ring on the counter? Why was her heart beating like a jackhammer? None of this felt right, and if it felt wrong it probably was. The final confirmation of this came when she thought she heard the ting of a phone being lifted. Had she? She wasn't sure. *Damn it!* The bastard could be calling the law.

She had to make a quick decision. If she did a runner, she'd have to leave the ring behind, but if she stayed he might try and keep her talking until the police arrived. How long would that take? Five minutes? Ten? Unless there was a patrol car in the district, in which case . . .

Lolly looked over her shoulder and out of the window. It was a busy road with lots of traffic. Vinnie was parked around the corner, out of sight. She was reluctant to abandon the ring – it was worth a few hundred – and Terry Street wouldn't be happy if she came back empty handed, but she didn't fancy getting nicked.

Stay or go? She had a bad feeling, chill fingers running down her spine. Perhaps it was best to cut her losses. At least she hadn't handed over both the rings. The more expensive one, a large diamond, was still in her bag. She was always cautious when she was flogging dodgy gear, testing the waters with a less valuable item first in case the buyer became suspicious.

Lolly was counting off the seconds now. If the law did come, she'd be caught in possession of two stolen rings. Not so easy to explain. She peered towards the back of the shop – still nothing – and made a decision. Her gut was telling her to scarper and so that's exactly what she did. Instinct was what propelled her out of the door and back onto the street, breaking into a run as soon as her feet hit the pavement.

Vinnie saw her coming and had the engine started when she was still twenty yards away. She jumped into the passenger seat and slammed shut the door. 'Drive!' she ordered, like some cliché of a bank robber fleeing the scene of the crime. 'Let's go! Get out of here!'

Vinnie took off with little regard for the cars behind and in front of him. He sped down the road, swung a right and was half a mile from the shop before he turned his head and said, 'Take it that didn't go too well, then?'

'He knew something was off. Disappeared out back with the ring and the next thing I know he's on the bleedin' phone, isn't he?' Lolly had automatically dropped back into her everyday voice. 'I didn't hang around for the law to show up.'

'They've got wise to you, love. Maybe word has got around.'

Lolly thought he could be right. She supposed she'd had a

good run, over a year now, but she couldn't afford to lose the income. Once a month or so, she and Vinnie left London and travelled out to the surrounding counties to try and offload some of Terry's more valuable acquisitions. For everything she shifted, she got ten per cent. Away from the capital, jewellers tended to be more trusting – or maybe just more gullible. 'Could be a one-off. Perhaps he's the suspicious sort.'

'You want to try somewhere else?'

She shook her head. Sometimes, when luck wasn't with you, you simply had to accept it. 'No, not today. I don't want to tempt providence.'

'So the ruby's gone for a burton?'

'I could have lost them both if I'd stayed,' she snapped defensively.

'All right, no need to bite me head off. I'm sure Terry will understand. Easy come, easy go, right?'

'You think?'

Vinnie barked out a laugh. 'Nah, he'll be well pissed off.'

And she knew he was right. She would have to get her story straight, perhaps embellish it a bit, before they got back to London. If Terry reckoned she'd panicked, overreacted, he might jump to the conclusion she was losing her nerve. Perhaps she was. Perhaps, at this very moment, the salesman and his colleague were standing behind the counter, ready to offer her a wad of cash and wondering where the hell she'd disappeared to. It wouldn't take them long to put two and two together.

She wound down the window – it was a balmy autumn day – and thought some more about Terry. On the whole, their relationship was an amicable one. It went back six years to when she'd been a skinny thirteen-year-old, orphaned and living with Brenda Cecil at the pawnbroker's. Terry had recruited Lolly to run errands for him. In those days he'd been working for the gangland boss, Joe Quinn, but Joe was long gone. Terry was the boss now.

The air blew through the car, freeing fine strands of hair from her carefully constructed topknot. She watched the Kentish roads go by. From the moment she'd woken up this morning she'd had one of those dread feelings in the pit of her stomach, like something bad was going to happen. A premonition? She wasn't sure if she believed in that kind of stuff. But perhaps that was why she'd reacted like she had in the shop, anticipating disaster even before it had occurred.

In all the time she'd been working with Vinnie, she'd never been caught. A few close shaves but nothing that came near to an arrest. She glanced over at him. Vinnie Keane was a great bear of a man, about six foot five, and built for intimidation. When it came to trouble, he didn't have to lift a finger. One look was all it took to frighten off even the stupidest of people. She couldn't claim they were friends, exactly – he was much older than her – but the two of them got along okay.

Her gaze flicked back to the road again, and it was then she saw the sign for West Henby.

On impulse, she said, 'Turn right, here, at the junction.'

'What for?'

'There's something I want to see.'

'Huh?'

'It won't take long. A quick detour. What's the matter? You in a hurry to tell Terry the good news about how it all went wrong and we lost his ring?'

'What's with the "we"? I'm just the driver.'

Lolly pulled a face. 'So much for solidarity. I thought you were supposed to have my back.'

Vinnie smirked, but did as he was asked and turned right onto the smaller road. It was another ten minutes before they came to the village of West Henby. She looked out of the window at the place that had once been so familiar to her. In the year since she'd last been here, nothing much had changed. Why would it have done? There were the same bustling streets, pubs and shops.

'Keep going,' she said. 'Straight through the village and then follow the road round.'

'What are we doing here?'

'Taking a trip down memory lane.'

Vinnie flicked the ash from his cigarette out of the window. 'Always glad to oblige,' he said drily. 'Where do you fancy next, your ladyship – the Riviera, New York?'

Lolly ignored him. 'Slow down. We're almost there. Okay, just beyond that tree. On the left. The gates. Do you see them? You can stop there.'

Vinnie pulled up, keeping the engine running. Lolly wound down the window and gazed along the long curving drive. It wasn't possible to see the house from here but she could see it in her mind's eye: a grand, three-storey white building with a central flight of steps and two big flower pots like Ali Baba jars flanking either side. And behind it, the grounds, including the wide, cold lake with its bulrushes and weeping willows.

'What are we looking at, exactly?'

'The past,' she said. 'This is where I used to live.'

'All right for some.'

Lolly could have told him that it hadn't been an easy time, that it was never straightforward being the cuckoo in someone else's nest, but it would have sounded self-pitying. Anyway, she wasn't in the mood for confidences. Mal Fury had taken her in after her mother's suicide, become her guardian when she was thirteen, and his wife had been less than happy about it. The only child Esther had wanted was her own, the baby that had been abducted all those years before. No one knew whether Kay was still alive or if she'd drowned in the lake on the day she was snatched.

Lolly wasn't sure how she felt about being back. Not nostalgic so much as . . . as what? The emotions she felt were strange, ambivalent. She had grown to love Mal – the only father figure she'd ever known – but her relationship with Esther had always been strained. Lolly's teenage years, enhanced by Mal's kindness, had been simultaneously blighted by the dark shadow of Esther's contempt.

'We done here?' Vinnie asked.

Lolly was about to nod when the thin wail of a baby's cry, plaintive and piercing, floated through the air. The hairs on the back of her neck stood on end. She sucked in a breath, her eyes widening. Where was it coming from? There were no other houses close by, and visitors never brought children here.

'Do you hear that?' she asked, turning to Vinnie.

'Hear what?'

'A baby. A baby crying.'

Vinnie shook his head. 'I didn't hear nothin'.'

'You must have. Turn the engine off.'

Vinnie obliged, and they both listened. Silence. He raised his eyebrows. Lolly frowned and got out of the car. She went up to the gates and pressed her face against the metal scrolls. She listened some more, straining her ears. Just the sound of the breeze rustling through the trees. Esther was the only person living here now, along with the staff. Mal's current digs were less salubrious: a small cramped cell in a London prison.

She peered along the empty drive, shivering in spite of the sun. Had she heard it? Perhaps it had just been a figment of her imagination, something dredged up from her subconscious.

The locals said this place was haunted, but then the locals said a lot of things.

Lolly didn't want to hang about in case Esther caught her. She retreated to the car, still none the wiser. 'Okay, I'm done here.'

'Feeling homesick?' Vinnie asked as he set off again.

Lolly glanced over her shoulder. 'No, just curious.' If home was where the heart was, then Kellston was probably more home than here. But she didn't really belong there either. She was one of those people caught between two worlds and at the moment both of them were rattling her nerves.

2

Friday 16 September. Kellston, East London

Lolly saw Terry Street as soon as she walked into the Fox. He was sitting in the same place he always sat, the place Joe Quinn had always occupied too – over on the left from where he had a good view not only of everyone coming in but of the whole pub. She wasn't looking forward to the meeting. He was expecting a wedge and he was getting nothing – minus nothing if you counted the ruby ring she'd had to abandon.

Vinnie cleared off to the bar, leaving her to it. She gave the news to Terry quickly, omitting the part about how she'd panicked and concentrating instead on the fact she'd been absolutely certain she'd been sussed.

'I could tell from the way he was looking at me. And when he cleared off with the ring . . . I didn't have a choice. It was stay and get collared or get the hell out of there.'

'You didn't try anywhere else?'

Lolly shook her head. 'I was thinking that maybe they've circulated a description. I'll have to change the way I look, change my story. Someone must have sussed me. Perhaps we need to go further out, get further from London.'

Terry didn't look impressed. 'Perhaps it's time to call it a day.'

But Lolly couldn't afford to lose the extra income, whatever the risks. It was what enabled her to survive. 'No, not yet. I don't think so. Give me a few days and I'll sort something out.'

It worried her that he might think she'd turned him over, concocting the story about the salesman. Vinnie could hardly corroborate the tale. For all he knew, she could have gone into the shop, flogged the ring and then dashed back to the car. Did Terry trust her? She hoped so, but you couldn't really trust anyone in his game.

'Sorry,' she said.

Terry pursed his lips. 'At least you hung on to the diamond.'

'I'll shift it, I promise.'

Lolly had the impulse to apologise some more but fought against it. She looked at Terry, remembering him as he'd been six years ago, cheeky and confident with big ambitions. Well, he'd got what he wanted: Kellston was his manor now, along with most of the East End and some of the West End too. He was smart, good-looking, dark-haired and dark-eyed, with a lot of charm. What set him apart from other men, however, was that indefinable quality that can only be described as charisma. When he walked into a room, everyone looked. When he spoke, everyone listened. It didn't do to underestimate him. Like most men in positions of power, he had a ruthless streak.

'Not losing your nerve are you, Lolly?'

She smiled and held his gaze. 'You know me, Terry, nerves of steel.'

'Good. Glad to hear it. Only I wouldn't like to—'

Lolly never got the chance to hear what he wouldn't like as at that very moment Vinnie came over. 'Sorry, boss, but I need a word.'

It was only then, as Terry rose to his feet, that Lolly became aware of the change in atmosphere in the pub. Something had happened. There was a frisson in the air, a charge like electricity. She tried to eavesdrop on the two men but Vinnie was leaning in close, almost whispering in Terry's ear. Seconds later they both took off.

Lolly, realising she still had the diamond ring in her possession, stood up to follow them but then changed her mind. Instead she made her way over to the bar. People were huddled in groups, exchanging information, passing comment. There was an urgency about the exchanges, a sense of both horror and excitement. She caught snatches of their talk, enough for her to gather that someone was dead. And not through any natural causes. She caught the barmaid's eye and beckoned her over.

'What's going on? Do you know?'

'It's bad. They've just found one of the girls, round the back of the station, at the arches.'

Lolly felt her heart lurch. It had to be one of Terry's girls – no one else was allowed to work round here – and instantly she thought of Stella. 'Do they know who it is?'

The barmaid shook her head. 'Not yet.'

'And is she definitely—'

But someone was waiting for a drink so that was as much as Lolly got out of the barmaid. She turned around and quickly forged a path through the crowd to the door. Outside there was an obvious police presence with a line of squad cars, lights flashing, heading for the scene of the crime. She watched them for a while before moving off in the opposite direction.

Lolly's mouth was dry as she crossed over, dodging the traffic, and hurried towards Albert Road. *Please God, don't let it be Stella.* They had first met when Lolly was a kid working for Terry. The house, a brothel, had been a place of sanctuary after her mum died, somewhere she could be with friendly faces for a while before returning home – if it could even be called that – to the awfulness of Brenda Cecil and her sons.

There was no reason for Stella to be at the arches. Why would she be? She wasn't a streetwalker. She worked out of the house, a relatively safe environment, with security and other girls to watch her back. Only the desperate used the arches, the junkies and the destitute. It was a dark and desolate place.

Usually Albert Road was flanked by kerb crawlers who wouldn't leave you alone but today, even though the body had only recently been found, there wasn't a car in sight. News travelled fast, and with so many cops in the area, the punters were keeping their distance. Lolly couldn't remember the last time she'd walked this way and not been harassed.

She dashed up to the house and rang the bell. She waited. No one answered. Anxiously, she jumped from one foot to the other. Where was everyone? There was nearly always someone in. She rang again and rapped on the door. 'Come on, come on,' she muttered. The suspense was killing her. She winced at the thought. Jesus, that was the wrong expression to use. *Please don't let it be Stella.* Reason told her it couldn't be, wouldn't be, but that didn't stop the fear from rolling over her in waves.

Finally, the door was answered by a redhead called Michelle. If she was surprised to see Lolly standing there in twinset and pearls, she didn't show it. Perhaps she was used to unusual sights or just had other things on her mind.

'Hi,' she said.

Lolly nodded, her heart in her mouth. 'Is Stella here?'

Michelle paused, one of those millisecond hesitations that made Lolly's blood run cold. *Oh, Christ.* She tried to prepare herself for the worst, but then the girl stepped back and gestured towards the rear of the house. 'She's in the kitchen.'

As Lolly went inside she raised a hand to her chest in relief. 'Ta,' she croaked. 'Thank God for that.'

'You've heard then?'

'Just now. I was in the Fox. I thought ... Do you know who it is?'

'Not yet, but Stella thinks it could be Dana.'

'What?' Lolly hadn't known Dana well – she was a fairly recent addition to the house – but the news still rattled her.

'I don't *think* it's Dana,' Stella said as they entered the kitchen. 'I know it. Why else hasn't she come back?' She gave Lolly a grim smile. 'Hello, love.'

'Hey, how are you?'

'Just waiting for the law to get here.'

Michelle shook her head. 'We don't know nothin' yet. Dana could be anywhere. Just 'cause she didn't come back last night don't mean—'

But Stella wasn't having any of it. 'It's her.' She pulled on the joint she was smoking, her eyes full of dismay. 'I can feel it. I've got the shivers all over.'

Lolly sat down across the table from her. She reached out and briefly covered Stella's hand with her own. 'Michelle's right. You can't be sure. Not yet.'

'I *am* sure. She'd be here otherwise, wouldn't she? She'd have called or something.'

'She could have had a skinful, stayed over with a mate,' Michelle said.

'She doesn't have any mates.'

'She wasn't working last night, then?' Lolly asked.

Stella shook her head. 'She went out about six. We don't know where.'

'She wouldn't go near the arches, though, would she? I mean, what would she be doing there?'

As though she couldn't bear to be still, Stella suddenly stood up, paced from one side of the kitchen to the other, walked over to the sink and leaned with her back against it. She smoked some more, taking long deep drags. Her outfit – a white mini-skirt, boots and electric-blue boob tube – seemed curiously at odds with the oppressive atmosphere of the room. 'Fuck knows. Maybe someone just took her there and . . . ' She swallowed hard, blinking two or three times as if to wipe away the picture that had just sprung into her head. 'You shouldn't hang about, Lol. You don't want to be here when the filth show up.'

'I don't care. It doesn't make any difference to me.'

But Stella was adamant. 'No, you push off. You don't want to get dragged into this. You know what those bastards are like; they'll have you down the station just for the fun of it.'

Lolly always tried to avoid the attention of the police, but some things were more important than keeping a low profile. 'They're not going to be interested in me.'

'I'm not on my own, hon. I've got Michelle here, and the others will be back soon. They've only gone to see what they can find out. Go on, you go home. I'll see you soon, yeah?'

Lolly was aware that in some ways Stella still thought of her as a child she had to protect, a kid who needed taking care of. But reluctantly she nodded, knowing that the older woman had enough to worry about without adding her to the mix. 'Okay, if you're sure, only—'

'I'm sure,' Stella said insistently. She made a flapping motion with her hand, wafting the smell of dope in Lolly's direction. 'Go on. We'll be fine.'

Lolly felt guilty leaving – she didn't believe Stella would be fine at all – but did as she was told. As she stepped onto the pavement, she glanced up and down Albert Road. It was still deserted. Not a car in sight, and not a single tom either. She began to walk, shivers running through her as she thought about Dana.

Violent death, although it filled her with fear and disgust, no longer shocked her. She had seen her mum's body, bloodied and broken, after she'd jumped from the top floor of Carlton House. That dreadful image could never be erased. Not long after, there had been Amy Wiltshire, killed at sixteen. And bad things didn't just happen in deprived, rundown places like Kellston. The Furys' baby, Kay, had been snatched from the grounds of the house in West Henby, and the nanny murdered. She thought again about that cry she'd heard, wondering if her mind had just been playing tricks.

Lolly had reached the corner and was about to turn onto Station Road when the cop car went past. She paused to follow it with her eyes, willing it not to stop outside Stella's. But as she watched the indicator light went on and the car pulled up outside the house. Her heart sank. Stella had been right. For a moment she thought about going back, but what good would it do? Instead she murmured a quick prayer and headed for home.

3

Friday 16 September. Kellston

Lolly got out of her good clothes, hung them carefully on hangers and changed into jeans and a black T-shirt. She made a cup of coffee and took it through to the living room where she sat down at the table by the window. To the left, wedged against the sill, were a couple of boxes, one containing various articles of jewellery, the other old watches in need of attention. Spread out in front of her were the pieces from a broken clock. She made a bit of cash from these repairs and restorations, but mainly they were a labour of love. She liked taking things apart and putting them back together the way Mal Fury had taught her.

She was hoping work would take her mind off the horror – there was something soothing, distracting about all the intricate parts – but her thoughts, refusing to be still, were bouncing around in every direction. There were some days that were so relentlessly bad, you regretted ever having got up in the morning. And hadn't she felt it, right from breakfast, that sense of impending disaster?

Lolly sipped her coffee and gazed down at the cars and buses going by. Her rented flat, above an Indian takeaway, was small but serviceable and she had made it comfortable. Everything in it was cheap or second-hand, bought from the market and charity shops, but that didn't matter to her. She didn't mind the traffic on the high street or the spicy smells that floated on the air of an evening. To her the flat was a refuge, a sanctuary, a place to call home.

Although she always expected the worst – experience had taught her to be prepared – the past year had gone comparatively well. But she had the feeling all that was about to change. An ill wind, wasn't that what they called it? Already it was blowing round her ears. She tried not to dwell on Dana, but it wasn't easy. She lifted her gaze to the sky where a plane was rising through the blue leaving a long white trail behind it.

Her eyes were still fixed on this when the doorbell went, two long rings. Could it be Stella? She quickly rose to her feet and hurried downstairs. As soon as she opened the door, her heart jumped into her mouth. Two uniformed cops were standing there. She thought of the stolen diamond ring sitting in her bag and her mouth went dry.

'Lolita Bruce?' the older of the two men asked.

It was a long time since she had heard anyone use her full name. She nodded, wondering if she looked as anxious as she felt. 'That's me. What is it? What—?'

'I'm Sergeant Glass, this is PC Carraway.' He flashed a warrant card in front of her. 'Would you mind if we came in?'

Lolly wasn't overjoyed by the prospect of having the law in her flat but could hardly refuse without looking like she had something to hide. 'Okay. Yes, of course.'

As she walked up the stairs in front of them, she tried not to panic. She made a fast, mental inventory of everything that was on the table. Was there anything dodgy on display? Occasionally, she would buy the odd damaged piece off Terry, a ring or a necklace, and restyle it into something new.

Lolly gestured towards the sofa in the living room. 'Sit down, please.' She only had one other chair, the one by the table, and she turned that around to face them. 'So what is it? What's going on?'

The sergeant had her fixed in his stare, his eyes boring into her. 'I understand Mal Fury is your guardian. Is that correct?'

Lolly's worries about being arrested or caught in possession of stolen property quickly evaporated, replaced by a colder, hard-edged fear. Instantly, she stiffened. 'Mal? Yes, that's right. What's happened?' Even as she was speaking her imagination was running riot, creating nightmare scenarios where he had dropped dead of a heart attack or been stabbed by some con with a grudge. 'Is he . . . is he all right?'

'We were hoping you could tell us that.'

'I'm sorry?'

'When was the last time you heard from him?'

Lolly frowned. 'I saw him a couple of weeks ago. Look, what's going on here? Why are you asking me . . . I don't understand.'

'Mr Fury failed to return to prison after work yesterday. It appears that he's absconded.'

'What?' Lolly said again. She shook her head, gave a mirthless laugh. 'That can't be right. He can't have. Why would he do that? He's out in a few months, a free man.' She was aware of the two cops watching her closely, but she didn't need to fake a reaction. 'That's crazy! It's just . . . Are you sure?'

'Did he have any worries that you were aware of, anything on his mind?'

'No, nothing. He was fine.' Mal had been serving the last part of his sentence at an open prison, working on a local farm and glad to be breathing fresh air again. She thought back to the visit, trying to remember if anything had been said, the slightest clue as to why he'd scarper, but she came up with a blank. 'There's no reason why he'd do this. It doesn't make any sense.'

The younger cop, Carraway, finally opened his mouth. 'And his plans for the future. What were those exactly?'

Lolly shrugged. 'The same as anyone else's: pick himself up, start again.'

'He's a jeweller, right?'

'Yes.' It was then Lolly recalled Mal talking about Antwerp, about how he might go there for a while, but she didn't mention this to the cops. Anyway, how would he get out of the country without a passport? 'That's what he was going to do, go back into the business, maybe open a new store eventually.'

'An expensive business to be in,' Glass said.

'I suppose.' She wasn't quite sure what he was getting at, maybe that Mal was rich enough to disappear without a trace. But she just couldn't get her head round *why* Mal had done it. With so little time left to serve, it was utter madness.

'Can you think of anywhere he might go?'

'No,' she said quickly. 'No, I can't think of anywhere.'

'You don't mind if we have a quick look around?'

Lolly stared at Sergeant Glass, her forehead scrunching into a frown. 'You can't think he'd come here. Why would he? He'd know you'd check. This is the last place he'd show up.'

But Glass was already on his feet. 'It's just routine.'

Lolly could have asked if he had a search warrant, but decided it was easier to get it over and done with. 'Go ahead. Help yourself.'

The two officers completed their search in less time than it took to boil an egg. There was no rear exit and the flat wasn't big enough to hide a cat, never mind a human being. Carraway emerged from the bedroom with disappointment written all over him, as though he'd expected to find Mal under the bed or huddled in the wardrobe. But it was Glass she was more concerned about. After checking the kitchen, he returned to the living room and hovered by the table, his jackdaw eyes drawn to the boxes. He reached out and poked a finger into one, delving between the items, looking for . . . for what? For something that might be on a list of stolen property, perhaps.

'It's just old stuff,' she said, perhaps a tad too defensively. 'I do it up and sell it.'

Eventually, he turned. 'You do know it's an offence to withhold information? If you have any knowledge as to Mal Fury's whereabouts—'

'I don't,' she said. 'I'm not withholding anything. I swear. I don't have a clue where he is. And I don't understand why he's done this. He must be ill, confused. He can't be thinking straight.'

Glass's face was thin, pinched-looking, as if the world and its lies pressed in on him. 'If he gets in touch, let us know. He's not doing himself any favours.'

'Of course,' Lolly said, although of course she wouldn't.

She showed them out, closed the door and went back upstairs. Immediately she went over to the window and looked up and down the street, her gaze searching the passing faces, wondering if Mal was around somewhere. What had possessed him? Something must have happened, something she didn't know about. If he was smart, he'd stay well away from Kellston.

She wondered if the law would put her under surveillance, hoping she'd make contact with him. With the murder at the arches, they might not have the manpower. Surely *that* was more important than tracking down an escaped prisoner who wasn't a danger to anyone. But then again, Mal's trial had been a high-profile one and his escape was likely to be all over the papers. The cops would want to grab him as soon as possible.

Lolly folded her arms across her chest. She didn't know what to do, but doing nothing didn't feel like an option. Her gaze fell on the phone box on the corner. She needed someone to talk to, someone to help her make sense of what had happened. Grabbing her purse, she dug out a handful of change and slipped it into her back pocket.

As she crossed the road, she kept her eyes peeled for a sign she was being watched but couldn't spot anything obvious. That didn't mean they weren't there, though. Someone could be watching from a window or a car. Maybe they would think she was calling Mal. Well, they'd be wrong.

She dialled the number for Nick Trent, but only got his answering machine. 'Hey, it's me,' she said. 'Can you drop by when you have a minute?' She paused and then added, 'It's about Mal.'

Lolly put the phone down, then picked it up again and called Stella. It rang and rang but nobody answered.

4

Friday 16 September. Dalston, London

Nick Trent got out of the car to stretch his legs and breathe in some diesel-laden London air. Surveillance could be a tedious business with lots of time spent twiddling your thumbs or sitting in traffic jams. For the past week he'd been tailing a man called Blake Sandler, a nasty bastard in his forties, a solicitor with links to organised crime and the National Front. The bloke also had a penchant for prostitutes.

Nick had no idea who the client was. His bosses, Marshall & Marshall, were two ex-cops who employed him to do as he was told and not ask too many questions. If he were to hazard a guess he would probably plump for the wife, looking to gather evidence before she began divorce proceedings. But then again it could be a business partner – the man had his fingers in lots of pies – or someone he'd crossed who wanted the dirt on him. There was always plenty of dirt when it came to the likes of Sandler.

The solicitor walked a fine line between law and criminality. He had bent coppers in his pocket, and drank with gangsters, thieves and lowlifes. He was the sort who could arrange for a jury to be nobbled or for witnesses to disappear. Bail was never a problem when Sandler was on the case.

Nick was parked up near a block of offices on the Kingsland Road at the Dalston end. Sandler had gone inside ten minutes before and there was no saying how long he'd be. There was no knowing who he'd gone to see either; the block had over twenty businesses in it. All Nick could do was be patient and wait. Despite hours of practice, patience still didn't come easily.

He was about to get back in the car when he noticed the red Mini parked ten yards behind him. Something clicked in his head. He was sure it wasn't the first time he'd seen it today. There was a girl with cropped fair hair sitting inside and she quickly turned her face away when he glanced over at her. So, he had company. Not a cop, he reckoned. Maybe another private investigator, but he didn't think so. Not unless she was a rookie. If he'd clocked her, it wouldn't be too long before Sandler did too. And that could be a problem. If he realised he was under surveillance, it would blow the whole job.

The little red Mini was distinctive, not like the battered white Ford he was driving. During a prolonged tail, both the car and the driver were frequently changed in order to minimise the risk. He made a decision, a quick one, sauntered over to the Mini and tapped on the window.

The blonde stared at him suspiciously before cracking open the window an inch.

'Yes?'

He leaned down. 'Sorry to bother you, but I was just wondering why you're following Mr Sandler.'

'I'm not.'

'So, it's just a coincidence, then, that I keep seeing you everywhere I go?' This was a slight exaggeration, but he wanted her to know that she'd been well and truly sussed.

The girl, who was extraordinarily pretty – wide grey eyes, porcelain skin – gave him a pitying smile. 'You're not much of a detective.'

'Meaning?'

'Meaning just that,' she said. 'It's *you* I've been following.'

Nick, who hadn't expected this particular answer, gave a start. 'Me?'

'You're Nick Trent, aren't you?'

'Yes, and you are?'

'Heather,' she said. 'Heather Grant. I want to talk to you about something.'

'I have a phone. I'm in the book. You could have called.'

'I hadn't made my mind up.'

'So you just thought you'd follow me around for a while?'

'Pretty much,' she said, as if it was the most normal thing in the world.

'You don't think that's a little strange?'

'No stranger than you following some random bloke.'

She had a point, he supposed. Nick had one eye on the office block while this exchange was taking place. He didn't want to be caught on the hop if Sandler suddenly appeared. 'And have you made up your mind yet?'

'You've kind of forced the issue, but . . . What time do you knock off?'

'About six. Would you mind telling me what this is about?'

She hesitated, clearly still undecided as to how much to share. 'Let's not go into that now. I'll meet you at seven. You know any cafés that are open late?'

Nick said the name of the first place that sprang into his head. 'Connolly's, on Kellston High Street. Do you know it?'

'I'll find it.'

'You could give me a clue before you leave.'

And then Heather Grant said something else he hadn't expected to hear. 'It's about the Fury baby. Your uncle worked on the case, didn't he?'

Nick narrowed his eyes. 'What are you, some kind of reporter?'

'No, I'm not a reporter.'

Then, before he could ask anything else, she wound up the window, started the engine and took off. He stood for a while gazing after her until the Mini disappeared around the corner. *What the hell?* That had come out of the blue. He was both suspicious and intrigued.

Nick went back to his car, got in and thought about it some more. It was over a year now since he'd last opened the file that his late uncle, Stanley Parrish, had left behind. Stanley had worked the Fury case for eleven years, sifting through the details of endless waifs and strays in the vain hope of finding Kay. It was possible, even probable, that the child had died on the day of the abduction – the pram had been found in the lake – but with no definitive proof the search had gone on.

Lolly Bruce had been one of those kids put forward, her origins shadowy enough to make her a candidate. Once it had been established that she wasn't going to be the goose that lay the golden egg, her temporary foster mother, Brenda Cecil, had made plans to dump her in the care system. That was when Mal Fury had stepped in and offered to become her guardian. Why Lolly? She'd been, by all accounts, an unprepossessing thirteen-year-old, small and mousy, with nothing much to recommend her. Or perhaps that was exactly why. Mal could see her future and decided to change it.

In the long run, Nick wasn't sure if Mal had done Lolly a favour or not. He had given her a roof over her head, fed, clothed and educated her, but removed her from her roots.

Now she didn't really know where she belonged. She seemed caught in a curious limbo. Even her name varied depending on where she was and who she was with. Mal's wife Esther had insisted she be called Lita and that was how she'd been known at school and in the Fury household. In Kellston, however, she was always Lolly.

Nick was fond of her, maybe more than fond, and made an effort to keep in touch. She was different to the other girls he knew, sassy and streetwise, tough but vulnerable too. She was a mass of contradictions, sparky and unpredictable. Challenging was probably the word. He grinned. Yeah, that just about summed her up.

He stared at the office block. Sandler charged by the hour so he'd probably stretch out his appointment for as long as possible. His thoughts shifted onto Heather Grant. What was her game? His uncle had come across every con artist and charlatan in the business and left a record in his file. Nick had read through it over and over again, absorbing the details, and he wondered what angle *she* was going to take.

Maybe she wasn't a reporter, or maybe she was. You could never believe what people told you. Her name might not even be Heather Grant. Interest in the Fury case had revived during Mal's trial. A fat reward for information leading to the discovery of the whereabouts of Kay Fury was still on the table, and anyone with an eye for the main chance would be looking to take advantage.

Still, the encounter had perked up an otherwise dull day. Nick liked to think he was smart enough not to be seduced by a pretty face, that he didn't keep his brains in his balls, but he wouldn't be the first man to suffer from an inflated sense of moral superiority. It was all too easy to be blinded by beauty and end up with scrambled eggs for brains.

He wondered why he'd chosen Connolly's as a meeting place. Maybe just the connection to Lolly. She only lived a short distance from the café and it would give him an excuse to drop by and have a chat. It worried him the way she lived, although he never told her that. She wouldn't appreciate it. But he knew she'd become reacquainted with Terry Street, an association unlikely to do her any favours in the long term. Terry only ever looked out for number one. If she wasn't careful she'd end up in the same accommodation as her guardian.

Nick checked his watch – twenty past four – and drummed his fingers on the wheel. How had Heather Grant even known about him? It wasn't as if he'd had anything directly to do with the Fury case. Eighteen months ago, he'd gone looking for answers to his uncle's death, a hit-and-run back in 1971, and started turning over some stones. That was how he'd met Mal Fury and Lolly. No one had ever been prosecuted over the 'accident', but he suspected the late Joe Quinn of being behind it. Stanley, whilst following a lead, had probably stumbled upon something Quinn didn't want exposed and had paid with his life. Nick didn't reckon that something was connected to Kay Fury.

None of this explained why Heather Grant should have an interest in him, and he meant interest in the loosest possible sense. Maybe she'd seen him with Lolly at Mal's trial. Or followed the trail from Stanley. Or . . . Well, he could throw theories around all day and it wouldn't make any difference. He'd find out soon enough.

Nick checked his watch again – twenty-five past four – and turned on the radio. Elvis Presley belting out 'Way Down'. His mum had liked Elvis, much to his father's disgust. His father, of course, disapproved of most things, or at least anything that brought a little joy and happiness into the world. Sadly, his mother had been of that generation who once they'd made their beds felt obliged to lie on them for ever.

The song finished and the news came on. A woman, believed to be a prostitute, had been found murdered in Kellston. Nick, who was in a cynical frame of mind, suspected that it wouldn't have made the headlines had it not been for the Yorkshire Ripper being on the loose. There was a certain attitude in the media, and even amongst the police, that the violent death of a tom was less important than that of a 'respectable' woman, almost as if it was an occupational hazard of the job they chose to do. Although this latest murder was a long way from the Ripper's usual hunting ground, his activities had made it newsworthy. There was slim chance it had been him, but the media never liked to miss an opportunity to scare the shit out of the public.

The radio didn't give the name of the victim. One of Terry's girls probably. He wouldn't be best pleased. And not out of any pity, but purely because someone had destroyed one of his assets. That's all the girls were to him, profit and loss, figures on a sheet. He'd want the bastard caught, though, just in case it became a habit.

Nick had been a cop once, although his career had been so short you only had to blink to miss it. He hadn't taken to the authority – too reminiscent, perhaps, of his father's iron rule – or to the attitudes. There was still a prevailing feeling in the Force that the end justified the means, even if the means weren't always pretty. Corruption was rife. There were too many cops taking backhanders from villains, 'losing' evidence, or stitching up those they believed to be guilty.

Nick didn't regret leaving the job – it wasn't for him – but he missed the regular salary and the security. His work for Marshall & Marshall was usually mundane, gathering evidence on errant husbands or ploughing through stinking paperwork garnered from dustbins. It was surprising what people threw out: letters, bills, statements, receipts. All useful stuff when it came to piecing together what money was coming in and what was going out.

It was another ten minutes before Sandler finally emerged from the office block with a jaunty stride and a smug expression on his face. What he was spending *his* money on was clear to see: Savile Row suit, stylish shoes, Rolex watch. He got into a yellow Jensen-Healey which cost more than Nick earned in a year. Still, it had the advantage of making him stand out. It was easy to tail a car like that in London without getting too close.

Nick started the engine, hoping Sandler was heading back to his office in Old Street and not to another appointment across the city. He was due to knock off at six, but that was unlikely to happen if he ended up miles away. As they joined the line of traffic, he checked his mirror for any sign of the Mini. No, she was well gone. It both pained and amused him to think that Heather Grant had been following him around for God knows how long before he'd noticed. It didn't say much for his detecting skills.

He wondered what Stanley would make of it all. The missing Fury child had occupied his uncle for years, one of those tragic mysteries that had never been solved. He'd hear Heather out, whatever she had to say, but he wasn't going to get involved. It was the kind of case that put you through the wringer, drained you dry and spat you out. Or worse. Yes, there were some situations it was wise to stay away from.

'Good thinking, Nick,' he murmured. 'Learn from the mistakes of others.'

He was sure Stanley would still be alive today if he'd never crossed paths with Mal Fury.

5

Friday 16 September. Kellston

Nick was in Connolly's by a quarter to seven. He ordered a coffee and a chicken sandwich at the counter and then sat down at the back. The café wasn't busy and he flicked through an abandoned copy of the *Sun* until his food arrived. He gobbled down the sandwich, partly because he was starving, and partly because he didn't want to be talking with his mouth full when Heather Grant turned up. That's if she *did* turn up. Perhaps she'd have second thoughts.

Still, it might not be a wasted journey even if she failed to show. He'd call in on Lolly and see how things were going for her. She wasn't on the phone so his visits were always hit-and-miss; it had been about three weeks since he'd last seen her. He sometimes wondered whether their friendship would survive if he left it up to her to make the effort and suspected not.

He liked to keep in touch, even if she didn't give much away. When it came to her private life he was pretty much in the dark; he had no idea if she was seeing someone, if she was in love or going steady, and if he ever attempted to probe she'd deflect his questions with ones of her own until he eventually gave up.

By a quarter past seven Nick was pondering on how much longer he'd wait for Heather Grant when the door to the café opened and she walked in. He raised a hand and she smiled. She was as pretty as he'd remembered, maybe more so, an English rose with perfect features. Taller than he'd expected although some of that height was down to high heels. She was wearing a flimsy pale blue summer dress and he tried not to stare at her legs as she approached the table. The other customers, all men, turned their heads to look at her. She walked with an easy grace, like a dancer.

'I'm late,' she said. 'I'm so sorry. Thank you for waiting.'

'It's fine. Would you like a coffee?'

'White, no sugar. Thanks.'

Nick went to the counter, got two coffees and carried them back. He settled into his chair opposite her and arched his brows as if inviting her to start.

Heather took a sip of coffee and looked at him over the rim of the mug. 'I suppose you think I'm crazy following you around like that.'

'I've known more conventional approaches.'

'Yeah, I didn't intend to . . . I just wanted to find a way of talking to you that wasn't awkward.' She gave a wry smile. 'I guess I blew that. I mean, I could have called you but then you might have hung up before you'd heard me out. And if I'd sent a letter, you could have ignored it. I wanted a chance to talk to you face to face, but then I kind of lost my nerve.'

'Because I'm so scary?'

She smiled again. 'Because I knew I was only going to get one chance and if I got it wrong . . . Well, I'd be kicking myself. So, I thought I'd wait for a suitable moment. Except that never really came along, and then you noticed me and that was that.'

'Okay, so this is your chance. Fire away.'

Heather hesitated, took a deep breath and said, 'Right, now

please keep an open mind. I know what you're going to think but . . . the thing is I'm doing some research into the abduction of Kay Fury.'

'You said you weren't a journalist.'

'I'm not. Well, I was, once upon a time, but not now. I'm writing a book about Kay's disappearance.'

'Hasn't that already been done?'

Heather gave a dismissive wave. 'Not seriously. None of those writers had any direct contact with Mal or Esther Fury, or much interest in finding out the truth come to that. Those books are just exploitative rubbish, pure sensationalism. I want to get to the real story. And that's where you can help if you're prepared to.'

'And why would I want to do that?'

'Because your uncle spent years on the case. And you've still got his file, haven't you?'

Nick was surprised that she knew this. 'Who told you that?'

'Are you saying it's not true?'

'I'm asking who told you.'

Heather pursed her lips. She inclined her head as if inwardly debating whether to tell him or not. Eventually, she nodded. 'Esther Fury.'

Nick frowned. 'You've talked to Esther?'

'Of course. I can't do this book without her cooperation. I wouldn't want to. It took a while but I finally managed to convince her. What's the point of another book full of lies and speculation? It's time for some honesty. This one's going to be different.'

Nick wondered what was in it for Esther, other than a good deal of publicity. For nineteen years she had refused to talk publicly about the abduction of her baby daughter. 'How did you get her to agree?'

'I can be very persuasive when I put my mind to it.'

Nick believed her. There was, perhaps, a financial arrangement between them. 'And you want access to my uncle's file.'

'Yes,' she said.

'No,' he said.

'And that will be because?'

Nick placed his elbows on the table. 'Because my uncle's file was written for his employer's eyes only. If Mal gives his permission, I'll happily release the papers.'

'And how likely is that?'

'You'll have to use your powers of persuasion.'

Heather seemed unfazed, her expression remaining placid. 'Okay, I get it. I can see where you're coming from, although it could be argued that Esther was Stanley's employer too.'

'Hardly,' he said. 'Esther couldn't stand him.'

Interest flickered on Heather's face. 'And why was that, do you think?'

Nick shrugged, already regretting that he'd let slip that piece of information. 'You'd need to talk to Esther about that.'

'What do you think of her?'

'I don't think anything. I've only met her once and that was fleetingly. Not long enough, really, to form a judgement.'

'But you still did.'

She was right, of course, but Nick wasn't going to admit it. He'd met Esther Fury – or Esther Gray as she was known in film circles – at a party at the house in West Henby. It had been a warm summer's evening and he'd gone there to talk to Mal about Stanley's death. He remembered the garden, full of glitterati, their champagne glasses clinking. He had thought Esther beautiful but brittle, the kind of woman who needed constant admiration and couldn't live without it.

Heather drank some more of her coffee. 'Look, I don't expect you to trust me, not right off, but I want you to know that I don't intend to be Esther's mouthpiece. Nor am I looking to screw anyone over or do a hatchet job. I'm going to make my own observations and draw my own conclusions. I do think, however, that your uncle deserves some recognition for all the hard work he did.'

Nick suspected she was only saying this to try and get him on side. Esther's opinion of Stanley Parrish had been a low one: she believed he'd actively encouraged Mal to keep on searching for Kay in order to line his own pockets. For every fraudster, every charlatan who came along, Stanley was able to put in a bill for the time spent disproving the claim. Although Nick hated to admit it, Esther could have had a point. Business at Stanley Parrish Investigations had never been what you'd call brisk. That didn't mean his uncle had been entirely cynical, though. As the file proved, he'd put endless time and effort into the work.

'So what got you interested in all this?'

Heather's mouth slid back into that easy smile. 'God, who wouldn't be? It's fascinating, don't you think? Like one of those dark fairy tales where the baby's snatched and nobody knows what's actually happened to her.'

'Except this is real life. No happy ending, so far as I can see.'

'You don't approve,' she said. 'I understand. But what if this book jogs someone's memory, or makes a witness come forward with new information? Isn't it worth writing it just for that?'

'You don't think Mal Fury has been through enough?'

'I can't see why he'd be unhappy about it, not if I tell the truth.'

Nick wondered if she really thought that or if it was just an easy way to justify what she was doing. 'And what if there is no mystery? Everyone knows Teddy Heath abducted Kay. There's every chance she died during the attempt, or shortly after.'

'That isn't what he told Mal Fury.'

'Well, he wouldn't, would he? Not if he was hoping to save his own skin. He had to claim she was still alive. He had to play the only hand he'd got and try to squeeze some money out of Mal while he was doing it.'

'That didn't work out so well.'

'No,' Nick agreed. 'It didn't.'

'I've been looking into Teddy Heath.'

'And what have you found out?'

'That he was a third-rate actor with drink and gambling problems. That Esther had a brief affair with him. That he probably took Kay intending to hold her to ransom, but then didn't dare go through with it after the death of the nanny.'

Nick pulled a face. She wasn't telling him anything he didn't already know, that the world didn't know. The story had come out at the trial and had been all over the papers. Mal had confronted Teddy Heath a couple of years after Kay's disappearance. By then the trail, at least as far as the police were concerned, had gone cold. There had been an altercation at Teddy's flat where Mal had lost his temper and decked him. Teddy, unfortunately, had suffered a fatal heart attack. Mal's first mistake had been to do a runner, his second to tell Esther what had happened.

'And?' he said.

'Oh, there's more. I've been doing a lot of digging.'

Nick waited but she didn't elaborate. 'You're not going to tell me.'

Heather ran her fingers through her short blonde hair. 'I thought you weren't interested.'

'I didn't say I wasn't interested.'

'But you're not prepared to share *your* information.'

'I've already explained that to you.'

'It's a bit of a one-way street, then, isn't it? I mean, I don't mind pooling, but if you won't let me see the file . . . '

'As I've already told you, I don't feel it's right to hand it over without having Mal's permission.'

'That's bullshit,' she said, 'and you know it. I bet you've read that file from cover to cover. Did you ask permission before you did that?'

'I'm not planning on publishing it.'

'Nor am I. But another pair of eyes never does any harm, does it? There could be something that's been missed.'

'I'll think about it,' he said. Then, because his curiosity had been piqued, he added, 'So what else have you found out about Teddy?'

Heather gave a light laugh and shook her head. 'That's not how this is going to work. Come on, give me *some* credit.' She took a small white card from her bag and passed it across the table. 'Why don't you call me when you've thought it over?'

The card just had her name and number on it, nothing else. He looked at it briefly and put it in his jacket pocket. Anyone could have cards printed, using whatever name they liked. 'Sure.'

'Oh, and there was one other thing. Would you be able to put me in touch with Lita? I'm presuming you know where she lives.'

'She won't talk to you.'

'Well, she might and she might not. That's her decision, isn't it? If you could give her my number, I'd appreciate it.'

Sensing that she was about to leave, Nick got in a question of his own. 'Why do you think Esther waited all those years before telling the law what Mal had done?'

'Because she was protecting him. She didn't want him to go to jail. She thought he was worth saving back then.'

'And then she changed her mind?'

'A woman's prerogative, apparently.'

'You asked me earlier what I thought of her. What do *you* think of her?'

Heather took a moment to consider her answer. 'I think she's selfish, arrogant, spiteful, self-obsessed . . . and kind of tragic. I think she and Mal had a toxic marriage and that they brought out the worst in each other.' She kept her gaze on his face. 'And if I remember rightly, you never got around to telling me what *you* thought.'

'Much the same,' he said. 'You've summed it up neatly.'

'And Stanley? What was his opinion?'

'I really couldn't say.'

'You mean you *won't*. Aren't you curious about what happened to Kay? I mean, she could still be out there somewhere. I think if there's even the tiniest chance she's still alive, we have to try and find her.'

Nick decided to play devil's advocate. 'And what if she doesn't want to be found? What if she's living a perfectly happy life in blissful ignorance of who her biological parents really are?'

'Everyone has a right to the truth.'

'Even if it causes damage?'

'You don't know what it's going to cause. It's not up to us to play God with someone else's life.'

'But that's exactly what you could be doing.'

Heather raised a hand to her head again, twisting a short strand of hair between her fingers. 'That's a weird way of looking at things. Wouldn't you want to know where you came from, who your real parents were? I know I would.'

'Maybe. I'm not sure. Especially if those parents were Mal and Esther. You could be placing the poor girl in the middle of a minefield.'

'Or giving her the chance to find out who she really is.'

'But it's not straightforward, is it, not black and white.'

'Nothing ever is.' Heather paused, glanced down at the table and then up again. 'Did you know Teddy Heath had a girlfriend?'

'I'm sure he had lots of them.'

'No, I mean a girl he might have been seeing at the time Kay was taken.'

'And who was that then?'

Heather gave a tiny shake of her head before pushing back her chair and rising to her feet. 'Have a think about that file,' she said. 'You've got my number. Thanks for seeing me.'

Nick watched her walk out of the café. Well, she certainly knew how to leave a man hanging, but he wasn't going to get pulled in. He was smarter than that, too smart to go chasing after ghosts. He still believed, like Stanley had before him, that Kay Fury was probably dead. No amount of wishful thinking was going to bring her back. And yet . . .

Nick quickly stood up and went over to the window at the front. The Mini was parked adjacent to the green. As Heather Grant was crossing the road, he scribbled down the car registration in his notebook. It wouldn't do any harm to check it out, to see if she was really who she said she was. Not that he was going to change his mind. Not in a million years. He was just curious, that's all.

6

Friday 16 September. Kellston

Lolly jumped when the bell rang. She'd been on edge all day, but with the murder, the visit from the law and the news about Mal, her nerves were frazzled. She hurried halfway down the stairs and then abruptly stopped, worried that Old Bill might be standing on her doorstep again. She couldn't face another load of questions. But then it could be Stella or Mal or Nick. She dithered for a moment but then continued on, opening the door with a cautious expression on her face.

'Oh, it's you,' she said with relief when she saw Nick Trent. 'Thanks for coming. I wasn't sure when you'd get my message.'

'What message?'

'I left it on your phone.'

'I've not been home yet.'

'So why are you . . . Never mind, it doesn't matter. Come in, come in.' She had a quick look along the street, left and right, before closing the door and following him up the stairs. 'Have you heard about Mal? I had the police round earlier.'

Nick glanced over his shoulder. 'What? No. What about him?'

'He's done a runner, apparently. Never went back to jail after work yesterday.'

'You're kidding. Why the hell would be do that? He's only got—'

'I know. It's crazy. A few months, that's all he's got left. Something must have happened. I can't figure it out. He's not stupid so why would he do such a stupid thing?'

They went through to the living room, but neither of them sat down. Lolly went over to the window, turned her back on the street and leaned against the ledge. 'He was fine the last time I saw him. At least he seemed fine. Maybe he just snapped. Maybe he couldn't take it any more.'

'It's weird.'

'It's that all right.'

Nick stood by the table, one hand in his jacket pocket. 'No, I mean it's weird because I was just talking to someone about Kay Fury. This girl approached me today, said she was a writer, that she was doing some research into Kay's abduction. Heather Grant, that's her name. Have you ever heard of her?'

Lolly shook her head. 'No, never.'

'She's writing a book, apparently – with Esther's approval. At least that's what she claims. She wants to take a look at Stanley's file.'

'And are you going to let her?'

'I shouldn't think so.'

Lolly nodded. She chewed on her lower lip for a moment. 'Do you think there's a connection between this Heather person and what Mal's done? Did she say she'd been in touch with him?'

'No, but then I didn't specifically ask. It's possible, I suppose. She told me she'd been doing some digging into Teddy Heath, that she'd discovered a girlfriend he had round about the time Kay was taken.'

'Do you believe her?'

'It could just be a ploy, a tasty bit of bait to reel us in.'

'Us?'

'She wants to talk to you too. But don't worry, I haven't told her where you live.'

'Good,' Lolly said. She thought for a while about what he'd said. There had been a theory that Teddy Heath couldn't have been working alone, that someone must have helped him. He was the type of bloke who couldn't take care of himself, never mind a baby. 'If Mal thinks she's got a lead, a good one, that might be why . . . but what's with the urgency? I don't see what can be so important that it's worth an even longer jail sentence when he finally gets caught. I mean, it would make more sense to wait, wouldn't it?' She sighed and scratched her chin, unable to fathom Mal's actions. 'And what can he even *do* when he's on the run? His picture was all over the papers during the trial. Someone's going to recognise him.'

'Maybe it hasn't got anything to do with Kay. Heather Grant turning up right now could just be a coincidence.'

'Some coincidence.'

'They happen.'

Whenever Lolly looked at Nick she was reminded of Stanley Parrish. They had the same long face and slightly mournful eyes. She had liked Stanley so far as she had known him, but then she would have liked anyone who had whisked her away from Brenda Cecil and her family. 'I can't imagine what else would make Mal do this.'

'Where would he go? Can you think of anywhere?'

'He was talking about Antwerp – he's got friends there – but how would he get out of the country without a passport?'

'There are ways, if you know the right people.'

'But if this is connected to Kay, why would he even want

to leave? He'd be more likely to head for West Henby, to try and see Esther. Except the law will be keeping an eye on that place, won't they? Actually, it's strange. I was there this morning and—'

'What? You were at the house?'

'Not in it, just passing by. We only stopped by the gates for a minute. I don't know, but I thought I heard ... No, it doesn't matter.'

'Heard what?'

Lolly shuffled her feet and gazed at the floor. 'I thought I heard a baby crying. It probably wasn't, probably just the wind or something.' She glanced up again, feeling self-conscious, not wanting him to think that her imagination had run away with her. 'I couldn't swear to it.'

Nick raised his eyebrows but didn't pass comment.

Lolly sighed. 'I don't know what to do.'

'What can you do?'

'Try and find him before he gets in even more trouble. Perhaps we should ring Heather Grant, see if she knows anything. Is that a bad idea?' She didn't wait for an answer. 'Or maybe not. No, it's just even more material for her book. That's if she's even writing one. She could be anybody.'

'We should wait a few days. Mal might realise he's made a mistake and hand himself in.'

Lolly turned and gazed out of the window. A squad car was coming down the road. Afraid it might stop outside the flat, she held her breath for a second, but it carried on towards the station. 'Did you hear about what happened at the arches?'

'Yeah, it was on the radio.'

'Stella thinks it's one of the girls from the house. Dana. That's what she's called. She didn't come home last night and ... ' Lolly's voice trailed off.

'Christ, it's a nasty business. I hope they catch him soon.'

Outside, it had grown dark. The evenings were starting to close in more quickly now and they came with a chill. Lolly would have put the fire on but she was counting the pennies. The meter seemed to eat money, its greedy little mouth gobbling up the coins as quickly as she dropped them in. She'd anticipated making a few quid from her trip to Kent with Vinnie, but that hadn't gone according to plan. Something else to worry about. She had some savings in the bank but they wouldn't last long, not with rent and food and bills.

'Do you fancy a drink? We could go down to the Fox.'

Lolly looked at Nick and shook her head. 'Not tonight.' Everyone would be talking about the murder and she didn't want to hear it. In addition, it was the market tomorrow and she had to sort out some stuff to sell. 'Sorry, I've got work to do. Another time, yeah? Do you mind?'

'Course not.' Nick took a small white card from his pocket and held it up. 'Do you want Heather Grant's number?'

Lolly hesitated, but then decided there was no harm in it. She didn't have to call the woman and probably wouldn't. She took the card, put it down on the table and picked up a pen to copy out the number.

'Keep it,' he said. 'I've already made a note of it. I'll do some digging and see what I can find out about her.'

'Will you let me know?'

'I'll drop by if I find out anything.'

'Thanks.'

Lolly walked down to the door with him.

'You sure you're okay?' he asked.

Lolly smiled and nodded and said all the right things. It was a habit she couldn't break: putting on a brave face and never showing weakness. She didn't think he was fooled, not for a minute, but he had the good grace to go along with it. They said their goodbyes and she closed the door.

Slowly she climbed back up the stairs. There was so much to think about, too much, and she felt weary just from the effort of trying. She collected a sweater from the bedroom, pulled it on and went into the living room. She sat down at the table and started rooting through the boxes for some good items to try and sell tomorrow, but her mind wasn't on it.

Ten minutes later she stood up again, switched off the light and went over to the window. She peered into the shadows, wondering where Mal was now. Would he try and contact her? No, it was too risky. But then again, if he was desperate enough . . .

Her gaze swept along the street. She pressed her nose against the glass and studied the dark edge of the green. Cars went by and groups of people. It was Friday night, go-out-and-spend-your-wages night, and everyone was on the move. All except her. She felt the weight of the past, thick and heavy, gathering in her head. Lies and secrets jostled for position.

Don't be afraid, she ordered herself.

But she was.

7

Saturday 17 September. Kellston

Lolly woke at the crack of dawn with her heart racing. She'd been dreaming of the lake at West Henby, of the weeping willows sweeping down to brush the water. It was a quiet, secluded place, but walking along the narrow path, she'd known that she wasn't alone. Someone or something had been there behind her, an invisible and malevolent presence that made the hairs on the back of her neck stand on end.

When she opened her eyes she almost expected to see the peacock wallpaper, to find herself back at the Fury house, but all she saw was plain magnolia. Relief flooded through her. She was home, she was safe. There was nothing to worry about. Well, that wasn't quite true, but at least there were no ghosts lurking in the flat. There was only the here and now.

She lay very still until the dream dissolved and reality took over. It was Saturday, market day, and she'd better get on if she wasn't going to be late setting up. She went to the bathroom, had a pee, a wash, brushed her teeth and then dressed at speed – blue jeans, sneakers, T-shirt and a sweater – before grabbing a slice of toast and a cup of coffee. Within fifteen minutes she was out of the door and crossing the road with a heavy holdall tugging at her arm.

There was a group gathered at the entrance to the market, thrusting leaflets at everyone who passed. Lolly's nose wrinkled as she realised who they were: National Front. Last month they'd been thwarted in their plans for a big demonstration in Lewisham when anti-NF protestors had turned up in even greater numbers. Now they were looking for other places to spread their evil.

Lolly stared straight ahead, ignoring the leaflets being flapped in front of her. She couldn't bear these people, couldn't understand them. They traded in hate and malice, in anger and division. As if there weren't enough problems in the world, they wanted to create even more.

She knew what it was like to be the target of bullies, to be singled out, to be judged for being different, and despised all those who encouraged it.

She was almost past the group when she heard the voice behind her.

'Well, if it ain't the little snitch herself.'

Lolly whirled around and found herself staring into the goblin-like features of Tony Cecil. Immediately, she stiffened. Brenda Cecil's older son was a skinhead thug with an axe to grind. He reckoned she'd grassed him to the law over a violent assault years ago – she hadn't – and was still bearing a grudge. If it hadn't been for Terry's protection of her, he wouldn't have hesitated in taking revenge.

She went to walk on but he grabbed her by the arm.

'Where do you think you're going?'

Lolly tried to pull away, but his thick fingers squeezed even tighter. She was scared of him but wasn't going to show it. 'Let go of me, you bastard, or I'll scream the bloody place down!'

Tony finally released her, his mouth twisting into a nasty grin. 'You see what she's like, mate?' he said to the bloke standing beside him. 'She's ain't normal. She's got a fuckin' screw loose.'

'The only crazy one round here is you.' Lolly rubbed at her arm, recalling all the other times he'd hurt her when she was a kid. 'Keep your hands off me in future or—'

'Or what? You going to go running to Terry? He can't watch over you twenty-four hours a day.' Tony laughed. 'And I shouldn't think he'd want to, ugly little bitch like you.'

Lolly raised her eyes to the heavens, feigning a nonchalance she didn't feel. 'You finished now? It's been lovely to talk but some of us have got work to do.'

'Nah, I ain't finished. Where's Jude Rule?'

Lolly paled at the mention of the name. Jude, her first love, the boy who'd used her, betrayed her and broken her heart. 'How the hell would I know?'

'Because you two were tight as a witch's arse.'

Suddenly FJ, Tony's younger brother, appeared beside him. He had the same haircut and the same cruel eyes. 'You remember Amy, don't you? She's the girl your fuckin' boyfriend murdered.'

'He didn't,' she said. 'It wasn't him.'

Tony snarled. 'Listen to her! Six years on and the lying cow is still defending the bastard. She can't help herself.'

'Just spit it out, yeah,' FJ said. 'We got things to do.'

'Like I said, I've got no idea.'

Tony pushed his face into hers. 'There's only one thing I hate more than grasses and that's fuckin' liars. Give us the address and we'll leave you alone.'

Lolly, feeling his rank breath on her, withdrew a step and glared at him. 'Are you deaf or what?'

'You gave that murdering shithead an alibi.'

'I just told the truth.'

'No one believes that, darlin'. You think we were born fuckin' yesterday?'

'Believe what you like. I haven't seen Jude in ages so if you want to find him you'll have to look for him yourself.' Lolly pushed her way past before they could say anything else. She held her breath, hoping they wouldn't come after her, and thankfully they didn't. That didn't mean they were finished with her, though. From now on she'd have to watch her back.

Lolly emptied the holdall and set up her stall. Her pitch was only a small one, squashed between second-hand books on one side and pots and pans on the other. She laid out the watches, necklaces, bracelets and rings, keeping the more expensive items near the back where they were away from thieving fingers. While she was doing all this her mind was still on the Cecil brothers.

The renewed interest in Jude was a worry. If the truth ever came out, she'd be dead meat. She had, of course, lied about being with him on the afternoon of Amy Wiltshire's murder, giving him an unshakeable alibi and sticking to it through police interrogations. She had done so because she'd believed absolutely in his innocence. At thirteen she'd thought she knew it all when actually she'd known nothing. And now? Now she could no longer put her hand on her heart and swear he hadn't killed her. It made her feel sick inside.

Lolly hadn't been lying, however, when she'd said she didn't know where Jude was. The last time she'd seen him had been eighteen months ago when he'd made it clear that his loyalties lay with Esther Fury and not herself. It shouldn't have come as any big surprise – he'd always been dazzled by movie stars, by beautiful women – but it had still rankled. He'd used her to get to Esther, raising her romantic hopes before dashing them again.

'Loser,' she muttered under her breath.

She wanted to forget about him, put him out of her mind for ever, but the more she tried the larger he loomed. The problem was that he'd been good to her once. When her mother had been ill, which was more often than not, she'd been able to find temporary solace – and some food and warmth – in the flat Jude shared with his father. There, on the fourteenth floor of Haslow House, she'd sat and watched old movies with him. He'd been three years older, sixteen to her thirteen, but had never talked down to her.

Lolly felt a lump come into her throat when she thought about those days. For all her struggles, she'd been happy. Watching the films flicker on the makeshift screen had transported her to another world and for a while she'd been able to put aside everything else. Memories flashed through her mind: the old corduroy sofa, peanut butter sandwiches, Humphrey Bogart narrowing his eyes at some glamorous but deadly woman. Quickly, she pushed the thoughts away. Now wasn't the time to be getting sentimental.

So far as she was concerned, Jude was on his own. She wanted nothing more to do with him. He must have moved out of Kellston or Tony Cecil wouldn't be asking where he lived, but she didn't care where he'd gone or who he was with. No, she didn't give a damn. And if that wasn't entirely true, she was certainly going to pretend it was.

Lolly turned her attention back to the stall and for the rest of the morning tried to drum up interest in her jewellery. She cut the prices, writing out a 'Sale' sign in the hope of attracting more customers and bringing in a bit of much-needed cash. By midday she'd sold two watches, some beads and a couple of rings, raising a grand total of nine pounds fifty pence. Not the worst she'd ever done but not the best either.

By midday she'd also found out, courtesy of the radio playing on the pots and pans stall, that the murdered prostitute had been named as Dana Leigh, and that Marc Bolan had been killed in a car crash. The bad news just never stopped coming. There was nothing about Mal but he had probably been pushed off the headlines by bigger events. She would have to try and see Stella later. God knows what state she'd be in. And she'd have to track down Terry too; she still had the diamond ring and needed to give it back.

The market was starting to pack up, the customers to drift away. Lolly stayed for another half hour before deciding to quit too. By now the music had stopped and the smell of frying onions was fading into the warm afternoon air. She packed her goods back into the holdall and stared along the central aisle before making a move. The Cecils and their National Front mates had left and so it was safe for her to leave too.

Leaflets were scattered on the ground near the entrance and she made it her mission to trample on as many of them as she could. They belonged in the bin but she wasn't going to waste her energy in gathering them up. Keeping an eye out for Tony and FJ she walked quickly up to the high street. She didn't fancy Jude's chances if they ever caught up with him, but that was his problem not hers. She had other things to worry about.

8

Saturday 17 September. Central London

Nick Trent was alone in the office, a situation he was taking advantage of. He'd put in a call to a contact he had at the Driver and Vehicle Licensing Centre, requesting information on the red Mini and its owner, and had just heard back. The car was registered to Heather Grant and the address on her licence was in Tufnell Park. He scribbled down the details, including her date of birth, expressed his thanks and hung up. Well, so far, so normal. At least she appeared to be who she said she was.

His next call was to a mate in CID, asking for a background check on Heather in case she had a history he should know about; the world was full of con artists and he wanted to make sure she wasn't one of them. He was aware that these favours were going to cost him one way or another, but figured it was still worth it. The check wouldn't be quick and while he waited he looked up the number for HMP Redwood.

Nick was winging it on this one. Impersonating a police officer was an offence and he'd be in serious trouble if he was caught out. He couldn't, however, see any other way of getting the information he needed. When the phone was answered he identified himself as DC John McEnery from the Yard and asked to be put through to the office.

'Sorry to bother you again,' he said once the transfer was made, 'but I need to double-check Mal Fury's visitors for the last couple of months. I don't suppose you have the information to hand?'

The screw on the other end of the line sounded more irritated than suspicious, as though he had enough on his plate without having to go over information he'd already provided. 'Hold on,' he said tetchily. 'You'll have to give me a minute.'

Nick drummed his fingers on the desk while he waited for the man to come back on the line. He was only pursuing this for Lolly's sake, to try and get a lead on why Mal had done a runner. What he couldn't find out, unfortunately, was what might have been sent through the post. It was doubtful they kept a record of every letter received, especially in an open prison.

Eventually the screw picked up the phone again. 'Okay, I've got it. You want me to fax it through?'

'No, that's all right. If you could just run through the names . . .'

'There's only two: Lolita Bruce and Heather Grant.'

'When did Heather Grant visit?'

'That would be ten days ago, on the seventh September.'

'Thank you,' Nick said. 'I appreciate it.' He put the receiver down and nodded to the empty room. 'Well, there you go,' he said. 'Surprise, surprise.' Now all he had to work out was what Heather had said to Mal to make him decide to go on the run. Something to do with Kay; it had to be. Maybe the stuff about Teddy Heath's girlfriend. Except it had to be more than that, something that was so urgent it just couldn't wait.

He dug out Heather's number, called and listened to her answering machine. He left both his numbers, office and home, said it was important and hung up. It could be worth handing over Stanley's file, he decided, if she was prepared to come clean about the conversation she'd had at the prison. A reasonable trade, although he couldn't be sure she'd tell the truth.

Nick didn't feel any particular loyalty towards Mal and was withholding the file as much out of sheer bloody-mindedness as anything else. Why should he contribute towards the creation of yet another piece of sensationalist trash? And even if Heather had greater aspirations when it came to her work, he wasn't convinced that a further book on the Fury tragedy was either appropriate or desirable. He was, however prepared to put these objections aside if she could shed some light on where Mal might be. He'd do it for Lolly's sake.

Having spent the last half hour on personal business, Nick thought he'd better get on with what he was actually being paid to do. He typed up his notes on yesterday's surveillance of Brent Sandler and chucked the sheet of paper into the relevant tray. Notes from the previous few days were still there, waiting to be collated, and out of curiosity he picked up the ones submitted by other operatives and had a quick look through them. There was nothing out of the ordinary – meetings, lunches, drinks, visits to prostitutes – until he came to Thursday night where he discovered that Mickey Ross had managed to lose Sandler at around eight o'clock in Shoreditch.

The lawyer had parked his car at a strip club called Marcie's, one of Terry Street's dubious establishments, gone inside and not come out again. The Jensen-Healey had still been parked there at closing time. Sandler must have slipped out the back way or walked out in plain view when Ross wasn't watching, abandoning the car and taking a cab home. Too much to drink, perhaps.

Nick wasn't surprised by any of this. Ross was a lazy, incompetent sod and had probably been napping. Whatever the reason, there was now a gap in the surveillance, lost hours that couldn't be explained. It was doubtful the client would ever get to know about this; one of the Marshall brothers would find a way to sweep it neatly under the carpet. Incompetence was hardly something to shout about.

He put the papers back in the tray, wondering again who the client was. His eyes strayed towards the larger office at the back where the Marshalls kept all the confidential files. They also kept the door locked when they weren't around. He toyed with the idea of trying to get in – some locks were easier to manipulate than others – but didn't want to take the risk of being caught in the act. He disliked being in the dark but preferred it to being unemployed.

The phone rang and he picked it up. 'Marshall & Marshall.'

It was his old colleague from CID. 'I've got the results on that check you wanted. Heather Grant, yeah? It's come up a blank, a clean sheet, nothing on her at all.'

Nick wasn't sure if he was pleased or disappointed. In some ways it would have been easier to find out she had a record as long as his arm, a history of conning people. At least then he'd have known who he was dealing with. 'Thanks, mate. I owe you one.'

'Too right you do.'

'I'll see you around.'

Nick sat back and thought about Heather Grant. Maybe she was exactly who and what she said she was, but he still didn't trust her. Why was that? Perhaps it was just instinct. Or the fact she hadn't mentioned visiting Mal. Or perhaps it was because everything to do with the Furys was hazardous. People tended to get damaged, even killed, when they got involved with them. He scratched his chin and sighed. He had the feeling he was heading straight for trouble, like a fly stepping into a spider's web.

9

Saturday 17 September. Kellston

Heather Grant parked a few yards down from the pawnbroker's but didn't immediately get out of the car. Instead she flicked through her notes making sure she was up to speed with exactly what she needed to ask. Her forthcoming interview with Brenda Cecil had taken some negotiation – the old cow hadn't been prepared to talk for free – and eventually they had settled on a ten-quid payment. Heather intended to get her money's worth.

Everything was going to plan at the moment. She was rooting around, stirring things up and getting results. Bad smells were rising from the cesspit. Sometimes you had to muddy the waters before anything became clear. As yet she didn't understand it all, couldn't see the whole picture but that would change in time. She was making progress and that was all that mattered.

Heather got out of the Mini, walked over to the shop and went inside. It was exactly one o'clock, the time they'd arranged, and Brenda was in the process of breaking for lunch. Cash was being transferred from the till to a canvas bag and there was a rustle of notes, a clatter of coins as the morning's takings were stashed away.

'You're here, then,' Brenda said, glancing up. 'Thought you might not be coming.'

Heather raised her eyebrows. First impressions of Brenda hadn't been good and she had the feeling they weren't going to improve. The woman was imposing, big and solid with a mountainous bosom and hands like hams. Her face had a puffy look, and her eyes were mean and sly. 'Sorry, I'm not late, am I?'

Brenda came out from behind the counter, flipped over the sign on the door to 'Closed' and pulled across a pair of heavy bolts. She turned and put her hands on her hips. 'A tenner. Wasn't that what we agreed?'

'That's right.' Heather took out her purse and passed over the note.

Brenda fingered the tenner for a second before holding it up to the light. Eventually she nodded. 'You'd better come through.'

Heather followed her along a narrow hallway to the lounge and from there to the kitchen at the very rear of the building. The smell of boiled cabbage and stale tobacco hung in the air.

After they'd sat down, Heather took out her Dictaphone and laid it on the table.

'You don't mind, do you? It'll save me making notes.'

Brenda eyed the machine with suspicion. 'You're recording this? No, I'm not sure if—'

'It'll make everything quicker,' Heather interrupted. 'I don't want to take up too much of your time. I know you've got a business to run so the sooner we're done, the sooner I can leave you in peace.'

This argument seemed to partly appease Brenda although she still looked wary. 'So, what do you want to know?'

'Okay, let's start with Lolita Bruce. Lolly. How did she come to be living with you back in '71?'

'I took her in, didn't I, after her mum topped herself. Someone had to help the kid out. Skinny, half-starved thing she was, barely able to string a sentence together. I thought I was doing the right thing but it turned out to be the biggest mistake I ever made.'

'Really? Why was that?'

'Because she didn't have a grateful bone in her body. Here's me, doing my best for her, feeding her, clothing her, giving her a roof over her head and what thanks do I get?' The corners of Brenda's mouth turned down with disgust. 'She only goes to the law saying my Tony attacked a man. A grass, that's what she is, a bleedin' snake.'

'Tony?'

'My oldest, love. He did time for that.'

Heather wasn't interested in Tony Cecil – he'd probably got what he deserved – but she made some token sympathetic noises before moving swiftly on. 'What made you believe there could be a connection between Lolly and the missing Fury child?'

'It was Angela, her mum. She talked about Mr Fury sometimes when she was having one of her episodes, said he was out to get her, that he had spies following her around. I hate to speak ill of the dead, but she weren't right in the head, not right at all. I didn't take no notice at the time but later, after she'd ... you know ... it got me thinking. Turned out there wasn't a birth certificate for the kid or nothin', like she'd just appeared from thin air, so I started to wonder if maybe she weren't Angela's at all.'

'And you contacted Mal Fury?'

'Not him, the other one, the private investigator. Stanley something, that was his name.'

'Parrish,' Heather said.

'Yes, that's it. He was the one who dealt with everything.'

'There was a big reward, wasn't there, for anyone who could provide information leading to the discovery of Kay?'

Brenda's face darkened, her voice becoming belligerent. 'That ain't why I took her in if that's what you're getting at. Don't you start accusing me of—'

'No, no, of course not. I wasn't saying that at all. Absolutely not. It was very good of you to look after her, extremely kind. There aren't many people who'd do the same in your position. I think it's admirable.'

Brenda seemed partly mollified by this, but her eyes probed Heather's face as if searching for signs of duplicity. 'I never did nothin' for money. All I wanted was to give the kid a decent home. You can put that in your book, love. I did it for *her* sake, not mine.'

Seeing as Brenda had charged ten quid just for the pleasure of a short interview, Heather found her protests laughable. But she was careful not to let it show. 'Of course. I'm sorry. I didn't mean anything by it.'

'If there was any chance she could be the Fury kid, then I had to find out. For all their sakes. It wouldn't have been fair otherwise, would it? Not on any of them. That's why I went to Mr Parrish, not for no other reason.'

'I understand.'

Brenda, having re-established the moral high ground, gave a firm nod. 'Some of us know right from wrong.'

Heather left a short respectful pause before asking, 'So, why do you think Mal Fury took her on? I mean, if it had been established she wasn't theirs, why would—'

'Who said it was established? All I know is what they told me. No *proof,* that Stanley said even though she was the right blood group. They could have been spinning me a line, couldn't they? Those sort can't be trusted.'

'Those sort?'

'You know what I mean. The rich, the ones who have all the power. They can do what they like and nobody asks any questions.'

'But surely Stanley Parrish wouldn't have continued the search if the Furys thought Kay had been found?'

Brenda's massive shoulders heaved into a shrug. 'I'm just saying, that's all. You can't believe a word that comes out of some people's mouths.'

'I suppose not,' Heather agreed, wanting to keep the woman on side.

'Still, they all got what they deserved in the end. Mal Fury's banged up and Lolly's back here. I reckon that Esther realised what a devious little bitch she was and chucked her out.'

'Yes, I heard she was back. You don't have her address by any chance?'

'If you're thinking of talking to her, I wouldn't bother. She's like her mother, she's got a screw loose. And she don't know how to tell the truth. She's a wrong 'un, love. You need to watch your step with her.'

'I'll bear it in it mind. But if you do have the address?'

'Just along the road here. I don't know what number. It's the flat over the Indian takeaway.'

'Thanks.'

'Walking around bold as brass after what she did to my Tony. It's a bloody disgrace. And it wasn't as if it was the first time. Do you know about Jude Rule?'

'I've heard the name,' Heather said cautiously. She had actually met Jude at West Henby, a young, good-looking but very intense man. A screenwriter who'd already had some success. He clearly had a strong attachment to Esther Fury although she wasn't sure of the exact nature of their relationship. The actress was older than him, over forty, although no one could deny that she was still a beauty. There had been something odd, obsessive even, about the way he had watched her, his eyes never leaving her face.

'Got away with murder, didn't he? Everyone knows he killed Amy Wiltshire – he was always sniffing round her – but Lolly swore she was with him when it happened. The two of them cooked up a story and stuck to it. That's when the law tried to pin it on Tony; hours he spent down that nick before they finally let it drop.'

Heather didn't know much about the Wiltshire case other than the girl had been sixteen when she'd been stabbed to death on the Mansfield estate. 'The police never charged anyone?'

'Bloody morons, the lot of them.'

'Lolly must have been pretty young then. What, about thirteen?'

'Old enough to know better. She gave that boy an alibi and let him go free. He should have been locked up. They should have thrown away the key. He'll do it again, you mark my words, some other poor girl, you can be sure of it.' Brenda's expression suggested she couldn't wait for the day to come. 'Jude Rule had Lolly wrapped around his little finger. She'd have let my Tony go down for murder rather than tell the truth. But he'll get what's coming to him one day, and so will she.'

The background information on Jude and Lolly was interesting, but it wasn't what Heather was here for. 'Going back to Stanley Parrish for a moment: what was your opinion of him?'

'What do you mean?'

'Was he doing a good job? Was he honest? Did he treat you fairly?'

Brenda gave a snort. 'He was working for the Furys, weren't he? It was *their* interests he were looking after, not mine. I did everything I could for that kid and what thanks did I get for it? I'll tell you this for nothing, I won't make the same mistake again. I look after my own these days and no one else. Blood's thicker than water, right?'

'And you never met either of the Furys, Mal or Esther?'

'Never.'

'You must have felt some sympathy for them, though. Losing a child in those circumstances, not knowing what's happened, must be a complete nightmare. I don't think I could cope with it.'

But Brenda's capacity for sympathy was limited. She placed her plump arms on the table and said, 'We all have our crosses to bear.'

'It still intrigues me as to why they decided to take on Lolly. Out of all the kids who'd been put forward, why her? What made her different to the others?'

'You'd have to ask them that. I've got my own suspicions, like I said.'

Heather didn't believe the Furys had ever thought that Lolly Bruce could be their missing daughter. And she knew for a fact that Esther had never wanted anything to do with her. It had been Mal who had taken the unilateral decision to become her guardian and bring her into the family home. And that, perhaps, had been the beginning of the end as regards the Fury marriage.

Brenda glanced at the clock on the wall. 'Is there anything else only I've got things to do? I can't sit here gassing all day.'

'Just out of interest, what do you think happened to Kay Fury?'

'I don't know, love, and I don't much care. It's a shame and all that, but it ain't my problem. I've enough of my own worries to be dealing with without adding to them.'

'Okay, I think that's it.' Heather turned off the Dictaphone and put it in her bag. 'Thank you for your time.'

As Brenda escorted her back through the house and shop, the older woman couldn't resist one final dig. 'Don't forget what I said about Lolly Bruce. She's a troublemaker. Some people are born bad, born bloody evil, and she's one of them.'

'Don't worry, I'll remember.'

Heather walked along the road to the Mini and climbed inside. Brenda Cecil was bitter and vindictive, and the interview had left a bad taste in her mouth. She brushed both shoulders in turn as if to wipe away invisible specks of dirt. How enlightening had their talk been? Well, she had learned a little more about Lolly, but that was about it. Still, every bit of information was useful.

It was over six months now since Heather had made an earth-shattering discovery, something that had flipped her world upside down. She was still trying to come to terms with it. That she had been lied to and deceived wasn't anything she'd get over in a hurry; the betrayal was still spreading through her blood like poison. If there was an antidote it wouldn't be found by sitting on her backside. She needed answers, clarity, understanding. She had to find the end of the thread and start pulling until everything unravelled.

10

Saturday 17 September. Kellston

Lolly left home at half past six and immediately crossed over the road. She always did this so she didn't need to walk directly past the pawnbroker's. Avoiding the Cecils was second nature to her now, and after the confrontation at the market this morning she was more wary than usual. If she'd had a choice she would have rented a flat much further away from the family, but at the time it had been the only affordable place available.

As she approached the junction she crossed back over and turned left onto Station Road. Her intention was to go and see Stella, popping into the Fox on the way. With any luck Terry would be there and she could return the ring to him. One less thing to worry about. But Tony and FJ were still on her mind. While she walked, she kept glancing over her shoulder, an involuntary movement like a nervous tic she couldn't shake off.

Even at this early hour the Fox was busy. Most of the tables were taken and there was a queue at the bar. Far from putting people off, the recent murder in the area appeared to have had the opposite effect with the locals gathering to discuss events and share in the horror. She could hear them talking about it, exchanging theories, as she looked over at Terry's usual table – currently occupied by a couple of lads and their girlfriends – before switching her view to quickly scan the room for Vinnie who was always head and shoulders above everyone else.

Lolly was about to leave when she noticed Stella, Michelle and Jackie standing by the corridor that led down to the Ladies. They were involved in some kind of altercation or at least Stella and Jackie were, their faces twisted, words spitting from their mouths like missiles. Michelle seemed to be trying to keep the peace and the two other women apart. All of them looked drunk.

Of the girls who worked out of the house on Albert Road, Jackie was the only one Lolly actively disliked; she was hard-faced and abrasive with a wide mean streak that ran straight through her soul. Lolly hesitated, not wanting to get caught in the crossfire, but then made her way across the pub. Loyalty, she decided, was more important than self-preservation. As she approached she could see that Stella's gaze was glazed and unfocused; she'd clearly been crying but now her grief had turned to anger. Her mascara had run leaving dark panda shadows under her eyes.

'You shouldn't have let her go!'

Jackie gave an empty laugh. 'Who am I, her bloody keeper? Don't put this on me, you bitch.'

'We're supposed to look out for each other.'

'Don't give me that. She had a mind of her own, didn't she? I didn't make her do nothin'.'

'It's no one's fault,' Michelle said. 'Except for the bastard who killed her. For fuck's sake, can't you two just drop it?'

Lolly went up to Stella and touched her arm. 'Are you all right?'

Jackie make a tsk sound in the back of her throat. 'Does she look all right?'

'Don't start on her,' Stella snarled. 'What's wrong with you?'

'Jesus, *you're* what's wrong with me. Have you heard yourself? I'm sick of listening to it.'

'Well, no one's forcing you. Why don't you just piss off and leave us alone?'

'I've had enough of this.' Jackie said. She waved a hand at Stella, threw Lolly a dirty look, turned on her heel and stormed off.

'What was all that about?' Lolly asked.

Michelle shook her head. 'I'd better go after her.'

Stella thrust a pound note into Lolly's palm. 'Get us a voddy, will you, love? A double. And buy yourself one. I need to sit down.' She staggered a few steps to a table that had just been vacated, slumped down onto a chair and fumbled for her cigarettes.

Lolly went to the bar and joined the queue. While she was waiting to be served she kept an eye on Stella in case she keeled over. How long had she been drinking for? Most of the afternoon by the look of her; she must have had a skinful before the pub even opened. Dana's murder, unsurprisingly, had knocked her for six.

Lolly ordered a single vodka – she reckoned Stella wouldn't notice the difference – and added a whole bottle of tonic to the glass. She got half a bitter for herself, carried the two drinks over to the table, handed over the change and sat down.

By now Stella's anger had dissolved and she'd become maudlin. 'Dana weren't no older than you, Lol. What kind of age is that for a girl to die?' She sighed into the vodka. 'Makes you wonder what it's all about. Had her whole life ahead of her and now . . . '

'I know. It's God-awful. Have you heard anything? Have they got any idea who did it yet?'

'They ain't said, but I reckon they think it was a punter.'

'And you don't?'

Stella gave a shrug, pulled on her cigarette and exhaled the smoke. 'Dana weren't stupid. She knew the score. She never worked away from the house.'

Lolly had only met Dana a few times and that had been in passing. The impression she'd got was of a young, slightly brittle girl who'd acted tough but probably wasn't. 'What did Jackie mean about not making her go? Go where?'

Stella examined the smouldering tip of her cigarette for a while, watching the grey end grow longer before finally flicking the ash in the general direction of the ashtray. It fell short and dropped onto the table, a tiny cylinder of dust. She frowned, as though she'd lost her train of thought.

'Jackie,' Lolly prompted. 'Why were you arguing?'

'Oh, yeah, *that.* I told her to keep an eye on Dana – I was worried about her – but she let her waltz off without even asking where she was going.'

'What were you so worried about?'

'She hooked up with some bloke a few weeks back, reckoned he could help her find her mum. Although I reckon the only person he was helping was himself. Taking money off her right, left and centre he was. Freddy he was called, or at least that's what he said.'

The name made Lolly's antennae twitch. She knew two Freddys, both connected to Brenda Cecil: one was her no-good wastrel of a husband, the other her son Freddy Junior, or FJ as he was known. 'Did you tell the law?'

'Yeah, I told them. Can't say they were interested though. Didn't bat an eyelid, did they? Truth is, Lol, they don't give a damn. To them Dana was just another lousy tom with a drug habit and shit taste in punters. They're only going through the motions. The only reason they're doing anything is 'cause they're worried about having the Yorkshire Ripper or a copycat on their patch.'

'You ever meet him, this Freddy?'

'Nah, never set eyes on him. He didn't come to the house, far as I know. Well, he wouldn't, would he? Might get asked some awkward bloody questions by the rest of us.'

Lolly sipped her beer and thought about it. 'So what was the deal with Dana's mum?'

'Dumped her on a church doorstep near Hackney Fields when she was a baby. Or somebody did. They never found out who. Didn't leave a note or nothin'. Not even to say what her name was. It was the nurses at the hospital who called her Dana. She grew up in care without a clue who her family was, and I guess that's always hard. Anyway, she reckoned someone had to know something and so she started digging, looking at the old newspaper reports and asking around in the area. Don't ask me how she met this Freddy 'cause I don't have a clue, but I reckon he saw a chance to make a few quid and grabbed it with both hands. He told her he'd got some leads but odds are he knew fuck all and was just stringing her along.'

'But why would he have killed her? I mean, if she was giving him money he was getting exactly what he wanted. She wasn't much use to him dead.'

'I don't know. Maybe he was just the kind of shit who gets a kick out of playing games with women. Once he'd had enough ... ' Stella stubbed out her fag and immediately lit another. 'Anyway, I'll get to the bottom of it. I'll find out who the bastard is.'

'And how are you going to do that?'

'I'll think of something.'

'You need to be careful, Stella.'

But Stella was beyond caring about her own personal safety. 'I'll get him,' she said. 'One way or another I'll nail the bastard.'

11

Saturday 17 September. Kellston

It was around eight-fifteen when Lolly departed from the Fox. By then Jackie had come back and a reconciliation had taken place involving tears, apologies and hugs. It was always like that with Stella and Jackie: daggers drawn one minute, best pals the next. Anyway, it meant that Lolly didn't need to worry about Stella getting home safely so she made her excuses and left.

Before heading for the flat, she walked along the road and put her head round the door of the Hope and Anchor. It was much quieter than the Fox, a spit and sawdust dive where the local villains gathered to recruit for jobs or make plans for new ones. There were no women inside, only a few blokes who gave her hard, unwelcoming stares as if challenging her to cross the threshold. Lolly didn't. Once she'd established that Terry wasn't there, she quickly withdrew.

It was dark now but the streets were bright enough and busy enough for her not to be too anxious. There was a murderer out there somewhere but she pushed it to the back of her mind. The police were more in evidence than usual with cars cruising down the high street and a number of foot soldiers patrolling the area. An exercise in making the locals feel safe.

Lolly did her usual thing of crossing the road before reaching the pawnbroker's. This meant walking past the shadowy expanse of the green, but it was still preferable to walking past the Cecils'. She kept to the outer edge of the pavement, keeping her eyes peeled for any sudden signs of movement, and stepped up the pace until she'd cleared the danger zone. All sorts lurked on the green at night: junkies and muggers and troubled kids from the Mansfield estate.

Lolly reached the flat and fumbled in her pocket for the key. The Indian was doing brisk business with a line of customers inside stretching almost to the door. Her stomach rumbled as she smelled the spice drifting in the air and she was briefly tempted. But no, she couldn't afford to be splashing out money on takeaways. It would be beans on toast for her tonight.

She found the key, put it in the lock and opened the door. It was then, just as she was going inside, that she heard the sound of footsteps coming up behind her.

'Hey, Lolly.'

It was eighteen months since she'd last heard that voice but she would have known it anywhere. Lolly spun round and there he was: Jude Rule. Her surprise was rapidly overtaken by shock and her mouth dropped open. He was a mess, his face beaten and one eye almost closed. Blood was in his hair and spattered on his clothes. Under normal circumstances she wouldn't have given him the time of day, but this hardly seemed the time to be bearing grudges.

'Christ, what happened to you?'

Jude gave a thin smile. 'Tony Cecil happened. But don't worry, I'm okay. It looks worse than it is. Can I come in? Would you mind?'

Lolly didn't have the heart to say no. Even after everything he'd done to her, she still felt something for him. Just pity, she told herself, as she nodded and beckoned him in. 'What are you even doing here? In Kellston, I mean. I thought you'd moved away.'

'I've still got the flat, but I don't use it much.' Jude trudged slowly up the stairs, each step clearly causing him pain. 'I only came back for a few days, to collect some stuff and next thing . . . '

'I saw Tony this morning. He was asking where you were. I'd have warned you if I'd known you were back.' Lolly wasn't sure if this was true or not, but that old desire to please had suddenly resurfaced. She didn't want him to think badly of her even though *he* was the one who should be feeling guilty.

In the light of the living room she could see his injuries more clearly. 'Do you want some ice for that eye?'

Jude shook his head and sat down on the sofa. 'The bastard had his brother with him. If it had just been Tony . . . '

If it had just been Tony, Lolly thought, the outcome would have been exactly the same. Jude wasn't a fighter. 'Two against one,' she said. 'You didn't stand a chance. What I don't understand is why he's coming after you after all this time. It's been six years, for God's sake.'

'Yeah, well, he was banged up for three of those, and by the time he got out I wasn't around any more. Someone must have seen me and tipped him off.'

'You want a coffee?' she asked. 'Sorry, but I haven't got anything stronger.'

'No, thanks. I can't stay for long. I only came to ask about Mal.'

Lolly, who had been labouring under the illusion that he had turned to her for refuge, for sanctuary, felt her stomach tighten. 'What?'

'I'm presuming you know where he is.'

'Then you're presuming wrongly.' She hissed out the words, glaring at him. 'How the hell would I know?'

'Esther's worried,' he said. 'She thinks he might come after her.'

Esther. Bloody *Esther.* Just hearing her name made Lolly grit her teeth. 'And why would he do that?'

Jude raised his eyebrows. 'Why do you think? She's the one who got him locked up, wasn't she?'

'Mal would never hurt Esther. It's ridiculous and you know it.'

'He pushed her down the steps, Lol. He could have killed her.'

'She *fell* down the steps. It was an accident. I saw it with my own eyes. You weren't even there.'

'She still got him sent down over Teddy Heath. You think he's happy about that? I wouldn't be if I was in his shoes.'

'If she's worried she should go to the police.'

'Oh, she's already talked to them, but who wants a load of plods hanging round the house? It doesn't do much for the ambience. Besides, they can hardly take care of her twenty-four hours a day.'

Lolly, who hadn't sat down yet, stared at him with suspicion. 'Tell me what's really going on.'

'I've already told you.'

'No, that doesn't make any sense. Mal's due to be released in a few months. If he wanted to have it out with Esther – and I'm not even saying he does – he could do it then. Why would he risk his future, his freedom, everything and take off now?'

'Because by the time he was released, she'd be gone.'

'What?'

'She's leaving,' Jude said. 'Going to the States. She has a couple of films lined up over there. If it all works out, she won't be coming back.'

Lolly scowled at him, raising her shoulders in a shrug. 'So what? There's such a thing as phones, aeroplanes. He doesn't have to abscond from jail in order to talk to her. She's an actress; it's not as though she can just disappear.'

'Maybe he doesn't fancy traipsing halfway round the world to see her.'

But Lolly wasn't buying it. 'There's something else going on. Tell me.'

Jude touched his damaged eye and sucked in a breath. 'Isn't that enough?'

'No,' she said. 'It isn't.'

'Why don't you just tell me where he is.'

'Because I don't know. And to be quite honest, even if I did, I wouldn't.'

Jude gave a slow shake of his head, his gaze sliding over the room, as though he might find some evidence of Mal having been there. 'You're not doing him any favours.'

Lolly was reminded of the two cops who'd come to visit. 'You want to search the place? He's not here if that's what you're thinking.'

'No, even Mal wouldn't be that stupid.'

Suddenly, Lolly didn't want him in her flat. Any sympathy she'd had was gone. He was still the same old Jude, without principles, without conscience. He didn't care about her in the slightest. Esther was still pulling his strings. The only reason he was here was to try and get information. 'You should go to A&E,' she said coldly, 'get yourself seen to. Your face is a mess.'

'I'll be fine. Look, Esther wants to talk to you. I've got the car outside. We can be there in an hour.'

Lolly wondered what went on in that head of his; maybe Tony Cecil had scrambled his brains. 'Are you kidding me?

Esther kicked me out, remember? I'd rather walk through a pit of snakes than speak to that woman again.'

'She's sorry about that. It was . . . a difficult time.'

'Yeah, a difficult time for *me.* Anyway, I can't help her. If she thinks I know where Mal is she's mistaken. And I'm not going all the way to West Henby to repeat what I've already said to you.'

'She's got other things she wants to talk about.'

'Like what?'

Jude averted his eyes, not meeting her gaze. 'Maybe she wants to apologise.'

'When hell freezes over. Come on, Jude, I wasn't born yesterday. What's she up to?'

Jude rose slowly to his feet. 'I have to get going. You know where we are if you change your mind.'

She noted the 'we', as though they were a couple, but her pride wouldn't permit her to delve any further. She didn't want him to imagine she had the tiniest bit of interest in his love life. Instead she asked, 'So, is that where you're living now?'

'For the moment, until we go to the States.'

'You're going too?'

'Why not? I'm sick of this country and all the people in it. I can't wait to see the back of the damn place.'

Lolly walked with him to the top of the stairs. Every time they met, it always turned to rancour. She wished he hadn't come tonight, wished she hadn't had to look at his stupid battered face. 'You should report him; Tony Cecil, I mean. You could have him for assault.'

'And spend the next three hours down Cowan Road? No thanks. I've got better things to do.'

There was a short awkward silence before Lolly said, 'Bye then. Watch how you go.'

Jude looked like he was about to say something in response, but his mouth closed almost as soon as it opened. He gave a cursory nod, went down the stairs and out of the door. She heard the click and then there was silence.

Lolly stood for a while gazing down at nothing.

12

Saturday 17 September. Mayfair

Vinnie Keane could see the whole room from his position at the bar. The pub was an upmarket joint in the heart of Mayfair, all shiny chrome and sparkling glass. The walls were covered in what passed for art, big blocks of colour that could have been painted by a five-year-old. It gave him a headache just to look at them.

The theatre crowd had come and gone, leaving a temporary lull. Now the pub was filling up again with a different crowd, men and women who would later move on to the swish clubs and casinos. The air was filled with the scent of expensive perfume. He sipped his overpriced Scotch while his gaze slid from face to face, never settling for long, never drawing any attention to himself.

Terry was sitting in the corner, still talking to Les Pool. It was a conversation that had been going on for over two hours now while the men tried to broker a deal over Soho territory. There had been trouble recently between the rival firms, resulting in fights and stabbings as they jostled for position. The situation was only pleasing to one party and that was the law. Old Bill was more than happy to have London's villains at loggerheads so long as it didn't develop into all-out warfare.

It was Terry's willingness to negotiate that made him different to his predecessor, Joe Quinn. Joe would have gone in, all guns blazing, the moment anyone stepped on his toes, but Terry had a smarter approach. If something could be resolved peacefully with a bit of give and take, then that's the way he would go. He'd rather spend his time making money than feuding.

That wasn't to say Terry was a pushover. There were plenty who suspected he'd killed Joe, and even if he hadn't the rumours didn't harm his reputation. In this business, a streak of ruthlessness was useful. Vinnie much preferred this boss to the last. You knew where you were with Terry. Joe had been a vicious bastard, feared rather than respected, and his death was no great loss to the world.

Vinnie glanced over to the other side of the bar where his counterpart was positioned. Rico was Les Pool's security, a tall, thin piece of shit with scars down his left cheek. They could have sat and drunk together but Vinnie preferred his own company. The bloke was weird, twisted, with a temper that would flare at the least provocation. One word out of place and he'd get the hump. Who needed that kind of crap? Nobody.

There had been bad blood between Terry and Les ever since Joe Quinn's murder. Les had seen an opportunity to take over Joe's manor, to fill the gap that had been left, and he'd marched in his army of thugs only to find Terry waiting for him. Vinnie smiled at the memory. A&E had been busy that night. After the battle a fragile peace had broken out but trouble was starting to escalate again.

Terry didn't need trouble at the moment. He had enough grief with the law crawling all over his patch. The killing of Dana Leigh would have a serious impact on business for a week or two, the punters keeping their distance until the fuss died down. And it wouldn't just mean a loss of earnings from the girls: the sales of weed and coke would suffer too. Customers didn't care for Old Bill looking over their shoulder.

Vinnie had barely known Dana and so felt no personal sense of loss at her death. He was sorry for her but had seen enough of life to know that for some girls it would never get any better than a futile, self-destructive cycle of turning tricks to fund their habit. One way or another, she'd have been dead before the age of thirty. It was possible, even probable, that Dana had been moonlighting, meeting punters away from the house so she could keep the money for herself. A risky business as she'd found out to her cost.

Brent Sandler came into the pub, shook hands with Terry and Les and took a seat at the table. Vinnie shifted on the bar stool and frowned. Sandler was someone else he couldn't stand, a creep, a slimeball who always had his hands on the girls. He'd been at Marcie's on Thursday night, taking the usual liberties, until he'd disappeared about nine leaving that flash motor of his in the club car park.

There were all sorts of stories about the bastard – none of them good – but Terry was happy to overlook his less desirable character traits. A bent solicitor always came in handy when you were dealing with the law: he could sort out sweeteners and make sure everything ran smoothly. Sandler had half the CID in his pocket and that kind of leverage was worth its weight in gold.

Vinnie drank his Scotch and slid his tongue along his lips. He had another more personal reason for hating the man and that was to do with his wife, Laura Sandler. The woman had class and he was smitten. It was three months now since the affair had started and it showed no signs of fizzling out. Most of the girls he dated were here one day and gone the next, a bit of fun, but she was different. When he thought about her something clenched in his chest.

Laura was dark-haired, brown-eyed, a real beauty, but what he felt went beyond the physical; she had got under his skin and he couldn't stop thinking about her. He knew he was playing with fire, that there'd be serious repercussions if the affair was exposed, but the sneaking around only added to the thrill.

Vinnie didn't give two fucks about Sandler – the bloke was beneath contempt – but Terry was a different matter. He'd do his nut if he ever found out and not because he had any scruples when it came to screwing other men's wives: Sandler was useful to him and business always came first. Vinnie liked to think that Terry would stand by him, the same way *he'd* stood by Terry after Joe Quinn's murder, but nothing was certain. Loyalty had shades of grey; it was never cut and dried.

Feeling Rico's eyes on him, Vinnie looked across the bar again. He held the lowlife's gaze, unblinking, until Rico gave up and glanced away. It was a small victory but it made him feel better. He drained his glass, put it on the counter and went back to thinking about Laura. Some women were worth taking risks for and she was one of them. He held her face in his mind, traced her features, thought about the way she moved when they made love. He was consumed, he knew, with a passion beyond reason. It was the kind of passion that didn't always end well.

13

Monday 19 September. Camden

Nick drank his coffee while he waited, wondering why it was that girls were always late. It was as if they worked to a different clock to the other half of the population, the mechanism ticking at a female pace. He hadn't heard back from Heather Grant until last night when she'd apologised for the delay and said she'd been away for the weekend. Not wanting to discuss matters over the phone, he'd suggested meeting up in Camden at eleven in a café near the Tube. It was only a couple of stops down the line from Tufnell Park if she chose to leave the Mini at home.

Nick always had Monday off when he'd worked a Saturday and he usually spent it catching up on those mundane chores like going to the launderette and giving his flat a clean. The latter never took long as he lived in a shoebox, the only place he could afford on his current salary. He could have shared accommodation – it would have been cheaper – but that came with its own problems, like having to put up with someone else's bad habits. Anyway, he spent so little time there its size didn't really matter.

Camden was one of Nick's favourite places in London. He liked the mix of people and its feeling of edginess. And okay so maybe it was a touch run down but he preferred that to the layer of gloss that covered some areas. However, this wasn't the only reason he hadn't chosen Connolly's like the last time. The risk of running into Lolly in Kellston was too great. All the things he admired about her – her straightforwardness, her feistiness – were things that could get in the way when it came to brokering a deal with Heather.

Although Nick felt some guilt about keeping Lolly out of the loop, he reckoned it was for the best. She was upset about Mal going AWOL and was likely to give Heather the third degree if she thought information was being withheld. He favoured a more softly-softly approach using artful persuasion rather than confrontation.

Just as Nick was checking his watch for the umpteenth time, the door to the café opened and Heather Grant walked in. Even in jeans and a shirt she managed to look elegant. Her face was as lovely as he'd remembered, her fair hair sleek and glossy. As she walked towards him his eyes quickly raked her slender frame, taking in everything from the fine gold chain around her neck to the pink pumps she was wearing on her feet. He could have justified this close scrutiny with the excuse it was important for detectives to hone their observational skills, but in truth he just enjoyed looking at her.

Heather pulled out a chair and sat down. 'Hello, Nick. Good to see you again.'

'How are you?'

'Curious,' she said. 'I didn't expect to hear from you so soon.'

'I'm curious too.'

'What's on your mind?'

'Mal Fury,' he said. 'I presume you've heard the news about him absconding?'

'Yes, I heard. It was in the papers – and Esther called me.'

'And the police?'

'The police,' she echoed, frowning slightly as if she didn't understand.

'Haven't they been in touch with you?'

A waitress arrived to take their order – more coffee for him, tea for her – giving Heather some time to consider her response. She waited a few seconds and then her mouth slid into a smile. 'Ah, so you know about the prison visit. How did you find out?'

At least she hadn't insulted his intelligence by lying to him. 'It wasn't that hard,' he said. 'But I'm surprised he agreed to see you. From what I know about Mal he usually stays well away from reporters, authors and the like.'

Heather gave a small shrug. 'Perhaps you don't know him as well as you think.'

'What did you tell the police?'

'The truth,' she said.

'And that is?'

'That I'm researching a book about Kay Fury. That I wanted to get Mal's take on things. What else?'

'It's the *what else* that interests me. I mean, it seems a bit of a coincidence that pretty soon after your visit he decided to do a disappearing act.'

'Coincidences happen.'

'I'm just wondering what you said to him.'

Heather inclined her head, her face the picture of innocence. 'I can't think of anything that would have made him take off. It's a complete mystery.'

'Why don't I believe you?'

'I've no idea. You must have a suspicious mind.'

'Did you tell him about Teddy Heath's girlfriend?'

Heather didn't answer.

'And what's Esther's view on all this?' he continued. 'She must have one. Why does *she* think Mal's gone AWOL?'

But Heather wasn't playing ball. Instead she said, 'I went to see Brenda Cecil. She doesn't have a very high opinion of Lolly.'

'I'm sure it's mutual. That woman was only ever out for what she could get. She's a nasty piece of work like those two sons of hers. If it had been down to her, Lolly would have ended up in care.'

'So, what's the deal with you and Lolly?'

Nick shook his head. 'There isn't any deal. We're just friends.'

'You're very protective of her.'

'That's what friends do: watch out for each other.'

'How chivalrous,' she said, the sarcasm not even thinly veiled.

'You don't think men and women can be friends?'

'Did I say that? All I meant was that you seem close.'

Nick suspected her of trying to provoke a reaction, of probing for his weak spots. She was certainly perceptive, unless his feelings were blatantly obvious. He hoped this wasn't true. He'd always been careful to keep relations with Lolly on a purely friendly footing and the last thing he wanted was a situation where the two of them became awkward with each other.

The waitress turned up with two mugs and put them on the table. There was a brief silence until the woman was out of earshot. Heather was the one to speak first.

'So where do we go from here?'

Nick decided to play his ace. 'I've brought a copy of Stanley's file with me.' He gestured towards a carrier bag lying on the seat beside him. 'You can have it if you'll share your information.'

Heather's eyes lit up. 'What made you change your mind?'

'I need to know what's going on in Mal's head, to try and figure out what he's going to do next.'

'Esther thinks he's coming after her. She's leaving you know, going to the States.'

'And you told Mal that?'

'I might have mentioned it,' she said. 'To be honest, I presumed he already knew.'

Nick didn't believe this for a moment. 'When is she going?'

'Soon. A few weeks, a month. But now Mal's on the loose, she's convinced she's going to be murdered in her bed.'

'And what do *you* think?'

'I suppose, in theory, he's got every reason to hate her – she sent him to jail, didn't she? – but I didn't get that impression when we met. He seemed more resigned than vengeful. And Esther's the original drama queen. Everything has to be about *her.*'

'Did you tell Mal about Teddy Heath's girlfriend?'

Heather's gaze flicked towards the white carrier bag. She didn't reply. She was going to stay tight-lipped until he delivered the goods.

Nick picked up the bag and put it on the table between them. Heather quickly reached out, but he brought his hand down, preventing her from taking it. He wasn't going to relinquish the papers until he'd got what he wanted. 'Teddy's girlfriend?' he repeated.

Heather smiled, hesitated, glanced at the bag again and said, 'Hazel, Hazel Finch. It took me six months just to find out her name. I must have talked to a hundred people, actors mainly, trying to jog their memories. Teddy wasn't what you'd call the monogamous sort; he changed his girlfriends as often as his underpants. It was one of his exes who suggested Hazel; she remembered Teddy bringing her to a party.'

'Did you manage to track her down?'

'Eventually. She was living in Harlow and wasn't best pleased to find me on her doorstep. Swore blind she hadn't even been with Teddy when Kay was taken, that they'd split up a long time before.'

'You don't believe her?'

'She seemed pretty jumpy, but then she could just be the nervous sort. The thing is, I watched the house for a few days before I even approached her. There was a girl living there too, fair-haired, about nineteen or twenty.'

'Her daughter?' Nick asked, a faint excitement stirring inside him.

'Well, *someone*'s daughter. Her name's Vicky, but I didn't get the chance to talk to her.' Heather gave a sigh of frustration. 'When I went back, a few days after I'd spoken to Hazel, no one was there and I've not had a sniff of them since. How odd is that? Unless it's another of those coincidences, I'd say I well and truly put the wind up her.'

'And Esther knows all this?'

'Yes, I told her.'

'And Mal?'

Heather nodded. 'But I was careful not to get his hopes up. I said it was just a lead, nothing more, that there was more chance of Vicky *not* being Kay than actually being her.'

'How did he react?'

'He was calm. He understood. I mean, he's been here before, hasn't he?' She glanced down towards the file. 'How many possibles are there in there? Hundreds?'

'Not far off. Some of them fell at the first hurdle – wrong blood group – and the others were dismissed later.' He took a sip of coffee and put the mug down. 'Did Esther think about informing the police?'

'Telling them what, though? Hazel could have had all sorts of reasons for leaving: maybe she just didn't want to get involved, didn't want people to know that she'd ever dated Teddy Heath. If the press had got hold of the story, they could have made something of it. Mud sticks, doesn't it? Or maybe she had a completely different reason for going – debt collectors on her back, a relationship breakdown, a new job ... '

'And the neighbours couldn't shed any light?'

'No, they kept themselves to themselves apparently, and they'd only lived there for nine months. There was something, mind: one of them told me that a man had been there looking for Hazel a few days earlier. He claimed to be an old friend and was trying to find out where she'd gone. He was very persistent. It made me wonder if ... I don't know, I could be completely wrong, but I wondered if Esther had hired a private detective.'

'I take it you asked her?'

'She said she hadn't, but I'm not sure I believe her. And recently she seems to have lost all interest in Hazel, saying I shouldn't waste any more time on her, that it's just another dead end.'

'You think she's trying to sideline you?'

'It's possible. This sudden decision to move to the States ... Well, perhaps it is to do with her job, but I'm not convinced. Something doesn't smell right.'

'How much of this does Mal know?'

'Most of it.'

It occurred to Nick that if Mal Fury thought Esther was in contact with Kay or even close to finding her, then that would provide a pretty good motive for what he'd done. By the time he got released from jail it could all be too late. Esther would be hundreds of miles across the ocean, taking the truth and maybe even their daughter with her.

'I've been down Somerset House,' Heather said, 'trying to find a birth certificate for Victoria Finch, but there's nothing matching in 1958. It could be she's not even registered under that name.'

'Or not registered at all.'

'Yeah, that's not going to help.'

'So what's the plan?'

'I'll just keep going, keep digging. Something might turn up. Did you get a chance to talk to Lita, to Lolly?'

'Not yet.'

Heather's eyes narrowed as if she could see straight through the lie. 'Well, when you do, let me know what she says.'

'I will.'

She placed her hand on the carrier bag next to his. 'Okay, I've stuck to my side of the deal.'

Nick hesitated, but then released his hold. 'Fair enough. It's all yours.'

'Thank you.' Heather pulled the bag towards her and then leaned her elbows on it as if Nick might try to snatch it back. 'You know what's so frustrating about all this?'

'Everything?' he suggested.

'Apart from that. If Mal had trusted Stanley with the truth, Hazel Finch could have been found years ago. If he'd just told him about what happened to Teddy . . . '

'That's a lot of trust. Don't forget you could hang for murder back then. Even if Teddy's death was an accident, a jury might not have seen it that way.'

'Wasn't it a risk worth taking if it meant his daughter might be found?'

'Unless he thought it was already too late, that Teddy would have covered his tracks. And he'd have been asking Stanley to be an accessory. Perhaps he didn't want to put him in that position.'

Heather wrinkled her nose as if neither of these explanations really stacked up. She gazed into the middle distance for a while before refocusing on Nick and expelling another long sigh. 'What if I'm barking up the wrong tree entirely? I'm not even sure how old Vicky is. Hazel might just be protecting her, and herself. No one wants to be linked to a murderer – he killed that poor nanny, after all – and with a man who stole a baby.'

'True. You should be careful.'

'Careful?'

Nick smiled. 'This is the kind of case that can take over your life. You'll end up living, eating, breathing and sleeping it.'

'I'm a lost cause already,' she groaned. After lifting her elbows, she tapped the bag with the fingertips of her right hand. 'Is there anything useful in here?'

'You'll have to read it and see.'

'What about the nanny? Did Stanley ever look into her?'

'Cathy Kershaw. Yes, he went to see her parents. He didn't think she was involved. The police had checked out that angle years before and come up with nothing. There was no indication that she'd even met Teddy.'

'But she could have. She was living in the Fury house, wasn't she?'

'Not mixing with the guests, though. Strictly below stairs if you know what I mean.'

'Teddy was a womaniser. He could have found his way downstairs.'

'She was a decent girl by all accounts.'

Heather rolled her eyes. 'Even decent girls get seduced.'

Nick almost asked if she was speaking from experience but bit his tongue. It could have come across as flirtation and he didn't want to give the impression he wasn't taking her seriously. Or that he was even faintly interested in her. This was strictly business, an exchange of information and nothing more.

'What about the other staff?' she asked. 'Didn't the police think there could be an inside connection?'

'Everyone was interviewed so far as I'm aware. A lot of the villagers were employed at the time and Esther sacked every single one of them. It didn't go down too well as you can imagine. Some of them had worked in the house for years.'

'Brutal,' she said.

'A knee-jerk reaction, I guess. What do you do when you can't trust anyone?'

Heather leaned forward and rubbed her face with her hands.

'Are you all right?'

She dropped her hands and nodded. 'Don't mind me. I'm just trying to get my head around it all.'

'Yeah, it's guaranteed to give you a headache. What's your gut feeling as regards Hazel Finch?'

Heather glanced down at her stomach as if to garner its opinions. She looked up again and grinned. 'Is that how you do your detecting?'

'Partly,' he said. 'It all counts.'

'Okay, well, I think she's got something to hide, but I can't be sure that something is Vicky. Although she certainly didn't want to talk about her. As soon as I broached the subject she clammed up – not that she was especially forthcoming to begin with. I made sure Vicky wasn't there when I knocked on the door which meant I never got the chance to see her up close. I took a few photos, though, from the car. Do you want to take a look? They're not that great.'

'Sure,' he said.

Heather took a small oblong paper wallet from her bag and passed it across the table. Nick slid out three glossy prints. She was right: they weren't that great. They'd been taken from a distance of about twenty feet and probably snapped too quickly for fear of being caught in the act. The girl had long, straight blonde hair and was dressed in flared jeans and a vivid orange T-shirt. In the first two prints her face was slightly blurry, but the third was clearer. He studied the features: the eyes, the nose, the mouth. Vicky's face was round, plump-cheeked and although she was pretty enough he could see no resemblance to either of the Furys.

'Not all girls look like their mothers,' Heather said, as though she'd guessed what he was thinking.

'You look more like Esther than she does.'

'I'll have to have a word with my parents, make sure there isn't something they want to tell me.'

Nick smiled and went back to studying the picture. 'You're right, though, insofar as there isn't anything to rule her out. Does she look anything like Hazel?'

'Not really. I mean, I wouldn't pick them out as being related in an identity parade.'

'And what about Esther? What does she think?'

'She said no, absolutely not, but she still held on to a set of the photos. Why do that if you're absolutely sure?'

'She can't ever be that. And Mal? Has he seen them?'

'I don't know. Probably. I took the best one with me to the prison, but they wouldn't let me show it on the visit. Rules and regulations, although God knows why a photo should be a problem. I had to leave it at reception so I've no idea if it was given to him or not.'

Nick slid the photographs back into the folder and returned them to her. 'But he did a bunk not long after you saw him.'

Heather stared at him. 'You think it's my fault he's absconded?'

'No, you can't blame yourself.'

'I don't,' she said sharply. 'He's a grown man. He can make his own decisions, no matter how stupid they are.'

'Absolutely,' Nick said. There was a shift in the atmosphere, a sudden chill. She had gone from amenable to hostile in under five seconds. 'I didn't mean anything by it.'

Heather's smile was slight and strained. 'I have to go,' she said, standing up. 'Thanks for the file. Let me know about Lolly, won't you?'

Nick nodded. 'Good luck.'

She left the café with the carrier bag swinging at her side. There was something defiant in her gait, something almost angry.

14

Monday 19 September. Kellston

Business was conducted on the ground and first floors of the house on Albert Road, but the girls who lived in had their own private space on the second floor. Dana's room was sparsely furnished with little in the way of personal belongings: some clothes hanging in the wardrobe, cosmetics and perfume on the dressing table, an old record player with half a dozen LPs. There wasn't much to show for nineteen years of life.

While Lolly sorted out the clothes, Stella was going through the drawer in the bedside table looking for any clues as to who the mysterious Freddy might be. To date all she had found of importance was a brown cardboard folder containing the history of Dana's time in care and a small collection of press cuttings relating to when she'd been abandoned as a baby. She had placed these on the bed beside her.

'Did the law take anything away?' Lolly asked.

Stella shook her head. 'They had a quick look round but that was it.'

Lolly folded up dresses and shirts and put them in a bag. She tried not to think too much about the girl who had worn them and how she had died: beaten, raped, strangled. Staying practical was the only way to deal with things. She was more than aware that her present life could easily have mirrored Dana's if it hadn't been for Mal's intervention. There but for the grace of God . . .

It didn't take them long to clear the room – a new girl would be moving in soon – and when they'd finished they stood together by the door and were silent. No words seemed adequate and it was too late for prayers. Dana was never coming back. The Good Lord would make his own judgement and hopefully it would be merciful.

Lolly's relationship with God was a tricky one. Like most people she tended to ask for his help when in trouble and forget about him when she wasn't. At the moment, what she felt was a combination of sadness, frustration and anger. What was the point of creating a world and then throwing a heap of grief into it? It seemed to her a questionable way of going about things.

Down in the kitchen, they placed the bags by the sink and sat down at the table. Stella rolled a cigarette; her hands were shaking and it took her twice as long as usual. Lolly started rooting through the rubbish they'd retrieved from the wastepaper basket: tissues, bus tickets, chocolate-bar wrappers, old magazines, just in case Dana had scribbled Freddy's phone number or address on them. Near the bottom of the pile she came across a National Front leaflet scrunched into a ball. She smoothed it out, stared at it for a while and then held it up.

'Look at this.'

Stella shrugged. 'What of it?'

'The Cecils are involved with the National Front, Tony and FJ. I saw them at the market on Saturday handing out these.'

'What of it?'

'Well, FJ's a Freddy, isn't he? Freddy Junior.'

'Except nobody calls him that.'

'*He* might, if he didn't want Dana to know his true identity. And he's more than capable of trying to rip her off.'

Stella puffed on the cigarette, frowning. 'There's a big difference between that and murder, love.'

'Tony's got form for GBH, he did time for it, and FJ's no better. The two of them beat up Jude on Saturday. They're thugs.'

'What? I didn't even know Jude was back.'

'He isn't,' she said. 'He was just . . . ' Lolly waved a hand, not wanting to go into the details. Even speaking his name sent sparks of anger through her. 'It doesn't matter. All I'm saying is that I wouldn't put it past them. Maybe Dana sussed what they doing, realised she was being conned and—'

'And so they decided to shut her up by killing her? Even if Dana had gone to the law – which she wouldn't have – she couldn't have proved nothin'. The worst they'd have got is a slap on the wrist.'

Put like that, Lolly could see that her theory didn't make much sense, but she wasn't prepared to let go of the Cecil angle just yet. 'What about Freddy Senior, then?'

Stella gave a mirthless laugh. 'Are you kidding? Freddy Cecil? He wouldn't have gone near Dana. If he'd so much as looked at a tom, Brenda would have ripped his balls off. Anyway, there are thousands of those leaflets doing the rounds. Dana could have picked it up anywhere.'

Lolly glanced at the leaflet one last time and then put it aside. Her suggestions had been coloured, she knew, by her loathing of the Cecils, what they'd done to Jude and her recent encounter at the market. She would still, however, keep Tony and FJ on her own private list of suspects. They were evil sods and capable of anything.

Stella started looking through the file, softly tutting while she perused Dana's history in care. Lolly moved on to the press cuttings and laid them out in front of her. There were seven in all, photocopies, and the stories came from local papers. There were pictures of a nurse holding Dana – possibly the nurse who had provided her with a name – and others of the church where the abandoned baby had been found. Dana had been about six or seven months old and wrapped in a pink blanket. Requests were made for anyone with information to come forward.

Follow-up reports failed to reveal any new leads. If anyone had known anything they had kept quiet, and the mother had never been traced. It was unusual, Lolly thought, for a baby to be abandoned at that age. More often they were newborns, left out of fear and desperation. Tests must have been done to establish that Dana wasn't the missing Fury infant. Had Mal and Esther been informed? If so, there would have been a few brief hours of hope before the crushing disappointment.

The mother could still be out there somewhere. If she was local, she would have heard about the murdered girl and possibly made the connection. Dana wasn't a common name. A shiver ran through Lolly. Not wanting to dwell on what the woman might be feeling, she tried to keep her practical hat on.

'I wonder where Dana met this Freddy.'

Stella looked up, a red flush of anger rising to her cheeks. 'I wish I bloody knew. In the pub most likely or through one of those scummy mates of hers.'

'I thought she didn't have any mates.'

'She didn't, not real ones. But she wasn't smart enough to know the difference. I told her time and time again: that lot only ever look after number one. So long as you're buying their junk, they'll be your best pal, but you won't see them for dust when the money runs out.'

Lolly knew that what she meant by junk was heroin. Although

Stella seemed to exist on a diet of fags, vodka, coffee and dope, she drew the line at the hard stuff. The drug had been growing in popularity recently and more pushers were moving into the area. They hung around the Mansfield estate, making what was already a bad situation ten times worse. Muggings and burglaries were on the rise as addicts struggled to feed their habit.

Worried that Stella might try and confront the dealers over Freddy – a move that could only ever end badly for her – Lolly put forward another suggestion. 'For all we know, Freddy could have been a punter.'

'Nah, she wouldn't talk about nothin' personal to a punter. They don't pay to have conversations, love. That's the last bleedin' thing on their mind.'

Lolly veered off in another direction. 'Where did she get these newspaper cuttings?'

'The library, I think. Most of them. And one or two from the *Gazette*.'

'Recently?'

'A few months back.'

'Perhaps that's how she met Freddy. I mean, she'd have had to have asked for help, wouldn't she? They don't leave these old newspapers lying around. They're in some kind of archive. Someone would have had to go and get them for her . . . well, unless they're on one of those microfiche things, but even then she'd have needed a hand operating the machine. Perhaps he works at the library or was just there when Dana came in. He could have overheard her talking and spotted an opportunity.'

Stella puffed on her cigarette while she pondered the possibility.

'Or the *Kellston Gazette* office,' Lolly continued. 'We could ask at both, see if anyone remembers her.'

'I suppose,' Stella said without much enthusiasm. She had,

perhaps, already formed her own opinion as to how Freddy could be tracked down and it didn't involve hanging around in dusty buildings. Standing up, she went over to the cupboard, took out a bottle of vodka and poured a couple of shots into a glass. 'You want one, Lol?'

Lolly wasn't a big drinker at the best of times, and two o'clock on a Monday afternoon wasn't one of them. 'No, ta.'

'The thing is,' Stella said, returning to the table, 'that lowlife had Dana right where he wanted. Kept saying he was close to finding her mum, that she was a local woman – as if anyone couldn't guess at that – but he needed a few more quid to grease some palms and get people talking. Where's the bloody evidence? I asked. How do you know any of it is true? I told her she couldn't trust no one round here, but she wouldn't listen. The stupid kid only ever heard what she wanted to hear.'

Lolly could understand Dana's selective hearing when it came to trying to find her family. Everyone wanted roots, a sense of belonging, and that need would have made her easy to exploit. 'What if it wasn't Freddy who killed her?'

'It was him all right. And I'll bet she had his phone number in her bag. He'd have made damn sure he got rid of that.'

'But I don't get all the secrecy. I mean, I do, from *his* point of view, but didn't Dana think it was odd?'

'She weren't thinking, hon, that's the trouble. And he had an answer for everything. Said they had to keep quiet, keep it under wraps, in case the papers got wind of it.' Stella drained her glass, stood up and poured another. 'He reckoned if they didn't keep it hush-hush, her mum might get spooked and do a runner.'

'But she still told you.'

'Only 'cause she was so excited she couldn't keep it to herself. She had this idea in her head, how she'd be welcomed with open arms and it would all be happy ever after.'

The front door opened and closed and Jackie came through to the kitchen. She scowled when she saw Lolly. 'You still here? Ain't you got a home to go to?'

'Leave it out,' Stella said. 'She's been helping me clear Dana's room.'

Jackie glanced towards the bags near the sink. 'Not helping herself, I hope.'

'I'm not a thief,' Lolly said.

Jackie's eyebrows went up, as though Lolly was being unduly sensitive. 'Didn't say you were, did I?'

'Near as damn it.'

The two of them glared at each other. Lolly, who had long since learned never to back down, held the stare until Jackie gave in and looked away. Having established that she couldn't be intimidated, Lolly pushed back her chair and rose to her feet.

'Okay, I'd better make a move. I'll go and check out the library, unless you want to come with me?'

Stella shook her head. 'Nah, I can't bear those places. They're too quiet, love. It ain't natural.'

'I'll let you know if I find out anything.'

'Thanks, hon. You take care of yourself.'

Lolly left the house and did her usual half-run, half-walk, making sure she didn't make eye contact with any driver cruising along Albert Road. It was still much quieter than usual, but business was starting to pick up. Even murder didn't keep the punters away for long. The police presence was minimal now with just the occasional patrol car doing the rounds.

She knew that Stella didn't have much faith in her theory, and maybe it was a long shot, but she reckoned it was still worth pursuing. It was a worry that Stella might do something rash, especially when she'd had a few. Confronting dealers was never advisable. The best of them were dodgy, and the worst . . . well, the worst would stick a knife in your guts if you caused them any trouble.

As she walked she wondered how Dana had found the money to feed her drug habit *and* pay Freddy. She had no idea how much the girls earned but imagined there wasn't a whole lot left over after Terry had taken his share and the rent had been paid. Dana, being young, had probably had more customers than the others – the older you were the tougher it was to make a living – but it must have been a stretch.

The library was a grand red brick building, halfway down the high street and next to the town hall. It was years since she'd last been inside. She would go there as a kid, especially in winter when her mum wasn't around and there were no coins to feed the meter in the flat. It had been a good place to stay warm and so long as you kept quiet no one bothered you.

Lolly halted by the entrance, trying to decide how to play it. People got suspicious when you started asking questions and she wasn't even sure what questions to ask. The staff might clam up if they realised she was retracing the steps of a murdered girl, and there was always the chance that Freddy either worked here or hung around a lot. Tipping off a murderer that you were hot on his tracks wouldn't be the smartest move in the world.

In the end, Lolly decided to simply make a request to see the local papers from the month and year Dana had been found – without mentioning Dana's name or why she was interested. From there she would play it by ear, have a good look round and see if anything happened. It wasn't much of a plan but it was the best she'd got.

Lolly had got herself all geared up and was about to go inside when she glanced along the high street and noticed

Nick's battered Ford parked outside the Indian takeaway. There was no sign of him so he'd either gone for a walk or was waiting in Connolly's. She hesitated, but only for a second. There was a chance he had some news about Mal and that was more important to her than trying to find Freddy.

15

Monday 19 September. Kellston and West Henby

There were only a few customers in the café; it was the post-lunch lull and the smell of burgers and onions still hung in the air. Lolly sipped an ice-cold Coke while she listened to Nick recount the details of his meeting with Heather Grant. She didn't interrupt but her expression grew darker while he talked. By the time he'd finished, her mouth was set in a thin straight line.

'You don't really believe this girl is Kay Fury, do you?'

'It doesn't matter what I believe. It's what Mal thinks that matters. Prison can screw with your head. There's no knowing what's going on in his mind. And the fact Hazel Finch and her daughter have suddenly disappeared is only going to reinforce whatever hope he might have left. Heather's story about Teddy Heath and Hazel seems to stand up, but that doesn't mean Vicky is Kay.'

'But even if she is, which is doubtful, what's he going to achieve by going on the run?'

'Perhaps he's scared the trail will go cold, that Hazel won't ever be found again. I don't know. You're trying to figure it out from a rational point of view and I don't imagine Mal's thinking straight at the moment.'

'Do you have the photos?'

Nick shook his head. 'But from what I could tell – and the pictures aren't that clear – she doesn't look like anyone in particular. Mal might have thought differently, though. Heather left one of the photos at the prison.'

Lolly could feel a small throbbing ache in her temples. She wasn't sure if this was down to the cold Coke or what Nick was telling her. 'Do you trust her? Heather, I mean. What if she's just stirring things up for her book? We don't even know if she's actually found Hazel. Those pictures she took could be of any random girl.'

'Oh, I'm sure there's plenty of stirring going on. I'm inclined to believe her about Hazel, but I could be wrong. So far as I can see she's dropped a bombshell, stood back and now she's waiting to see what rises from the dust. And I reckon she said a lot more to Mal than she's letting on, especially about Esther leaving. Did you know she was moving to the States?'

Lolly nodded. 'Jude told me.'

'You've seen Jude?'

'Briefly. He asked me to go to West Henby with him, said Esther wanted to talk to me.'

'And?'

'What do you think? There's nothing that woman can say that I want to hear.'

Nick's mouth turned down at the corners. 'Yeah, I get that, I understand, but perhaps you *should* go. What if she knows something important? What if Mal shows up there? You're the one person who might be able to talk some sense into him.'

Lolly hadn't considered that. 'You think he might?'

'I think it's likely. Heather's planted a seed in his head, the possibility that Esther might already be in contact with Hazel and Vicky. He'll want to see her, find out what's really going on.'

'But Esther's going to call the law the minute she sets eyes on him.'

'He could be prepared to take that chance.'

Lolly's natural instinct was to stay well away from Esther, but perhaps Nick was right. And even if Mal didn't show there was still a chance of finding out what Esther was up to. She decided, on balance, that it wasn't worth throwing the opportunity away. 'All right. I'll go. I'll go first thing tomorrow.'

'Why wait?' Nick said. 'If Mal's going to turn up, it's going to be soon. Let's do it now. I can give you a lift.'

'Right now?'

'Have you got something better to do?'

Lolly thought about the library and her plans to look for Freddy, but that was probably going to be a wild goose chase. Anyway, this was more pressing. If there was a chance of seeing Mal she had to grab it with both hands.

'Give me five minutes. I'll go and pack a bag.'

By half past three, Lolly and Nick were in Kent. The afternoon was sunny and warm and they drove with the windows halfway down. Carly Simon was on the radio singing 'Nobody Does It Better'. As they travelled along the winding roads there was a hint of autumn in the air, a feeling of change as the leaves on the trees began their transformation, a slow fade from green to yellow and rust.

Lolly, who had no idea of the kind of welcome she was going to receive – and welcome probably wasn't the right word – tried to distract herself by thinking about other things. But the dreaded encounter refused to be dismissed. No sooner had she pushed it away than it crept straight back into her head again.

Esther always made her nervous. She had an intimidating beauty and a cold kind of cruelty that could cut to the bone.

'What if she won't see me?'

'Why wouldn't she? She invited you, didn't she? She told Jude she wanted to talk.'

'And I said no.'

'So you changed your mind. It's not a crime. She won't care. She wants something and that gives you the upper hand. Perhaps she thinks you know what Mal's up to or where he is – or both. Just don't give too much away.'

'I haven't got anything to give away.'

Nick grinned. 'Yeah, well, she doesn't know that. And with a bit of luck she'll want to keep you under the same roof while she tries to figure it out. Keep your enemies close and all that. If Mal's going to confront her, it's going to be soon. You need to make sure you're there when it happens.'

Lolly didn't relish the thought of an extended stay or of facing Esther on her own. 'Will you be able to hang around for a while?'

'For a few hours,' he said. 'I have to work tomorrow.'

'You could stay over, drive back in the morning. There's plenty of room, and if Esther wants to talk so badly, she isn't going to quibble over one more guest in the house.'

'Let's see how it goes.'

Lolly reckoned it would go badly which was why she wanted some support, but she wasn't going to beg. Hopefully, Nick would agree once he saw how the land lay – which was always rocky when it came to Esther. They were getting close now and nerves were fluttering in Lolly's chest. 'You know what I don't understand?' she said. 'Why Heather Grant told you all this stuff in the first place. What's the benefit to her?'

There was a short pause before Nick said, 'I made a deal.'

'What kind of deal?'

'She wanted Stanley's file, remember? I figured it was worth handing over a copy to find out what she knew.' He gave her a sidelong glance. 'Do you think that was the wrong thing to do?'

Lolly considered it. 'Depends on whether you got the better part of the deal.'

'I've no idea,' he said. 'Not yet. But at least we've got a clue to why Mal's done what he's done.'

'He could be miles away by now.'

Nick nodded. 'He could be, but I don't think he is.'

The sun slid behind a cloud as they pulled up in front of the tall wrought-iron gates. There was a security system in place with a buzzer. Nick reached out of the window and pressed it.

They waited. Nothing happened. 'No one's home.'

'There's always someone home, or there used to be.'

Nick pressed the buzzer again. This time there was a clicking noise and a distant tinny female voice came out of a speaker.

'Who is it?'

'Nick Trent and Lolly Bruce.' He quickly corrected himself, remembering the name she was known by here. '*Lita* Bruce. We're here to see Esther Fury.'

There was another delay, as though the woman – Lolly was pretty sure it was the formidable housekeeper, Mrs Gough – was in two minds as to whether to let them in. But eventually the gates rolled back and they were allowed to enter.

As they travelled along the winding path, Lolly was reminded of the first time she'd ever come here with Nick's uncle, Stanley. It had been evening then, dark, and her first sight of the house, brightly illuminated, had taken her breath away. She had so many memories of the place, good and bad, and they all jostled for position in her head. Deep breaths, she told herself. Esther no longer had any power over her, no control. She was her own person now, as grown up as she'd ever be and reliant on nobody else.

But there was Jude to think about too. Would he be here? She was over him, completely, but still didn't want to see him with Esther. There would be a kind of humiliation in it, a torment that she couldn't bear. First love always stayed with you even if it was unrequited.

Nick parked on the drive, switched off the engine and turned to her. 'You ready?'

'As I'll ever be.'

'Let's do it then.'

16

Monday 19 September. West Henby

Although Mrs Gough had been informed of their arrival, the door was still firmly shut when they reached the top of the steps. Lolly rang the bell. A full minute passed before the housekeeper deigned to answer it. Her expression was tight and disapproving. She gave no indication of ever having met Lolly before and instead looked them both up and down like they were a pair of unwanted pedlars come to sell their wares. If she'd had the choice she would probably have slammed the door in their faces.

Eventually, though, she managed to squeeze the words from a reluctant mouth. 'I suppose you'd better come in. Follow me. Mrs Fury is in the sun room.'

As they walked in her wake, their footsteps echoing through the large hallway, Lolly glanced at Nick and rolled her eyes. Then, in an act of deliberate mischief, knowing that the woman had no desire to engage with her, she asked, 'So, how are you, Mrs Gough? Are you keeping well? It's been a while.'

The housekeeper flinched but didn't even glance over her shoulder. 'Quite well, thank you.'

'That's good. It must be over a year since I saw you last.'

Mrs Gough upped her pace as if to outrun Lolly's hollow pleasantries. She sped through to the back of the house where she flung open the doors and formally announced, 'Mr Trent and Miss Bruce,' before marching back the way she had come.

Lolly and Nick went in. It was warm in the sun room, the glass walls and roof retaining the last of the afternoon heat. A pungent smell of lilies filled the air. Esther was reclining in a wide wicker chair, her feet on a stool and her ankles crossed. Dressed in a cream linen skirt and a white shirt, she looked impeccable as always. She didn't bother getting up but managed to stretch her lips into a smile.

'Lita, darling, what a surprise! How wonderful to see you! I was *very* disappointed when Jude told me you weren't coming. Do come in and sit down.' She made a regal gesture with her hand towards the chairs in front of her. 'And you've brought a friend. How lovely.'

'Nick Trent,' he said, reaching over to shake her hand. 'Pleased to meet you.'

Lolly had no idea if Esther recognised Nick or not. The two of them had only met once before and that had been at a party when Nick had dropped by to talk to Mal about the death of his uncle. She doubted if his presence had even registered.

'Delighted,' Esther said. She studied him for a moment, dismissed him as being of no particular interest, and returned her attention to Lolly. 'Do sit down,' she repeated. 'You're making the place look untidy.'

Lolly took a seat. Despite all her best intentions, she was starting to feel like a thirteen-year-old girl again. Esther had that effect on her. Before she could revert to a juvenile state, she blinked hard, straightened her spine and resolved to hold her ground. 'Jude said you wanted to speak to me.'

'I do.' Esther paused and glanced at Nick. 'But it's rather

private, I'm afraid. Perhaps your friend would like to take a stroll in the garden. It's quite lovely at this time of day.' She bestowed one of her charming smiles on him. 'Would you mind awfully?'

'He's not going anywhere,' Lolly said firmly. 'Whatever you tell me I'll tell him anyway so he might as well stay and hear it for himself.'

Esther's smile quickly faded. 'I really don't think that's acceptable.'

Lolly rose to her feet and called her bluff. 'Okay, if that's how you feel. Believe me, I've got better things to do than to waste my time arguing.'

'Nobody's arguing, darling,' Esther said. 'Don't be so dramatic. If it's that important to you then of course he can stay.' She looked at Nick. 'I'm presuming you know the meaning of the word discretion, Mr Trent?'

'Call me Nick,' he said, 'and yes, I know the meaning.'

'Good. These are difficult times as I'm sure you understand.'

Lolly sat back down again. She had gained a small victory but it had only been a minor skirmish. The true battle was just beginning. 'I'm presuming you want to talk about Mal?'

'Do you know where he is?'

'If I did, I wouldn't be here.'

Esther arched her eyebrows as if not entirely convinced of the truth of this statement. 'He's not in his right mind. He can't be. He needs help, my dear. So, if you *are* protecting him, for whatever misguided reason, you're really not doing him any favours.'

'I have no idea where he is,' Lolly said. 'Why do you think he's absconded?'

Esther's expression grew sly. 'How on earth would I know? You're the one who visits him in prison, not me.'

Nick leaned forward and rested his palms on his knees. 'Why don't we cut to the chase here, Mrs Fury? You've been talking to

Heather Grant, and so has Mal. There's every chance he's got it into his head that Vicky Finch is your missing daughter. Now, because you're leaving the country, he suspects this could be more than a coincidence. He's concerned, perhaps, that you'll try and take Vicky with you and wishes to prevent this happening. You want to know how much, if anything, Lita knows about his plans. That's why you asked her to come here. Would you say that's a reasonably accurate summary of the situation, give or take a detail or two?'

Lolly was impressed. Most men were either entranced or intimidated by Esther, and Nick appeared to be neither. It was a novelty, and he went up a few notches in her estimation. She waited for the response.

Esther took a while. Eventually she said, 'Heather Grant might have got carried away. I asked her not to say anything to Mal until she'd made more enquiries, but she ignored me. Personally, I don't believe Vicky Finch is my daughter.'

'Do you think Mal will come here?' Nick asked.

Esther gave a visible shudder, although Lolly wasn't sure if it was genuine or not. The woman was an actress after all.

'Who's to know? If he does, I'll have no choice but to call the police.'

Nick sat back and folded his arms. 'Why don't you go away, stay somewhere else for a while?'

'Why should I? This is my home. I refuse to be terrorised by that man.'

'Terrorised?' Lolly repeated sceptically.

'Oh, you can defend him as much as you like, but that's exactly what he's doing. He's tried to kill me once and I'm sure he won't hesitate to try again. He wants me to be frightened, to be always looking over my shoulder, to jump at every sound in the night. No, I'm not going to let him drive me out.'

Lolly saw a flaw in this reasoning. 'But you're moving away anyway, aren't you? You're going to live in the States.'

'So what?' Esther snapped. 'If I do, it will be in my own time and when I'm good and ready.'

'Maybe Lita should stay a few days,' Nick suggested. 'It might help calm things down if he does show up.'

Esther gave a scornful laugh. 'Like a bodyguard, you mean? No, I don't think she'd be much use for that. She couldn't scare away a fly.' But then she seemed to have a change of heart. 'Well, perhaps it wouldn't do any harm.' She looked at Lolly and sighed, 'You'll have to fend for yourself, though. I'm too busy to be waiting on you hand and foot.'

Lolly made a noise, half snort, half splutter. The very idea of Esther waiting on anyone was a joke; she was a pampered princess who never lifted a finger. 'You don't have to worry about that. I'm quite capable of taking care of myself, thank you.'

Esther glanced at her watch. 'I'm afraid I have to go out. I have an appointment and it's too late to cancel. If you'd let me know you were coming . . . We'll meet up again at dinner. Will you stay for a bite to eat, Nick?'

'Thank you. I'd like that.'

'Seven o'clock, then. It won't be anything fancy, just a cold platter, but we can probably rustle up a decent bottle of wine. I had to let the cook go and it doesn't seem worth hiring another.'

'She's gone?' Lolly said. This was a blow to her. Mrs Docherty had been her ally in the past, someone to run to when things got too much. Comfort could always be found in the kitchen: a friendly face, hot buttered toast and a strong cup of tea.

'Over a month ago now. The woman was a dreadful gossip, you know, forever spreading rumours in the village.' Esther stood up and smoothed down her skirt. 'Right, I'll see you both at dinner. Do make yourselves at home.'

Nick waited until the door had closed behind her. 'So, what do you think?'

Lolly, who knew Mrs Gough wasn't beyond a spot of eavesdropping, gestured towards the garden. 'Let's go outside. I could do with some air.'

She chose the path that went past the tennis court and led eventually to the lake. The last of the summer roses were still blooming, their petals velvety, their scent wafting on the breeze.

'Esther's up to something,' Lolly said. 'She isn't scared of Mal. She never was. It's almost as though she wants a confrontation.'

'A set-up of some sort?'

'I wouldn't put it past her. She hates him enough. And Mrs Docherty, the cook, was never a gossip. She worked here for years. Mal wouldn't have kept her on if she couldn't be trusted.'

'Something could be going on that Esther doesn't want other people to know about.'

Lolly wondered if that something could be as simple as Esther's relationship with Jude. Even in these so-called liberated times, the age gap would still be frowned upon by many. He was, after all, almost young enough to be her son. But on reflection she didn't think this was the reason. 'If that's the case, why let *me* stay? She could have made an excuse, said it wasn't convenient.'

'The million dollar question.'

They sat down on the wooden bench near the lake's edge and gazed out across the water. It was quiet here and peaceful, but the tranquillity belied its history. Lolly still found it hard to believe that such dreadful things had happened in this place, murder and abduction, horrors that had ripped lives apart.

'Perhaps you shouldn't stay,' Nick said. 'It might not be such a good idea.'

But Lolly wasn't backing out now. She hadn't come all this way to turn tail and run at the first sign of trouble.

17

Monday 19 September. West Henby

Heather Grant had taken a risk, a big one, but she had no regrets. Sometimes you only got once chance and you had to grab it with both hands. She was not concerned with consequences and there was no punishment that could have deterred her. Once she had started off down the road, there had been no question of turning back.

Pushing Mal Fury to the point where he would jump had been the easy part. The evidence she'd gathered on Hazel Finch and her daughter had been compelling. She had sent some of it by post, enough to convince him that a face-to-face meeting would be worthwhile, and then presented the rest in a small visiting room with high windows and an oppressive atmosphere.

Seeing Mal for the first time had shaken her. It was not the same as looking at a photograph. This man was so much a part of her life and yet he had no idea. It had made her tremble just to think of it. She had furtively searched his face, his eyes, trying to read him, trying to understand who he really was. He had been charming, patient and polite, and she had been careful to never let her mask slip.

Slowly she had built up a picture for him – Hazel's anxiety, her reluctance to discuss her daughter, her abrupt disappearance – before throwing in the news about Esther's imminent departure.

'It seems odd, don't you think? I mean, why now? Why so suddenly? She never mentioned going away before. I could be wrong but I think she could have tracked down Hazel herself.'

'If she had, why wouldn't she tell you?'

'Exactly. It doesn't make sense. Not unless . . . It's as though she wants to cut me out of the picture, cut both of us out. She knows I'm in contact with you. I've told her that. What if she *has* found Hazel, maybe even had Vicky tested. If the girl's definitely not Kay, if she has the wrong blood group, then why not share the information, draw a line under the whole business?'

'There's no accounting for what Esther does or doesn't do.'

'Okay, but I don't believe she'd keep quiet about this. What would be the point? I'd find out eventually. There's something else going on. I'm sure there is. I mean, why doesn't she want me at the house now? I've been coming and going for weeks and suddenly I'm persona non grata.'

Mal had frowned at this piece of information. 'She won't see you?'

'I turned up a few days ago and she said she'd changed her mind, that she didn't want to be involved with the book any more, that she was off to the States and that was that. It's crazy. There hasn't been a problem up until now. I asked if we could talk about it, but she wouldn't even let me over the threshold. There were people inside. I could hear voices.'

'It could have been anyone.'

'That's why I hung about for a while. I drove out and parked up in the lane. I waited for over an hour and eventually a car came out, Esther's car. She was driving but she wasn't alone.' Here, Heather had paused for dramatic effect, lowering her voice so no one else could catch what she was saying. Then she had dropped the bombshell. 'Look, I can't put my hand on my heart and swear to it, not a hundred per cent, but I'm pretty sure she was with Vicky Finch.'

Once the seed had been planted all Heather had had to do was sit back and wait. It had come as no surprise to her that Mal had gone AWOL a week after her visit. What did surprise her, however, was that there was still no sign of him. How long did it take to get from Surrey to Kent? There were trains and buses but he'd need money for those. Still, he struck her as a resourceful sort of man. There were ways of getting hold of cash even inside prison.

She stood up, went over to the window and looked out across the vast garden. She'd lied to him, of course, about . . . well, quite a lot when she thought about it. But what the hell. It had been the only way to get him here, to make sure he was present for the big revelation. Everything was about to change and she was the one who would make it happen.

Her eyes grazed the lush green lawn, the rose bushes and the paths winding off in every direction. From between the trees she could even catch a glimpse of the lake. An ache ran through her. Esther hadn't turned her away and never would so long as the possibility existed of her daughter being found. For a long time, Esther Fury had refused to hope but now her heart was slowly opening again.

Heather pondered on how different her childhood could have been. The people she'd believed to be her parents had been dour, strict and unyielding. God's law was the only law and it was of the Old Testament variety. Disobedience was not to be tolerated and wrath was quick to follow. She had learned to keep her head down, to keep her thoughts and opinions to herself. She had learned patience and built resilience.

Henry and Edith Grant had not been mixers, keeping themselves to themselves, shunning society and all its evils. She had been raised in a home that might as well have been a prison, the list of things she wasn't allowed to do far outweighing those that she was. Apart from the hours spent at school, she'd had no respite from the claustrophobic and suffocating atmosphere.

As she'd grown older, they'd continued to control every aspect of her life and it was only when she was seventeen, when Henry had died, that she'd finally begun to free herself from the shackles. She had, despite Edith's objections, left Devon, done a short journalism course and managed to get herself a job as a trainee reporter on a North London paper. Liberated, she'd blossomed and developed, discovering the joys of friendships, of good food, fashionable clothes, music, alcohol and sex. For the first time in her life, she'd been happy.

All that had changed six months ago when Edith had succumbed to a fatal stroke.

Returning home, Heather had set about the business of clearing the house. This hadn't been an arduous task: the house was small and the contents few. The Grants had not believed in accumulating material possessions. It was only when she'd come across the envelope lying at the back of a drawer – her stomach churned as she thought about it – that the truth had been revealed.

The facts, like a mighty earthquake, had shaken the very foundations of her life. Although they went some way towards explaining why she'd been treated as she had, the level of deceit both stunned and shocked her. It was the very worst kind of betrayal, flesh and blood turned to dust. She had gone through the contents of the envelope and wept.

Even now, the breath caught in the back of her throat when she recalled it. So many lies, so much treachery. She had not known what to do next. Her instinct had been to run straight away to Mal and Esther Fury, but something held her back. Perhaps it was only fear. She'd needed time to absorb everything, to readjust, to think of the best approach. It was then the idea of the book had come to her, a means to an end, a way of infiltrating their lives without revealing who she really was.

Heather could feel her heart thumping in her chest. She pressed her face against the coolness of the glass. 'Where are you, Mal?' she whispered. 'Where are you?'

18

Monday 19 September. West Henby

It was a surprise to Lolly to find not just Esther in the dining room when she and Nick entered at seven o'clock, but also Jude Rule and a very attractive girl she had never seen before. As Esther made the introductions, Lolly was startled to learn that the stranger was Heather Grant. Nods and smiles were exchanged, some of them more strained than others.

Jude was seated to Esther's left, Heather to her right. When Nick took the seat beside Heather, Lolly had no choice but to sit beside Jude.

'I thought you weren't coming,' he said in an almost sulky tone.

'I changed my mind.'

'And why was that?'

'Why not?' she replied with a shrug.

Esther glanced up. 'There's no need to interrogate the poor girl, Jude. She's here, isn't she? That's all that matters.'

Lolly was tempted to ask *why* it mattered – it never had in the past – but decided now wasn't the time for confrontation. Listen and learn, she advised herself. Let Esther think she was in control. All she had to do was play along and perhaps, eventually, everything would become clear.

Esther, Nick and Heather made small talk while they ate. There was cold chicken and ham, potatoes and salad. The crisp white wine flowed freely. Lolly studied Heather Grant whilst pretending not to, trying to gauge the girl's character and form an opinion. She seemed pleasant enough, smart and amusing, at ease in her surroundings. But that didn't mean much; charming people weren't always what they appeared to be.

Jude, on the other hand, was definitely on edge. She wasn't sure if this was down to her and Nick turning up out of the blue or if he had something else on his mind. His face had healed a little since their last encounter but his left eye was still circled by dark purplish bruises. He played with his food, shifting it around the plate, and refilled his glass before she had even taken a sip from hers.

While the others were discussing a recent film that had come out, Lolly leaned towards him and asked, 'So when are you off to the bright lights?'

Jude's gaze was on Esther and it was a few seconds before he transferred it back to Lolly. 'Huh?'

'I was asking when you were going to the States.'

'It hasn't been decided yet.'

'But soon?' she suggested.

'That depends.'

'On what?'

Jude stared at her. 'What do you think? Everything's up in the air at the moment.'

'You mean, Mal? Or the Hazel Finch business?'

Jude didn't answer. His gaze slid back to Esther, as though she might disappear, evaporate into the evening air, if he didn't keep his eyes on her. Even while he was talking to Lolly his attention was elsewhere.

She tried a different question. 'Are you living here now?'

'It isn't safe for Esther to be on her own, not at the moment, not with *him* out there. She needs protecting. He isn't sane. You do understand that, don't you? You think you know him but you don't, not the *real* Mal Fury.'

Lolly thought that was rich coming from someone who barely knew him at all. Jude had probably spent less than a few hours in Mal's company, and all his opinions had been coloured by the lies that came straight out of Esther's spiteful and vindictive mouth. She was about to respond when she became aware of a sudden change in atmosphere at the table. The small talk had been dropped and the conversation had moved on to more controversial matters.

If Esther had been unaware of Nick's connection to Stanley Parrish when he'd first arrived this afternoon, she'd certainly got up to speed since – courtesy of Heather, no doubt – and was currently holding forth on his uncle's inadequacies. 'I can't lie,' she said. 'I never liked the man. I found him to be both incompetent and exploitative.'

Nick kept his composure, smiling thinly. 'Well, I suspect he could have done a better job if he'd been apprised of the facts. Had he known about Teddy Heath's confession, he could have tracked down Hazel Finch years ago. As it was, he was left in the dark.'

'He was *always* in the dark, sweetheart,' Esther said. 'That was the problem.'

'And whose fault was that?'

Esther gave him a long hard look before her eyes softened and she flapped a hand. 'Oh well, let's not fall out over it. It's understandable you'd want to defend him. I am curious, though.

Are you here in a professional capacity, trying to finish off your uncle's work, or just as Lita's boyfriend?'

Lolly started, not expecting her personal life to be drawn into this. She opened her mouth to refute the assumption, but then smartly closed it again. There was nothing going on between her and Nick, nothing more than a friendship, but to clarify this too quickly might feel like an insult to him. As though she was saying ... saying what? That he was not the kind of man she would ever go out with. And what business was it of Esther's anyway? By the time she had sloshed all this around in her head, Nick was already answering.

'Just moral support,' he said, giving away nothing more than he had to.

Esther looked from one to the other. 'Oh, *moral support,* is that what they're calling it these days?'

Lolly wondered if Esther had been drinking before she even came to the table. There was colour in her cheeks and her voice was an octave higher than usual. Heather Grant had a grin on her face; she was listening intently, hanging on to every word, probably trying to memorise it all for her book.

Nick ignored the comment and turned to Heather. 'No news on Hazel Finch, I presume?'

'Nothing. Not yet. I could kick myself, I really could. I should have played it differently, or at least kept a watch on her. I must have scared her off. She could be anywhere; it could take months to track her down again.'

'I wouldn't bother trying,' Esther said. 'It's a waste of time. She might have been Teddy's girlfriend at some point but ... Oh, let's not talk about it any more. Lita, darling, we didn't get the chance to have a proper chat this afternoon. What have you been up to since you decided to move back to London?'

Lolly felt a flush of indignation warm her face. Esther said it as if the move had been voluntary, conveniently ignoring the fact she'd been kicked out of the house with no warning and nowhere to go. The minute Mal had been locked up, she'd been out on her ear. But there was a time and a place for recriminations and this wasn't it – not with Heather Grant mentally taking notes. 'This and that. I've got a market stall where I sell watches, jewellery and the like.'

'Ah, a market stall. How novel!'

'It keeps me busy.'

'Well, it's good to know that expensive education didn't go to waste.'

Lolly glared across the table, trying not to lose her temper. Angry words leapt into her mouth but she swallowed them back down. Esther was goading her and she wasn't going to rise to the bait. Instead she smiled and said calmly, 'Education *never* goes to waste, or at least that's what the headmistress used to say.'

'I'm sure she did, my dear. Especially with the fees she was charging.'

Before things could escalate, Heather said, 'I've always thought running a stall would be rather fun. Better than working in an office. All the different people you meet and—'

'You wouldn't want to meet the people in Kellston,' Jude interrupted. 'They're lowlifes, the whole bloody lot of them. It's a shame Hitler didn't finish the job and raze the place to the ground.' He picked up his glass and drank some more wine. 'Scum, that's what they are.'

'No offence taken,' Lolly said sarcastically.

'I didn't mean you – just the rest of them.'

'I'm honoured.'

Heather stopped eating, her fork poised halfway to her mouth. 'You never did say what happened to you, Jude. Were you mugged or what?'

Jude, having been reminded of his bruising, tentatively touched the swelling under his eye. 'On that shithole of an estate. You can't go out after dark on the Mansfield without some toe-rag trying to rob you.' He gave Lolly a quick sideways glance as if she might be about to contradict his version of events. 'Or daylight, come to that. It's a jungle.'

Lolly said nothing. This wasn't out of any loyalty to Jude – she had none – but because she didn't want the whole Amy Wiltshire story coming out. She wasn't proud of having given a false alibi and certainly didn't wish to broadcast it.

'Isn't that where you grew up, Lita?' Heather asked.

'Yes,' Lolly said, but didn't elaborate. Heather must have been reading Stanley's file as she doubted whether Esther or Jude would have furnished her with the information. She was wary of saying too much, not wanting to feed the girl's curiosity.

'Is it as bad as Jude says?'

'There are worse places.'

Esther leaned forward and touched Jude lightly on the arm. 'You're not cut out for the mean streets are you, sweetheart?'

Jude pulled his arm away. 'And what's that supposed to mean?'

'Just that you prefer the nicer things in life. There's nothing wrong with that. Fighting off muggers isn't really your forte.'

Jude stared at her while his less than sober mind tried to work out exactly what she was saying. Then his face twisted. He pushed back his chair and stood up, swaying a little. 'You really can be a bitch sometimes.' Then he lurched out of the room, slamming the door behind him.

Everyone fell silent.

Lolly suppressed a smile. Trouble in paradise? She couldn't say she was sorry.

'Oh dear, I seem to have touched a nerve.' Esther laughed,

more amused than upset by the exchange. 'It's the creative temperament, I suppose.'

'I suspect he thought you were insulting his manhood,' Nick said.

Esther raised her eyebrows. 'People can be *too* sensitive, don't you think?'

'Difficult times. I guess you're all on edge.'

'Some of us handle it better than others. In my experience, things usually get worse before they get better. Still, not to worry; I'm sure we'll survive one way or another.'

'Let's hope so,' Heather said. She raised her glass and made a toast. 'To a happier future.'

Lolly thought of Mal and her inner smile quickly faded. As if a shadow had fallen across the room, dark and disquieting, she was struck by a sudden sense of foreboding.

19

Monday 19 September. West Henby

Mal Fury hunkered down beneath the willows, smelling the earth and the water and the damp night air. He wasn't sure what time it was, only that it was late. The lights in the house were off and the only sounds he could hear were the scrabblings and snufflings of small nocturnal creatures. He held his breath and strained his ears. It was another noise he was listening for, the tread of policemen or security guards or anyone else who might be patrolling the property. It was dogs, however, that he feared most. They didn't need to see him to pick up his scent.

It felt like a long time since he'd walked off the farm in Surrey, more like weeks than days. And it had taken planning – and some bribery. Jed, a local man he'd worked beside for months, had provided him with what he needed: a small amount of cash, a train ticket via Victoria, a change of clothes, a rucksack, food supplies and the loan of a bike to get him to Sutton station. In exchange, Jed had got his gold Cartier watch.

There had been no guards to watch him on the farm. Open prisons relied on trust. Mal often worked whole afternoons on his own with only the pigs for company so there would have been nothing odd about the fact that his absence wasn't immediately noticed. Jed had agreed to give him a few hours start before raising the alarm.

Even with this promise, the journey had been a fraught one. With his rucksack and casual clothes, he'd hoped to look like any other tourist, but with no way of knowing whether the search for him had begun he'd felt like a hunted man. In London, at Victoria station, he'd mingled with the crowd, anxious in case his description had been circulated or he ran into someone he knew. The half hour wait had felt like an eternity.

Mal had not got off at West Henby – too big a risk of being spotted – but had gone on to the next stop. From here he'd begun the long trek back, cutting across the fields to stay out of sight. A few miles outside the village was a derelict farmhouse and that was where he'd stopped. It had been his place of refuge for the past few days while he waited for the initial fuss to die down. If he was lucky, the police would think he wasn't coming and concentrate their efforts elsewhere. That's if they were even bothered.

It was Mal's belief, and he hoped he was right, that the law wouldn't waste too many resources on him. He was hardly a dangerous criminal. Esther would have kicked up a fuss, though, and in order to placate her they would probably be keeping an eye on the place. This was why he'd waited until cover of darkness before scaling the high wall at the rear of the estate, the way he'd done when he was a kid, still knowing off by heart where all the footholds were.

Mal rubbed his face with his hands. He was tired and hungry. It was good to be home but he was still exiled from his own house. He had no key, no way of gaining entrance. A crazy idea jumped into his head of simply ringing the bell, of rousing Mrs Gough from her sleep, pushing past her when she opened the door and going upstairs to confront Esther. Except it wouldn't happen like that. Mrs Gough was more likely to call the police than answer the door at this time of night. He squeezed shut his eyes and opened them again. What was he thinking? He hadn't come this far, done so much, to throw it all away on an impulse.

No, patience was what was required now. If he wanted the truth, he would have to bide his time, watch the house and see who came and went. If Heather Grant was right then Esther was hiding the fact that she'd found their daughter. Was that possible? Of course it was. It was why he was here, wasn't it? When it came to his wife *anything* was possible.

There was a section of his brain, the rational part, that had railed against the plan to escape. *Don't do anything rash*, that sensible voice had urged. But here he was anyway. In prison, ideas could sit in your head and fester. What Heather Grant had said made sense to him: Teddy having help from a girlfriend; that girlfriend being Hazel Finch; Vicky being around the right age to be Kay. And then Esther changing her mind about the book, making plans to go abroad, being seen with Vicky Finch . . . well, not a hundred per cent seen but close enough. It was an accumulation of evidence that couldn't be ignored.

In the end, he had gone with his gut. His instincts had won the day. If he'd waited for his sentence to be completed it could have been too late. Esther might have taken Kay abroad, placed her somewhere Mal would never find her. And every day that passed, every minute of every hour, she would be trying to poison their child against him. He had to find out the truth whatever the cost, whatever the consequences. It was killing him not knowing.

Slowly Mal got to his feet, his knees complaining. He wasn't as young as he used to be and sleeping on the ground for the past few nights had made his joints creak. He walked along the water's edge, moonlight spilling over the path, until he came to the summerhouse. The door was locked but he knew where the key was, under the terracotta pot with the white geraniums. He lifted it with care – sound travelled in the dead of night – and fumbled underneath until his fingers touched the cool metal.

The summerhouse smelled musty inside, as though it hadn't been used for a long time. No one would have been here since he went to jail. Esther never used it. She had never come near the lake, not since the day Kay had been taken. The horror was too much for her. But he'd often come to sit and contemplate, to stare out across the water in the hope that one day the lake might accede to his demands and give up its secrets.

There were two wide wicker chairs and he slumped down in one of them, stretching out his legs. He thought some more about his daughter. She would be nineteen now, the same age as Lita. The photo Heather had left for him hadn't corresponded to the visual image in his head, but he was starting to adjust to it.

Mal ran his palm over his chin, prickly with stubble, and dreamed about having a shave. He needed a shower too although he'd have to make do with a swim in the lake. Not tonight, though. He was too tired to negotiate the reedy water, too chilled with fatigue to risk plunging into its depths.

He bent and undid the laces on his boots, kicked them off and flexed his toes. His stomach, hollow with hunger, rumbled its displeasure. It crossed his mind to creep round to the back of the house and rummage through the bin for scraps, but he didn't have the energy. Tomorrow. He would deal with the demands of his body in the morning.

Mal sat back and closed his eyes. The stress of the last few days, the constant fear of discovery, had left him feeling drained to the point of exhaustion. But he had finally made it. He was home. Was he crazy? Perhaps. But not completely out of his mind. What he had done, was doing, might seem irrational to others, like a madman chasing ghosts. Not to him. It was necessary, vital. He had lost his daughter once and he wouldn't let it happen again.

He heard an owl hoot, an eerie sound that sent a shiver through him. His shoulders tensed and his eyes flew open. The sound came again, echoing through the night. Folklore had it that the owl was a harbinger of doom, of death. He stared through the window into the dark.

20

Tuesday 20 September. West Henby

When Lolly woke in the morning the first thing she noticed were the printed peacocks strutting across the wall. She studied them for a while, their little heads, their fabulous tails, just as she had so many times in the past. The room felt simultaneously strange and familiar. It did not belong to her any more and yet a part of her was engrained within it. When she wasn't at boarding school this was where she'd slept, dressed, cried, dreamed and planned. It knew all her secrets, her joy and her pain.

She threw back the covers and padded over to the window. The sky was pale blue and cloudless. Looking out over the grounds, at the lake, she thought of Mal and hoped he was a long way away. In Antwerp, perhaps, finding refuge with friends, people who would shield and protect him. And yet she couldn't quite believe it. He'd gone AWOL for a reason and it wasn't to revel in the charms of Belgium.

Lolly took a shower and got dressed. She was standing in front of the mirror, combing her hair, when she heard footsteps along the landing. Quickly she opened the door and looked out. It was Nick.

'Are you off?' she asked.

'Once I've found some coffee.'

'I can help you with that.'

It was early and the house was quiet. Mrs Gough was probably the only other person up, but there was no sign of her as they descended to the basement. It was chilly in the kitchen. In the old days Mrs Docherty would have had the range going, making the place snug and warm while she organised breakfast. The place felt empty without her.

Lolly put the kettle on, took the coffee from the cupboard and spooned it into the percolator. 'Would you like something to eat? I could do you scrambled eggs.'

'Just coffee, thanks.'

'Are you sure? What about some toast?'

'No, really. It's too early for food. I'll grab something when I get into town.'

While she was waiting for the kettle to boil, Lolly sat down opposite him at the big wooden table. 'I still don't get it, why Esther wants me here. It's weird, don't you think? The woman can't stand me and she knows I wouldn't tell her anything about Mal even if I could.'

'All the more reason to come back to London with me,' he said. 'Whatever's going on, you don't want to be involved.'

Except Lolly *was* involved. Mal had taken her in, been good to her, and she couldn't cut and run when things got tricky. If he did show up she had to be here. 'I'll give it a few days, see what happens. What do you think of Heather? Do you trust her?'

'No.'

'Me neither. Or Jude, come to that. And don't get me started on Mrs Gough.'

'So you're going to stay in a house where you can't trust anyone?'

Lolly grinned. 'That's about the sum of it. Still, at least I know where I stand.'

'With a dagger in your back if you're not careful.'

Fifteen minutes later, Lolly walked down the steps and onto the drive with Nick. She was sorry to see him leave. Once he was gone she'd be well and truly on her own. A daunting thought but she tried not to let the worry show on her face. This, as it turned out, wasn't difficult; she'd had years of practice at hiding her feelings.

'Call me if you need to talk,' he said as he climbed into his car. 'Any time. And let me know when you want to go home. I'll come and pick you up.'

'That's okay, I can get the train.'

'It's no bother. The offer's open. I'll leave it up to you.'

She waved him off and stood on the drive until the car was out of sight. Despite the sun, the morning was chilly and she wrapped her arms around her chest. Later, when it had warmed up a bit she'd take a walk in the garden, maybe even go down to the village and find her old friend, Theresa. If there was any gossip to be had – and she was sure there was plenty – Theresa would be more than happy to share it.

Lolly breathed in the crisp air, trying to clear her head. She hadn't drunk much wine last night but hadn't eaten much food either. There was a fuzziness around the edges of her thoughts. After a while she went back inside, washed up the cups, cleaned out the percolator, and wondered what to do next.

With most of the household still sleeping, Lolly decided to take the opportunity to have a look around. She went from room to room, each one with its own memories. She had known this house when it was quiet as the grave, when the only sound was the soft ticking of the old clocks and had known it too when it was full of voices, of music, of talk and shrill laughter, of people filling every available space.

The parties had been Esther's idea or perhaps more precisely Esther's revenge. Mal had not wanted company, had not wanted his house taken over by the glitterati and their hangers-on. He preferred peace, or the closest he could get to it. These constant invasions were, however, the price he'd had to pay for bringing a kid Esther neither wanted nor liked into the family home.

Lolly had always understood why Esther loathed her. She was a poor replacement for the child that had been lost, a changeling, a mockery. Every misspoken word, every clumsy action only served as a reminder of what might have been. Even when the rough edges had been smoothed out, when she was able to speak without making Esther wince, when she could walk gracefully and almost pass for a lady, nothing had changed. She was, and always would be, an interloper.

Lolly sighed and went into the library, one of her favourite rooms. She looked at the brown leather chair Mal had sat in. The arms were worn, paler than the rest, and there was a slight dip in the seat. This was the place he would retreat to when the parties were in full swing, to work or read or drink his whisky in peace.

She went over to the tall bookcases and ran a finger along the spines of the books. She would pick out one to read; it would pass the time while she waited for the rest of the world to wake up. There was everything here from art to zoology and a good selection of novels too. She was on the point of plucking out a volume on the history of clocks and watches when the door suddenly opened and Mrs Gough strode in with a duster in her hand. When she saw Lolly, she stopped dead in her tracks.

'What are you doing here?'

'Just browsing,' Lolly said. She knew exactly what the housekeeper was thinking. Many of the books here were valuable, first editions, and girls like her couldn't be trusted. 'That's all right, isn't it?'

'So long as you're careful and put them back where you find them.'

'Of course.'

Mrs Gough didn't retreat – she must have had plenty of other rooms to clean – but instead began to run a duster over Mal's desk. All the time she kept her eyes on Lolly, watching her as closely as she could without actually hovering at her shoulder.

Lolly refused to be driven out. This was a battle she wasn't going to lose. In order to add a little interest to the proceedings she said, 'You must be busy, getting ready for the States. Are you looking forward to moving?'

Mrs Gough stopped wiping, her cloth poised in mid-air. There was a distinct air of fluster about her, a redness creeping over her cheeks. Then, after a short hesitation, she straightened up and replied sharply, 'Me? What on earth makes you think *I'm* going to that place?'

'Oh, I see. I just presumed—'

'Well, you presumed wrong. I can't go gallivanting halfway round the world, not at my age.'

Lolly, who had always been of the opinion that Mrs Gough would follow Esther to the end of the earth if called upon to do so, was puzzled by this. But then it struck her: the decision had *not* been the housekeeper's. Esther wasn't just leaving behind the house, her home, but Mrs Gough too. After years of loyal service, the woman was about to be dumped.

'Oh,' Lolly said again. 'I didn't realise. What will you do?'

'Do?'

'When Mrs Fury leaves.'

'It won't come to that. She'll see sense in the end. This is where she belongs.'

'You think she'll change her mind?'

But Mrs Gough wouldn't be drawn any further. She pushed

out her jaw and her mouth pursed. 'I haven't got time to stand here gossiping all day. Some of us have work to do.' And with that she gave a single flap of the duster, turned on her heel and flounced out.

As soon as she'd gone, Lolly sat down in the leather chair and thought about what she'd learned. She might have had some sympathy if Mrs Gough had ever showed her an inch of compassion. As it was, she had only ever been treated with cruelty and disdain. She reckoned Mrs Gough had modelled herself on Mrs Danvers from *Rebecca*: all darkness and spite and hostility. The comparison didn't do much to ease Lolly's already troubled state of mind.

Finding herself too restless to sit still, Lolly stood up, flew upstairs to get a sweater and then went out into the garden. It was her intention to walk around the lake but she hadn't got further than the tennis court when she came across Heather Grant sitting on a bench. If she'd had the option she would have turned back and avoided her, but it was too late. She'd already been spotted. She walked up to the bench and forced a smile.

'Hi. I didn't know anyone else was up yet.'

'Actually, I'm in hiding. I'm trying to avoid Mrs Gough.'

This piqued Lolly's interest. 'Why, what have you done to her?'

'Nothing, as far as I know, but every time I turn around she's there. It's like having a permanent shadow. Everywhere I go, she's two steps behind.'

'I know the feeling,' Lolly said.

'To be honest, she gives me the creeps.' Heather put a hand to her mouth as if she might have spoken out of turn. 'Sorry, I didn't mean to—'

'Don't apologise on my account. She creeps me out too.'

'But she's known you for years.'

'That doesn't mean she likes me.'

'Does she like anyone?'

'Just Esther.' Lolly could have gone on to say that she thought Mrs Gough's attachment to her mistress bordered on obsession but was wary of sharing too much. Even Mal had only ever been tolerated, more a necessary evil than someone to be liked or respected.

Heather patted the space beside her. 'Why don't you sit down?'

Lolly hesitated, thought about making an excuse, but then decided to take up the offer. If she was going to find out what was going on round here she couldn't do it by avoiding contact with everyone else. But she made a mental note to be cautious. Talking to Heather, she imagined, was like talking to the law: anything could be taken down in evidence and used against her.

'Mrs Gough reminds me of that monster thing in Greek mythology. You know, the three-headed hound who guards the gates to Hades. What's his name?'

'Cerberus,' Lolly said. Amongst the books in the library were several on Greek mythology, all full of gruesome tales she had devoured as a young teenager.

'Yes, that's it. Wasn't it his duty to stop the dead from escaping?'

Lolly gave her a sidelong glance, wondering if this was just a straightforward question or if she was implying something darker. 'I think so.'

'Yes,' Heather said, leaning back her head to catch the sun's rays on her face. 'That must be a full-time job.'

Lolly thought of Kay and a shudder passed through her body. Quickly she changed the subject. 'So how's the book going?'

'Slowly but I'm getting there. It's like putting together a jigsaw when half the pieces are missing.'

'I thought you'd be out looking for Hazel Finch.'

'Oh, I've got someone else on that. At the moment I need to grab as much time as I can with Esther. She's always got meetings or script readings or something that means she's too busy to talk. That's why I'm staying; it's the only way I can get to see her. I'm lucky if I manage to snatch the odd half hour.'

'I'm surprised she agreed to it – the book, I mean.'

'Well, I'd like to say it was because she was so impressed with my investigative prowess, but I suspect it was mainly to spite Mal. She knew he'd hate the idea.'

'Hasn't she hurt him enough already?'

Heather gave a low laugh. 'Women like Esther don't know the meaning of enough.'

'You don't like her.'

'I don't like or dislike her. That's simply the way she's made. And I'm not here to pass judgement; I just want to get to the truth.'

Lolly thought the reply disingenuous. Everyone had an opinion, positive or negative, when it came to Esther, and she didn't imagine Heather was any different. 'And what about Mal? What do you think of him?'

'The same. I've only met him once. I feel sorry for him, for them both, but they haven't exactly helped themselves. If Mal had come clean, if he hadn't covered up his part in Teddy Heath's death, Hazel might have been found years ago.'

'You don't always make smart decisions when you've just killed someone, even if it is an accident.' Lolly stretched out her legs and crossed them at the ankles. 'Do you really think Vicky Finch is Kay?'

'It's possible.'

'Possible rather than probable?'

'I'm just trying to be cautious. I don't want to get anyone's hopes up too much.'

A bit late for that, Lolly thought. 'But Mal believes she is?'

'I don't know what he believes. Like I said, I've only met him the once. I told him what I know, the facts, nothing else. I didn't embellish them. I'm not the sort of writer who makes things up to get a reaction.' Heather shifted on the bench, glancing at Lolly. 'I'm not convinced that what he's done is any kind of response to what I said on the visit. He was perfectly calm, not fired up at all. I got the impression he thought it would be another dead end.'

Lolly wasn't sure if she was telling the truth or just covering her own arse. 'But he still walked.'

'It could have been over something completely unrelated. Perhaps there were things going on in jail, a situation he had to get away from.'

'He was fine when I visited.'

'Would he have told you if anything was wrong?'

'He was fine,' Lolly repeated firmly.

Heather nodded. 'Well, if it was something I said, he must have taken it out of context.'

'Did you talk to him about Esther?'

'In what respect?'

'What *she* thinks, whether she believes this Vicky could be Kay.'

Heather assumed a look of concentration, frowning slightly as if trying to recall the details of the conversation. 'No, I didn't go into that.'

'And he didn't ask?'

'I don't believe he's particularly interested in what Esther thinks.'

Lolly thought this might be true in a general sense but not when it came to their daughter. Esther had always been the sceptic, the disbeliever, the one who was convinced Kay had died on the day she was taken. If she was starting to change her mind then that would have a profound effect on Mal's point of view.

'I wonder where he is,' Heather mused.

Lolly gazed along the path as if Mal might suddenly stride into view. 'A long way away, hopefully.'

'You don't think he'll come here?'

'And get himself arrested? Why would he do that?'

A hint of cunning entered Heather's eyes. 'You can't be that sure or you wouldn't be here yourself.'

'Esther wanted to see me.'

'And now she has, but you're not exactly rushing home.' Heather grinned. 'Come on, you think he might show up, don't you?'

'No,' Lolly insisted. 'I think he'd be mad to come within twenty miles of the place.'

'Well, we all get a little mad sometimes, especially when the stakes are high.'

Lolly didn't reply.

There was a short silence before Heather asked, 'So what's your take on Jude Rule?'

Lolly bristled. 'What's Jude got to do with anything?'

'You've known him a long time, haven't you? Since you were kids.' Heather must have clocked the look on Lolly's face because she quickly added, 'It's completely off the record. I swear. Nothing to do with the book. I'm just curious. I mean, you came to live here, then you left, then *he* came here. How did that come about?'

'I don't know. I haven't seen him in ages.'

'Why's that, then?'

Lolly tried not to show her irritation. She didn't want to talk about Jude, didn't even want to think about him. 'We just lost touch.'

But Heather wasn't giving up. 'And what's the deal with him and Esther? I can't work out whether they're an item or not. One minute he seems to hate her guts, the next he's following her around like an adoring puppy.'

'You're asking the wrong person. I don't know anything about their relationship.'

'He's good-looking, I suppose, but kind of intense. I get the feeling there's all sorts bubbling under the surface. What was he like when he was younger?'

'The same as he is now.'

'The jealous sort, huh?'

'I didn't say that,' Lolly snapped. Even though it was true, she didn't want words being put into her mouth.

'Sorry, I didn't mean anything by it. Only I was talking to Brenda Cecil and she had some pretty nasty things to say about him and Amy Wiltshire.'

'What? Why on earth were you talking to her? You can't believe a word that woman says.'

'She says much the same about you.' Heather laughed. 'But don't worry, I've met her type before. A real piece of work, right? No, I was just trying to get a bit of background information on Stanley Parrish, what he was like, and one thing led to another and . . . well, she obviously bears a grudge against you and Jude. Women like her don't forget in a hurry.'

Lolly, whose intention had been to interrogate Heather, felt like the tables had been turned. She felt uneasy, slightly panicked, as though the past was coming back to haunt her. Brenda wouldn't just have spoken about the murder but also about the alibi Lolly had given and how she had got Jude Rule off the hook. In order to defend herself, she had to defend Jude too. 'None of it's true. It was her own son who was in the frame. He was the one who was going out with Amy. She's just looking for someone else to blame.'

'I'm sure you're right and I don't envy you having to live with her even if was only for a few months. That can't have been easy.'

'It was years ago. I don't ever think about it now. I don't *want* to think about it.'

Heather took the hint and moved on. 'Is Nick still in bed?'

'No, he's already left. He's got work. He had to get back to London.'

Heather looked relieved, as if she was glad to have him out of the way. 'Oh well, I'd better go and see if Esther's up yet. What are you going to do with yourself?'

'I'm not sure. I might take a walk, stretch my legs.'

'I'll leave you to it, then.'

Lolly stayed a while longer, mulling over the encounter. It had been less a casual conversation and more a battle of wits. Unfortunately, she wasn't convinced that she'd come out on top. Heather had her own agenda and God alone knew what it was. She looked over at the house and then along the path that led away from it. What she should probably do, she thought, is go back inside and loiter at some doors. If she was going to find out what was going on, she wouldn't do it sitting on her backside.

But the lure of fresh air and solitude was too much. The espionage could wait until later.

Lolly stood up and set off towards the lake.

21

Tuesday 20 September. West Henby

It was getting warmer now, the sun rising higher in the sky, and Lolly took off her sweater and draped it round her shoulders. She followed the curve of the lake, taking care to keep an eye on the ground where there were stones and knotty roots waiting to trip the unwary. The water was calm, a wide sheet in muted shades of blue and grey, ruffled only by a light breeze. As she walked she had to push aside the slender graceful fronds of the weeping willows, dodging the showers of raindrops that fell from the higher branches. It had poured during the night and the air smelled of wet earth.

As a thirteen-year-old, she'd been both frightened and fascinated by this place, repelled and attracted. Ghosts lurked in every corner: in the trees, amongst the reeds and bulrushes, but most of all in the lake itself where the nanny, Cathy Kershaw, had met her brutal death and Kay Fury had been snatched from her pram before it could sink beneath the surface for ever. Had the baby still been alive at that point? It was impossible to know. Lolly thought of the cries she'd heard when she and Vinnie had parked up by the gates last week. She was still no closer to finding out who or where they'd come from.

Lolly tramped on. Eventually the summerhouse came into view, its paint old and peeling, the wooden window frames starting to rot. No one bothered to repair it because no one came here any more. She approached and would have walked on past if she hadn't noticed something odd: the door was slightly ajar. When she'd lived here, the place had always been locked. As a kid, she'd often pressed her nose against the smeary windows, peering in at the abandoned room with its table and chairs and dusty cushions.

Lolly stopped and frowned. She stood for a moment, listening for any sound but there was nothing but the birds in the trees. She looked to either side and over her shoulder. Eventually she took a step forward, tentatively pushing open the door with her fingertips. There was a mustiness about the room, a dank cellar sort of smell. The floor was littered with nature's debris, leaves and mouse droppings and dead flies. Cobwebs had gathered in every corner.

Suddenly she began to notice all sorts of things that didn't belong here: a bright red rucksack parked under the table, a raincoat flung over the back of one of the chairs, an empty bottle of juice. Her mind was still absorbing all this when she heard a noise behind her. Lolly swung round, her heart in her mouth, and almost screamed.

The man loomed over her, tall and threatening. His face was thin, unshaven and his eyes were hollow. His wet hair, slicked down, gave his head an almost skull-like appearance. She instinctively recoiled, her pulse starting to race. Her first thought was a tramp, someone seeking shelter, but then something clicked in her brain and she realised who it was.

'Jesus Christ!' she exclaimed, lifting a hand to her chest.

'You almost gave me a heart attack. What the hell are you doing here?'

Mal gave a wry smile. 'Where else would I go?'

'Anywhere but here. It's not safe. The police are looking for you.'

'I should think they've already searched the grounds, haven't they?'

'That doesn't mean they won't come back.'

'I'll take my chances.'

Now that the initial shock had subsided, Lolly gazed up at him, her eyes full of concern. 'Are you all right? How long have you been here? God, you look worn out.' Actually, he looked worse than that: exhausted, grey and haggard. 'You can't stay, Mal. What if somebody finds you?'

'Somebody already has.'

'Yeah, well, you're lucky it was me. Anyone else would have called the law.'

'I need to know what's going on.'

'What do you think *I'm* doing? You didn't have to . . . Jesus, they were going to let you out in a few months. Couldn't you have waited until then?'

'And let Esther disappear with my daughter? Or whatever else she's got up her sleeve. You know what she's like. Is she there? Is Vicky in the house?'

Lolly shook her head. 'No, only Esther and Heather Grant and Jude. Oh, and Mrs Gough of course. And there's no evidence that Vicky is your daughter. You do realise that, don't you? I've no idea what Heather told you but you shouldn't pin your hopes on it.'

Mal had a towel in his hand, an old one that must have been lying around the summerhouse for years. He ran it over his head and then held it to his nose. 'This towel smells worse than I do.'

'Are you listening to me?'

'I have to talk to Esther.'

'You can't. She's just waiting for you to turn up so she can have you arrested again. Is that what you want?'

'Then I'll wait. I'll watch the house. Vicky's going to come here eventually.'

Lolly sighed. She could see there was no point in arguing with him. All she could do was try and contain the situation until she figured out a better plan. 'When was the last time you had something to eat?'

'I don't know. Yesterday? The day before?'

'Look, I'll go and get you some food. But be careful, yeah? Stay in the summerhouse until I get back.'

Mal nodded.

'Promise me? Promise you won't go near the house?'

'For now,' he said.

Lolly, seeing this was the best she was going to get, nodded too. 'Okay, I shouldn't be too long but it depends on who's around . . . and what's left in the fridge. I might have to walk into the village.'

'Mrs Docherty always keeps the place well stocked.'

'Mrs Docherty isn't here any more. Esther got rid of her.'

'What?'

As soon as she'd spoken, Lolly wished she hadn't. She didn't want to add more fuel to whatever conspiracy theories were already flying around in his head. 'Or perhaps she retired. I'm not sure. Anyway, Esther's not employed a replacement yet so I guess Mrs Gough is dealing with it all. Don't worry, I'll find you something.'

'I could do with some clean clothes too.'

Lolly stared at what he was wearing. His shirt and trousers were covered in grass stains and dirt, like he'd been sleeping rough for a few nights. 'I may have to sort that out later. And I'll bring a blanket too.'

'Thanks, Lita. I'm sorry to drag you into this.'

'Just don't do anything . . . I don't know, anything stupid. Keep your head down, yeah?'

'I'll stay out of sight.'

'Good. I'll see you soon.'

Lolly glanced over her shoulder as she walked off down the path. She was relieved that Mal was safe, not dead in a ditch at least, but how was she going to keep him that way? It was a question that troubled her as she hurried back towards the house.

Lolly heard the one thing she wanted to hear as she crept down the stairs that led to the basement: silence. 'Thank you, God,' she murmured. She looked in through the kitchen door and then back up the stairs making sure the coast was clear. When she was certain no one was in the vicinity she rushed inside and made a beeline for the fridge.

The contents were disappointing. In Mrs Docherty's day, it would have been crammed full of goodies but clearly Mrs Gough was more frugal. There were pork chops – today's lunch perhaps – but not much else apart from milk, butter, eggs and the remains of last night's dinner. She removed a few slices of cold chicken and ham and wrapped them in foil.

In the pantry she had more luck, finding bread and cheese, tomatoes and apples. She took as much as she dared. There were guests in the house, people who were going to get hungry, so hopefully Mrs Gough wouldn't question a bit of food going missing. The last thing she wanted was to raise suspicion.

After rummaging through the cutlery drawer she chose an old knife and put it to one side. She had a moment's hesitation – was it wise to furnish Mal with something that could be used as a weapon? – but then dismissed the thought. For one, the knife was too blunt to inflict any serious damage, and for two she couldn't imagine him deliberately hurting anyone. It made her feel guilty to have even considered it.

Lolly's next stop was the utility room where she dug out a large carrier bag and unlocked the door that led outside. It would be safer to leave this way than to go through the house again. She noticed a crate of empty bottles, alcohol and juice, and picked out the cleanest. Returning to the kitchen, she rinsed the bottle, filled it with water and then stuffed it in the bag with all the food. She looked down at the contents: not exactly a feast but it would do for now.

Lolly was about to leave when she heard footsteps on the stairs. And then a voice – Jude's voice.

'Esther? Are you there?'

It was too late to make a run for it. Instead Lolly shoved the bag under the table, switched on the kettle and tried not to look too guilty.

'Oh, it's you,' he said, coming in. 'Have you seen Esther?'

'No.'

'I don't suppose there's any coffee on the go?'

'No.'

'Be a pal and make me one, would you? Seeing as the kettle's on and all.' He sat down at the table, groaned and raked his fingers through his hair. 'I need caffeine urgently. I've got a stinking headache.'

'What you've got is a hangover, and what you need is aspirin. Why don't you go and find Mrs Gough? I'm sure she'll have a stash somewhere.'

'I will,' he said. 'Once I've had some coffee.'

Under normal circumstances Lolly would have told him to

make the damn coffee himself but she didn't want him hanging round for any longer than necessary. It was too risky to pick up the bag and walk out. He might wonder what was in it. He might even start asking awkward questions. She glanced down at the carrier, praying he wouldn't stretch out his legs and come into contact with it.

'I think Esther's with Heather,' she said. 'Have you tried the sun room?'

'I suppose they're working on that bloody book again.'

Lolly found a jar of instant coffee and shovelled a few spoonfuls into a mug. 'You don't approve?'

'Why should I care? It's nothing to do with me. I just don't see what good it's going to do raking everything up again. There's nothing to be gained by it. You've got to move on, haven't you, leave the bad shit behind.'

Lolly wondered if he was only thinking of Kay or whether Amy Wiltshire was on his mind too. Had he moved on from the 'bad shit' he'd been involved in, a girl he'd been obsessed with, a murder that had never been solved? 'Here,' she said, placing the mug of coffee in front of him. 'I'm presuming you want it black.'

'Ta.'

Lolly leaned against the range and folded her arms. Her head was full of Mal, of what he might do, and it was a struggle to contain her impatience. She had to get back to him but couldn't do that until she'd got rid of Jude. 'You don't think there's anything in this Vicky Finch business then?'

'What are the odds?'

'Heather Grant seems to think it's possible.'

'Well, she would, wouldn't she?'

She heard the edge in his voice and said, 'You don't like her.'

'Do you?'

Lolly shrugged. 'I barely know the girl.' And then, because

a bit of stirring never did any harm, she added, 'She seems very interested in you, though.'

'What do you mean?'

'She was asking about you this morning, what you were like when you were younger.'

'And what did you say?'

'That you were just the same as you are now. She asked about you and Esther too, said it was strictly "off the record" but I don't believe that for a second. And she's been talking to Brenda Cecil.'

If Lolly had wanted to shock him she couldn't have made a better job of it. Jude started, his face turning greener than it already was. 'Brenda Cecil? What? Why the hell has she been doing that?'

'I've no idea. Perhaps you'll have a nice little cameo in her book.'

This suggestion clearly didn't make him feel any better. 'She's got no right. That book has nothing to do with me.'

'Seems she thinks otherwise.'

Jude leapt up from the table. 'We'll see about that.' Abandoning his coffee, he strode out of the kitchen and stomped up the stairs.

Lolly took her opportunity. Reaching down, she grabbed the bag and dashed through to the utility room. As she was opening the door she noticed an old tartan rug, probably used for picnics in the past, and quickly draped it over her arm so it covered the carrier. If she ran into anyone or if someone was watching from a window it would just look like she was going out to sit on the grass.

It was an effort to walk at a leisurely pace. The fear of being watched made her feel self-conscious and suddenly putting one foot in front of the other in an orderly fashion seemed like the most difficult thing in the world. It took all her willpower to resist glancing back over her shoulder.

It was a relief when she rounded the corner and was out of view of the house. But she didn't relax entirely. Instead of going straight to the summerhouse she stopped at the bench, sat down and listened. Was anyone following her? She kept her ears pricked for footsteps, for the snapping of twigs, for anything that would indicate she had a tail. Only when she was sure she was alone did she stand up again and continue on her way.

There was no sign of Mal when she arrived. She tried the door but it was locked. She rapped lightly with her knuckles, thinking that they should have arranged a code – but then again, who else was likely to come knocking? A few more seconds passed before she heard movement from inside. There was a click as the key turned in the lock and then the door opened.

22

Tuesday 20 September. West Henby

Mal, who was starving, tried to eat with a modicum of restraint. He could feel Lita's eyes on him as he devoured the food. Hunger could turn into a form of madness, he thought, a dangerous desperate craving that drove everything else from your mind. Even in prison he'd been fed and watered on a regular basis. Jed's supplies had soon run out and the pains had been gnawing at his guts ever since.

'There must be somewhere else you can go,' Lita said. '*Anywhere* else. You'll end up back in jail if you stay here.'

Mal shrugged. He didn't care about jail; he'd survived it before and he would again. What he did care about was getting caught before he found out the truth, but there was no point dwelling on that. What choice did he have? He'd come this far and there was no turning back. He talked between mouthfuls, chewing too quickly. 'A few days, that's all. I have to know what's going on.'

'That's what I'm trying to find out. Why can't you get away from here while I do it? Lie low for a while. What about London? No one's going to notice you there. A hotel or a B&B. I can help sort something out. You could get lost in the crowd, disappear.'

Mal smiled but shook his head.

Lita sighed. 'What exactly did Heather say to you?'

'That she'd tracked down Hazel Finch and the woman was pretty jumpy when the subject of Teddy came up. That she has a daughter called Vicky about the right age to be Kay.' Mal picked up the bottle and took a gulp of water. 'And that she'd seen Esther leaving here with Vicky Finch.'

This last piece of news seemed to startle Lita. 'What? When? She never told me that. Do you believe her?'

'Why would she lie?'

'I don't know. To provoke a reaction? To get you to do exactly what you have done? It's all good publicity for her book. And Jude never said anything about Vicky being here.'

'Perhaps he doesn't know – it was a couple of weeks ago – or perhaps Esther's told him to keep his mouth shut.'

'Or perhaps it's all a pack of lies.'

Mal didn't want to believe this. He had a single thread of hope left in his life and wasn't about to relinquish it. 'We'll see.'

'What else did Heather tell you?'

'Not much. Let me think. That Esther had stopped cooperating on the book, that she didn't want to be involved any more.'

'There!' Lita said triumphantly. 'That's not true! The two of them are inside right now, cooperating till the cows come home. Heather's even staying here. Doesn't that prove something?'

'Only that Esther must have changed her mind. There's nothing new about that.'

Lita shifted on her chair, crossing and uncrossing her legs. She frowned, probably turning over fresh arguments in her head. 'Look, even if this girl does turn out to be Kay, you're not going to be able to spend any time with her if you're on the run. How's that going to work?'

'Ten minutes, that's all I want. Just so she knows I care, that

I care *enough* to give up my freedom for her. God knows what Esther's told her about me. I just want a chance to put the story straight and then I'll hand myself in. It's not too much to ask, is it?'

'And what if it's all for nothing?'

'Then at least I'll know. I'd rather sit in a cell with the truth than always be wondering.' Mal sat back and looked at her. 'You shouldn't be involved in this. I don't want to drag you into trouble. You don't owe me anything. You do understand that, don't you?'

Lita made a dismissive gesture with her hands. 'You're not dragging me into anything.'

'All I'm asking is that you keep quiet about my being here. Just for now.'

'Of course I will.'

'And thanks for the food. I'll save some of it for later. You shouldn't hang about. Someone might notice you're missing.'

'I'll come back as soon as I can.'

Mal opened the door to the summerhouse, just a crack, and peered along the path. He waited for a while, listening. 'Okay.'

Lita slipped out and set off back along the bank. He watched her progress, thinking about the first time he'd seen her in the flesh, the evening Stanley Parrish had brought her to West Henby. She was still as slight, as skinny, as she'd been then, and as hard to read. She was loyal, though, sticking by him through all the bad times. He loved her like a daughter although he never told her that. It was impossible to say whether her life would have been better or worse if he'd left her in Kellston; that was something he would never know.

Mal stepped out of the summerhouse, closing and locking the door behind him. He had meant to ask how she had persuaded Esther to let her stay but the question would have to wait. Lita hadn't been back here, so far as he knew, since she'd been thrown out after his arrest. Perhaps Esther just wanted to rub her nose in it when she produced their *real* daughter. It was the type of malicious thing she'd do.

He walked with care, making as little noise as possible, and circled round until he had a view of the front of the house. Then he crouched down in the undergrowth. From here he could keep an eye on all the comings and goings. Patience was what was needed and he had plenty of that. He wasn't going anywhere.

23

Tuesday 20 September. Old Street, London

Nick Trent ate a bacon sandwich as he sat in his car and flicked through the local paper, one eye on the news and the other on Sandler's office. Three hours had passed since the solicitor had shown up for work and he hadn't budged since. Nick had the feeling it was going to be one of those days where sod all happened and boredom turned his brain to mush.

In order to keep the little grey cells exercised, he turned his attention to Lolly and the Mal Fury business. He wasn't happy about leaving her alone at the house; there was something about the place that made him uneasy. There was too much pain within its walls, too much anger and grief. Or perhaps it was just Esther who disturbed him with her cool beauty and imperious ways.

He couldn't think about the Furys without thinking about Stanley too. The last part of his uncle's life had been defined by the case and there was little doubt in Nick's mind that he would still be alive today if he'd never accepted Mal Fury as a client. It was odd how a single decision could change your life for ever. And now he felt like he was following in his uncle's footsteps, getting involved in something that would never work out well.

Nick closed the paper, whistling out a breath between his teeth. He wasn't, strictly speaking, involved in anything other than looking out for Lolly. Not that she'd appreciate the sentiment. She was the type of girl who believed in taking care of herself, and she'd had plenty of practice. From an early age she'd learned that other people, even those you were closest to, couldn't be relied upon. Would she call him? He hoped so. Perhaps he should call her. Or would that seem too pushy? Perhaps he'd give it a few days.

Nick was saved from any further agonising on the subject by the appearance of Brent Sandler. At last, some movement. Although negotiating London traffic wasn't his favourite pastime it was better than doing nothing. He threw what remained of his sandwich onto the passenger seat and started the engine.

Sandler was only feet from the yellow Jensen-Healey, briefcase in hand, when it happened. A dark-coloured Jaguar with tinted windows passed Nick's car and slowed as it approached the office car park. There were two loud bangs like the sound of an exhaust backfiring. It was over in a matter of seconds. By the time the car had accelerated away, Sandler was lying on the ground with two holes in his chest and no further use for his briefcase.

Shock rendered Nick temporarily immobile. He stared through the windscreen, trying to process what he'd just seen. 'Shit!' He switched off the engine and jumped out but already passers-by were gathering round the body. A woman started screaming. He stood and watched, knowing there was nothing he could do. Sandler was dead, beyond help. What he'd just witnessed was a professional hit and those guys rarely got it wrong.

He quickly got back in the car and set off in pursuit of

Sandler's killers. He wasn't planning any heroics, just a registration number if he could get it. The reality of the cold-blooded murder was only just beginning to sink in. He should have paid more attention to the Jag and it was probably too far ahead of him now to catch up. But he tried anyway. It was only when he came to Old Street roundabout and realised he had no idea which exit they'd taken that he knew it was a waste of time. He could drive around for ever and not catch a sniff of them.

So what next? What he should do is return to the scene of the crime and report to the attending officers. He'd have to identify himself and explain why he'd been tailing Sandler. What would follow would be hours down the police station, the writing of a witness statement and a bucketload of grief. Most cops didn't like private investigators at the best of times and this certainly wasn't one of them.

Nick saw a phone box and pulled up beside it. He got out of the car, digging in his pockets for change. He put through a call to Marshall & Marshall and it was the older of the brothers, Phil, who answered.

'It's me, Nick. There's no easy way of saying this but someone just took Brent Sandler out. He's been shot. He was leaving his office and—'

'Fuck! Where are you?'

'Still on Old Street. I went after the vehicle but no joy.'

'You sure he's dead?'

'Yeah, I'm sure. I'm just on my way back there now. Thought I'd better warn you before I talk to the cops.'

'Hang on,' Phil said. 'Give me a minute. I need to talk to Roy.'

Nick waited. Phil must have covered the receiver with his hand because he couldn't hear the ensuing conversation. He looked out of the phone box at the traffic going by. He tapped his fingertips on the metal shelf and went over the shooting in his head. He'd have to be clear about things, exactly what he'd seen, before he gave a statement. The pips went and he slid another coin in the slot.

Eventually Phil's voice barked down the line. 'Nick?'

'Yeah, I'm still here.'

'Get yourself back to the office.'

'What, now? I can't just leave the scene of a crime.'

'You've already left it, haven't you?'

'Well, yeah, but I'm not far away.'

'Far enough. Get your arse back here now!'

Nick didn't have an opportunity to open a debate. He heard the click of the phone going down and the connection was cut. This wasn't good news, not for him at least. It was possible the Marshalls were going to keep shtum about the surveillance and try to protect their client.

And that wouldn't go down too well with the law if they found out.

If or *when*? Nick pondered on this as he drove towards the office. He was a direct witness to a crime and the police would hang him out to dry if he didn't come forward and they later found out he'd been right on the spot. He had no idea if anyone had noticed his presence; he'd been parked about ten yards from the solicitors', close enough for someone to have clocked him, but with all the fuss he couldn't be sure.

'Shit, shit, shit,' he muttered.

There was an air of controlled panic at the office of Marshall & Marshall. Roy was on the phone and Phil was pacing, fag in one hand, sheets of paper in the other. They both glared at him when he walked in, as though he was personally responsible for Brent Sandler taking two bullets to his chest.

Roy slammed the phone down. 'This is a real mess. The bloke

wacked in broad fuckin' daylight. He *is* dead, by the way. Died instantly. I just checked it out. Tell us what happened.'

Nick leaned against a desk while he talked. It didn't take him long to run through events and when he'd finished he said, 'Look, are we going to the law or not? Because if we don't and they find out I was there, there's going to be hell to pay. I mean, Christ, we've been following the guy for over a week. Withholding evidence: it's a crime, right? And I'm the one who—'

'Aagh,' Roy said, 'stop fuckin' stressing. Of course we're going to let them know. Haven't got much choice, have we? We just need to get a few things straightened out first.'

Nick didn't much like the sound of that. 'Straightened out?'

'We have to decide whether we tell the client or not.'

'Who is the client?'

Roy and Phil exchanged a look before Roy shook his head. 'You don't need to know that. Probably better if you don't at the moment.'

Nick knew what was going through their minds. 'You think the client could have arranged the hit, right? But they'd have to be pretty stupid to do that. As soon as the police find out Sandler's been under surveillance, they're going to be first on the list of suspects.'

'Perhaps they are stupid. Or perhaps they think we won't divulge that kind of information to the law. Client confidentiality and all that. They could be counting on us keeping our mouths shut.'

'That's a big risk to take.'

Another look flew between the brothers. Phil sucked on his cigarette, seeking solace in nicotine. 'It won't do much for our reputation if we start handing over the names of our clients.'

Roy was quick to respond. 'And it won't do much for our

business if we don't. We can't afford to have Old Bill on our backs. If they think we're holding out on them . . . No, we've got no choice. We're better off cooperating.'

Nick pushed himself off the desk, relieved that he wouldn't have to spend the next few weeks waiting for a knock on the door, but apprehensive about what lay ahead. 'I take it that means we're going down the nick.'

24

Tuesday 20 September. Kellston

Vinnie Keane left the Fox at one-thirty p.m. only to find himself faced with a reception committee. The four cops were probably the tallest Cowan Road could muster but he was still head and shoulders above them all. Not that he was planning on having a scrap. Being hassled by the law was part and parcel of his everyday life and he simply raised his eyebrows.

'Gentlemen,' he said. 'What can I do for you?'

What he could do, apparently, involved accompanying them down the station with his hands cuffed behind his back to answer some questions about a shooting in the city. Being innocent of any such crime, Vinnie presumed they were just whistling in the wind, pulling in a few faces in order to make it look like they were doing something and hoping they might get lucky.

He only started to sweat when he found out who the victim was: Brent Sandler. That's when he knew it was more serious, *bloody* serious in fact. He had over an hour to reflect on his predicament before his lawyer, Ross Perlman, showed up. By then his usually calm demeanour had begun to fray a little at the edges. Before the formal police interview took place he was allowed some time alone with his brief.

Perlman studied him over the rim of his glasses. 'Tell me how you knew Sandler.'

'I didn't, not really. He did work for Terry, legal stuff. I don't know all the ins and outs.'

'Well, whatever he did, I doubt if much of it was legal.'

Vinnie didn't argue the point. 'You got any fags?'

Perlman took a pack from his pocket and slid it across the table along with a box of matches. 'Any enemies you know of? Anyone he could have pissed off enough they'd want to see him down the morgue?'

'I should think there's a long list, especially amongst the toms of London. He wasn't what you'd call the respectful sort. But no, I can't point the finger at anyone in particular.' Vinnie ripped the wrapper off the cigarettes, pulled one from the carton and lit it. 'Why have the filth come up with my name? What's going on here?'

'You heard of a firm of PIs called Marshall & Marshall? Couple of ex-cops.'

And now Vinnie knew he was buggered. He felt his chest tighten as he pulled on the cigarette and blew a stream of smoke out of his nose. 'Yeah, I've heard of them.'

'According to plod, you were paying them to have Sandler followed. Is there any truth in that or are our boys in blue making up fairy tales?'

Vinnie could have denied the allegation but it wasn't going to erase his signature from the contract he'd signed. He should have known better than to use the Marshalls. Cops, ex-cops, they were all the same, and they all stuck together. 'Okay, so I arranged a tail, but that doesn't have anything to do with his death.'

'So what does it have to do with?'

'It's personal.'

'So is a twenty-year stretch for murder. *Personal* doesn't wash, Vinnie. You need to start talking and fast.'

'Okay, so I didn't trust the guy. Terry was getting in deep with him and I thought he was making a mistake. I figured have the bloke followed for a while, see what he's up to, who else he's getting cosy with. You've got to watch your back in this business. That's all there was to it. I was just trying to prove a point to Terry.'

'Pretty expensive point.'

Vinnie shrugged.

'Where were you at eleven-thirty this morning?'

'At home.'

'Alone?'

'Yeah, alone.'

'No alibi, then?'

'Christ, if I was going to waste Sandler I'd make sure damn sure I had one lined up. And I wouldn't do it in broad daylight when I knew the guy had a tail on him.'

Perlman sighed. 'You might not want to repeat that in the interview room. The thing is you knew all his movements, what he was doing, who he was seeing, his everyday routine.'

'In general, but I couldn't know he'd be outside his office at any particular time.'

'Unless you'd set him up with a fake appointment. That's where he was going when he was shot, to see a prospective client who doesn't exist.'

'How do you know all this?'

'Because I've done my homework, Vinnie, pulled in a few favours. I don't want us facing any nasty surprises when we go into that room. Talking of which, did you ever meet Sandler's wife, Laura?'

It was a question Vinnie had been dreading. 'Once or twice,' he said casually. 'At least I think it was his wife. Sandler wasn't the faithful type. He liked to spread the joy if you know what I mean.'

'That can't have made her happy.'

'I've no idea how it made her feel.'

'You sure about that?'

Vinnie smoked some more, staring at his brief. 'What are you getting at?'

'Plod's been busy over the past few hours, Vinnie. And not just with Marshall & Marshall. They've been talking to the grieving widow too.'

'And?'

'If you're trying to protect her, I wouldn't bother.' Perlman tapped the end of his pen against his teeth. 'You're involved with her, right? There's something going on between you.'

'I didn't say that.'

'You're not saying much. From what I've gathered, *she's* being very vocal, though. I get the impression she's going to throw you to the dogs.'

'Bullshit!'

'Tell me the truth, Vinnie, or how the fuck am I supposed to help you?'

Vinnie stubbed out his fag in the ashtray and immediately lit another. 'What do you mean, *throw me to the dogs*?'

'She doesn't want to go down for conspiracy to murder. That's a long time out of a young woman's life. She's denying having any kind of a relationship with you.'

'She's telling the truth.'

'Is she?'

Vinnie knew that Laura must have panicked when she was told about her husband's death. Of course she wasn't going to admit to the affair; it would put her right in the frame. The wife, the nearest and dearest, was always first on the list of suspects and he didn't intend to make things worse for her. When you loved someone, you took care of them. 'Like I said, I barely know the woman.'

Perlman glanced at his watch. 'Time's almost up. You got anything you want to add before we go in?'

Vinnie shook his head.

'You know the drill. Just keep your cool, right? I get the feeling this won't be plain sailing.'

Perlman had been right. Two hours later Vinnie was sitting in a police cell, still reeling from the interview and wondering how his day had gone down the toilet so fast. He hadn't been charged yet, but it was only a matter of time. The law were already convinced of his guilt, were already building a case. A few more hours and they'd throw the bloody book at him.

Jail was an occupational hazard of his job, but this was something different. He was staring down the barrel of a life sentence. The evidence might only be circumstantial but it could be enough to convict him. His big mistake had been in agreeing to organise the tail on Sandler so Laura could get the information she needed to file for divorce. No, that wasn't exactly right. His big mistake had been getting involved with Laura in the first place.

Denying the affair was one thing – he understood that – but she'd gone a step further. Now, apparently, she was saying that he'd harassed her for months, that he'd been obsessed with her, that he'd seen Brent Sandler as an obstacle to them having a relationship. Delusional was the word being bandied about. She was claiming she knew nothing about the surveillance, that she'd loved Brent, that they'd had a happy marriage.

Vinnie put his head in his hands. There were only two explanations for what she was doing: either Laura had arranged to have her husband killed, or she thought he had. He wanted to believe the latter – at least that explained the betrayal – but slowly, minute by minute, he was coming to a different conclusion. He had no alibi because he'd been waiting at his flat for her, waiting for an eleven o'clock liaison that had never materialised. Why hadn't she come? There was only one answer. He screwed up his face as the truth hit him full square in the guts: he'd been a sucker, he'd been taken for a ride, he'd fallen for the oldest trick in the book.

25

Tuesday 20 September. West Henby

Heather had been building up a picture of Teddy Heath, trying to get him fixed in her head, to understand his actions, his motives, what made him tick. What she had learned so far was that he'd been a shallow, careless sort of man, driven by his own wants and needs. Handsome, amusing, narcissistic. A womaniser. A drunk. A gambler. Charming in a louche sort of way, but without morals or principles. Bitter at his own lack of success and resentful at the success of others.

She looked at what she had written but still felt like she hadn't truly grasped him. Perhaps he was beyond reach, one of those people who lack any kind of empathy or soul. An empty vessel. Frustration tugged at her. It was important that she understood him and yet she couldn't. She had spent the morning with Esther, discussing her affair. How had it happened? Why? She had been looking for answers but the ones she'd been given seemed evasive and inadequate.

Esther had assumed a role, that of the unloved, abandoned wife, and played it to perfection. Mal was often away, working in London while she was left on her own in the country. It had always been about the chase for him she'd claimed, and once he'd got his prize, once they were married, he had rapidly lost interest. She'd been lonely and Teddy had paid her attention. It had been a terrible mistake, of course it had, and she had ended things almost as soon as they'd begun.

Heather had no idea how much of this, if any, was true. She glanced up from the desk in the library and gazed out across the garden. Women like Esther needed constant adoration. It was the oxygen that kept them going, their lifeblood. Teddy and Esther had had a lot in common – both indifferent to the feelings of others, both self-obsessed. Together they'd created a noxious situation that had eventually ended in tragedy.

For a while Mal and Esther had been the golden couple, the handsome jeweller and the glamorous actress. One of those power couples like Mick Jagger and Jerry Hall. Heather had a pile of newspaper articles and photographs printed at the time of the Fury marriage. She lowered her gaze and slipped some pictures out of her file. The pair looked happy, beautiful, the way people are supposed to look on their wedding day, but she didn't think they'd have stayed together if it hadn't been for what happened to Kay. Grief had bound them in a way love never could.

She caught a movement outside and glanced up. Jude Rule was crossing the lawn with his hands in his pockets. His expression was cross and sulky, more like a teenage boy than a twenty-something adult. He was probably still brooding over the Cecil business. He'd come storming into the library this morning with a face like thunder.

'Leave me out of your damn book!' he'd demanded. 'What do you think you're doing? What's it got to do with me? Why are you poking your nose into things that don't concern you?'

'Who said I was putting you into the damn book?' she'd replied coolly. 'Don't flatter yourself.'

'So why have you been talking to Brenda Cecil about me?'

'I didn't bring the subject up, she did.'

'And Lolly? You've been talking to her too.'

'Oh, for heaven's sake, stop being so paranoid. We were just chatting. I didn't have her strapped to a chair with a gun to her head. That's what people do, Jude: they *talk* to each other. There's nothing sinister about it.'

Heather kept her eyes on Jude as he walked to the end of the lawn, stopped and stared through the trees. She wondered if he really did have something to hide or was just afraid of rumours getting out of control. Neither of them had mentioned Amy Wiltshire but they'd both known that was what the confrontation was all about.

It struck her as odd that Lolly – or should she call her Lita? – had mentioned their conversation to Jude. On the whole the two of them seemed to avoid each other. There was a kind of weird tension between them, defensive and antagonistic at the same time. Sometimes she caught Lolly looking at Jude, as though she hated him, a fierce sort of loathing that possibly had its roots in something less hostile. There were old feelings, perhaps, on Lolly's side at least.

Jude was different to Teddy Heath but equally destructive in his own way. Teddy, she imagined, had not harboured strong emotions for anyone or anything. He had drifted through life, grabbing what he could, indifferent or oblivious to the consequences of his actions. Jude, on the other hand, dwelled on everything, obsessing over the smallest detail. There was something dark about him, something slightly dangerous.

Heather gave a small shake of her head, freeing her mind of him. She put the photos of Mal and Esther back in their folder, pulled the Stanley Parrish file towards her and opened it at the familiar place. She must have read this part fifty times already but kept returning to it, studying each line, each word, each sentence, as though there could be meaning she had missed on the other occasions.

She had no real sense of Stanley Parrish, other than his having been a meticulous man. He'd recorded every detail, every conversation and summarised his own view in short, pithy paragraphs. She wondered where she'd been on the day he'd come to see her parents. At school, perhaps, or in another room. Why had they even agreed to see him? There was only one answer she could think of: because it would have looked suspicious if they hadn't, as if they had something to hide. She didn't recognise the London address he had listed. It must have been before they'd moved.

For all Stanley's care and attention, he had still been fooled by them. He hadn't looked beneath the surface, hadn't probed deeply enough, hadn't asked the right questions. They had got away with it and she was the one who had paid the price. She would have remained in ignorance if it hadn't been for that envelope and its shattering, explosive contents. Why had her mother, her *so-called* mother, kept it all? Out of sentiment? Conscience? Or maybe she'd simply forgotten she had it, stuffed as it was in the back of a drawer that was hardly ever opened.

Heather swung her chair round and stared at the shelves full of books, at the wood panelling, at the fittings and fixtures of a rich man's sanctuary. She gazed at the leather chair Mal must have sat in, at the small Chippendale table he would have placed his drink on. Mistakes had been made and she was here to rectify them. She couldn't stop thinking of how things might have been. It occupied her day and night like a craving that could never be satisfied.

26

Tuesday 20 September. West Henby

Lolly was spending the afternoon on military manoeuvres. It was all very well finding her four targets, but she also had to establish whether they were likely to stay where they were for the next fifteen minutes. Esther seemed settled in the sun room and Heather was hard at work in the library. Jude was sitting on the grass outside. Mrs Gough, however, remained a worry. Although she was currently down in the kitchen, there was no saying how long she'd stay there. The woman patrolled the house at regular intervals like a guard dog sniffing out irregularities.

Confident that the coast was at least temporarily clear, Lolly dashed up the stairs to the second floor, walked as quietly as she could along the landing and stopped outside the door. Lolly had never been inside Mal's bedroom before and even though she had permission it was not the kind of permission she could readily use to explain her presence to anyone else. The fear of being caught made her heart race.

'Get on with it,' she murmured.

The longer she stood here, the greater her chances were of being discovered. Before nerves could give her second thoughts, she turned the handle, stepped inside and closed the door behind her. The room was very much a man's space, simple and uncluttered, with only the essentials. It was comfortable and elegant without any kind of ostentation. There was a view over the garden from the two windows.

Lolly went straight to the wardrobe, grabbed a shirt, trousers and a sweater and threw them on the bed. She added a jacket and a decent everyday pair of shoes. If he had to leave in a hurry, and was wearing these clothes, she figured the shoes would look less conspicuous than the boots he had on. Next, she raided the drawers for black socks and underpants, the latter making her feel less than comfortable. There was something not quite right about rummaging through your guardian's pants, even in an emergency.

Lolly made a quick sortie into the bathroom, wondering whether or not to take his shaving gear. There was an electric razor in the cabinet but the battery was probably flat. She didn't dare try it in case she was wrong and it buzzed into life, creating a noise that might travel. Anyway, perhaps he was better off growing a beard, some form of disguise. In the end, all she took was a comb and a bar of soap.

Now Lolly had collected everything, the only task left was to get it downstairs to her own bedroom. It would help if she could find something to put the items in, a bag or a suitcase, but a fast search revealed nothing suitable. She should have thought to bring one with her. In the end she dug out a sheet from a drawer under the bed, wrapped it around the clothes, gathered the ends together and lifted it up like a sack.

Lolly listened at the door before she cautiously opened it, peered out and listened some more. Silence. When she was sure it was safe she stepped tentatively out of the room and tiptoed along the landing. She was almost at the head of the stairs when she heard the sound of ascending footsteps. Jesus! Talk about bad timing.

Frantically, she looked around. Esther's room was the nearest but she didn't dare go into that. What if it was Esther coming up the stairs? Just the thought of being found inside turned her blood to ice. With no other choice she doubled back to Mal's room, flew inside and pressed her ear to the door.

Logically, she could see no good reason for anyone to come into the room. But then she began to think of reasons. Mrs Gough probably still kept it clean and dusted even though Mal didn't sleep here any more. And perhaps Esther came sometimes to . . . well, perhaps just to remember that she'd once had a husband who lived in this house.

Lolly held her breath, her pulse racing, as the footsteps approached. And then, horror of horrors, they stopped right outside the door. Her mouth went dry. What now? She should make a dash for it, perhaps, go and hide in the bathroom. It might not prevent her being discovered but at least she could dump all the clothes in the laundry basket. Then she could make up some story about . . . God, she couldn't think of anything.

Lolly's brain was shrinking, going into panic mode. Stay or shift? The problem with any sudden movement was that it might alert the person outside to her presence. And now, anyway, she was too paralysed by anxiety to make a decision. She prayed. She waited. It felt like an eternity, eons rather than seconds, before the footsteps finally resumed and whoever it was walked on. A female, she reckoned, from the lightness of the tread, but that only narrowed it down to three.

Lolly slowly released the breath she was holding. She didn't try and leave straight away – there was a chance the woman would return the way she'd come – but instead walked over to the bed and sat down. Her legs were shaky, her heart still pounding. A close shave. If she'd left the room slightly earlier she would have run straight into the person at the foot of the stairs. Explaining why she was carrying a sackful of unusual swag might have been tricky.

While Lolly was waiting for her heart to recover, her gaze fell on the bedside table. Mal's black leather wallet was lying there, probably in exactly the same spot he had left it on the day of his fateful row with Esther. She picked it up and flicked it open. Inside was his driving licence, credit card and a wad of cash. The money could be useful to him. She didn't dare take it, though. If she was caught she'd look like a thief. Carefully, she replaced the wallet where she'd found it.

Once Lolly's nerves had been restored she set off again along the landing. This time she made it down to her room without event, sighing with relief as she closed the door behind her. Step one successfully completed. Now she just had to get the stuff to Mal.

27

Tuesday 20 September. Kellston

Stella rubbed her eyes, yawned and got up from the bed. She looked at her watch – almost four o'clock – and frowned. She had only meant to lie down for ten minutes after lunch and that had been over three hours ago. Although lunch suggested food, hers had been of the liquid variety, a few much needed shots of vodka. The inside of her mouth felt stale, her teeth rough and furred. She stared at the basin for a moment but couldn't be bothered to wash her face or pick up a toothbrush. All that routine stuff was too much effort now.

What was the point? she kept asking herself. Nothing was going to bring Dana back; the poor kid was gone for ever, obliterated, wiped out, dust to dust and all that. But she wasn't going to let it go. The knot in her stomach tightened. The familiar anger flared and burned. She hated him, the arsehole who'd done it, and not just with any old hate – this was deep and lasting and vengeful. Making the bastard pay was the only thing that kept her going. Trying to out-think him, to get inside his head, to figure out what he'd do next.

'Freddy,' she muttered. 'I'll bloody well find you and when I do . . . '

Downstairs some of the girls were gathered round the kitchen table. They stopped chatting as she came into the room, averted their eyes, pretended they hadn't been talking about her.

'Don't mind me,' Stella said.

'You all right, hon?' Michelle asked.

'No, I'm not fuckin' all right.'

Michelle raised her eyebrows. 'Only asking. No need to bite me head off.'

'Don't ask bloody stupid questions then.'

Stella had considered making a coffee but now had a better idea. Instead she opened the cupboard, took out a bottle and poured herself a stiff vodka. Hair of the dog. Just what was needed.

Jackie, who could never resist throwing in her two pennyworth, said, 'Go easy, Stel. That stuff ain't going to help.'

'And who asked you?'

'All I'm saying is . . . '

'Keep it to yourself. I don't want to hear it.'

Stella grabbed the glass and marched out through the back door to the yard. Why couldn't they just leave her alone? She lit a fag, walked to the end of the yard and opened the gate. While she drank and smoked, she gazed along the length of the empty alley. All she could think about was Dana and the shithead who'd murdered her. And what were the pigs doing about it? Fuck all so far as she could see. She had a mind to go down Cowan Road and have it out with them. Except she'd probably just end up in the slammer.

Already she had a picture of Freddy in her head, a man old enough to have learnt how to manipulate women, but still young enough to have been able to make a connection with Dana. He was out there somewhere, probably eyeing up his next victim; his type never stopped at one. Well, if he thought he'd got away with it, he had another think coming. She wouldn't rest until she'd hunted him down.

28

Tuesday 20 September. West Henby

Dinner was at six o'clock. As soon as Lolly entered the dining room she could sense the atmosphere, something off-kilter, something not quite right. Her gaze raked the faces. Esther was in an unusually good mood, her eyes shining, her gestures even more dramatic than usual. Jude had on his angry expression. He glared across the table at Heather, his bad mood a consequence perhaps of Lolly's earlier attempt to stir things up between them. She had no regrets about that.

'Lita, darling,' Esther said. 'What have you been doing all afternoon? We've barely seen you.'

Lolly was instantly wary, afraid of falling into a trap. Esther was never interested in anything she did. She felt the anxiety that comes with keeping secrets and fearing they might suddenly been exposed. 'Oh, nothing much.'

'You must find this place very dull after the bright city lights.'

Lolly thought of Kellston, probably one of the least bright areas of London, and raised her eyebrows. 'Of course not.' She had a choice between sitting beside Jude or Heather and plumped for the latter, the lesser of two evils.

'London's so vibrant, isn't it?' Esther continued. 'Always something to do, somewhere to go.'

'*Your* London, perhaps,' Jude said crossly. 'You have no idea how the other half live.'

'Well, I'm sure you won't hesitate to enlighten me.'

Lolly's eyes took in the fare on offer. Tonight's meal wasn't that different to last night's, except the chicken and ham had been replaced by a cold game pie. Either Mrs Gough had been down to the village or there had been a delivery to the house. This was good news. Lolly had decided to delay seeing Mal until this evening and now, hopefully, the larder had been replenished and she would have more supplies to take him.

Heather joined Esther in extolling the charms of London: the cinemas, the theatres, the parks, the art galleries. Jude said the city was a cesspit. While the three of them debated the point, Lolly picked at her meal, nerves blunting the edge of her hunger. She glanced towards the window. The light was beginning to fade but it wouldn't be dark until about half past seven. That should, theoretically, give her enough time to raid the kitchen, sort out the clothes and get down to the lake. She could hardly go walking in the pitch black, at least not without raising suspicion.

Lolly glanced at Heather. She would have liked to confront her over the claim that she'd seen Vicky Finch with Esther but could hardly do so without revealing her source. It was annoying and frustrating. What was the girl playing at? And then there was the lie about not working on the book with Esther any more. Mal's theory that Esther had just changed her mind didn't wash. There were manoeuvrings going on here, scheming and duplicity. She was certain of it.

As the meal progressed, the conversation petered out. Soon the only sound that remained was the scraping of knives against china. Esther released a sigh into the quiet of the room. 'Everyone's so glum tonight. I do hope you'll cheer up before tomorrow.'

Lolly, who'd been lost in thought, pricked up her ears. 'Why, what's happening tomorrow?'

'The party, of course!'

'What party?'

'Didn't I mention it? I'm sure I did. One last fabulous do before I say goodbye to the old place. You'll stay for it, of course. You must. You don't have to go rushing back to London, do you?'

It seemed to Lolly, looking round, that she was the only person surprised by the news. She had no idea if this was a genuine oversight on Esther's part or if everyone had conspired to keep her in ignorance until the last minute. Although she had no immediate plans to leave – and really couldn't so long as Mal was here – she felt a sudden sense of unease. 'Erm . . . I'm not sure.'

'But you've got to be here, darling. I've got a very important announcement to make.'

This didn't do anything to allay Lolly's fears. 'What sort of announcement?'

'Well, if I tell you now, there won't be anything *to* announce, will there? Let's hope the rain keeps off. It'll be lovely if we can spread out into the garden.'

Lolly couldn't think of anything worse than a crowd of champagne-fuelled guests wandering around the grounds. What if one of them stumbled on the summerhouse? What if they peered through the window and noticed something odd? Or heard something. Or even forced the door. It was flimsy, rotting, and the lock might easily give way.

Mrs Gough came in and started to clear the plates off the table. She performed the task with a kind of stiff-backed disdain, as though the job was beneath her. In the old days Mrs Docherty had done all the fetching and carrying.

'Leave those for now, Mrs Gough. Be a dear and bring us some coffee in the drawing room.'

The housekeeper gave a pained smile, nodded and said, 'Very well, Mrs Fury.'

Once she had left the room, everyone else stood up. Only Lolly loitered as the others headed for the drawing room. Heather stopped at the door and looked back. 'Are you joining us?'

Lolly shook her head. 'Maybe later. I've got a phone call to make.'

'You will stay for the party, won't you?'

Lolly lowered her voice and asked softly, 'Do you have any idea what this announcement is?'

'Not a clue.'

As soon as she was alone, Lolly darted over to the door, closed it and set about gathering up some of the food that was left over. She quickly wrapped a large piece of pie, bread and a hunk of cheese in a napkin, hoping that Mrs Gough hadn't noticed what was remaining during the brief time she'd been in the room.

Once she'd finished, she went over to the door again, opened it, checked that no one was in sight and hurried along the corridor and up the stairs. Back in her bedroom she placed the booty on the dressing table, pleased that she'd saved herself a trip to the kitchen and possibly a long delay while Mrs Gough was dealing with the dishes.

Lolly dug out Mal's clothes from the back of the wardrobe. She hadn't dared leave them on view in case Mrs Gough had come snooping. Now all she had to do was get out of the house and down to the lake without being spotted. With Esther, Jude and Heather safely ensconced in the drawing room the only person she had to worry about was the housekeeper.

Another problem remained, however: how to transport the clothes to Mal. There was a suitcase on top of the wardrobe but she didn't dare take the chance. Creeping out of the house with luggage would look mighty odd unless she was leaving. No, she had a better idea.

Lolly took off her own sweater and put on Mal's instead. It was fine knit, cashmere, far too long and big for her but not too lumpy. She slipped the shirt on top of that and tucked them both into her jeans. She put on her thigh-length raincoat, did up the zipper and went over to the full-length mirror to examine her reflection. Well, she didn't exactly look slimline but she reckoned she'd get away with it. The coat was big enough to cover a multiple of sins.

Before leaving, Lolly pushed the underwear and socks into her left pocket and the food into her right. She would take the rest of the things first thing in the morning: the jacket, trousers and shoes. If she woke early enough, she could be up and about before anyone else rose from their beds.

'Here we go again,' she murmured.

Lolly walked softly down the stairs and was passing the drawing room, heading for the rear of the house, when the door suddenly opened and Jude came out.

'Where are you off to?' he asked.

Lolly was starting to wonder if she was cursed by bad luck. Every time she tried to do something surreptitious, she seemed to run into obstacles of the human variety. 'What?' she asked, playing for time.

'Where are you going?'

Lolly could have answered, quite simply, that she was going for a stroll in the garden but worried that it might seem odd.

It wasn't dark yet but it was getting that way, dusk settling all around, the sky low and grey. 'The village,' she said. 'I'm going to see a friend.'

'At the pub? Actually, I might join you. I wouldn't mind getting out of here myself for a few hours.'

'No,' Lolly said, mortified at the thought. 'I'm going to Theresa's. Just for an hour. I haven't seen her since I got here and . . . ' She glanced down at her watch. 'I'd better go or I'll be late. Will you let Esther know?'

'Aren't you going to use the front door?'

What's with the twenty bloody questions, she wanted to ask. Instead she said, 'I was just looking for an umbrella in case it rains. Never mind, I'm sure it won't.' Lolly turned and walked back the way she'd come. She could feel his eyes on her as she opened the door and closed it behind her.

As she hurried down the drive, Lolly wondered if Jude suspected anything. Had he noticed the bulk under her coat? Had she seemed shifty, evasive? She replayed the exchange in her head but couldn't come to any firm conclusion. In case he was watching her, she felt obliged to keep walking down the drive until she came to the bend and passed out of sight of the house. At this point she veered onto the grass and started circling back round towards the lake.

Lolly dived into the trees and followed the curve of the perimeter wall. The detour had cost her an extra five minutes and she walked with fast, furious strides, wanting to get to Mal before darkness fell. It was spooky in the twilight. Everything looked different from the daytime, shapes contorted, familiarity replaced by strangeness. The birds had fallen silent, their song replaced by other sounds, tiny rustlings that made her jump and turn and peer into the undergrowth.

By the time she reached the lake and joined the narrow

path, she was slightly out of breath. She slowed her pace as she approached the summerhouse. There was no sign of life. A part of her hoped he'd gone, seen sense and scarpered. He was better off out of here, a thousand miles away. She was scared of what might happen if he stayed.

Lolly went up to the door and knocked very lightly. Her hopes were instantly dashed. She heard the key turning in the lock and a few seconds later the door opened. Even though this wasn't the first time she'd seen Mal she was still shocked by his appearance. The suave sophisticated man had been replaced by a down-and-out, ragged and dishevelled with emptiness in his eyes. But as soon as he smiled this impression left her and she saw the real Mal again.

'Ah,' he said, 'it's always lovely to have visitors. Please excuse the state of the place; I've only just moved in.'

Lolly grinned, went inside, took the food out of her pocket and placed it on the table. 'Game pie. Very tasty. And some bread and cheese.'

'You're an angel. What would I do without you?'

'Starve to death, I suppose.' She emptied her other pocket of the pants and socks. Then she took off her jacket, removed the shirt and sweater and laid them over the back of a chair. 'I'll bring the rest tomorrow.'

He smiled again when he saw how she'd hidden the clothes. 'They'll be recruiting you to MI5.' He reached out a hand and touched the soft cashmere. 'Thanks. It's been a while since I wore anything decent.'

Lolly put her coat back on – it was getting chilly – and perched on the edge of the chair. 'Are you warm enough with the rug? Should I bring you a blanket?'

'No, the rug's fine. Do you have any news? Have you found out anything?'

'Only that we have a problem. Esther's throwing a party tomorrow night.'

'That's not a problem.'

'Of course it is. There'll be guests swarming all over the place, especially if it stays dry. Make sure you keep the door locked.'

'What's the party for?'

'I've no idea.' She didn't mention the announcement, afraid that this would only encourage him to take unnecessary risks. Especially if he thought it was about his daughter. 'Does Esther need a reason?'

'No, I suppose not. Don't worry, I'll stay out of sight.'

'You won't do anything daft, will you? You won't try and get in the house or talk to Esther?'

'No,' he said. 'I won't do anything daft. I promise.'

Lolly had always trusted Mal, always taken him at his word. So why, on this occasion, did she not believe him?

29

Tuesday 20 September. London

It was evening before Nick Trent finally made it home. He threw his car keys on the table, switched on the kettle and took a couple of aspirin. His head was banging from too many hours spent in a police interview room being asked the same questions in a number of different ways. It was probably a good thing that he hadn't known the identity of the client at the time or he might have overthought what he'd said. Providing evidence that could lead to the conviction of Terry's Street's enforcer was hardly conducive to free and open speech.

Naturally, the police had been less than impressed about him leaving the scene of the crime even after he'd explained why he'd done it. They'd huffed and puffed and raised their eyebrows, trying to imply that he'd been involved in an attempt to cover up the surveillance of Brent Sandler.

'Why would we want to do that?'

'So you didn't have to do this,' the DI had said. 'You lot prefer to keep out of it when the shit hits the fan.'

You lot meaning private investigators, of course. Nick had kept his cool, stayed polite and told them what he knew.

Which, as it happened, wasn't that much. No, he hadn't seen the driver of the Jag, the windows had been tinted, and it had all happened so quickly. No, he wasn't sure of the exact colour of the car, but definitely dark blue or black. No, he hadn't managed to get the registration or see what direction it had gone in after Old Street.

They'd moved onto his surveillance of Sandler, asking about the man's movements, where he went and who he saw. 'It's all in the notes,' Nick had said.

'Humour me,' the DI had replied. 'I'd rather hear it straight from the horse's mouth.'

And so Nick had told him what he could remember.

Sandler's visits to prostitutes seemed to interest him a lot. 'You reckon he was cheating on his wife, then?'

'I really couldn't say.'

'But you could hazard a guess.'

'I'm paid to report the facts, not to guess. I didn't follow the bloke inside. It could have been business or pleasure.'

'And what kind of business might he have had?'

'He was a solicitor, wasn't he? I should think working girls need a good brief every now and again.'

It was when the DI had started asking about Terry Street, if he'd seen the two men together, whether their relationship seemed amicable, that Nick had started to wonder if Terry was in the frame for the killing. Not good news. No one wants to be pointing the finger at an East End gangster – not if they value the air they breathe. It was only later he'd discovered that it was Vinnie Keane.

While he poured hot water over a sachet of tomato Cup-a-Soup, Nick mused on whether this amounted to the same thing. Had Terry ordered the killing of Brent Sandler for some reason? Maybe he'd even been driving the car. Nick had stopped wishing by now that he'd paid more attention to the Jag and was glad that he hadn't. Although he believed in the basic principles of law and order, he had no desire to put his own life on the line for the likes of a scumbag like Sandler.

Nick took his mug through to the living room where he noticed the light was flashing on the answer machine. He pressed the button and waited for the tape to rewind.

'Hi, it's Lolly. Look, Esther's having a party tomorrow and I wondered if you'd like to come. I know it's short notice and you're probably busy so don't worry if you can't, only . . . Well, come if you can. It's starting about seven. Okay. Bye, then.'

Nick played the message again. It was the 'only' that interested him, what she hadn't said rather than what she had. Had she found out something? Or did she just enjoy his company so much that she couldn't bear to party without him? Okay, so the latter was stretching it a bit but the fact that she wanted him there was encouraging.

Under normal circumstances he'd have been working tomorrow but with the abrupt cessation of Sandler's surveillance he was actually at a loose end. Roy Marshall had suggested he take the day off and he hadn't objected. With his police statement done and dusted, he was free to go where he liked.

It was a strange time for Esther to throw a party with her husband on the run and all this business with Hazel and Vicky Finch, but there was no accounting for how her mind worked. And who held a party on a Wednesday night? Only the rich, he thought, the people who weren't ruled by nine-to five drudgery and alarm clocks going off at the crack of dawn.

Nick considered calling Lolly back, confirming that he'd be there but then he'd feel obliged to tell her about Vinnie Keane. He wasn't sure how close the two of them were but they certainly knew each other. He'd seen them together a few times in the Fox. Perhaps, with everything else that was going on, this particular piece of bad news could wait until tomorrow.

He sat down and sipped his Cup-a-Soup. With luck, he'd be dining better tomorrow. Or perhaps it would just be endless canapés, vol-au-vents and insubstantial things on sticks. Anyway, a few hours in the country was just what he needed, a break from city strife and a chance to relax. Hopefully there wouldn't be any drama.

30

Wednesday 21 September. West Henby

By mid-morning there was a small army occupying the house, with cleaners, florists and caterers all jostling for position. The downstairs rooms were being hoovered, dusted, buffed and polished, the smell of Mr Sheen mingling with the heady scent of lilies and roses. Crates of champagne were being unloaded from a van and stored in the basement. Outside, the lawns were being mowed and lights strung through the branches of the trees.

Lolly was glad she'd got up early and gone to see Mal before the place was overrun. She'd given him another pep talk on the wisdom of keeping his head down but whether he'd taken any notice was questionable. She felt nervous about Esther's forth-coming announcement and prayed for rain so that it would be delivered inside the house and not from the garden where he might hear it. A good downpour would also stop the guests from wandering around the lake. She didn't trust him to stay in the summerhouse.

Her prayers, however, weren't about to be answered any time soon. The sky was cornflower blue without a cloud in sight. Still, it was Britain, and the weather could easily turn before the party started. She would try and stay optimistic.

Most of the staff hired for the do came from the village. Although they disliked Esther, it was extra money, cash in hand, and for that they'd even put up with Mrs Gough ordering them around. Lolly went from room to room until she found who she was looking for, a pale girl, a few years older than her, with long red hair and freckles. She checked that Jude was nowhere around before approaching.

Theresa jumped when Lolly tapped her on the shoulder and let out a yelp when she saw who it was. 'Lita! Jesus, what are you doing here?'

'I wish I knew. Esther asked me to come.'

'Christ, I'd have told her to shove her party where the sun don't shine. After what she did to you ... I wouldn't have stepped foot in this house again.' Theresa laughed, leaned forward and gave her a quick hug. 'I'm glad you did, though. When did you get here? How have you been? You should have called me. Are you staying for long?'

Lolly didn't get a chance to even begin answering her questions before Mrs Gough put her head round the door and promptly put a stop to the conversation.

'You're not being paid to chat, Theresa.'

'Sorry, Mrs Gough.'

'Sorry doesn't get the table laid.'

'No, Mrs Gough.'

The housekeeper gave them both a dirty look before she withdrew, but only as far as the hall where she continued to keep her beady eyes on them.

'When do you get a break?' Lolly asked quickly.

'Lunchtime, twelve o'clock.'

'Let's have a catch-up then. I'll meet you on the back steps.

And look, if anyone asks can you do me a favour and say I was round your place last night, just for an hour or so about half seven?'

Theresa gave her an enquiring look, but immediately nodded. 'Course I will.'

'Thanks.'

Lolly left the room and said to Mrs Gough, 'Anything I can do to help?'

The housekeeper pursed her lips. 'Not distracting the staff would be a start. That girl does little enough as it is.'

Lolly took that as a no and headed for the library. The house would be in chaos for the next few hours and it was the only place to get some peace and quiet. Unfortunately, Heather and Jude had beaten her to it. They were standing by the window and seemed to deliberately move apart when she opened the door. 'Oh, sorry, I didn't know anyone was in here.'

'That's all right,' Heather said. 'I was just off.'

As she left, Lolly went inside and walked over to the bookshelves. She could feel the remnants of an atmosphere in the room, something simmering, but couldn't quite grasp its nature. She glanced over at Jude.

'Is everything all right?'

'Why shouldn't it be?'

'I don't know. You didn't seem best pleased with Heather yesterday. Have you sorted things out?'

'As much as you can sort out anything with Heather.'

Lolly thought about this while she went back to looking at the books. After a while, when Jude still hadn't moved, she asked casually, 'Do you have any idea what this announcement is about tonight?'

'What announcement?'

'Esther said she was making an announcement. At dinner last night. She said—'

'Oh *that*. Esther's always making declarations of one kind or another. I wouldn't worry about it.'

Lolly felt a jolt of alarm. 'Why should I be worried?'

'You shouldn't.'

'So you know what it's about.'

'No.'

Lolly stared at him. 'So how do you know I shouldn't be worried?'

'Well, it's not going to be anything to do with *you*, is it?' He said it with a hint of derision, as though she was so far from significance that she barely warranted a second thought, never mind an announcement. 'Forget about it.'

For a second Lolly was back on the Mansfield estate, a kid again, sitting in Jude's flat and watching him out of the corner of her eye while he watched the big screen up on the wall. It was those women who'd fascinated him – Lana Turner, Veronica Lake, Rita Hayworth – with their ability to charm and seduce and destroy. And hadn't he been the same with Amy Wiltshire? Lolly had been as inconsequential to him then as she was now. Even though her love for Jude had long since been extinguished – well, most of it – she still felt a pang, a hint of that old rejection.

Lolly, annoyed by her own reaction, immediately went on the offensive. 'It was Esther who asked me to come here, remember? Or rather asked you to do it for her. And it's not as if she even likes me, so I can only presume she's got another motive. Do you have any idea what that might be?'

Jude's mouth curled into a half smile. 'Because she likes to have an audience.'

'Is it about Vicky Finch?'

'I've told you. I don't know. You'll just have to wait and see.'

'You *do* know,' she insisted. 'You're just not telling me.'

'Why should I? You're not telling us about Mal.'

Lolly flinched at the retort and quickly tried to cover it up by shifting awkwardly from one foot to the other. Her mind started racing. Did he know Mal was here? Had he found out about the summerhouse? Followed her last night, perhaps. Or seen her leave the house at the crack of dawn this morning. She forced herself to hold his gaze while she said, 'That's because I've got nothing to tell. I don't have a clue where he is or why he took off.'

Jude gave her a doubting look. 'You two were always tight.'

'What would you know about it?' She tried to make her next comment sound as if she was affronted by Mal's failure to inform her of his plans. 'And clearly we're not *that* tight or he'd have told me what he was going to do.'

'If you say so.'

Lolly, deciding this didn't merit a reply, picked a Graham Greene novel at random off the shelf and walked out of the library. It was only when she was halfway up the stairs that she glanced down at its title and winced. It was called *The End of the Affair.*

At midday Lolly and Theresa were sitting on the grass eating hamburgers washed down with Coke while they caught up with each other's news. There had been an addition to Theresa's family since the two of them had last met, a baby she'd called Michael. Money was tight – there wasn't much work in the village, but they got by. Lolly glossed over her life in London, only talking about the legitimate stuff she did and leaving out the dodgy parts.

Inevitably the talk turned to Mal and his escape from prison. Theresa gazed around the garden.

'I keep expecting to see him walk across the lawn or down the drive. It doesn't seem right, him not being here. I hope he doesn't get nabbed by the cops; the poor bloke deserves a break. I wonder where he is now.'

Lolly shook her head, forced to lie in order to protect him. 'I don't know, but I hope it's a long way away.

'You've heard about Mrs Docherty, I suppose? Esther gave her the push last month. She told her it was because she was moving to the States but the house isn't even on the market yet.'

'I don't think she can sell the house without Mal agreeing to it. And she told me it was because she was a gossip.'

'That's such a load of crap. She hardly said a word about what went on here.'

'Went on?' Lolly enquired.

Theresa grinned and lowered her voice. 'Well, all the comings and goings. The *men*. First, that Claud – he left his wife for her, you know – and then there was some actor, I can't remember his name, and then—' She stopped suddenly, looking flustered, as if she feared being tactless.

'Jude?'

Theresa, sensitive to Lolly's feelings, grimaced. 'I don't know if anything's going on between them. It probably isn't. But people talk, don't they? He spends a lot of time here these days.'

'It's all right. You don't have to worry about breaking my heart. I don't care what he does, or who with.'

'Good. You deserve better. What happened to his face, by the way? Did Esther give him a slap?'

'He says he got mugged in London.'

'I think I prefer my version.' Theresa took a swig of Coke and put the bottle down on the grass. 'That girl who's been staying, the blonde. Who is she?'

'Her name's Heather Grant. She's writing a book about what happened to Kay.'

'She's very pretty. Maybe Esther's got competition.'

'What makes you say that?'

'I've seen them together in the pub a few times. Just her and Jude. Very cosy, if you know what I mean.'

'Cosy?' Lolly repeated. 'You think . . . '

'Well, not actually *doing* anything, but it's all in the body language, isn't it?'

Lolly recalled that sudden moving apart she'd observed when she went into the library. 'He gave me the impression he didn't like her much.'

'What's liking got to do with it? Men don't have to like women to fancy them.'

Lolly thought this was true, especially of Jude. He'd despised Amy Wiltshire but he'd still wanted her. Lust rather than love. She supposed any red-blooded man would have the hots for Heather, but whether the girl felt the same was another matter altogether. Heather struck her as determined, focused and the only thing she appeared to have on her mind at the moment was her book. Anyway, it would be a risky business to mess about with Jude while she still needed Esther's cooperation. Thinking of the book reminded Lolly of Vicky Finch.

'I don't suppose you've seen another blonde girl here recently, have you? In the past few weeks. About my age.'

Theresa shook her head. 'Who is she?'

'Oh, just someone Heather knows. Her name's Vicky.'

'No, but that doesn't mean anything. I'm hardly ever here, only to help out at parties and there haven't been many of those in the past few months. The house could be full of guests and I wouldn't be any the wiser. Is it important?'

Lolly didn't want to go into the whole Hazel/Vicky business and so she shook her head. 'It doesn't matter.'

'Hey, I forgot to ask. What's with the alibi for last night? I hope you were up to no good.'

'I wish,' Lolly said, laughing it off. 'I just fancied a walk, a chance to get away from everyone for an hour or so, but then I bumped into Jude who gave me the third degree about where I was going and yours was the first name that popped into my head. You don't mind, do you?'

'Of course not. Why would I? And you're welcome to come round any time. Do you know how long you're staying for?'

'I haven't decided. A few days. It depends how it goes.'

'Odd though, Esther inviting you here after everything that's happened. What is it, some kind of olive branch?'

'Since when has Esther ever offered those?'

'Exactly. I'd watch my back if I was you. She's not exactly renowned for the sweetness of her nature.'

'Tell me about it.'

'You must be worried about Mal, though. Where do you think he is?'

Lolly didn't like lying to her old friend but she had no choice. 'Your guess is as good as mine. Somewhere safe, I hope.'

Theresa might have pressed her further if the other workers hadn't started to stir, gathering up their litter and heading back inside the house. 'Here we go again,' she said, rising to her feet. 'I'll see you tonight if Mrs G. doesn't sack me in the meantime.'

Lolly stood up too. 'Before you go, could I just ask you something? You weren't here with Michael on Friday, were you?'

Theresa looked puzzled. 'God, no, why would I bring Michael here? You know what Esther's like about kids. She won't have them anywhere near the house. Why do you ask?'

'Oh, it's nothing. Someone said they thought they'd heard a baby crying, but they must have got it wrong.'

'There hasn't been a baby here since . . . ' Theresa's voice trailed off as her gaze strayed towards the lake. She gave a shiver and wrapped her arms around her chest. 'No, not here. Not ever.'

The two girls stood in silence for a moment and then went their separate ways.

31

Wednesday 21 September. West Henby

At seven o'clock, Lolly was up in her old bedroom searching through the wardrobe for something to wear. She still had a lot of things here. When she'd left – or perhaps, more accurately, been thrown out – she had gone in a hurry taking only a small suitcase and the bare essentials. She could have returned for the rest, but pride had stood in her way. She had sworn she wouldn't set foot in the house again until Mal was a free man and back where he belonged. She glanced towards the window. Well, he was certainly home but not in the circumstances she'd imagined or hoped for.

Lolly's fingers quickly separated the hangers as her eyes flew from one garment to the next. Eventually her gaze settled on the dark red silk dress she had only worn once. That occasion had been another party, the last party she'd attended here. Even though she tried her best, it was impossible to forget the excitement she'd felt that night, the fluttering in her chest, the anticipation at the knowledge that Jude was coming. Jude was back in her life.

Although she couldn't have known that he was only using

her to get to Esther, Lolly still cursed her naivety. How had she been so stupid? Blinded by desire, she hadn't seen what should have been staring her straight in the face. A pink flush spread across her cheeks, a hot mix of anger and humiliation. What a fool! He had trampled on her feelings, leaving her shattered and bereft. Even now, she wasn't completely over it. She said she was, *swore* she was, but the memory still haunted her.

Lolly went to the full-length mirror, held up the dress and examined her reflection. The dress certainly couldn't be described as lucky but that was why she wanted to wear it, to purge those demons and prove that her present was not controlled by the past. A putting aside of all things negative. On top of that, it was a damn nice dress and it suited her.

There was something else Lolly had worn that night, her eighteenth birthday present from Mal. It was another item she'd left behind, too afraid of it getting lost or stolen in London. She went over to the dressing table, opened the box, drew out the ruby necklace and fastened it around her neck. The red stones glowed like fire. The rubies had come from Burma and had probably passed through many hands before they'd finally ended up at Mal's shop in Hatton Garden.

Before she could change her mind, Lolly pulled the dress over her head, put on her shoes, brushed her hair and took one last look in the mirror. The girl who stared back seemed more defiant than pretty but she would have to do. Her last job was to spray on some perfume, a fine mist of Chanel No. 5.

Just as she was about to leave, she remembered Terry's diamond ring still lying in her handbag. Was it safe to leave it here? She didn't want to lug the bag around all night but she'd curse herself if the ring got nicked. On the whole, Esther's guests were probably trustworthy but thieves came in all shapes and sizes, and with no lock on the bedroom door anyone could wander in. She took out the ring, put it on her finger and held out her hand. Well, it was somewhat ostentatious, but people would presume it was fake.

By the time she got downstairs, the guests were already streaming in. Their smart shiny cars rolled down the drive and gathered at the side of the house until the area began to resemble an outdoor luxury showroom. She watched for a while, wondering who'd get out when the uniformed chauffeurs opened the doors. Mal had always spent more time with these men than he had with Esther's guests, talking engines and speed, performance and handling, before he sent them off to Mrs Docherty to be generously fed and watered.

Lolly grabbed a glass of champagne and went from room to room, not so much mingling as people-spotting. There were famous faces everywhere: actors, directors, producers, writers, even the odd politician or two. Esther's star, in a long decline after the abduction of Kay, had risen again over recent years, and the scandal of the trial had only added to her popularity.

Was popularity the right word? Perhaps what she meant was notoriety.

As it was still warm, the guests inevitably spilled out onto the lawn. Lolly joined them, throwing fast nervous glances towards the line of trees, certain that Mal was lurking there somewhere. He wouldn't be able to resist. She kept an eye on the pathways in case anyone decided to wander off towards the lake.

There was no sign of Nick yet. He probably wasn't coming. It had been short notice, after all, and she couldn't expect him to drop everything and dash down to Kent. Everywhere she looked she seemed to be surrounded by couples, men and women holding hands or with arms linked at the elbow, standing together with their shoulders touching. Although Lolly knew she didn't *need* anyone – she was more than capable of taking care of herself – she still felt a pang of envy. It would be nice to have someone to share things with. Even at the tender age of nineteen, she was beginning to suspect that she was one of those girls who would never find another half.

Lolly was still musing on this when a cut-glass voice sliced through her thoughts. 'Lita, darling. Heavens, I never expected to see you here!'

Lolly turned to find Anna Leighton standing behind her. The two had first met the summer Jude had come to West Henby and bad times had followed for both of them. Anna was a dark-haired, curvy, sultry beauty, her looks more exotic than would have been expected from her East End origins. 'Likewise.'

'Claud insisted, I'm afraid. Says there are people he simply has to talk to. It's such a bore. And how are you? I heard Esther threw you out. You should have taken the evil bitch to court. You've as much right to be here as she has.'

Lolly was unsurprised by Anna's vitriol. Her husband Claud had briefly left her for Esther and, presumably, only come crawling back after Esther had tossed him aside. She could have divorced him, of course, but rich powerful husbands were hard to come by and Anna had a pragmatic nature. Having clawed her way out of poverty, she had no intention of returning to it.

'And what about poor Mal,' Anna continued. 'How exciting to be on the run. I've heard he's been seen in South America.'

'Oh,' Lolly said. 'Really? Seen by whom?'

'Hugh Devine. Swears blind he spotted him in Buenos Aires, clear as day, walking down a street in Palermo, but he's such an old soak he could have been hallucinating. Still, I like to think it's true. One in the eye for the law, right? And at least over there that spiteful cow can't cause him any more grief.' Anna glanced towards the open French doors, through which Esther was currently passing as she made her way into the garden. 'Talk of the devil.'

Esther floated down the steps in a long white dress so sheer it was almost diaphanous. She looked like an angel. Her eyes were sparkling, her fair hair piled up on top of her head with a few loose tendrils framing her face. She had a glow about her, an air of triumph, or perhaps it was just self-satisfaction. She was, without doubt, a woman who knew exactly how to make an entrance.

Jude was by her side, impeccably dressed, his clothes definitely more Savile Row than Kellston market. His face was solemn, unsmiling, but that didn't detract from how handsome he was. Lolly hated herself for even noticing. He was sticking to Esther like glue, like a man afraid of superior suitors.

'What did I tell you?' Anna said. 'I warned you about that boy. You shouldn't have let him anywhere near her.'

Lolly, who'd suffered enough without having her nose rubbed it in, quickly retorted, 'I could say the same for you.'

Anna glared at her for a moment but then burst out laughing. 'Touché. We're both as dumb as each other.'

'Thanks.'

'Claud never could keep his eyes off her, or his hands come to that. Still, she'll get what's coming to her. What goes around, comes around. Isn't that what they say?'

'Just because they say it doesn't mean it's true.'

Anna's mouth curled into a smile. 'Oh, in this case I think it might be.'

32

Wednesday 21 September. West Henby

It was after eight o'clock and Lolly was on her second glass of champagne when she saw Nick Trent strolling across the lawn. He had made the effort and put on a suit but didn't look entirely comfortable in it. Even as he walked, he pulled at his tie as if it was some alien creature that had wound itself around his neck. She liked that he was different to the other men, that he didn't quite fit in, that he was, like her, an outsider. Neither of them really belonged here.

'Ah, hello. You made it, then.'

'You know me,' he replied drily, 'I never like to miss a party. I see the glitterati are out in force.'

'All the beautiful people. Do you remember? That's what you called them the day you first came here.'

'Did I? Yes, perhaps I did.'

'And I was rude to you, I think. Not about that. I was in a bad mood because . . . ' It had been because she'd been sitting with Jude on the grass, and Esther had come over with Nick and asked her to take him to see Mal. 'Oh, I don't know, something or other. Come on, let's go inside and get you a drink. Are you hungry?'

'Starving.'

As they walked towards the house they passed Claud Leighton, Anna's husband, who was talking to a suave-looking man smoking a cigar. Claud glanced at Lolly but didn't acknowledge her. He either didn't remember her or didn't wish to renew the acquaintance. She suspected the latter. One had to take sides in Esther's wars and there was nothing to be gained in taking Lolly's. Esther may have thrown him over but he still needed her; she was hot property in the film world and he was a director who needed stars.

Lolly turned her attention back to Nick. 'So, how have you been? Busy?'

'I don't like to whine on an empty stomach. I'll tell you about it later. How about you? Have you found out anything yet?'

'Only that Esther's making an announcement tonight.'

'That sounds dramatic.'

'That's what's worrying about it. I've asked the others but they say they don't know what it's about.'

'You don't believe them?'

'I don't know what to believe any more.'

As they climbed the steps she noticed Jude and Heather standing at the top. There was something conspiratorial about them. They had their heads close together and were talking quickly. She tried to read their lips but it was useless. Jude put his hand on Heather's arm but she shrugged it off. A group of guests, tipsy and laughing, moved across her line of vision and by the time they'd shifted there was nothing left to see. Both Jude and Heather had disappeared.

It was crowded in the drawing room where the food had been laid out. Nick piled up his plate from the cold buffet and Lolly took a couple of sandwiches. After Nick got a drink they went back outside, plate in one hand, glass in the other, where they could talk without having to raise their voices.

Illumination from the house spilled out in white oblongs, chasing the darkness to where the lawn met the trees. Here the branches were strung with fairy lights. A brazier had been lit and they settled near it, sitting down on the grass. Nick took off his tie, put it in his pocket and undid the top button his shirt. 'You don't mind, do you? I hate to lower the tone but I feel like I'm being strangled.'

'I'll try not to die of embarrassment.'

Nick grinned and glanced at her hand. 'That's quite a sparkler you're wearing. Did you win the pools?'

Lolly spread out her fingers to show the ring to full advantage. 'It's not bad, is it? A fake, of course, but a decent one. You wouldn't know it's not a diamond, not at a glance anyway.'

'It had me fooled but that's not saying much. I know as much about jewellery as I do about celebrities. How exactly do you spot a fake?'

'Are we talking jewellery here or . . . '

Nick laughed, his gaze travelling quickly round the people in the garden. 'All that glisters is not gold, right?'

'If Shakespeare said it, it has to be true.'

'I take it there's no sign of Mal?'

The sudden change of subject caught her off guard. Lolly shook her head, simultaneously reaching for a sandwich so she didn't need to meet his gaze. 'He'd be mad to come here.'

'He was mad to go AWOL, but it didn't stop him.'

'I think it was to do with something Heather said. She claims she didn't raise his hopes about Vicky but I think she might have done. She's kind of . . . evasive about it all. Anyway, if I remember rightly, you were going to have a good whine about something.'

'You might not want to be eating when I do.'

Lolly put the sandwich down. 'It's all right, I've got a strong stomach.'

'You're going to need it.' He took a swig of champagne and looked at her. 'Well, I've been following this bloke around – surveillance, the usual stuff – and yesterday I was parked up outside his office and just as he came out of the door a car drew up and somebody shot him.'

'What?'

'Yeah, right in front of me. Two shots straight through the heart.'

'Christ,' Lolly said. 'Is he dead?'

'As a doornail. And I had to spend the afternoon down the nick being given the third degree. Not my favourite way of passing the time, I can assure you.'

'I can imagine. Are you okay? Seeing something like that must be awful.'

'It all happened so quickly, I didn't really have time to think about it.'

'And now?'

'I'm doing my best to forget about it.' He lifted up his glass. 'You can always rely on champagne to blot out the bad stuff.'

'So who was he, this bloke?'

'A dodgy solicitor called Brent Sandler. He likes to . . . *liked* to walk the thin line between what's legal and what isn't. Although, to be honest, I reckon he crossed it a fair few times. He tended to mix with the more dubious elements of society. Have you ever heard of him?'

Lolly shook her head. 'Why would I?'

He pulled a face and she knew he had more to tell.

'Nick?'

'I didn't know who the client was at the time, who was paying the firm to have Sandler followed. We don't tend to be told that unless it's relevant. Just do the job and don't ask too many questions.'

Lolly had a sinking feeling. 'Is this something to do with Terry?'

'It could be,' he said, 'but Terry wasn't the client. It was Vinnie Keane. And he's been arrested over the murder, probably charged by now.'

'Vinnie? God, what?' Lolly was genuinely shocked. She knew Vinnie was no stranger to violence but this was something else. 'Why would he do that?'

'Perhaps Terry told him to – he could have fallen out with Sandler – but that's not what I'm hearing. I don't know all the ins and outs but rumour has it that Vinnie was involved with Sandler's wife, Laura. It gives him a pretty good motive for getting rid of the man.'

'But you don't have to kill someone to ... Why couldn't she just divorce him?'

'I suppose there could have been financial reasons, or emotional ones. Sandler wasn't what you'd call an ideal husband. He seemed to prefer the company of prostitutes to his own wife.'

'Delightful.' Lolly thought about all the selling trips she'd made with Vinnie. They'd never talked about anything personal, just exchanged a bit of banter to pass the time. And yet she felt she knew him well enough to question his guilt. It didn't seem plausible to her. Something didn't add up. 'Surely, if he was planning on killing Sandler, he wouldn't pay someone else to follow him around. I mean, that would put him right at the top of the suspect list. Vinnie might not be the smartest man who walked the earth but he's not stupid.'

'Everyone can be stupid when it comes to love.'

'You think he did it then?'

'I suppose we'll find out soon enough. Sorry to break the bad news. I know he's a friend of yours.'

Lolly wasn't sure if she'd class him as a friend exactly but she'd grown fond of him in the past year. 'It's not your fault. Thanks for letting me know.'

Nick rose to his feet and said, 'I'm just going for a . . . Where is the loo, by the way?'

'Straight through, past the library and it's on your left.'

While Nick went to relieve his bladder, Lolly contemplated this latest bit of news.

Mal had just escaped from prison and now Vinnie was going in. It was like a revolving door. He'd be banged up for a long time if he was found guilty. Could love ever be worth that? She sighed into the night air, picked up her champagne and drained the glass.

A couple of minutes later Jude came striding towards her. 'Have you seen Esther? I can't find her anywhere. She's not in the house. I've looked in her room, everywhere.'

Lolly, who had no interest in Esther's whereabouts, gave a shrug. 'She can't be that far away.'

'Someone said she was out here.'

'I don't think so. I haven't seen her. Not in the past twenty minutes or so.'

Jude seemed disproportionately jumpy and anxious. What was he afraid of? That Esther had sneaked off with another man, perhaps. That even at this moment she was kissing someone more desirable – or doing more than kissing. She might have felt sorry for him if he'd ever expressed one iota of regret for how he'd treated her. As it was, she just gave another shrug. 'I'll let her know you're looking if I see her.'

'People are starting to wonder where she is. I think I'll check the lake.'

Lolly frowned. 'She wouldn't have gone there. She *never* goes there.'

But Jude was insistent. 'I'll try anyway.'

Lolly jumped to her feet, afraid that he might stumble upon Mal and the game would be up. Jude wouldn't hesitate to raise the alarm, to call the law if he caught so much as a glimpse. 'I'll go,' she said. 'It's dark and I know my way around better than you. Why don't you try the drive? She might have . . . I don't know, walked down to the gate for some reason.'

Jude hesitated, perhaps wondering why she was suddenly being so helpful. 'No, I'll come with you.'

'What's the point in both of us going? It's better if we split up. You try the drive or look inside the house again. Perhaps she's back now.' And then, before he could protest, she walked away as quickly as she could in her high heels. Lolly held her breath, hoping he wouldn't follow, and was relieved when she glanced over her shoulder to see him cutting across the lawn towards the drive.

Lolly was certain Esther wouldn't be anywhere near the lake but she'd go as far as the bench, stay a couple of minutes, make sure there was no sign of Mal and then go back. She kept her eyes peeled as she walked through the trees. The further she got from the house, the darker it became until the only light was from the moon. The sounds of the party, the music and the chatter gradually grew more distant. An uneasiness was starting to stir in her. It wasn't like Esther to desert her guests, especially when she was the centre of attention.

Lolly smelled the water before she saw it, an earthy musty odour. She continued along the path until the lake was revealed. Streaks of pale silver danced on the surface. A light breeze rustled through the reeds. She fought against all those bad feelings that creep up on you when you're alone in a dark place, the most powerful of them being that you are *not* alone.

Knowing that the bank could be slippery even when it hadn't rained, she approached with caution. The willows shimmered in the moonlight. She glanced to her left and right. It was then she heard the noise. She couldn't say exactly what it was, only that it didn't belong here. The hairs on her arms stood on end. Her first instinct was to retreat, to run away, but instead she stood immobile.

Gradually the noise turned into something identifiable, a low, soft kind of keening. Lolly trembled. Then, as if she had no choice in the matter, she moved to the right following the sound. One foot in front of the other until she reached the source. It was the whiteness she noticed first, spread out across the bank, standing out in the dark. Gradually, the rest came into focus, the long pale legs, the arms, the head thrown to one side, the face that was like alabaster. She drew in a breath, horrified. Esther. And beside her another figure, rocking back and forth, his arms wrapped around his knees.

Mal looked up, his eyes full of grief and pain and fear. 'She's dead, Lita,' he said. 'She's dead.'

33

Wednesday 21 September. West Henby

For a moment, Lolly couldn't speak, couldn't react. Paralysed by shock, she stood and stared at the scene in front of her. Her mind made several swift connections – a body, a man beside the body, a violent act, a crime of anger or of passion.

'Jesus,' she murmured. 'God, no.'

'I didn't kill her,' he said, so softly she could barely hear. 'I found her in the water.'

Lolly, propelled by a surge of adrenalin, lurched forward and then hunched down beside him. She reached out her hand to touch the underside of Esther's wrist. No pulse. The flesh was cold and wet and lifeless. Her gaze slid up to Esther's face, the eyes partly open, glazed and unseeing. There were marks around her neck, bruises from where someone had tightened their fingers.

'When? How did you . . . ?' Lolly was having problems stringing a sentence together. She gulped in a breath and tried again. 'When did you find her?'

'I didn't kill her.'

'I believe you. When did you find her, Mal?'

As if he couldn't quite process what she was asking, a few seconds passed before he answered. 'Not long. Five minutes. I heard people arguing, two, three, I'm not sure, but I know one of them was Esther. I was by the summerhouse. I could hear them but I couldn't see anything. I thought there was a splash.' He spoke quickly, his forehead puckering into a frown as he struggled to make sense of it all. 'And then it went quiet. I stayed out of the way for a while in case . . . and then I walked along here and saw her. She was in the water, *under* the water, just here by the bank. I dragged her out but . . . '

'What were they arguing about? Do you know? Did you catch any of it?'

Mal shook his head. 'Just voices.'

'Male, female? Come on, Mal, *think*.' Lolly knew that unless he could provide another suspect, someone with a motive, the law would jump to the same conclusion she had. Even now she wasn't completely sure of his innocence. She wanted to believe him, needed to, but just because he said he hadn't killed her didn't mean that it was true.

Mal's hand rested on Esther's shoulder. 'I can still remember the first time I saw her. She was the most beautiful woman I'd ever seen. She's still beautiful. She's still—'

Lolly gripped his arm, trying to convey a sense of urgency. She was starting to think about Jude and how long it would be before he came looking for her. 'What are you going to do?'

'Do?' He had the same look on his face that he'd worn in the courtroom, as if nothing really mattered any more, as if he'd lost the will to even bother to defend himself. 'I suppose you'd better go and fetch someone. I'll stay with her.'

This was the point Lolly made up her mind. She suddenly knew that he couldn't have killed Esther. He didn't have it in him. Despite everything the woman had done, all the misery she'd inflicted, a part of him had carried on loving her. She was his wife, the mother of his child. Even in anger, he would not have put his hands around her throat.

'I will,' she said, 'but you can't stay here. Don't you see how it's going to look? They'll lock you up and throw away the key.'

'I'll tell them what happened. I'll tell the truth.'

'You think they care about the damn truth? You're on the run, you're here and Esther's dead. They won't believe a word you say. She sent you to jail and now you've got your revenge. That's how they'll see it, Mal. You've got to get away.'

'And go where? I'm not running. I can't.'

Lolly had to find a way to get through to him. Quickly she scrambled to her feet. 'And what are you going to do if there is some truth in what Heather Grant says? You think your daughter's going to visit you in jail? You'll be banged up for years, Mal. If you can't do it for yourself, do it for her.'

Mal's gaze slid from Lolly to Esther and back to Lolly again. 'But if I'm on the run I still won't be able to see Kay.'

'Not for a while, no. But once they've found out who really did this, you can hand yourself in, do whatever time you have to do. It won't be that much. It's a better option, isn't it, than being stitched up for a crime you didn't commit?'

Slowly Mal stood up. He looked dazed and confused. 'Do you think Kay's still alive?'

'I don't know,' she replied honestly. Lolly could see he wasn't thinking straight and she wasn't sure if she was either. What if she was urging him to do the wrong thing entirely? If he was caught near West Henby, it would look worse for him than if he'd stayed. But it was too late to start backtracking now. 'The drive's full of cars; they're parked almost to the gate. Someone might have left their keys in. You'll have to be careful, though. Jude might be around. Go the long way, through the trees.'

'Perhaps I should just go over the wall.'

Lolly nodded. 'It's up to you. I'll give you as long as I can. I'll get rid of the stuff in the summerhouse – no one needs to know you were ever here – and then I'll go back to the house and raise the alarm.' She suddenly thought of something else. 'You'll need money. God, your wallet was in your bedroom. I should have taken out the cash and . . . ' But should haves weren't much use now. She could only think of one other option. Taking the diamond ring off her finger she thrust it into Mal's hand. Then she unclasped the ruby necklace and gave that to him too. 'You should be able to raise some cash with these.'

'I can't—'

'You can. You have to. Just take them, okay? Please.'

Mal nodded and slipped them into his pocket. 'Thank you.'

'Do you remember my friend Stella's address, where I stayed when I went back to London?'

'Albert Road,' he said.

'That's it. Number twenty-four. Write to me there when you can, when you're somewhere safe. Just in case the law start messing about with my mail.' She leaned forward and gave him a quick hug. His clothes were wet and he smelled of the lake. 'Take care of yourself. I'll see you soon.'

Mal didn't move immediately. He gazed down at Esther as if by sheer force of will he could raise the dead.

'Go!' she insisted.

And, finally, he did.

34

Wednesday 21 September. West Henby

Mal went part way round the lake before moving into the trees and circling round to the front of the house. He had the same two thoughts revolving in his head: it was a mistake to run/to run was his only option. He could still change his mind, hand himself in to the police and explain how he had stumbled on Esther's body. But Lita was right. They wouldn't believe him. He'd be cuffed, charged and down the local nick before he even had time to protest his innocence.

Esther was dead. It did not seem possible. Despite everything that had happened, all the drama, the betrayal, he had still been sure that one day they would reconcile. The ties that bound them had always been stronger than their differences. And now it was over. And now, if Kay had been found, she would never get to know her mother.

He felt an ache in his chest like his heart was breaking.

Mal ploughed on. He didn't need to think about where he was going. He had grown up on this land and knew every inch of it. Over the wall or try for a car? He still hadn't decided. But a car had to be a better bet. It would be tough going on foot and if the police brought out the dogs . . .

When he could see the end of the drive he stopped and stared through the darkness. There was a security guard positioned by the gates, a bored-looking bloke in uniform, leaning against the pillar while he smoked a cigarette. He wasn't worried about him. The guard's job was to stop uninvited guests coming in, not to prevent anyone from leaving.

Mal moved quietly back through the trees, only coming out into the open when he was parallel to the wide curve in the drive. This was the blind spot where he couldn't be observed from the house or the gates. It was fortunate that the party was a big one and guests had been forced to park where they could. He cut across the grass and began to examine the cars, one by one. What he wanted was something solid, reliable and not too distinctive. But he would take what he could get.

Mal wondered if he could actually hotwire a car. He'd had it explained to him in jail on numerous occasions – it didn't seem too complicated – but theory and practice didn't always coincide. To add to the difficulty there wasn't much light. No, he'd be crazy to even try. Already the instructions about which wires to connect were blurring at the edges.

As he hurried along the line, he glanced at each car to check that the keys hadn't been left in the ignition. Lita's idea was not as crazy as it might sound. People felt safe in an environment like this and didn't always take the precautions they normally would. Tonight, however, no one was being careless. He was almost at the end of the curve, about to give up, when he suddenly hit the jackpot: a white Hunter with the keys left on the dashboard.

He blinked hard, barely able to believe his luck. For a split second he thought he was imagining it, his mind playing tricks like a dying man in a desert stumbling on a mirage. Then he yanked the door open and climbed inside. He started the Hunter – there was half a tank of petrol – did a three-point turn and set off towards the gates. A gentle pace. Not too fast. Not like a fugitive running for his life. He kept the headlamps on full so the security guard would have trouble seeing him properly.

Before he even reached the gates, the man heard the car coming and opened them. Mal swept through and turned right into the lane. He was breathing heavily, sweat pouring off him. Once he was clear of the house, he put his foot down and sped into the night.

35

Wednesday 21 September. West Henby

Lolly knew she didn't have much time. She took off her shoes and raced barefoot to the summerhouse. The door was unlocked and she dropped the shoes and barged straight in. The trouble was, it was dark, darker than outside and she had to wait a moment for her eyes to adjust. In those seconds she wondered if she'd made a huge mistake. What had she just done? If Mal was caught nicking a car, driving a stolen car, leaving the scene of a crime, he'd look guilty as sin. And she'd be the one who was responsible.

Before doubt could paralyse her, she set to work gathering everything up. She grabbed the rucksack and filled it with the clothes he'd left, the old boots, food, knife, water bottle. Was there anything else? Only the rug and that wouldn't fit in. She folded it neatly and placed it on a chair. Hopefully, no one would remember where they last saw it.

Lolly had one last check round, made sure nothing had been overlooked and then picked up the rucksack and took it outside. She locked the door and put her shoes back on, walked rapidly towards the bank and chucked the key into the water.

It wouldn't stop the police from getting into the summerhouse but there was no point in making it easy for them.

Once this was done she scoured the ground for stones, the heavier the better. She piled them into the rucksack until she was sure it was heavy enough and then she lifted it up, swung it several times to get some momentum and flung it as forcefully as she could into the lake. It made a splash that sounded to her frightened ears as loud as an explosion.

Lolly didn't hang about. If she could have avoided seeing Esther's body again, she would, but she didn't have any choice in the matter. She had to get back to the house as fast as she could. How long had she been away for? It felt like hours but couldn't have been more than fifteen minutes. Even that might be enough for the law to wonder what she'd been doing. The thought of the police, of all the questions, made her feel sick to the stomach.

Lolly wanted to avert her eyes, to hurry past the body, but something made her stop. It felt wrong, disrespectful somehow, to not even look. Esther hadn't been good to her, never kind, but she'd been a part of her life. She didn't linger for long – there was nothing useful to be said or done – but she murmured a short prayer and crossed herself even though she wasn't Catholic.

It was a relief when the bench came into sight. By now everything was starting to catch up with her. The adrenalin had subsided to be replaced by brutal reality. She felt cold and shaky and her nerves were in tatters. How was Mal doing? If he'd managed to get hold of a car he could be miles away by now. He would still be a suspect but without evidence they couldn't prove he was ever here.

She listened out for footsteps coming in the opposite direction. Jude, she presumed, would still be searching. She had two choices: either she raised the alarm, said she'd found Esther's body, or she waited for someone else to find it. Neither option was especially appealing but the latter, she decided, would give Mal more time. Although it wasn't a pleasant thought leaving the body lying there, it was the living she had to think about now.

From the bench it was only a short distance along the path and through the trees to where Nick was waiting but instead of going directly there she circled round to the front of the house, had a quick look down the drive – no sign of any commotion – went through the front door and joined the guests inside. She negotiated the length of the busy central hallway from one end of the house to the other, exited through the back door and walked down the steps to the lawn.

Nick was sitting in the same place near the brazier, looking up at the stars. Lolly dropped down onto the grass beside him. Knowing that she would have to account for the time she'd been missing, not just to him but later to the law, she said, 'Sorry, it's packed in there. And Jude's been running around looking for Esther. He can't find her anywhere. I went down to the lake . . . well, as far as the bench, but she wasn't there. I told him she wouldn't be. And then I went to the loo and had to wait for ever.' Did her voice sound weird, croaky? She cleared her throat. She'd only thought up the story five minutes ago. It wasn't exactly watertight but it would have to do.

'Yeah, there's quite a crowd. I got you another drink. When do you think Esther's going to make her grand announcement?'

'Thanks.' She had to stop herself from grabbing hold of the glass and downing it in one. 'I don't know. Whenever she feels like it, I suppose. I saw Rory Gill when I was inside, you know that actor who was in *The Last Tycoon*.'

'I haven't seen it. I always find Fitzgerald depressing.'

Lolly tried to concentrate, tried to stop her gaze from darting towards the house every five seconds. Where was Jude? What was he doing? At some point, she presumed, he would go and search round the lake himself. She had a knot in her stomach. She knew what was coming and it filled her with dread. 'Yes, he can be a touch dark.'

'Is that the one about the film industry?'

'That's it. Hollywood.' She racked her brains for something more interesting to say but couldn't come up with anything. In the event she didn't need to. A piercing sound came from beyond the trees, half scream, half yowl, like an animal in torment.

And Lolly knew the waiting was over.

36

Wednesday 21 September. West Henby

It didn't take long for the police to arrive. They swarmed over the grounds, secured the crime scene, blocked the gates and rounded up the guests. News of the killing created clamour and panic, outrage and tears. Faces quickly filled with shock and disbelief. For Lolly it all had a dreamlike quality. She knew she had to keep her wits about her but her wits felt blunt and useless.

Esther was dead. Esther had been murdered.

The guests and staff were herded into a couple of the downstairs rooms, their names and addresses written down. No one was supposed to leave the house but it wasn't long before senior officers were being lobbied, phone calls made and strings pulled by the more influential of thc partygocrs. Whatever pity they felt for Esther was outweighed by their desire not to be inconvenienced.

Lolly waited with Nick in the drawing room. He didn't say much but his presence was reassuring. As their initial shock subsided, people began to look around, to make up their minds about the likely perpetrator, to whisper and confer. It felt like one of those scenes in an Agatha Christie novel where all the suspects are gathered before the killer is finally revealed. Well, perhaps not *all* the suspects. She could hear Mal's name being muttered and knew that he was being put firmly in the frame.

With everything that had happened, Lolly hadn't had the chance to think about who the actual murderer was. Jude, with his dark obsessive love, was the first name that sprang to mind. Had he let her go alone to the lake in the hope that she would be the one to find Esther's body? She remembered how jumpy he'd been but that could have been down to all sorts of reasons, not least his unease at Esther having disappeared. But then there was Amy Wiltshire. If Jude had killed her then he could have killed Esther too.

Jude, however, wasn't the only person with a motive. There was Heather Grant, angry perhaps at being sidelined over Vicky Finch, although there was no evidence that this was actually the case. But she could have been aggrieved that her big scoop was about to be snatched away from her. Or interested enough in Jude to dispose of the competition. Lolly wasn't sure if she believed there was an emotional relationship but she remembered the two of them standing on the steps, conspiring over *something.*

Mrs Gough wasn't beyond suspicion either. After years of loyal service, Esther was throwing her on the scrap-heap. Rage could easily spring from festering resentment. Perhaps she had preferred to see Esther dead than living without her on the other side of the ocean.

Lolly looked around until her eyes came to rest on two other possible candidates: Anna Leighton and her husband, Claud. Both had good reason to hate Esther. Lolly could still hear Anna's words: *What goes around comes around.* And Claud, after leaving his wife, had been unceremoniously dumped. Male pride didn't always take kindly to that sort of thing.

The police had requisitioned the library as their main interview room, probably because it had a desk and a suitable air of gravitas. Lists must have been drawn up with the most likely suspects at the top – those closest to the victim. Other rooms were being used too as the law tried to process all the guests and staff. Lolly was called at exactly ten to ten. As she walked into the library she tried to wipe all memory of seeing Esther's body from her mind. She had not been there, she had not seen Mal, she had not been anywhere near the summerhouse.

DI Latham was in his fifties, a slight, skinny, grey-haired man who already looked exhausted from the sheer pressure of having to deal not just with a murder but with so many egos gathered under one roof. He had the unenviable task of trying to control a large group of people who were used to getting their own way and did not take kindly to being told what to do by a provincial policeman.

There was another officer with him, DS Barry, armed with a notepad. He was younger, bright-eyed, less careworn than his boss and had an air of barely contained excitement. Whether this was down to a house full of celebrities, a juicy murder or just a genuine love of the job was hard to tell.

'Lolita Bruce?' Latham asked, as if he didn't already know her name.

'Yes,' she said.

He waved a hand towards the chair that had been placed in front of the desk. She sat down and he gave her some spiel about knowing how upsetting this must be for her and how they would try and get through it all as quickly as possible.

'You're the ward of the Furys. Is that right?'

'Mal Fury was my guardian,' she said.

Latham's eyebrows went up. 'Just Mr Fury?'

'That's right.'

'Not Esther too?'

Lolly wondered how often she would need to repeat it. 'Just Mal,' she said.

Barry quickly scribbled something down, as though he thought this detail was important.

'Did you and Esther get on?' Latham asked.

'Not really,' Lolly replied truthfully. She was aware that Mrs Gough had already been interviewed, the DI being smart enough to know that it was the staff who were the eyes and ears of any house. And the grieving housekeeper wouldn't have been slow to express her opinion of Lolly. 'I suppose we tolerated each other.'

'Even when she threw you out?'

Lolly gave a thin smile, sure now that Mrs Gough had been talking. 'I wouldn't say she threw me out exactly. It simply became impossible for me to stay here. I took Mal's side, you see, when things came to a head with him and Esther. It would have been awkward living under the same roof.'

'And are you still taking his side?'

'What do you mean?'

'He can't have been happy when his wife got him sent to jail.'

Lolly could see where this was heading and tried a spot of deflection. 'Do you know, this might sound strange but I think it was a relief. He'd been living with the secret for so long, always looking over his shoulder, that he was glad to finally have it out in the open.'

Latham kept a poker face, but Barry's mouth twisted into something akin to a sneer.

'It's true,' she insisted. 'He didn't bear a grudge. He didn't hate Esther. They'd been through too much together. And if you're thinking he killed her, there's not a chance. He'd never do that.'

'So why did he abscond?' Barry asked.

'I've no idea. Perhaps prison was just getting too much for him.'

'So you think it's a coincidence that a short while after he goes on the run, his wife ends up dead?'

'Perhaps someone saw their opportunity and took it. With Mal on the run, he was always going to get the blame. He's the perfect scapegoat, isn't he?'

'Or just a murderer,' Barry said.

Latham threw him a look. 'Miss Bruce is right. We can't go jumping to any conclusions, not until we have all the facts.'

Lolly wondered if they were doing that good cop/bad cop thing where Latham tried to lull her into a sense of security while Barry went in for the kill. Her palms were starting to sweat and she could feel the thump of her heart in her chest.

Latham nodded and said, 'You've been staying here, is that right?'

'Esther invited me down so I came.'

'Despite the fact you weren't on good terms?'

'We weren't really on any terms. I suppose I saw it as an olive branch, as a chance to put the past behind us. It seemed churlish to say no, so . . . '

There was a silence which Lolly didn't try to fill.

'Getting back to this evening. When was the last time you saw Esther?'

'It was just after Nick got here. Nick Trent. He's a friend of mine. We were on the lawn and she came out into the garden. That would have been about eight o'clock.'

'And who was she with?'

'She was with Jude, but there were lots of other people around too.'

'Did you speak to her?'

'No.'

Barry tapped his pen against his teeth. 'Were they a couple, Jude and Esther?'

'I'm not sure.' Lolly had no idea how much, if anything, they knew about her history with Jude or his history as regards Amy Wiltshire, and she certainly wasn't going to enlighten them. 'That was their business, not mine.'

Another silence while they both stared at her.

Then Latham said, 'I understand Jude asked you to help him look for Esther. What time would that have been?'

This was the part Lolly had been dreading most. Her lips had gone dry and it took an effort of will to stop sliding her tongue across them. She sensed a trap in the question and hesitated before she answered. 'No, I don't think he actually asked me to help. He just came over to ask if I'd seen her. That would have been about eight-thirty, a quarter to nine? Nick wasn't there. He'd gone into the house to use the loo.'

'But you offered to go and check the lake.'

'Well, he said he was going to go but that didn't seem like the best idea. It's dark by the water and the bank can be slippery. I know it better than he does so I told him I'd do it while he checked the drive.'

'Why the drive?' Barry asked.

'I don't know. He seemed to have looked everywhere else. I thought she might have got chatting to someone who was leaving and—'

'Why would anyone be leaving at that time? The party hadn't been going for long, had it?'

'Some people don't stay for long, only an hour or so. They have work early in the morning or other places to go. They just come to show their faces. Anyway, I was pretty sure Esther wouldn't be down by the lake. She never went there, not since . . . not since what happened to Kay.'

'But you went all the same.'

'I was trying to be helpful and I only walked as far as the bench. It's at the end of the path. You turn right and there it is.'

'Did you call out?'

Lolly could feel the stares of the two officers boring into her. She kept her own gaze on Latham, trying to keep eye contact and not appear evasive. 'No. I had a quick look round but I couldn't see or hear anyone. I only stayed for a minute and then I went back.'

'And you didn't meet anyone else on your way there or back?'

'No, no one.'

'And after that?' Latham asked. 'What did you do next?'

'I went to the house. I needed the loo and . . . It was busy inside so that took a while and when I got back to the garden, Nick was there. It was about ten minutes later that Jude found her and . . . ' Lolly took a deep breath. 'Sorry, it's only just sinking in. It still doesn't feel real.'

'That's all right. Take your time,' Latham said.

It had not really occurred to Lolly until now how big a suspect she could be herself. She had only been thinking about shielding Mal but from an outside point of view she had as much reason as anyone to want Esther Fury dead. 'That's it, really. I can't think of anything else.'

There was a knock on the door and Barry got up to answer it. She could only catch snatches of the exchange, but enough to learn that a car had been reported as stolen. It was good news. That meant Mal had a decent head start and a chance of getting away.

37

Wednesday 21 September. West Henby

It was Nick's opinion that whoever said lightning never strikes twice was talking though their backside. Two murders in two days and he'd been present at both of them. He was starting to feel like the kiss of death. When he'd mentioned it to the officers – better out in the open, they were going to find out anyway – they'd looked at him as if there was no such thing as coincidence.

Latham had placed his elbows on the desk and smiled grimly. 'You seem to be a touch unfortunate, Mr Trent.'

'I can't argue with that.'

'Always in the wrong place at the wrong time.'

'Well, I wouldn't say always.'

The interview hadn't taken long. He'd told them what he knew, which was very little, and had been suitably vague about Lolly's absence when she'd gone down to the lake. 'I went for a slash and when I got back she wasn't there. She came out of the house a few minutes later.'

'A few minutes?'

'Give or take.'

'And how did she seem?'

'Just the same as when I'd left her.'

This hadn't actually been true. Lolly had been on edge, nervous, her gaze continually darting towards the house, as though she was waiting for someone to come out. He had put it down to anxiety over Esther's forthcoming announcement but now he was not so sure.

'So you're a private detective,' DS Barry had said, barely concealing his contempt. 'What's *your* take on all this?'

'It's not my job. I don't have a take on it.'

'Were you in the Force for long, Mr Trent?'

'No.'

'Not fond of rules and regulations, huh?' Barry had said, thinking he had him sussed.

'Not fond of working with people who jump to simplistic conclusions.'

The corners of Latham's mouth had twitched. 'Let's stay on subject, shall we?'

Nick had kept his answers short and told them no more than he had to.

It was another couple of hours before Lolly was allowed to leave the house to travel back to London. All the other guests and staff had been interviewed and dismissed, and only Jude, Heather and Mrs Gough remained. There had been some debate by the police over whether Lolly should be allowed to leave at all but with nothing to directly implicate her in the murder permission was eventually granted.

Nick went with her to her bedroom on the first floor where she quickly grabbed her overnight bag and began packing her clothes.

'Can I help?'

She shook her head. 'I'll only be two minutes.'

'You don't need to rush.'

'I want to get out of here.'

'What about the rest?' he asked, noticing that she only seemed to be taking what she had brought with her.

'I don't need the rest.'

The clothes she was leaving behind, and there was a wardrobe full, looked expensive and it occurred to him that they were Lita's rather than Lolly's. They belonged to a shy, obedient, lost girl who had once lived in this house, but that girl barely existed now. She had grown up and returned to her roots. Kellston was her home now. He could have asked if she was all right, but the question seemed redundant. How could anyone be all right under the circumstances?

Nick glanced around the room, taking in the luxury of it, the deep pile carpet and the fancy bed, the en suite bathroom. His gaze settled on the wallpaper. For the want of nothing better to say, he murmured, 'I'm not sure if I could wake up to these peacocks every morning.'

Lolly stopped what she was doing for a moment and stared at the wall. 'I always rather liked them.'

The birds were like the Furys, Nick thought, or at least the Furys of time past: beautiful but showy, creatures who liked to strut and preen. Was that unfair on Mal? A little, perhaps, but he often struggled to understand Lolly's affection for him. Mal was a man who'd used his wealth to salve his conscience, taking in an East End orphan to recompense for having Teddy Heath's blood on his hands. Of course, she would never see it that way and perhaps it was better that she didn't.

Lolly went to the bathroom, picked up her toothbrush and toothpaste, dumped them in the bag, zipped it up and put it over her shoulder. 'Okay, I'm ready.' Then, as if something had just occurred to her, she put the bag down again. 'Hold on.' She went over to the chest of drawers, reached into the very back of the middle drawer and took out a pair of socks. Slipping her hand into one, she pulled out a small bundle of notes and held them up. 'Five pounds, she said. 'I just remembered. It's the money I had with me when I first came here. I was saving up for a headstone for Mum.'

'That's a lot of money for a thirteen-year-old.'

'Terry Street used to pay me to run errands for him.'

Nick didn't ask what kind of errands they were. 'Why did you hide it?'

'I was scared someone might steal it off me.' She gave an empty laugh. 'I was scared of a lot of things back then.'

He watched as she gave the room a final look, her eyes roaming everywhere, as though she was drinking it all in and storing it in her memory. Then she heaved out a breath and said, 'Right, let's go.'

As they were walking down the stairs, Nick saw Mrs Gough and DS Barry huddled together in the hallway. The housekeeper was leaning in towards the policeman, her face hard, her mouth spitting out words ten to the dozen. Trouble, he thought. And he didn't have long to wait to find out what it was. As soon as their feet touched the hallway floor, Barry strode over to them, managing to look both officious and smug at the same time.

'If it's all right I'd like to look in your bag, Miss Bruce, before you leave.'

'No, it's not bloody all right,' Nick said. 'What the hell for?'

'Do you have an objection?' Barry asked, addressing Lolly.

But Lolly simply held out the bag towards the sergeant. 'Help yourself. I've got nothing to hide.'

'You don't have to do this,' Nick said. 'He's got no right.'

'The sooner it's done, the sooner we can get out of here.'

Barry took the bag over to the wide hall table, opened it and began taking out the items one by one. Mrs Gough watched from a distance, her eyes gleaming with spite. What was she expecting the police to find? A stash of family silver, perhaps. However, it didn't take the sergeant long to establish that there was nothing in the bag but clothes and toiletries. He ran his hand around the inside lining, prodding and poking, searching for anything hidden. When this produced no results, he threw a glaring look at Mrs Gough, returned the clothes to the bag and handed it back to Lolly.

'Thank you, Miss.'

'Can we go now?' Nick asked.

DS Barry waved his hand towards the door. 'We'll be in touch.'

Mrs Gough stood, unrepentant, as they passed her. She stared at them, her lips set in a thin straight line.

Once Lolly was outside she strode quickly towards the side of the house. The space which only a few hours ago had been filled with fancy expensive motors was now occupied by a fleet of squad cars. Nick unlocked the doors to the Ford and they got in. She said nothing as they headed down the drive. Ironically, the whole place now looked like a movie set with arc lights set up to illuminate the garden. The police were still searching, combing the ground, looking for evidence.

The security guard at the gates had been replaced by a couple of uniformed cops. They stared at the car as it approached, but then waved it through. Lolly gazed straight ahead, tense and silent. Nick left her to her thoughts. There were questions he had to ask but they could wait.

They had travelled several miles, leaving West Henby behind, before she turned her head and asked, 'Who would have killed her? Who would have done that?' She didn't wait for an answer before saying, 'They're going to blame Mal.'

'They've got to prove he was there first.'

'It could have been Jude. Just because he found her doesn't mean he didn't do it. You saw what he was like with her the other night. He's always been . . . '

'Been what?'

She shrugged. 'Jealous? Possessive? I don't know. Did you mention the announcement to the law?'

'No, did you?'

'No. I wonder what that was about. Perhaps it was why someone killed her, to stop her saying whatever she was going to say.'

'That would narrow it down to a pretty small group of suspects.'

'It's pretty small already, don't you think?'

The roads were quiet and they made good progress. Soon they were on the M20 and Nick could put his foot down. 'I heard a car got nicked from the house.'

Lolly gave him a quick glance. 'Did it?'

He suspected she already knew this. 'Kind of suggests that whoever killed Esther wasn't an invited guest. If they were, they'd have come in their own car. Still, at least they didn't take mine. That would have been a pain in the arse.'

'It might not have had anything to do with Esther. All those expensive cars parked up without an owner in sight . . . Someone could have just slipped into the grounds and helped themselves.'

'Even with the guard on the gate?'

'It's not impossible.'

Nick felt her discomfort and although he didn't want to make matters worse, he had to get to the truth before she buried it too deeply. He took a deep breath and said, 'Mal was at the house, wasn't he?'

Lolly's head jerked round, her eyes widening. 'What?'

'When did you find out? Yesterday? Tonight?'

'He hasn't been there. What makes you think that? He wouldn't come to the house. It's the first place the law would look for him.'

'Mal isn't bothered about the law. He's only got one thing on his mind and that's his daughter. You've seen him, haven't you?'

'No! Jesus, of course I haven't!'

'Shit, Lolly, it's me you're talking to. If you want me to help, you're going to have to tell me what's going on.'

'I don't need any help.'

Nick fought against the temptation to roll his eyes. 'Okay, so why don't you tell me what happened to the jewellery you were wearing? One so-called fake diamond ring and a necklace. One moment you're wearing them and the next ... And why you were so damn long down at the lake? When I went for a slash, it only took me five minutes. You were gone for what, fifteen? It doesn't take that long to walk to the bench and back.'

'I told you. I went to the loo after. It was busy in the house, crowded.'

'And the jewellery?'

'I took it off.'

'And put it where?'

'In my bedroom.'

'And why would you do that?'

Lolly glared at him. 'What is this, the bloody third degree?'

'You'll get worse off the law if someone else noticed. Like I said, I'm just trying to help. You gave the jewellery to Mal, didn't you? Something he could liquidate while he was on the run.'

Lolly turned her face away and stared out of the side window. Eventually, after what seemed like an age, she said softly, 'He didn't kill her. He found her by the lake.'

'Christ,' Nick said. 'You'd better tell me everything.'

38

Wednesday 21 September. West Henby

DI Bob Latham stood on the bank of the lake and gazed out across the water. It wasn't the first time he'd been here. Nineteen years ago, as a freshly promoted DS, he'd stood in much the same place, thinking much the same thing as he was thinking now: that life was hard and cruel and full of pain. Nothing had happened in the intervening years to make him alter that opinion.

Back then it had been Cathy Kershaw's murder that was being investigated. She'd been pulled from the lake by a frantic Mal Fury, but to no avail. The girl was already dead. There had been an expectation that the baby would be found in the water too, but after a long search and an eventual draining of the lake, nothing was discovered. Little Kay Fury had disappeared for good.

Latham turned his thoughts to the present. Esther's body had been moved to the morgue, ready for the autopsy first thing in the morning. She'd been examined by the pathologist at the scene and although the bruises on her neck had initially suggested strangulation, it now appeared more likely that she'd been held under water and drowned.

At the moment Mal Fury was heading up a short list of

suspects. How couldn't he be? On the run, angry, bitter, a man whose wife had betrayed him. But Latham wasn't going to jump to conclusions. Until he had definitive proof that Fury had been on the premises, he was keeping a more or less open mind. There were others who'd harboured grudges too. Esther Fury had been the sort of woman who provoked strong emotions.

DS Barry was striding along the bank towards him. Latham adjusted his features so they didn't betray the dislike he had for the younger officer. The sergeant was one of those ambitious types who had his sights set on the top of the pile and didn't care who he trampled over to get there.

'Everything all right, guv?'

Latham didn't bother replying to the question. Cops like Barry couldn't understand the concept of standing back for a moment, of trying to get some perspective. Fools rush in where angels fear to tread . . . wasn't that the saying? Not that he classified Barry as a fool exactly, but he wasn't what you'd call the thoughtful type either. 'Anything from forensics?'

'Nothing useful from the scene as yet. If the perp did leave footprints they were all churned up by Jude Rule.'

'What do you make of him?'

Barry lifted and dropped his shoulders. 'He seems upset enough. Shocked. Bit of an odd relationship, though. She was old enough to be his mother.'

'You wouldn't say that if it was the other way around. Older bloke, younger woman. No one bats an eyelid, do they? But I get your meaning. We'll run some checks on him, see if he's got any form.'

'He's not in the frame, is he? This has got to be down to the husband. Has it on his toes, makes his way back here, sees her by the lake, grabs his opportunity and it's job done. Then he nicks the Hunter and he's away.'

'They're all in the frame until we know otherwise.' Latham had a nose for when people were lying to him and it had been twitching excessively during some of the interviews. 'She was down by the lake, wasn't she? The ward, Lolita Bruce.'

'She wouldn't be strong enough to hold Esther Fury under water.'

'You'd be surprised what people can do when they're angry. She and Esther had history and it wasn't the warm fuzzy sort. Rule was going to search round the lake himself, remember, until Miss Bruce insisted on going instead.'

'History?'

'You don't find it odd that Mal Fury was her only guardian? Not the two of them. And you heard what Anna Leighton said.'

'Oh, *her*. She's the type who likes the sound of her own voice.'

It was true that Anna had been nothing short of verbose, almost revelling in the interview, as if it was her chance to be in the spotlight. A gossip, too, but gossips could be useful in this business. She had seemed neither shocked nor dismayed by Esther's death.

'Esther took what she wanted whenever she wanted it,' she'd said. 'It was only a matter of time before someone . . . Well, she had no regard for other people's feelings, did she? Husbands, boyfriends: they were all fair game. She had an affair with Claud, you know. And look at Jude Rule. He dropped poor Lita like a hot potato as soon as *she* took an interest in him.'

Latham had gathered it all in and stored it away. It was his job to sift through information, to separate the wheat from the chaff, but that sometimes took a while. He knew, of course, how powerful an emotion jealousy could be. It could rip through reason, through sanity, and make the soul black as coal. Lolita Bruce was not above suspicion. But then neither was Jude Rule. He sensed something toxic about the entire household, an undercurrent of bad feeling, of secrets and lies.

It was a fact that people often lied during a murder inquiry, sometimes deliberately, sometimes through a misguided desire to be helpful, telling you what they thought you wanted to hear, rather than what they actually knew or had observed. That a party had been in full swing didn't help matters either, the house and garden full of guests, and the guests full of champagne. Only the staff had been sober and they weren't saying much.

Barry, who was not fond of silences, quickly filled the one that had fallen between them.

'I've had another word with the security guard, but he's still claiming he didn't see the driver's face. Had the headlights on full, apparently. He can't even be sure if it was a man or a woman. It had to be Mal Fury, though. Don't you think?'

Latham suspected he was right. Everything pointed in that direction, and yet he still had niggling doubts. 'It doesn't seem very organised, does it? If you're planning to kill someone, don't you make sure you've got a better exit strategy? He couldn't have known he'd find the keys in the Hunter. What if he hadn't? What would he have done then?'

'Gone over the wall, I suppose.'

'And then he's on foot. How far could he hope to get?'

'Well, he got from Surrey to here without us picking him up. And perhaps he hadn't planned on killing her tonight, but an opportunity came along and he took it. Then he panicked and had to get away by whatever means he could.'

Latham could see no real flaws in this argument. Perhaps he was overcomplicating things. A vengeful husband, a treacherous wife: all the ingredients for murder. And yet those doubts wouldn't go away. 'What about the summerhouse? Have we got inside yet?'

'The housekeeper can't find the key.'

'Better just break in, then.'

39

Thursday 22 September. Kellston

When Lolly woke on Thursday morning, the first thing she did was curse herself for telling Nick Trent the truth. Could she really trust him? Now that he knew Mal had been at the house, there was nothing to stop him going to the law. He was an ex-cop after all. She should have kept her stupid mouth shut. The problem was, she hadn't been thinking straight. Esther's murder had knocked her for six and she had let her barriers down.

'Idiot,' she muttered.

In the cold light of day, she knew this wasn't the only thing she had to worry about. What if someone else had noticed the missing jewellery? As she got out of bed, she went through a list of likely candidates. Fortunately, she hadn't talked to many people and most of the guests had probably been too preoccupied by their own appearance to pay much attention to hers. There was Anna Leighton, of course. She was the type who always took note of what other women were wearing, but after Esther's murder even she might have had other things on her mind.

Lolly went to the bathroom, had a pee, washed her hands

and then brushed her teeth. But none of this distracted from the fear that was growing inside. Mrs Gough was her biggest worry. That woman had eyes in the back of her head. And there had been that business with the bag, when DS Barry had asked to take a look in it. What had all that been about? Probably just Mrs Gough trying to put the knife in, hoping that Lolly had taken something she shouldn't. It couldn't have been about the necklace and ring as neither of those items belonged to the Furys.

While she made a brew, her thoughts stayed with the jewellery and inevitably shifted on to Terry Street. Jesus, she was going to have to tell him that she didn't have the diamond ring any more. That wasn't a conversation she was looking forward to. And he wasn't going to be in the best of moods with Vinnie banged up. The best course of action, she decided, was to try and avoid him for as long as possible.

Lolly drank her tea while she wondered what to do next. She was pretty sure the law would be back at some point, knocking on the door, asking more questions. What she wanted to do was go to the phone box across the road and ring Nick to find out for certain that he wasn't going to talk. But the call would be a waste of time. He'd be at work and the best she'd be able to do was leave a message. No, she'd wait until this evening when he was home again.

Once she had finished stressing over Nick she quickly moved on to Mal. Where would he go? He must have dumped the white Hunter by now; it wouldn't be safe to go on driving around in it. If he sold the jewellery this morning, he should be able to raise enough cash to get far away, not abroad – he had no passport – but somewhere the police wouldn't think to look for him. The news of Esther's murder would be on the TV and radio, although the papers wouldn't be publishing the story until tomorrow. He would have to find a place where he could keep his head down until the real killer was discovered.

With so much on her mind, she needed a distraction. It was then she thought of Dana Leigh. With everything that had happened, her promise to Stella to check out the library had gone right out of the window. Well, now was as good a time as any. She found a notepad and pen, shoved them in her bag and set off for the high street.

Lolly had only got as far as the green when the door to the pawnbroker's opened and Tony Cecil stepped out. She hoped he wouldn't notice her, but that hope was quickly dashed. He clocked her right off and zigzagged across the road, nonchalantly dodging the cars with a big fat grin on his face.

'Hey, babe,' he said, once he'd caught up with her. 'Seen your mate, recently?'

Lolly thought it smarter to keep shtum about knowing what he and his brother had done to Jude. 'Who do you mean?'

'Who the fuck do you think I mean? You ain't got that many friends, darlin'. It shouldn't be too hard to figure it out. But, shit, what the hell, I'll give you a clue anyway: that murdering scumbag who killed Amy and got away with it. Jude fuckin' Rule.'

Lolly kept on walking. 'I don't know why you keep asking me. Haven't you got anything better to do? And the answer, in case you're wondering, is still no.'

'That's a shame. What with his little accident and all. He should be more careful.'

Lolly stopped outside the library and stared at him. 'Just leave me alone, okay?'

'I wish I could but . . . well, you're living on the same street as me, and I have to look at your ugly mug every time you walk past.' Tony's grin suddenly grew wider. 'Any sign of that guardian of yours yet? I've heard he's wanted for murder now. It was all over the radio this morning. Topped his missus, didn't he? Shit, it's funny how murder just seems to follow you around.'

Lolly had heard it on the radio too. They had only said that Mal was wanted for questioning, but the implication had been obvious. 'You shouldn't believe everything you hear.'

'I reckon you're the kiss of death, love. It ain't safe to be around you.'

'So what are you standing there for?'

Tony gave a snigger. 'You think I'm scared of a two-bit tart like you?'

'Maybe you should be.'

'Maybe *you* should start telling the truth about that fuckin' alibi you gave Jude Rule.'

'As opposed to *your* alibi. What was that exactly? Oh yes, that you were with one of Terry's girls at the time. And we all know how true that is. I mean, girls aren't really your thing, are they, Tony?'

That wiped the smirk off his face. His features contorted and his eyes flashed with anger. 'You want to say that again?'

She leaned in towards him. 'You heard.' And with that she turned on her heel and went into the library.

Even as she was walking through the door, she wondered if she'd done the right thing. Now he had even more reason to hate her. Personally, she didn't give a toss who Tony slept with, whether he was gay, straight or anything in between, but *he* cared. And went out of his way to hide his sexuality from his peers. That's why he'd gone out with Amy in the first place; a good cover for what really rocked his boat.

She'd been told, years ago, that he'd actually been in a gay club at the time of Amy's murder, but because he'd have rather died than admit to it, Terry had fixed him up with a more palatable alibi. Better to be shagging a whore than kissing another bloke. That had been back in the day when it was in Terry's interest to keep Brenda Cecil sweet. She'd been a useful fence for some of his stolen gear.

Lolly sighed as she walked through the cool lobby of the library. Tony was a psycho, nuts, and there was no knowing what he'd do next. All she could hope for was that he'd stay well clear of her now that he knew she knew his secret. But what were the odds? He was just as likely to try and shut her up for ever. With that disturbing thought revolving in her head, she pushed through the doors to the main room and made her way to the counter.

40

Thursday 22 September. Kellston

Freddy Mund spent a lot of time in the library. He was not that interested in books, other than those in the true crime section, but he liked to people-watch. You got all sorts in a place like this. It was a stopping-off point for mums, kids and students, a second home for pensioners and tramps. Although many of the faces were familiar to him now, he never talked to anyone. Not that you were supposed to talk in a library, but people still did, in those funny half whispers that were never quite as quiet as the speaker imagined.

This morning Freddy was reading about Dr Crippen. The man's big mistake had been to lose his nerve and do a runner after the police had been to see him. It wasn't the sort of mistake *he* would ever make. You had to have a cool head to get away with murder. You had to carry on as normal. Panic was the enemy, the knee-jerk reaction that gave you away. If Crippen had just stayed put and brazened it out, he wouldn't have ended up with a noose around his neck.

He tentatively touched his throat, wondering how it would feel to be standing on a scaffold, knowing that you were about to die. Not that he was ever going to find out. There was no death penalty now, well, except for treason and you didn't get much of that these days. He wondered if Crippen had been sorry for what he did or just sorry he got caught. The latter, he suspected.

Freddy looked up as a girl walked past and approached the counter. She was smallish and skinny, wearing faded blue jeans and a navy T-shirt. He stared at her arse for a moment before lifting his gaze again. Her long brown hair was tied back in a ponytail.

'Hi,' she said to Mrs Levy. 'I was wondering if you kept old copies of newspapers here?'

'How far back do you want to go?'

'Oh, about nineteen years or so.'

'You'll need the microfiche, then. Do you know how to use it?'

'Is it complicated?'

'I'll show you,' Mrs Levy said.

Freddy put his head back in his book as the two of them went by. He was having one of those déjà vu moments. This was just like the day Dana had come in, except Dana had talked more loudly, as though she didn't understand the library rules. Dana had been taller too, with long fair hair that swayed when she walked. It was her hair he'd liked best, shiny like silk and tumbling down her back in waves. He'd wanted to reach out and touch it, but that was against the rules too.

Mrs Levy explained how the machine worked and left the girl to it. Freddy watched her while he pretended to read, quick furtive glances in case she sussed him. He was too far away to see what she was looking at, but a part of him already knew. *Nineteen years*, she'd said, just like Dana. Could it really be a coincidence?

Freddy closed his book, stood up and drifted down the aisle, stopping every now and again to peer at the shelves, edging ever closer to her until he was standing right behind. That was when his worst fears were confirmed. His body tensed as he saw the article she was reading, a piece about a baby abandoned in Hackney. Quickly he turned and went back to his seat.

He stayed very still, almost rigid, trying to work out what was going on. Was it some kind of trap? A set-up? Perhaps the girl was a plant, sent by the law to see if he would do exactly what he'd done with Dana: sit down at the machine next to her and strike up a conversation.

Mrs Levy might have seen and remembered, might have grassed him up. His eyes darted around the room, but he couldn't see anyone who looked like an undercover cop. But what if the girl was the cop?

Freddy opened his book again. He was starting to sweat, and his pulse was racing. Don't get in a funk, he told himself. *Don't do a Crippen.* It was important to stay calm at times like this, to think things through, to not do anything stupid. It was more likely the girl was a local reporter, researching Dana's origins just as Dana had researched them herself. The link between the abandoned baby and the murdered prostitute had only just come out and journalists were playing catch up.

He sneaked another glance at her, unsure as to what journalists looked like. She seemed too young, but then everyone looked young these days. He transferred his gaze to Mrs Levy. Had she even made the connection between the blonde girl who'd come in a few weeks ago and Dana Leigh? The photo in the paper hadn't been a good one.

When he thought of Dana, Freddy felt a pain in his chest. She'd been special, one of the chosen, and now he'd never see her again. It wasn't fair. He never had any luck. One after another, the girls proved to be a disappointment in the end. You did your best to help, but it always got thrown back in your face.

They didn't understand the meaning of gratitude. If only Dana had listened to him, taken his advice, she'd still be alive instead of laid out in the morgue like a piece of meat.

It was over an hour before the brown-haired girl turned off the machine and prepared to leave. Freddy didn't want to have to follow her out and so he put his book back on the shelf and walked as fast as he dared towards the exit. Once outside, he crossed the road and waited from a safe distance. He was still suspicious, still wary, but no one could accuse him of doing anything wrong.

His worries about the police had subsided. If they had something on him, they'd have been round to the flat days ago. So far as he knew he wasn't even on their radar. Of course, there had been that bit of trouble with the redhead, but that was a while ago, and not even in Kellston. Since coming back here, he'd been clean as a whistle. Well, almost.

Sometimes opportunities just dropped into your lap, like they were meant to be. God-given. How could he refuse? Dana had needed hope and he had given it to her. That's the kind of bloke he was. And yes, okay, so he had taken *some* cash off her, but that was only to cover expenses. Time is money – isn't that the saying? And if that was the case he should have asked for a damn sight more. Hours he'd spent studying those newspaper reports, looking for clues to pull out, twist and dangle in front of her.

It was another ten minutes before the girl came out of the library. What the hell had she been doing? Talking to Mrs Levy, perhaps. He felt his anxiety levels jump up a notch. What if she'd been asking about *him*? She could have noticed him watching her. 'Do you know the name of that man, the one who was sitting at the table near the counter? He was wearing a green sweater.' And Mrs Levy might have leaned across the counter and replied softly, 'Oh, *that* one. No, I don't know his name, but he's always in here, working his way through the crime section. Murder, rape, strangulation, poisoning: he can't get enough of it.'

Freddy played over this hypothetical scenario in his head as he trailed the girl down the high street. Was Mrs Levy allowed to reveal his reading habits? It didn't seem very professional, but then librarians were hardly doctors or priests. They didn't have an obligation to keep quiet about anything.

He had made Dana swear not to tell a soul about him. 'Most folk can't keep their mouths shut,' he'd explained. 'If word gets around that you're looking for your mum, it could ruin everything. She might get scared and do a runner. People don't always want the past catching up with them.'

He'd liked that trust she had in him, and the way her eyes widened every time he gave her a new snippet of information. She'd been kind of stupid, but in an endearing sort of way. That was the trick with women: find their weak spot and exploit it. They all had one. Sometimes it was right there on the surface, like Dana's, but other times you had to dig a little deeper. That was part of the challenge: ferreting around until you hit pay dirt.

The girl stopped at the traffic lights, preparing to cross over. Freddy turned left onto Station Road and paused by the newsagent's, pretending to study the display in the window, but really waiting for her to catch up with him. The lights were slow and he had time to study his reflection in the glass. He didn't hate what he saw, but he wasn't proud of it either. Ordinary was probably the closest description. He was thin and lanky, and his round pale face had a curious flatness to it. Like he had no cheekbones. Whenever he saw himself, his mother's words always jumped into his head.

'You might be plain on the outside, Freddy, but you're beautiful inside.'

As if anyone wanted to hear that. Being beautiful on the inside didn't count for much in the real world. And who said that kind of thing to their kid? She had no sensitivity, that was the trouble. She spoke it as she saw it, called a spade a spade and never thought twice. There were things he could have said to her, hurtful things, but he never did. Inside him was a tangled knot of slights and wounds, all quietly festering.

The girl passed by and carried on up Station Road. He trailed behind, keeping his distance. By the time they'd gone two hundred yards a nasty suspicion was starting to form. Could she really be heading for Albert Road? He didn't have long to wait for an answer. As she approached the corner, she picked up the pace and abruptly turned left.

Freddy wasn't happy about this latest development. He didn't follow her but stood on the corner and counted off the houses until he saw which one she went into. Twenty-four. For fuck's sake. What was going on? That was where Dana had lived. Was the girl a tart too? She must be. And she must have known Dana or why else would she be poking her nose into business that didn't concern her?

He shuffled his feet, unsure as to what to do next. He'd never been inside the house, not wanting the other girls to see him, and wondered what it was like. When he thought of brothels he had a picture in his head, an image from a Wild West film where half-dressed women danced around or draped themselves over men, sitting in their laps. Somehow, he didn't think it was quite like that in the back streets of Kellston.

Freddy didn't like whores. They were rancid, dirty creatures who preyed on the lusts of men. Usually he stayed well away and had only made an exception in Dana's case because she'd been young and damaged and in need of someone to take care of her. It was a shame it had worked out so badly, but it wasn't his fault.

He gazed down the road, trying to figure out what the brown-haired girl might be up to. You didn't go to the library and look up old newspaper articles just for the fun of it. Maybe Dana had told her more than she should. Or was he stressing over nothing? He scratched his head while he tried to balance out the probabilities. When push came to shove, what could Dana have told her that would be any threat? His name? But lots of people were called Freddy. And it was no secret that she'd been abandoned as a baby. The only secret lay in his attempts to help her find her mum – and the money he'd been taking off her. If the cops found out about that it wouldn't look good.

The sky had gone overcast and it was starting to rain, a fine drizzle that gathered on his hair and slid under the collar of his shirt. His forehead scrunched into a frown. Most of what he'd told Dana about himself had been lies, but she could have given this other girl a description, said she'd met him in the library. But a description didn't amount to anything. He hardly stood out in a crowd. No, he didn't need to worry. But still he did.

Five minutes passed, then ten. Freddy was about to leave – there was nothing more he could do here and he didn't care for getting wet – when the door to number twenty-four opened again and the girl came out. It caught him by surprise and he couldn't decide which way to go and so stayed where he was. He watched as she hot-footed it up the road, ignoring a car that was cruising beside her. The driver leaned across to make her an offer she clearly could refuse.

He turned his face away as she walked past, pretending to look in the opposite direction. She went a few yards up the high street and then crossed over as the traffic ground to a halt at the lights. He kept to his side of the road and followed her at a cautious pace. Where was she going? Back to the library? That didn't make much sense.

Once she'd cleared the green, the girl stopped, looking to the left and right while she waited to cross the road again. Freddy didn't understand this either. Why cross back when she'd only just crossed over? Couldn't she make her damn mind up? He strode on purposefully, eyes to the fore, pretending not to be paying attention to her.

Unwilling to get too far ahead, he paused at the Indian takeaway and studied the menu in the window. It was all weird, foreign stuff. Why would anyone want to eat it? He didn't like spices or sauces. He preferred good British food with gravy. Although he had nothing against coloured people per se, he found it objectionable that they should want to inflict their cuisine on him. He glanced discreetly over his shoulder. The girl was still waiting.

It took her a while to find a gap between the cars and buses, and when she did finally manage it he was prepared and ready to continue the tail. Why not? He might as well find out as much as he could about her. But as she grew closer, a nasty feeling started growing in his guts. He watched her out of the corner of his eye. She seemed to be heading straight for him. She was, she definitely was. Shit! He didn't know whether to walk off or brazen it out, and by the time he'd turned the two options over, it was too late and she was almost on him.

Freddy girded himself for confrontation. Denial was the stance he would take, along with a dollop of indignation. *Why on earth would I be following you? Can't a man stand and read a menu without being accused of . . .* But even as he prepared himself, rearranging his features into a suitably affronted expression, she was taking a key out her bag and approaching the door to the right of the takeaway.

He let out a sigh of relief as she opened up and went inside. A close shave. And then he laughed. It was funny to think she might be looking for him, trying to track down Dana's mysterious Freddy, and he'd been standing right beside her. His amusement soon receded, his face growing solemn. Was she a threat? He didn't have enough information to establish that yet. Still, at least she was small. If the worst came to the worst, he couldn't see her putting up much of a fight.

41

Thursday 22 September. Kellston

Lolly threw her bag onto the table and collapsed on the chair with a groan. What now? Talk about unlucky! She leaned forward and put her head in her hands. The library had been a waste of time – she hadn't been able to find out anything useful – but she'd gone to see Stella anyway, hoping her old friend might have some more encouraging news about the hunt for Dana's killer, or even about Vinnie.

Michelle had told her Stella was out, but just as Lolly had been about to turn around and go, Terry Street had appeared and beckoned her inside. She went over the encounter in her head, grimacing at the memory.

'Just the person,' he said. 'I need a word.'

'With me?' Her heart sank. Christ, he was going to ask for the ring back and she didn't have it. She attempted a smile, but her lips were dry. 'Sure.'

Terry, unsurprisingly, was in a foul mood. It was written all over his face. First one of his girls had been murdered, and now Vinnie was banged up. 'Let's talk in the front room.'

The front room was where the punters waited, a depressing

sort of place with yellowing net curtains, a worn carpet and a couple of sofas that had seen better days. As they went through, Lolly tried to think of what she could say. That she'd lost the ring? That it had been stolen? That she didn't have it on her but would return it asap? None of these, apart perhaps from the latter, was going to go down well.

Terry sat down at one end of the red sofa and she took the other end. He lit a fag and took a couple of puffs before he spoke again. 'You've heard about Vinnie, yeah?'

Lolly nodded. 'I can't believe it.'

'Did he say anything to you about Laura Sandler?'

'Me? No, not a word. But he never really talked about personal stuff, girlfriends and the like.'

'She wasn't his girlfriend. She was Brent Sandler's bloody wife. And the bitch has put Vinnie right in the frame. She's claiming there was nothing going on between them but that he's been after her for months, harassing her, trying to get her in the sack. Reckons he topped Sandler so he could have her for himself.'

Nick had told Lolly some of this, but not all the details. 'Jesus. That doesn't sound like Vinnie. He's not what you'd call the obsessive sort. He wouldn't have killed Sandler, would he?'

Terry didn't answer the question. 'What was he like when you were with him last week?'

'Same as always.'

'And you're sure he didn't say anything?'

She thought about it, but nothing relevant came to mind. 'I'm sure.'

Terry looked disappointed. 'He should never have gone near the tart. What was the stupid bastard thinking?'

Lolly suspected Vinnie had only been thinking with one part of his anatomy and it certainly wasn't his brain. 'Has he been charged yet?'

'Yeah, he's been charged, charged with bleedin' murder. And you know what the filth are like. He'll be going down for a long stretch if they get their way.'

'Someone must know who really did it. Who else hated Sandler enough to want him dead?'

'Apart from his wife?'

'Yeah, well, she'd be top of my list.'

Terry stood up and paced around the room for a while, adding his fag ash to the already grubby carpet. She could see how pissed off he was. Vinnie was his right-hand man, the one person he could really trust. Realising he might not be around for the next twenty years was a tough pill for him to swallow. After a while, as if he had just remembered she was still there, he said, 'Okay, ta.'

Lolly was almost out of the room, relieved that *that* question hadn't come up, when something jogged his memory.

'Oh, you got that ring on you, Lol?'

She stopped and turned around, her chest tightening. She'd been dreading this moment and now it was here. 'Erm . . . no, I haven't got it with me.'

'Okay, I'll drop by later and pick it up.'

Lolly was tempted just to nod – she didn't have to answer the door – but she knew she'd have to tell him the truth eventually. She swallowed hard and forced herself to speak. 'No, I mean I don't have it any more. At all. I'm sorry. I had to . . . Someone I know was in a lot of trouble and . . . I'll pay you back, I promise. Every penny.'

Terry was staring at her like she was someone he'd never met before, a stranger who'd robbed him while his back was turned. Two angry stripes of red appeared on his cheekbones. 'You haven't got it?'

'I'm sorry. I'm really sorry.'

'It wasn't yours to give away.'

Lolly could have retorted that, strictly speaking, it wasn't his either seeing as the ring was nicked, but now wasn't the time for smart talk. It was the time to grovel. 'I know, and I wouldn't have done it if there'd be any other way. I'm not trying to rip you off, Terry, I swear. You know me better than that.'

His voice was cold. 'Who did you give it to?'

Lolly shook her head. 'I can't tell you that. I'm sorry. But I'll make it up to you. I'll do anything.'

As soon as the words were out of her mouth, she regretted them. Saying you'd do anything for an East End gangster wasn't the smartest move. She could see the ice in his eyes, the way his mouth had formed a thin, straight line. And she saw what she had never seen before on his face: disappointment and contempt.

'All right,' he said, 'I'll tell you what you can do: find out what the fuck Laura Sandler's game is.'

'How am I supposed to do that?'

'That's your problem, love. Do whatever you have to.'

Lolly nodded. What else could she do? 'Okay. I'll try.'

'Trying's no good to me. I need results.'

'I'll get them,' she said, with as much conviction as she could muster. 'I will.'

'And soon,' he said. 'Don't let me down again.'

'I won't. I promise.'

And then she fled before he could think of something worse to do to her.

42

Thursday 22 September. The Irish Sea

Mal stood on the deck of the ferry, looking down at the choppy waters of the Irish Sea. From West Henby he'd headed north towards Wales, driving through the dark. When you were in this much trouble you needed your friends, but not the law-abiding kind. Gareth Thomas, a fence for over thirty years, had been his cellmate for nine months. He was the type of man who didn't ask too many questions and who knew the value of a diamond ring when he saw it.

A deal had been struck whereby the two of them would go over to Dublin together – the police would be looking out for someone travelling alone – sell the ring and split the proceeds. Gareth had contacts in Ireland, business associates who wouldn't rip them off. Once the deal was done, they would go their separate ways. The white Hunter was safely stashed in a lock-up.

Mal had been provided with a hat – 'You'll need it. It always bloody rains in Ireland' –and a pair of spectacles with plain lenses. With his fair hair covered and the glasses on, he was less likely to be recognised. He didn't know if Gareth believed in his innocence when it came to Esther's murder or if he was just pretending to. And he wasn't entirely sure if the man was motivated by loyalty or avarice. Perhaps it was a combination of the two.

He felt the swell of the waves beneath the ferry. His stomach shifted, and not just from the movement. He still didn't know if he was doing the right thing. Running away was gutless and cheap, the act of a coward, but he had no faith in the police finding the true culprit. Why would they even bother to investigate when he was neatly in the frame? However, running didn't help that situation. Perhaps he should have had the courage to stand his ground and protest his innocence.

'If you're having second thoughts, you can always hand yourself in to the Garda,' Gareth said with a grin. 'Although I'd appreciate you keeping my name out of it.'

'You have my word.'

'Well, that's good enough for me. But don't do anything rash, will you? It's early days. Give it a while and see what happens. Wait till the smoke clears, so to speak. You don't want to be making decisions you'll regret down the line.'

Mal gripped the rail, his knuckles white. There was another option besides running or handing himself in, and that was to end it all. He could excuse himself, pretend to go for a slash and find a quiet place at the rear of the boat. No one would notice if he climbed over the rail and dropped into the sea. By the time Gareth raised the alarm – if he even did – it would be too late.

For some reason Lord Lucan sprang into his head. It was three years now since he'd disappeared after murdering the family nanny. There were rumours he was living in Africa or France, although others believed that he'd jumped off a ferry crossing the English Channel. Mal wondered what that moment was like, those few seconds you were falling before the icy water closed around you. Too late then to change your mind.

His Adam's apple bounced in his throat. He feared death, but he feared life too, or at least the kind of life he would be forced to live if Esther's killer was never found. He would be in perpetual exile, always looking over his shoulder, always waiting for the knock on the door. He would never be Mal Fury again, never go home, never look across the lake or get to place flowers on the grave of his parents. And, worst of all, never get the chance to see Kay again if she *was* still alive. He shuddered at the thought. It was, in its way, a different kind of death.

Gareth bent and placed his forearms on the rail, gazing out towards the horizon. He wasn't old, barely fifty, but already his hair was streaked with grey. Thin red veins ran like a road map across his nose and cheeks, each one branching off another. He had a drinker's belly and a smoker's cough. In the normal scheme of things, they would probably never have met, but prison spawned unlikely friendships.

'We'll be there soon.'

'How soon?' Mal asked.

'Half an hour. You'll like it well enough in Dublin. Just keep your mouth shut when it comes to politics or religion and you'll be fine. I'll give you some names in case you need papers. If you want to move on at some point, get a passport, they're the ones to contact. Tell them Gareth Thomas sent you and they'll see you right.'

Mal couldn't think of where he would go with a passport, but he nodded anyway and expressed his thanks. They fell into silence. There was only the slap of the waves against the boat and the throb of the engine. He could feel a weight pressing down on him, a darkness descending.

The reality of Esther's death, of what it meant, was starting to eat away at him. Their marriage had been torrid, confrontational, destructive, and yet love had existed in it somewhere.

He could not imagine a world without Esther, and yet he was already living in that world. The question was whether he wanted to.

Gareth coughed and lit another cigarette, shielding the flame of the lighter with a cupped hand. Mal glanced at him, shifted his gaze to the sky and then down at the sea. He studied the water, grey and merciless, stretched out beneath him. There might be, he thought, a kind of salvation in its depths. He stepped away from the rail and cleared his throat.

'I need a slash,' he said. 'I won't be long.'

43

Thursday 22 September. Tufnell Park, London

Nick was parked a short distance down the road from Heather Grant's flat in Tufnell Park. He was presuming she'd come home from West Henby at some point today and was hoping it would be sooner rather than later. The street was quiet, pleasant, tree-lined and virtually empty. Having already read the newspaper from cover to cover, he was reduced to staring through the windscreen at a black cat sauntering along the pavement.

First thing this morning he'd called the office and arranged to take a few extra days off. Lolly was in trouble and he wanted to do what he could to change that situation. Quite what this was he hadn't figured out yet, but he was working on it. If the law discovered she'd helped Mal Fury to escape, she would be done for aiding and abetting and whatever else they might decide to throw at her.

The big question was whether Mal was actually guilty of Esther's murder. His jury at least was still out on that one. But if Lolly was right and Mal hadn't done it, then someone else must have.

'Smart thinking, Nick,' he said aloud. 'This is why you're such a rich and successful detective.'

Apart from Mal, his own list of suspects was fairly small and Jude Rule was at the top of it. This was why he wanted to talk to Heather. Maybe she could help shed some light on what had actually gone on last night. Although he hadn't entirely dismissed her from the list either. From what Lolly had told him, Heather had been filling Mal's head with all sorts of ideas, few of which bore much resemblance to the truth. He couldn't really see her holding Esther under water until she expired, but stranger things had happened.

He was on the point of going in search of a caff – even brilliant detectives needed to eat every now and again – when the red Mini drew up outside the house. As Heather got out of her car, he jumped out of his too, locked it and walked towards her. She saw him and frowned.

'What are you doing here?'

'I need to talk to you about last night. I realise it's not a good time but . . . '

'No, it isn't.' She walked round to the back of the Mini, opened it and took out her suitcase. 'I've told the police everything I know.'

Nick noticed that she looked pale, shattered, as though she hadn't slept. Her face was pinched and there were dark circles under her eyes. 'Ten minutes,' he said. 'I won't stay any longer.'

She seemed about to protest, but perhaps even the effort of doing that was too much for her. 'You'd better come in, then.'

'Thanks. I appreciate it.' He indicated towards the case. 'Would you like me to carry that?'

'I might be tired,' she said, 'but I'm not helpless.'

Heather's flat was a ground-floor conversion, spacious and comfortably furnished. He wondered how she could afford it, unless she had a flatmate or well-heeled parents. She dumped her suitcase on the living-room floor, sighed and said, 'I suppose you'd like a coffee.'

'Ta. If you don't mind.'

'It'll have to be black. I don't have any milk.'

'That's fine.'

He followed her into the kitchen where she kept her back to him and busied herself with the kettle, mugs and a jar of Nescafé.

'Are you all right?' he asked. 'It's always shocking when something like this happens. Takes a while for it to sink in.'

Heather turned, teaspoon in hand, and stared at him. Her eyes were mocking. 'Oh, is that what this is about? You've just come to check that I'm okay?'

'Partly,' he said.

'Well, now we've got that covered why don't you tell me what the other part is.'

Nick stood beside a wide oak table, wondering whether he should sit down or not. 'I wanted to get your take on things. I mean, you've been staying with Esther, spending a lot of time with her.'

'Not that much time. She was always busy.'

The kettle was boiling and Heather turned away again. She poured water into the two mugs, gave the instant coffee a stir and passed one of the mugs over to him. As if to make it clear that this wasn't going to be a long conversation she returned to the counter, leaned back against it and folded her arms across her chest.

'Is Jude still in West Henby?' he asked.

'No, I dropped him off in Kellston. He couldn't really stay at the house, could he, not after . . . '

'I suppose not.'

'He's devastated.'

'Is he?'

'Of course he is. I mean, yes, they had their differences – Esther wasn't the easiest person to get along with – but he really did love her.' Heather stopped for a moment, tilting her head slightly to the left. 'Look, I can see where you're going, but he'd never have killed her, not in a month of Sundays. We all know who did it. Even Lita does, deep down. She just doesn't want to face up to it. And I understand that. It's hard to come to terms with, especially when you care about someone.'

Nick thought she might have a point, but he hadn't come to agree with her. 'There's no evidence Mal was even there.'

'Where else would he be? Come on, Nick, are you saying it's just a coincidence that one minute he's escaped from prison and the next his wife has been murdered?'

'Could be that someone chose to take advantage of that situation.'

'What are the odds? And why exactly would Jude kill her?'

'I don't know. There was a certain amount of tension when I saw them together.'

'Some couples thrive on that kind of thing.'

'Were they actually a couple? I was never entirely sure.'

'When she felt like it,' Heather said. 'When there wasn't anyone else on the scene.'

Nick raised his eyebrows. 'Very modern.'

'We didn't speak much, to be honest.'

'Not even down the pub?'

The fact that he knew about this clearly came as a surprise. Her eyebrows lifted and she gave a low laugh. 'My, someone's been gossiping. There's nothing going on, if that's what you're thinking. He's not my type. It was just somewhere to go, something to do when Esther was out.'

He was tempted to ask what her type was but felt it would be impertinent. 'What did you talk about?'

Heather shrugged. 'I spent most of the time trying to find out what Esther knew about the disappearance of Hazel and Vicky, if anything, and he spent most of it trying to find out what was going into my book. There was nothing romantic about it. The very opposite, in fact.' She took a sip of coffee and put the mug back down. 'How come Lita sent you to ask all this stuff? Why didn't she come herself?'

'She didn't send me. I'm just trying to figure out what really happened last night.'

'Why? You barely knew Esther. Why don't you just leave it to the police?'

Nick couldn't tell her the truth – that Lolly had lied, had covered for Mal. 'I'm a suspect,' he said. 'We all are until they find out who killed her. And I don't like being in that position. The sooner it's sorted, the better.'

Heather gave a snort. 'Why on earth would you be a suspect?'

'Because I was there. Because I'm Stanley Parrish's nephew. Because he died as a result of looking for her daughter.'

'You could hardly blame her for that.'

'People aren't always rational. I could have been bearing a grudge.'

'And were you?'

'All I'm saying is that it's not clear cut. There were lots of people at the party who could have had a reason to kill her, guests and staff. She didn't exactly make herself popular.'

'So why are you concentrating on Jude?'

'Do you know where he was when Esther was murdered?'

'I don't know when she was murdered. Not precisely.'

'But you noticed that Esther had gone missing?'

'Not for half an hour or so.'

'And where was Jude in that half hour?'

Heather shook her head, expelled a sigh. 'God, I'm not his keeper. He was around, here and there. I was talking to other people. I wasn't paying attention to what he was doing.'

'But you were talking to him on the back steps around ten past eight. What was that about?'

'Jesus, you're as bad as the police.' She frowned, considering his question for a moment. 'Let me think. I suppose that must have been when Jude started looking for her. Yes, I think that was it. He just asked me if I'd seen her. It was no big deal. There were lots of guests and people were spread out through the house and garden.'

'But he was worried, or acting like he was?'

'No, I wouldn't say worried exactly. You know what he's like.'

'Jealous, possessive, controlling?'

'They're your words, not mine. No one controlled Esther.'

Nick, sensing that he wasn't making much headway, changed direction. 'What about this announcement she was going to make? Do you know anything about that?'

'I presume it was to do with the film.'

'What film?'

'She'd just got a big part in some Hollywood production. I heard her telling Mrs Gough about it. I wasn't earwigging – well, I suppose I was – but I just happened to be walking past the room and the door was open so . . . Anyway, Esther asked her not to tell anyone else, said she wanted it to be a surprise.'

'Nothing to do with Vicky Finch, then?'

'What would she have to announce about her?'

'I don't know. That her long lost daughter had been found?'

'Except she hasn't. And even if she had, Esther wouldn't be announcing it at a party, would she? She wouldn't want a pile of fuss before she'd even got to know the girl properly. The press would be crawling all over the place.'

Nick could see the logic in this, although he wasn't sure if Esther had ever acted logically. 'I suppose.'

Heather glanced at her watch. 'Are we finished here? Only I'm completely done in. I can barely think straight as it is.'

'Yes of course. I'm sorry.' He wanted to challenge her about what she'd said to Mal, the claim that she'd seen Esther with Vicky, but he couldn't, not without revealing that Lolly had spoken to Mal recently. Instead, as she walked him to the door, he said, 'What are you going to do about the book? Will you still go ahead with it?'

'I've no idea. It's too soon to make that decision.'

He paused on the doorstep. 'You've got my number. Give me a call if you remember anything useful.'

'Don't waste your time, Nick. You know who did it. We both do.'

44

Thursday 22 September. West Henby

DI Bob Latham stood by the entrance to the summerhouse, gazing into the interior. 'Are they sure?' To him the area looked still and undisturbed, but scene-of-crime officers had been going over the space since first light and discovered some anomalies.

DS Barry nodded. 'Someone's been here. There's definite signs of occupation including crumbs on the floor. Bread and cheese, they think.'

'Do we know when?'

'Recently. In the last few days. There's evidence of mice too so the fact the crumbs are still there . . . '

'But the door hasn't been forced.'

'No. Either there was a key hidden somewhere or somebody opened the door for him.'

'And that wouldn't have been Esther Fury or the housekeeper.'

'Unlikely,' Barry agreed. 'And there was a rug found here too. Mrs Gough thinks it used to be kept in the utility room, but she can't recall when she last saw it.'

Latham could see a picture emerging: a desperate man who

had escaped from prison, made his way here and holed up until he got the opportunity he needed. No electricity or running water. Only his own tormented thoughts for company. Had he brought the food with him or had someone provided him with it? It would have been too risky, surely, for him to have taken it, or the rug, from the house.

An appeal to the public had already gone out on the radio. The newspapers, apart from publications like the London *Evening Standard* and *Evening News*, wouldn't be able to publish until tomorrow. Later today the story would be shown on the TV news. Doubtless, they would be inundated with false sightings, everywhere from Land's End to John O'Groats.

The ferries and airports were on red alert – they couldn't rule out a fake passport – but as yet there hadn't been a sniff of him. There was no sign of the white Hunter either.

'Where would you go?' he asked Barry. 'If you'd just committed murder, which direction would you head in?'

'Dover, I suppose, if I thought I stood a chance of getting across the Channel. Or a big city: London, Birmingham. Hide in the crowd until things calm down a bit.'

Latham nodded. Back at the station the team were already starting to sift through a long list of known associates, many of whom had been present at the party last night. The owner of the Hunter had come under particular scrutiny – it wasn't impossible that the keys had been left in the car deliberately – but he had turned out to be a film producer of some renown who had never even met Mal.

'There's something else come up,' Barry said. 'We just heard back from Kellston. Jude Rule was interviewed over another murder six years ago: a girl called Amy Wiltshire who was stabbed to death on the Mansfield estate.'

The case rang a bell with Latham. So far as he could

remember there had never been a conviction. 'Lots of people must have been interviewed.'

'Yes, except he was pretty high on the list of suspects at the time. The girl's best friend pointed the finger, said he'd had a "thing" about Amy, that he was always following her around. And here's the interesting part: guess who gave him an alibi?'

'Enlighten me.'

'None over than Lolita Bruce. Swore blind, apparently, that she was with him for the entire time.'

'Any reason to suspect she was lying?'

Barry shrugged. 'That pair seem to be unlucky. Caught in the middle of two murder investigations. What are the odds?'

'Pretty short if you live in Kellston, I should think.' Latham moved away from the summerhouse and strolled down towards the lake. Barry walked beside him. They stood and stared out across the shimmering water.

'I thought you had Mal Fury pegged for this,' Latham said.

'I did. I *do*. But maybe those two were involved as well. I'm not sure about that Jude Rule. There's something not quite right about him.'

'Better lock him up then.'

Barry, not renowned for his sense of humour, scowled. 'You know what I mean. His relationship with Esther Fury wasn't what you'd call normal, was it? And the Bruce girl was down by the lake. How come she never heard anything, saw anything? It doesn't add up.'

Latham had his own thoughts on the matter, but he kept them to himself. 'We'll talk to them both again, see what they've got to say now the dust has settled.' His gaze scanned the water until it settled on the weeping willows. A sigh came from deep within him. 'If I believed in such things, I'd swear this place was cursed.'

45

Thursday 22 September. Kellston

Lolly was only half listening to what Nick had to say. She sat at the table chewing her fingernails while he told her about his visit to Heather Grant. The words floated around in her head, jumbled up with Terry's more aggressive ones. What was she going to do? There was no way she could raise the money to pay Terry back and very little chance of getting information on Laura Sandler either.

'She doesn't think it was Jude, although she wasn't with him at around the time it happened so it's just an opinion and I'm not sure how much that's worth. For all we know they could be in it together. Or she could be covering for him.' Nick scratched his chin. 'I don't know why she'd do that though. And she reckons the grand announcement was about a film part Esther had got, nothing else.'

Lolly made a vague noise, something to confirm that she was taking in what he said.

'I know you're worried, but no news is good news. He's probably miles away by now.'

'Huh?'

'Mal. He's probably miles away. So long as he keeps his head down, he should be okay. And if you stick to your story that you had no idea he was at the house, the police can't prove otherwise.'

'No, I suppose not.'

'We'll just have to hope the real killer made a mistake, left a clue behind, some kind of evidence that proves it couldn't have been Mal. Do you think we should try and talk to Jude? Heather says she dropped him off at the Mansfield.'

'What's the point? He's not going to tell the truth, is he? Not if he killed her.'

Nick gave her a long, steady stare. 'I know it's a shock, Esther being dead and everything, but so long as you hold your nerve you'll be all right.'

Lolly rubbed her face with her hands. She didn't want to ask for help, but she was running out of options. 'Do you know where Laura Sandler lives?'

Nick looked understandably bemused. 'What on earth do you want to know that for?'

'I have to talk to her – about Vinnie.'

'And say what? Christ, Lolly, you can't go near that woman, not unless you want to get yourself arrested. She'll view it as intimidation.'

'How could anyone be intimidated by me?'

'You're a friend of Vinnie's, and Vinnie has just been charged with her husband's murder. How do you think it's going to look if you approach her? She'll be straight on the blower to the law.'

'I have to try.'

'And say what? "Hey, is it true that you had your old man topped and set up Vinnie Keane to take the rap?"'

'I wasn't going to put it quite like that.'

Nick shook his head. 'There's no good way of putting it.

Haven't you got enough to deal with at the moment? Vinnie's a big boy. He can take care of himself.'

'And how's he supposed to do that when he's banged up?' Lolly could see that she'd have to come clean or she'd never find out where Laura lived. She took a deep breath and bit the bullet. 'Thing is, I've got a bit of a problem. You remember the necklace and ring I gave to Mal? Well, the diamond ring wasn't fake and it wasn't strictly speaking mine. I was holding on to it for someone else.'

Nick sighed. 'Why do I get the feeling I'm not going to like what you're going to tell me next?'

'You won't,' she said. The ring belongs to Terry Street and as you can imagine he's not overjoyed about my generosity. I couldn't tell him about Mal so now he thinks . . . God, I'm not sure what he thinks, but I'm not top of his list of favourite people at the moment.'

'So he wants you to find out what, if anything, Laura Sandler is up to?'

'That's about the sum of it.'

'How much is the ring worth?'

'A lot. About a grand.'

Nick winced. 'Jesus.'

'And as that's not the kind of money I can spirit out of fresh air, I'm figuring the Laura option is the best one going at the moment.'

'I thought you were friendly with Terry.'

'I was . . . sort of. Let's just say things have cooled a little since he found out what I did. Look, all I want is her address, nothing else. Then I'll . . . '

'Then you'll do what? Get yourself arrested, probably.' Nick stood up and put on his jacket. 'It's madness and you know it.'

Lolly watched him, unsurprised by his imminent departure.

Why should he help? First, she'd landed him in the middle of an inquiry over Esther's murder, and now she was asking him to give her details that could jeopardise his job. He wasn't, she was certain, supposed to divulge the kind of information she was asking for.

Nick stood, looking down on her. 'Well?' he said.

'Well what?'

'Are you coming or not? I'll take you to the house on one condition.'

'Anything,' she said, leaping to her feet.

'We just keep an eye on the place, see who comes and goes, nothing else. You don't go near that woman. Do you promise?'

'I swear. Thank you.'

Nick gave a wry smile. 'Please don't make me regret this.'

46

Thursday 22 September. Primrose Hill

Nick had found a parking space about fifty yards down from the Sandler residence and it was from this position that they'd been watching and waiting ever since. He hadn't asked Lolly why she'd been holding the ring for Terry. There were some questions you preferred not to know the answer to. And he'd only decided to bring her here because she'd have probably found out the address from someone else, come to the house and done something crazy. Crazy being anything that involved trying to talk to Laura Sandler. At least this way he could keep an eye on her.

Primrose Hill, near Regent's Park, was leafy and expensive. The house was large, detached and more than any average solicitor could afford, but of course Brent Sandler hadn't been any old solicitor: he'd been making a tidy living from helping out the likes of Terry Street.

As yet there was no sign of the grieving widow and to pass the time – surveillance could be a tedious business – they'd been going over the case against Vinnie.

'If it was Laura,' Lolly said, 'who would she get to do something like that?'

'Oh, she wouldn't be short of volunteers, not in London – so long as the price was right.'

'But you can't just pick up the phone and order a hit. I mean, you have to *know* people, don't you? And it has to be someone you can trust.'

'Brent Sandler was mixing with all sorts. She probably got introduced to some of them.' Nick thought back to the file on Sandler, to the detailed list of all the places he'd been and all the people he'd met. Unfortunately, they hadn't been taking much notice of the wife. 'Maybe she had Vinnie lined up for the job but realised he wouldn't play ball.'

'So she set him up instead?'

'It's a possibility.'

Lolly was quiet for a while and then she said, 'You still think Vinnie could be guilty.'

'I didn't say that. But you can't dismiss the possibility. On his own or in collusion with her. And she's never going to admit to having an affair. That would put her right in the line of fire.'

'The police must still suspect her. I mean, she's the one with the most to gain, isn't she? Money, property, freedom ... ' Lolly stared at the house. 'That place must be worth a fortune for starters.'

'They'll be more inclined to believe her than him, especially with Vinnie's background. Although I doubt she's off the hook just yet. They'll be looking to see if there's a link between the two of them. If she's smart, she'll have made sure she didn't leave a trail: no meetings in public, no phone calls to his number, no love letters or anything like that. If all this was carefully planned, she'll be clean as a whistle.'

'And Vinnie will just be a murderous fantasist.'

'That's about the sum of it.'

It was warm in the car. Lolly wound down the window and put her elbow on the sill. 'What else do you know about Brent Sandler? Did he have any enemies, do you think?'

'Men like Sandler always have enemies. But all I was doing was following him around. I didn't get to listen in on any conversations.'

'What about the girls, the prostitutes? You told me he seemed to prefer their company to hers.'

'He went to Marcie's a lot. It's one of Terry's clubs in Shoreditch.'

'Is it worth trying there, do you think?'

'I can't see anyone wanting to get involved.'

'But off the record,' she insisted. 'They must know Vinnie, at least some of them. Surely they'd want to try and help him.'

Nick wasn't so sure. In his experience, working girls preferred to steer clear of trouble rather than invite it in. 'It depends how much they liked him ... Although even then they'll be cautious, afraid of saying something they shouldn't. They won't want to get on the wrong side of Terry, and they won't want to get dragged into a murder investigation.'

'Terry's not going to object to them helping.'

'Unless they say something that incriminates him, like the fact that most of his clubs are nothing more than knocking shops. He's got a business to protect, remember, and he isn't going to want the law rooting around in it.'

'He won't want Vinnie going to jail either.'

'Well, that's an occupational hazard in their line of work.' It came out sounding harsher than he'd intended, and he quickly qualified it by saying, 'But I get what you mean. I suppose even villains like Terry have some sort of loyalty.'

Lolly glared at him for a moment and then transferred the glare to the house, as if by sheer effort of will she could get

Sandler's widow to emerge. 'What does Laura Sandler even look like?'

'Tallish, slim, dark-haired, mid-thirties probably. Attractive. She looks a bit like Jackie Kennedy, the younger version. Stylish, well-dressed, usually wears sunglasses.'

'Not that you were paying attention or anything.'

'She might have slipped into my line of view occasionally.'

'Well, I wish she'd slip into it today.' Lolly fidgeted in her seat, crossing and uncrossing her legs, glancing at her watch. 'How do you bear this, just sitting around for hours on end?'

'It gives me time to contemplate life.'

'And have you come to any conclusions about it?'

'It's more of a work in progress.' He smiled, took out his wallet and said, 'There's a deli round the corner. Why don't you go and buy some supplies – they do sandwiches, coffee – while I keep an eye out.'

'Why, don't you trust me to stay here on my own?'

'I just thought you might like to stretch your legs. I'll go if you don't want to.'

She hesitated and then took the note from his hand and got out of the car.

Two hours passed and no one went into the house and no one came out. Sandler's yellow Jensen-Healey was parked in the drive and behind it was a pale blue MG, presumably Laura's car although he'd never seen her drive it. The presence of the MG suggested that Mrs Sandler was at home, but there was nothing more to back this up, not a sign of movement from inside, not even the twitch of a curtain.

The conversation had moved on to Esther's murder and they were going over the same ground they had last night, trying to figure out who had motive and opportunity to kill her. The latter was tricky as the party had meant a fluid movement of people between the house and the garden, and neither of them could remember seeing the major suspects at the relevant time.

'Mal said there was arguing, but he couldn't catch what it was about.'

'And the other voice or voices?'

Lolly shook her head. 'It was only Esther's he was certain of. I still can't figure out what she was even doing by the lake. She hated that place, wouldn't go near it normally.'

Nick still wasn't sure that he believed Mal Fury's version of events; it could easily be a story made up on the spur of the moment, a story rooted in panic rather than the truth. It seemed to him that Lolly, so untrusting of most people, had a kind of blind loyalty to a few. He still hadn't decided if this was a strength or a weakness or even if it mattered.

'The Leightons both had reason to hate her,' he said. 'And so did Mrs Gough. All those years of devoted service and for what? So Esther could discard her and swan off to Hollywood. Would anyone have noticed if she'd disappeared last night for ten, fifteen minutes?'

'Half the village had reason to hate Esther. She sacked all the staff after Kay was taken: housekeeper, cook, maids, handyman, gardeners. That was their livelihoods up in smoke. They relied on the house for an income.'

'But that was years ago.'

'People don't forget. They still resent her for it.'

'And Jude?' he asked. 'What would his motive have been?'

'You've seen what he's like. Maybe he was scared of being dumped or replaced.'

'You think he's capable of murder?'

Lolly glanced at him and then away. 'I don't know. Perhaps

we're all capable if we're pushed hard enough.' She stared through the windscreen at the house, sighed and said, 'This is a waste of time, isn't it? Nothing's going to happen.'

'You want to call it a day?'

'I should be trying to clear Mal's name, not sitting around here. She's hardly going to do something stupid now, not if it was all planned.'

'It's unlikely. Should we go and talk to Jude?'

She displayed the same reluctance she had earlier, but eventually nodded. 'There's no point in both of us going though. Why don't you go and check out the girls, call in at Marcie's and see if you can dig up anything new on Sandler?'

'What if it *was* Jude? You shouldn't go there on your own.'

Lolly shook her head. 'He'd never do anything to me.'

Nick looked at her closely, wondering how she really felt about Jude Rule. Although she acted indifferent, as though she no longer cared, he suspected this wasn't the case. Whatever feelings she had once harboured – and Jude had certainly meant a lot to her – might be carefully buried, but they were not entirely dead.

47

Thursday 22 September. Kellston

Freddy Mund loved his mother but he didn't like her. What was there to like? It was fair to say she had a nasty side, a streak of spite running through her. Her sharp tongue was usually reserved for the neighbours or the tallyman who came to collect his dues every week, but she wasn't averse to venting her spleen on her son too. He didn't take it to heart – he was used to it by now – but he still despised her for it.

'What are you even doing here?' she asked. 'Haven't you got work to do?'

'It's the end of the summer. No one wants gardeners at this time of year.' He had put a card up in the library in spring and got a few takers, mainly because he was cheap. He wasn't an expert in the field of horticulture but he knew a plant from a weed and could do all the heavy work, the hedge cutting and the lawn mowing. The big advantage was that he worked for cash and so didn't need to declare it to the social. He didn't declare it all to his mother either; she'd only take the lion's share and spend it on gin.

'Well, you can't sit round here all day cluttering up the place. If you haven't got work, you should go out and look for it.'

'I've not been here all day. And I have been looking. Been out all morning, haven't I? I'm entitled to some dinner.'

His mother curled her lip as though this entitlement was debatable. 'Food costs money, Freddy. It doesn't appear out of thin air.'

'It does if you nick it from the Spar.'

'I wouldn't need to nick if you brought in a decent wage.'

He stared at her, wondering not for the first time how it was they were even related. She was fat – or big-boned as she liked to put it – and he was thin. Her eyes were brown and his were grey. Her face was long and flabby, his round and flat. Even their hair was different: hers, dyed a curious gingery colour, was wavy and had a streak of grey at her scalp where the roots were growing out.

Bored of the conversation, he went over to the window and stared down at the estate. Rain was spitting against the window, a steady drizzle that had been falling since the morning. From the second floor there wasn't much to see but the wide concrete square and the paths that led to the other two towers. The Mansfield was a dump, a decaying, crime-ridden, rat-infested slagheap which even the law thought twice about visiting.

'What are you looking at?' she asked, worried that she might be missing out.

'Nothing.'

'How can you be looking at nothing?'

'What else is there to see here?'

Freddy thought about Dana. Everything had been more interesting when she'd been alive. There had been a reason to get up in the morning, a sense of purpose. He'd liked all the sneaking around, the secret meetings, the clandestine nature of their relationship. Just for a while he had been important, even necessary, to somebody else. In many ways, he thought, Dana had been lucky: he often wished that *his* mother had left him on a church doorstep. At least then he wouldn't have had to put up with her nagging for the past thirty years.

He was about to move away from the window, to sit down again, when he saw her – the brown-haired girl from the library. It gave him a jolt. What was she doing here? For one irrational moment he thought that she was coming to see him, to *accuse* him, and he sucked in a breath and quickly shifted to the side.

After a moment he peeked out through the window again. No, she wasn't coming in this direction but towards Haslow House. She was walking slowly with her head down, as though she was deep in thought or checking out the ground for lost change. He did that himself sometimes. It was surprising what you found. Now the fear had subsided, curiosity was replacing it. What was she doing here? Who was she going to see? He had to know.

Freddy grabbed his jacket off the back of the chair and slipped it on. 'I've got to go out.'

'You've only just got in.'

That was his mother all over, never happy when he was there, never happy when he wasn't. 'I've just remembered. Mrs Barlow said she might have some odd jobs for me. When I was free. Which I am now. Might as well check it out.'

'It's raining.'

'Not much.'

'She can't expect you to work in the rain. You'll catch pneumonia. What sort of person . . . '

But Freddy was already shutting the front door. He jogged along the corridor and down the two flights of steps. When he reached the ground, he strode through the foyer and went out into the damp afternoon air. The brown-haired girl wasn't far from Haslow now. She was acting differently to the way most women did on the estate, not scuttling along, not always glancing over her shoulder. As though she wasn't afraid of anything or anyone. That was odd. It piqued his interest. She was either very stupid – the estate was a dangerous place – or unusually confident.

He walked quickly to catch up with her. Perhaps she was going to see a client. Was she a whore? He still wasn't sure. She didn't dress like a whore – she wasn't even wearing high heels – but that wasn't proof one way or the other. He couldn't think of any other reason why she'd have been in Albert Road. No respectable woman went near the place. The reporter angle came back into his head, the idea that she could be some busybody journalist, but he didn't think that was the case. If pressed, he couldn't have explained why not. It was just a hunch.

By the time she went inside the building he was only a short distance behind. As he reached the entrance he saw her step into a lift, saw the metal doors closing. He walked into the foyer and stood watching as the little red light charted the ascending lift's progress up the floors. It was unlikely, he thought, that it would stop anywhere else before it reached its destination. Who else would want to go up rather than down? No one unless they had a friend higher up.

The lift stopped at the twelfth floor. He stared at the light for thirty seconds. Nothing happened. When he was sure that this was where she must have got off, he got into another lift and pressed the button marked 12. He didn't know which flat she'd gone to but if he hung out on the walkway she would emerge eventually. He would simply watch and wait. Why not? It was what he was good at.

48

Thursday 22 September. Kellston

Everything about the Mansfield estate, from the cracks running through the tall concrete blocks to the stink of the lifts, was familiar to Lolly. Despite the oppressive atmosphere, the dark air of despair and hopelessness, she still felt comfortable here, at home. This was where she had lived until she was thirteen, a place she knew like the back of her hand, and although she was aware of its dangers she felt impervious to them. It was as though the past protected her from any current threats, wrapping her in a blanket of safety and giving her a free pass. There was only so much bad stuff that could happen to a person and she'd already used up her quota.

She still paused, however, when she got out of the lift. Too many memories were flooding her mind, a torrent of history. Jude's flat had always been her haven in difficult times, a refuge from the emptiness and loneliness of her own home. It had not been her mum's fault – she hadn't been a bad person, only a tormented one – but she had needed solace and Jude had provided it. He'd given her food and shelter and company. Through a constant stream of old movies, he'd transported her to another world and for a while she had been able to forget about this one.

Being back here reminded her of something else too: how much she had cared for him. She was loath to call it love and yet it had been more than a childish crush. At the time she would have died for Jude, would have laid down her life, but such dramatics were never called for. In the event all that had been required was that she lie for him and this she had done with skill and alacrity. It was too late for regrets. She had chosen to believe in his innocence over the death of Amy Wiltshire and any doubts she might have now were futile.

It was odd, she thought, how much harder it was to face him here than at West Henby. She was afraid of what she might feel when she walked into that flat, anxious that the past might overwhelm her. For a second, she was almost tempted to turn tail and run, but then she remembered why she was doing this: if she couldn't find out who really killed Esther, Mal's name would never be cleared.

As she walked on she tried to wipe everything but that from her mind. She went up to the door and knocked before she could have second thoughts, three determined raps that echoed along the empty corridor. There was a long delay before she heard signs of movement from inside, a period of time she had to force herself to wait.

Jude eventually opened the door. He looked a mess, unshaven and unwashed, his cheeks sunken. He was wearing jeans and a shirt with stains down the front. She could smell the alcohol on him but couldn't tell if it was from last night or today. He stared at her through bleary eyes.

'Lolly,' he said. 'What do *you* want?'

'I just came to check you were okay. Heather said she dropped you off here.'

'No, I'm not okay. Why the fuck would I be okay? In case you've forgotten, Esther's just been murdered.'

'No, sorry, I didn't mean ... Can I come in?'

He hesitated but then shrugged and headed towards the living room.

She closed the door behind her and followed him. The room was sparsely furnished with hardly anything in the way of furniture, just a sofa, a small table with a typewriter on it, and a chair. He clearly hadn't spent much time here recently. The house at West Henby had become his home and all that was left in the flat were the bare essentials.

'Is there news?' he asked. 'Have they caught the bastard yet?'

Lolly bit her tongue, not wanting to get in a row. 'If you mean Mal, then no. But he didn't kill her. He wouldn't have.'

Jude gave a hollow laugh. 'What's wrong with you? Jesus! Can't you see what's staring you in the face? Of course he bloody killed her. And now he's run away like the pathetic coward he is.'

She studied him, trying to work out if he really believed this or was just trying to cover his own tracks. In truth, she couldn't tell. He was obviously upset, distraught even, but that didn't mean he was innocent. 'So where's the evidence? There's nothing to say he was even at the house. Did you see him there? Did anyone?'

'He was there, right under our bloody noses. The law were sniffing round that old summerhouse this morning. They reckon that's where he'd been hiding.'

'What?' She was shocked by the fact they'd discovered this so quickly. 'Are you sure? They told you that?'

'Didn't need to, did they. It was obvious. Someone had got in there and they hadn't forced the lock. I heard that DS Barry talking. There'll be fingerprints and everything.'

'Fingerprints don't mean anything,' she said, aware that her own would be in there too. 'It's *his* summerhouse. There are bound to be prints.'

'Mrs Gough said it hadn't been used for years.'

Lolly wondered if the police could tell if prints were old or new. Did they change, alter with age, deteriorate? She had no idea. 'What would she know? She wasn't following him around twenty-four hours a day.'

Jude lifted and dropped his shoulders again. 'That woman knows everything. You should realise that by now.'

'*Thinks* she knows everything,' Lolly corrected him. 'And what she doesn't know, she just makes up. She's a spiteful old cow. She hates Mal and she'll do her best to get him locked up again.'

'I reckon he's doing a pretty good job of that himself.'

Lolly looked at him for a moment before her gaze shifted to the window and the magnificent panorama; you could see right across London from this height, even to the dome of St Paul's. But she hadn't come to admire the view. 'Anyone at that party could have killed her. We're all suspects.'

'So who stole the car if it wasn't Mal?'

She looked back at him. 'Someone else,' she said stubbornly.

'Well, that's handy. Bit of a coincidence though. And if Mal was at the summerhouse, why did he clear off?'

'Wouldn't you?' she retorted. 'He'd get the blame and that would be that.' Then she rapidly added, 'That's if he was ever there in the first place.'

Jude pushed his hands into his jeans pockets and leaned against the table. 'He's the only person who wanted her dead,' he said flatly. 'Did you hear anyone arguing down by the lake? When you went there to look for her.'

She shook her head. 'There must have been some kind of altercation though. A row. Don't you think?'

'Not if he took her by surprise.'

'But why would she even go there? That's what I don't get. She hated the place.'

'How would I know?' he snapped. 'Maybe she saw him, saw Mal in the garden, and followed him there.'

'She'd be more likely to call the law. Or at least tell someone. You or Mrs Gough.'

'Maybe she would, maybe she wouldn't. She'd had a few drinks. She might not have been thinking straight.'

'What do you know about that announcement she was going to make?'

Jude glared at her. 'What's with all the questions? Shit, I've already been interrogated by the cops and now you're at it too. I've had enough. What the hell do you want, Lolly?'

'The truth, I suppose.'

He snorted and turned away from her, going over to the window.

She stared at the back of his head. She wondered what a guilty person looked like, sounded like. Scared, angry, defensive? Perhaps not that different to an innocent one. There was always the fear of being falsely accused in circumstances like these. And there was always guilt and regret – things that should have been said, should have been done. She couldn't tell whether his conscience was clear or not, just as she hadn't been able to after Amy had been killed.

'Maybe those forensics people will be able to shed some light. I mean, whoever did it must have left some clues. They can find out all sorts these days.' Lolly studied his body language but it told her nothing, other than the fact that he would rather she wasn't there. 'What will you do now?'

Jude glanced over his shoulder. 'Do?'

'Will you still go to the States?'

He waved a hand towards the room and said dismissively, 'There's nothing to stay here for.'

Once upon a time the comment would have stung but now it barely touched her. Their futures had diverged long ago and anyway she had never held the place in his life that he'd held in hers. To him she had always just been the scrawny kid from upstairs, at worst someone to be pitied, at best someone to sit and watch a movie with. Back then he wouldn't have realised how she felt about him but later . . . yes, later, she was sure he would have known.

'Esther's announcement,' she said. 'You never told me what it was about.'

'I've no idea.'

'You're not curious?'

He looked over his shoulder again. 'What does it matter now?'

Lolly was about to ask about the film, about what Esther had allegedly said to Mrs Gough, but a knock on the door interrupted their exchange.

As though he hadn't heard it, Jude didn't move for a moment. Then he sighed, took his hands out of his pockets and walked towards the hallway. 'I bet that's the bloody law again.'

But it wasn't the law. And by the time Lolly realised who it was the two Cecil brothers had forced their way past Jude and were standing right in front of her.

49

Thursday 22 September. Kellston

'Well, look who it is,' Tony Cecil said, pushing his ugly face into Lolly's. 'It's the filthy little liar who said she didn't know where Jude Rule was. Got your memory back, I see.'

She didn't immediately respond but kept her eyes on him. She felt afraid, intimidated, but was trying her best not to show it. It was one thing to stand your ground in public, where there were other people around, witnesses, quite another behind closed doors.

'You lay one finger on me and you'll regret it.'

'Oh, I doubt that, sweetheart. I doubt it very much.' Tony turned to his brother. 'You reckon I'll regret it?'

'Nah, I don't reckon so.'

'Get out of my flat,' Jude said, 'or I'll call the law.'

Tony withdrew his face from Lolly's and grinned. 'He's going to call the filth, FJ. Are we worried?'

'Yeah, dead worried. I'm going to pee my fuckin' pants.'

Jude made a move towards the phone but he wasn't fast enough. FJ was already there, yanking out the cord from the wall. 'Ah, shit,' he said, holding the dead receiver to his ear. 'There seems to be a fault on the line.'

'So what now?' Tony asked, his gaze shifting between Lolly and Jude. 'Doesn't look like the filth are going to make it after all. You got a back-up plan?'

'Just get out,' Jude said weakly. 'Leave us alone.'

Tony started strolling round the room, looking at everything. As there wasn't much to see this didn't take long. 'Christ, and I thought I lived in a dump. Can't you afford any furniture, mate?'

Jude didn't reply.

'What's the matter, you deaf or something?' Tony raised his voice, speaking loudly and slowly. 'I said can't you afford any furniture?'

'I'm moving out,' Jude said.

Two red spots had appeared on his cheeks, but Lolly wasn't sure if that was down to anger or humiliation. She hoped he wasn't going to do anything stupid.

'Not without saying goodbye though? I mean, you wouldn't just leave without letting us know, would you? We should throw a party, celebrate. Have a few beers. Everyone likes a party, don't they?'

Jude suddenly launched himself at Tony, swinging wildly with his right fist. It was a clumsy attempt. Tony easily blocked him, laughed and then pushed him away. Jude staggered back, lost his balance and ended up in a heap on the floor. Quickly he scrambled to his feet, his pride more damaged than anything else.

Lolly wondered if the Cecils had heard about the murder, about the party last night, but so far as she was aware they didn't even know about Jude's connection to Esther. She grabbed hold of Tony's arm. 'What do you want? You've already beaten the shit out of him once. Isn't that enough?'

'Ah, look at that, FJ. The little slapper's trying to protect her man. Ain't that sweet?'

'True to the end,' FJ said. 'Shame she wasn't as loyal to the family who took her in.'

'Yeah, you're not wrong there.' Tony grabbed her hand by the wrist and forcibly removed it from his arm. He didn't let go but squeezed it tightly, his fingers crushing the flesh. 'And no, it's not enough,' he said to her. 'It's not nearly fuckin' enough. I want to hear those words come out of his mouth: *I killed Amy Wiltshire.*'

Lolly, wincing, tried to free herself but the harder she tried the tighter he held on. She could almost feel the bruises forming. 'You want him to lie. What does that achieve?'

'Let go of her,' Jude said.

'Or what?'

'I'll report you. I'll have you done for assault.'

Tony laughed again. 'Your word against ours, mate. And how are you going to walk to the cop shop with two broken legs? You going to crawl there or something?' Abruptly he swung Lolly round in front of him and gripped her throat in the crook of his elbow. 'Say you killed her. Say you killed Amy or I'll snap your girlfriend's fuckin' neck in two.'

Jude stood there with his mouth gaping open. 'Let go of her. Let go,' he said again, as though if he repeated it often enough Tony might eventually take notice.

'Make me.'

It was at times like these, Lolly thought, that you needed a Vinnie in your life. Someone who acted first and thought about it later, someone who could flatten the likes of Tony Cecil with his little finger. Pressed up against her assailant the stink of sweat and stale tobacco quickly reached her nose. She sensed the excitement in him, the thrill he got from hurting others. He was more than capable of carrying out his threat.

'An eye for an eye,' Tony said. 'Ain't that how it goes?

Sounds reasonable to me. You took Amy, I'll take Lolly. Fair enough, huh?'

Lolly thought he was barking up the wrong tree if he imagined Jude gave a toss about her. And Tony hadn't really cared about Amy either. This was just an opportunity for him to inflict some pain, to flex his muscles and show off to his brother. Her eyes darted sideways. FJ, still with the phone in his hand, was watching, waiting to receive orders. He always took the lead from Tony. He was like a pet dog, forever at heel, blindly following wherever his master took him.

'Terry's going to rip your heads off,' she said, hoping they hadn't heard about the falling out.

Tony sniggered. 'You think I care about that bastard? I'm not afraid of him.'

'You should be. I mean, alibis can be given and they can be taken away.'

'What's that supposed to mean?' FJ said, frowning.

'Ask your brother. Ask him what he was really doing the day Amy was murdered.'

Tony snarled and clamped his hand over her mouth. 'Shut up, bitch! She don't mean nothin'. She's just an evil little cow who needs teaching a lesson.'

Lolly knew mentioning the alibi had been a big mistake. Now Tony was even angrier, more determined than ever to shut her up for good. Seeing that help wasn't likely to come any time soon from Jude, she acted on impulse, kicking out at Tony's lower leg, hitting him as hard as she could with her heel while she struggled to free herself from his grasp. The surprise of the attack temporarily loosened his hold and he had to remove his hand from her mouth to try and get her under control again. She grabbed her opportunity and started screaming, using every last inch of her lung power to make the sound travel.

Tony grabbed hold of her hair, yanked her head back and hurled her to the floor. She landed with a heavy thump, the impact of the fall both winding and silencing her. Immediately he was on her again, twisting her over, straddling her, pushing her face into the carpet. 'Bitch! Bitch! Fuckin' bitch!' She was blind. She couldn't move, couldn't breathe. Panic coursed through her veins. Her heart was thrashing, fear rising in her throat like bile. She could feel a darkness descending as the last of her strength ebbed away.

And then, just when she thought it was over, Jude finally did something. She heard it rather than saw it, a heavy cracking sound followed by some groans and then a clattering bump as an object hit the ground. Immediately the weight of Tony's body slid away as he toppled sideways. She turned her face the other way to gulp in air, to fill her empty lungs again. It was then she saw the weapon lying beside her – Jude's typewriter.

Scrambling to her feet, she looked down at Tony. For a moment she thought he was dead – Christ, that was all they needed – but then his lips moved and the groaning started up again. Blood was trickling through his hair from a cut on his scalp, but it didn't look terminal. No brain damage, at least, although it wouldn't be easy to tell the difference. FJ didn't seem to know what to do. With his brother out of action, all his bravado had seeped away. He put the phone back on the table and crouched down by Tony.

'You okay, bro? You okay?'

It was a while before Tony responded. He seemed groggy, concussed perhaps. He lifted a hand to his head, tentatively touched the wound, winced and then examined his fingers.

'Shit!'

Jude was standing in the middle of the room with a slightly bemused expression on his face, as though he wasn't entirely sure what had happened or how. Then he gave a start, bent and picked up the typewriter, more concerned with its well-being apparently than Lolly's. Still, she wasn't complaining. He'd saved her skin and she was grateful for it. Now all they had to do was get rid of the brothers before Tony revived enough to get mad and have another go.

As FJ hauled Tony up, there was a loud knocking at the door. When no one else showed any sign of answering it Lolly went through to the hall. She still felt unsteady on her legs, wobbly, as if the oxygen hadn't quite made it to her lower limbs yet. Two uniformed cops were standing on the doorstep.

'Everything all right here, Miss?' the taller one asked, trying to peer round her. 'We had a report of a disturbance.'

'Oh,' she said. 'I . . . erm . . . '

Before she could continue they'd gently pushed her aside and gone into the living room.

'Ah, look who it is. Been in the wars have you, Tony?'

'He had a fall, didn't he,' FJ said. 'Banged his head. It ain't nothing. We was just going.'

He took his brother's arm and tried to bustle him out but the cops blocked the way. 'Not so fast, son. We need a few words first.'

Tony glared at the officers. 'I tripped that's all, nothing for you lot to be arsed about.'

The smaller cop looked at Lolly. 'Someone screaming is what they said. A woman. Would that have been you, Miss?'

The number one rule on the Mansfield estate was never to grass no matter what the circumstances. It only ever made matters worse. Which wasn't to say she wasn't tempted – she'd be more than happy to see Tony get his just deserts – but old habits die hard. And anyway, more trouble was the last thing she needed at the moment. 'Yes, it was me. It was just when he fell and I saw the blood, I thought he was dead or something. That's when I screamed, you see. Sorry. I didn't mean to cause a fuss.'

Neither cop seemed convinced. The taller one asked, 'What's your name?'

'Lolly Bruce.'

'And is this your flat?'

'It's mine,' Jude said.

'And you are?'

'Jude Rule.'

'Would you like to tell us what happened?'

Jude hesitated, perhaps as tempted as Lolly had been to tell the truth, but eventually he simply shrugged. 'It's like she said. We were messing about and Tony tripped. That's when Lol screamed. She panicked. That's all it was, nothing else.'

'You see?' FJ said. 'We were just messing. Can we go now?'

'I'm fuckin' bleeding here,' Tony said.

The tall cop ignored him. He studied Lolly for a while. She smiled back, trying to look relaxed. He glanced at the other three, knowing everyone was giving him bullshit and also that there was sod all he could do about it. Eventually when he could see that nobody was going to budge on the story he gave a cursory nod. 'Okay, but maybe you could be a bit more careful when you're *messing about* in future.'

'We will,' Lolly said. 'Sorry.'

The two officers escorted the Cecil brothers out. Jude closed the door behind them and returned to the living room. He picked up the phone, sighed and put it down again. It was only then that he addressed Lolly, but not to ask how she was or to offer a mug of hot sweet tea after the shock of it all.

'What did you mean about the alibi?'

She slumped down on the sofa, wanting to cry but

forcing herself not to. There was something adrift with him, she thought, with the way his mind worked. Anyone normal would have offered her some comfort, fussed around her, made sure she wasn't hurt.

'Nothing. I was just winding him up.'

'Well, that was a good move,' he said sarcastically.

Lolly touched her head where Tony had almost yanked out her hair. 'Thanks for reminding me.' She could have told him about Tony's sexual preferences, about the secret he preferred to keep hidden, but thought it might do more harm than good. If Jude gave even a hint of knowing, Tony wouldn't be slow to silence him. She gave herself a mental shake. Christ, even now she was trying to protect him. What was wrong with her? But then again, she owed him for the timely blow with the typewriter so maybe that made it all right.

'They'll come back,' she warned. 'They've got it in for both of us.'

'I'm getting out of Kellston. If you've got any sense you'll do the same.'

'And go where?'

'Anywhere the Cecils aren't. This place is a dump anyway. I should have left when my dad did.'

'Will you go and stay with him?'

'What, with him and his tart? No thanks. I'd rather sleep under a bridge. Once I've got my visa sorted I'm out of this country for good.'

Lolly didn't hate the place the way he did. She just hated some of the people in it.

Standing up, she went over to the window to check the coast was clear and that the Cecil brothers weren't still hanging around. There were questions she hadn't asked, about Esther, about the murder, but she'd lost her taste for investigation. 'I'd better go,' she said. 'If I don't see you again, good luck with everything.'

Jude was playing with the typewriter, checking out the keys. He glanced at her and nodded. 'Yeah, you too.'

As she walked towards the hall, he said, 'Hey, Lolly?'

She turned, thinking he might have something more heart-warming to say. 'Yeah?'

'In case you're wondering, I didn't kill her. Esther, I mean.'

'No, of course not.'

He nodded again, half smiled and went back to his typewriter.

And what about Amy? she might have asked, but she didn't.

50

Thursday 22 September. Kellston

Freddy had strolled around the twelfth-floor corridors, trying to figure out which flat the girl had gone into. He'd listened at a few doors but hadn't heard anything other than TVs and radios and a baby crying. Then the Cecil brothers had shown up. Those two were always on the hunt for trouble, psycho skinheads with blood on their boots.

He'd watched from a safe distance until they'd entered the flat. The same one as the girl? At the time, he hadn't been sure. It could just have been coincidence that they'd all turned up on the same floor. A few minutes had passed and then the screaming had started. Now he wasn't going to go knocking on that door, not with the brothers on the other side of it. He wasn't a fool. No, he'd scarpered outside onto the walkway.

But he wasn't the only one who'd heard the screams. Some old crone, the type who didn't like her afternoon nap being disturbed, came rushing out from the floor underneath and leaned over the balcony to roar at a couple of cops who must have been there to harass another resident. They'd come clattering up the steps, probably hoping for a murder in progress. Freddy, who wouldn't normally get involved, had made an exception in this case and pointed them in the right direction.

Then he'd stood back and waited to see what would happen next. The cops hadn't stayed long, leaving with the brothers in tow. No ambulance. No battered corpse. No sign of the brown-haired girl. He was wondering how much longer to wait when his patience was finally rewarded. She came out of the flat and headed for the landing.

Freddy followed behind, his heart starting to race. Was he going to talk to her? He hadn't decided yet. But opportunities like these didn't come along every day.

Lolly didn't take much notice of the man who got into the lift with her. They went through the odd procedure that probably occurs in most British lifts when strangers are forced together in a confined space: a slight nod of acknowledgment without actually making eye contact. Her fingers hovered over the buttons. 'You want the ground floor?'

'Ta.'

The doors closed and her nose was instantly assailed by three equally powerful smells: dope, pee and the musky aroma of cheap aftershave. She tried not to breathe too deeply. Her body was hurting in several different places including her scalp, her knees and her wrist. What if the lift doors opened and the Cecils were waiting for her? She could have taken the steps instead but twelve flights were a long way to walk when your legs were still feeling shaky.

The man cleared his throat, glanced at her and said, 'Those two should be locked up.'

Lolly, startled, looked at him properly for the first time. An innocuous looking man in his thirties – fawn trousers, fawn shirt, beige cardigan and cream raincoat – with a curiously childlike face. 'Locked up?' she echoed.

'The Cecil brothers. They should be behind bars. Best place for them.' And then, before she had the chance to respond, he added, 'I was the one who called the police, you know. Well, not called exactly – they were already here – but I told them which flat it was.'

'Oh, well it wasn't anything really. But thanks.'

'I heard the screaming.'

'Oh,' she said again.

'I'm Alan, by the way, Alan North.'

Lolly raised her eyes to the bank of lights above the metal doors, watching the progress of their descent and willing the lift to move faster. She knew it would be rude not to give her name in exchange, but the bloke, although he was probably harmless, freaked her out a bit. 'I'm Lita,' she said eventually, choosing her West Henby name rather than her Kellston one.

'That's pretty.'

Lolly forced a smile. 'Thank you.'

'Do you live on the estate?'

'No, I was just visiting a friend.'

'And you're all right? You're not hurt or anything?'

'I'm fine.'

'It's rough, this place. You should be careful.'

The lift finally came to a shuddering halt and the doors opened. 'Well, nice to meet you,' she said quickly as she scooted out. She thought he said something in return but by then she was already legging it across the foyer. She'd had enough of men for one day.

Freddy watched her leave, pleased with the exchange even though it had been a short one. Next time he bumped into her he'd have an excuse to stop and chat. *Lita.* He rolled the name over his tongue, murmured it, liked the sound. She was quite pretty close up in a girl-next-door kind of way. And she had nice hands. He always noticed hands. Hers were small with slender fingers and tidy nails.

The rain was coming down harder now, but he didn't rush home. He wanted to savour the moment. It was a shame they hadn't had the chance to talk more. It was clear, however, that she wasn't on good terms with the Cecils. That was excellent news for him. Those boys were dangerous, and damsels in distress were his speciality. Although he was no closer to finding out what her connection was to Dana Leigh, he had taken the first step in getting to know her.

His face fell as he thought about Dana. It wasn't his fault what had happened. Sometimes women pushed you too far, made you lose your temper, made you do things you later regretted. It would have all been different if she'd just listened, for God's sake. How many times had he told her? Well, there was no point crying over spilt milk. What was done was done. It was time to move on.

51

Thursday 22 September. Shoreditch and Harlow

It was that time of day, late afternoon, when trade was slack at Marcie's. There was a ghost town feel to it, a sense of abandonment. It was only when Nick looked more closely that he was able to make out a few customers huddled in the corners. Music was playing and a girl was on stage slowly divesting herself of her clothes with all the enthusiasm of a grandmother forced to relinquish her cardigan on a cold winter's day. The smell of cigarette smoke and cheap perfume drifted on the air.

He chose a table near the back and sat down. A waitress wearing a skimpy black mini dress was on him straight away.

'What can I get you, sweetheart?'

He ordered a beer, the cheapest drink available, and watched her face fall. Another cheapskate she was thinking, and she was right. 'Could I have a word, if you're not too busy?'

Interest flickered in her eyes again. She sat down opposite him, hoping perhaps for an offer she couldn't refuse. 'Never too busy for a handsome young man,' she said. 'What can I do for you?'

Nick tried to keep his gaze on the horizontal and not let it slide down to her ample cleavage. This was easier said than done as she deliberately leaned forward and batted her eyelashes. 'I'm investigating the murder of Brent Sandler,' he said. 'I understand he used to come here.'

Instantly she drew back, her eyes narrowing. 'What are you, a cop?'

He took out his ID and slid it across the table. 'Private investigator. I'm trying to clear Vinnie Keane's name. I don't think he killed Sandler.'

She examined the ID closely and then handed it back. 'You working for Terry then?'

'I'm working for Vinnie,' he said. He shrugged. 'Although I suppose that means I'm working for Terry too in a roundabout sort of way.'

She thought about this for a moment, but then shook her head. 'I don't know why you're asking me. I don't know anything. Why would I?'

'Because you're a smart girl and you keep your eyes and ears open.'

'You know what else smart girls do?' she said, pointing towards her mouth. 'They keep this zipped.'

'Even if it means Vinnie Keane going down for life? The law have got him right in the frame. If they have it their way, he'll be spending the next twenty years behind bars.'

The girl wrinkled her nose. 'I wish I could help but . . . '

Before she could give him the brush off, he said, 'Look, I'm just trying to find out some more about the man. Sandler, I mean. I've heard he wasn't the most popular punter in the world.'

She left a long pause before she said, 'I can't stay here with you, not unless you buy me a drink. House rules, I'm afraid.'

Nick could already feel his wallet growing lighter. 'Go on then, but I'm not Rockefeller so try not to go mad.'

She grinned, stood up and sashayed over to the bar in her high heels. A few minutes later she was back with a tray. One glass of beer and one glass of champagne. 'Okay,' she said, sitting down again. 'Sandler. But this is off the record, right?'

'Off the record,' he agreed.

'Well, he had a temper on him, I can tell you that much. None of the girls wanted anything to do with him.' She glanced around the room, making sure nobody was paying attention. 'Trouble is, you can't pick and choose in this business. Yeah, he was a prize bastard. Liked to play rough if you get my meaning.'

'Terry wouldn't stand for that, would he?'

'It depends.'

'On what exactly?'

'Let's just say Terry gave him more leeway than the other punters. They did business together, didn't they? He wanted to keep him sweet.'

'Even if that meant overlooking his ... erm ... nastier tendencies?'

She sipped her champagne, or what passed for champagne in this joint, and nodded. 'Within reason.'

'Were you working last Thursday night?'

'I work every night, apart from Sunday.'

'Sandler was here, wasn't he? He left his motor out in the car park, didn't drive home. Do you know what time he left, who he left with?'

'Last Thursday,' she repeated, frowning. 'Let me think.'

Nick drank some weak beer while she tried to separate this particular night from all the other probably identical ones. 'It was the same night that girl was murdered in Kellston,' he said, trying to jog her memory. 'Dana Leigh.'

Her face tightened. 'You think he had something to do with that?'

'Not that I know of, although . . . but he didn't take his car so it seems unlikely. Unless he got a cab to drop him off, did the deed and got another cab home. It's not impossible but a bit risky. One of the drivers could have remembered him.'

'He was the type,' she said. 'A real woman hater. I wouldn't put it past the sod.' More champagne disappeared down her throat. 'You know, I reckon he might have spent some time with Candy. Or was that Wednesday? No, I think it was Thursday. That's who you need to talk to.'

'Is she here?'

'No, not today. She only usually does Friday and Saturday but we were short last week so she covered for another girl. She'll be at Dean Street this evening, after seven. I don't know the number but it's over a record shop. You'll find it; her name's on the bell.'

'Okay, thanks. Will she talk to me, do you think?'

'She might. I can't make any promises. She likes Vinnie though, everyone does.' A couple more customers came into the club and she pushed back her chair. 'I have to go. When you see him, tell him Stacey said hello.'

'I'll do that,' he said.

While Nick finished his beer, he looked round the room. It wasn't any more appealing now than when he'd first come in. A different girl was on the stage, going through the same routine of taking off her clothing, step by step. There was nothing sexy about it, nothing even faintly erotic. Or maybe he just wasn't in the mood. Murder tended to do that to you.

He paid on the way out, an outrageous bill that made his eyes water. But he didn't argue. The bruiser on the door, although not quite Vinnie's size, was built for trouble. Had it been worth the money? He'd find out later.

Back on the street he pondered on what to do next. With time to kill before he could see Candy, he considered going back to Primrose Hill and putting in a few more hours. He weighed up the pros and cons, mainly cons, and decided against it. If Laura Sandler had been involved in the murder of her husband she wouldn't be putting a foot wrong until she knew the law were off her case.

Eventually he decided to head for Harlow and see what he could find out about Hazel and Vicky Finch. It was one of those loose ends that needed tying up. He knew what Heather had told him, but what she had told him might not be the whole truth. If he'd thought he could have asked her for the address this morning, but then again that might not have been the best idea. It would only have alerted her to the fact that he was checking out her story.

While he drove, his mind was skipping from one subject to another and focusing on none of them: Esther's murder, Sandler's murder, Vinnie's affair, Mal's disappearance, Lolly's trouble with Terry. It was hard to know what to prioritise. He still found it hard to believe in Mal Fury's innocence and he wondered how Lolly would cope if he was found to be guilty. She would stand by him, he thought, no matter what he'd done.

Harlow was one of those post-war new towns in west Essex that had been built to offer decent living accommodation after the ravages of the Blitz. The housing estates were separated by green spaces, and there were plenty of recreational facilities: sports centres, a swimming pool, even a skating rink. It had been designed, Nick suspected, to some kind of utopian ideal, a place where the poor could prosper, but he wasn't entirely sure they'd pulled it off. Although all seemed calm on the surface, he sensed a kind of fraying round the edges. Everything that had once been new and fresh was gradually starting to decay.

When he got to the town hall it was already after four. With less than an hour to spare before it closed he rushed inside the high-rise building, located the right floor, took the lift, entered the department, requested access to the electoral register and then began to trawl through the lists.

It was another twenty minutes before he found what he was looking for. Hazel Finch was registered as living at 41 Elmington Road. He scribbled down the address in his notepad and then checked out exactly where it was from the map on the wall. Once he had the directions firmly in his head, he headed back to the car.

Traffic was starting to build up as he negotiated the streets. People were returning home from work, tired and impatient and fractious. He drove carefully, keeping an eye on his fellow drivers. His car was battered enough without another prang to add to the collection. Anyway, he wasn't in a hurry. If Heather was right, the Finches had already abandoned the nest.

Elmington Road was a yellow brick terrace of two-up two-downs with small front gardens. He found a parking space a few doors down from forty-one, turned off the engine and studied the house. It looked neat and tidy from the outside, the paint-work fresh, the net curtains white. No sign of life, although it was too early for any lights to be on. He peered up at the first floor – more nets along with dark-coloured curtains – and wondered if there was the slightest chance of Vicky Finch being Kay Fury.

A light smattering of rain fell against the windscreen. It would be a tragedy, he thought, if the long-lost child was to be discovered just as her birth mother had been murdered. Almost simultaneously another thought jumped into his head: if Vicky *was* Kay the one person who would want to stop the truth coming out would be Hazel. But, so far as he knew, she hadn't been at the party, and anyway wouldn't Heather be the more likely target? Unless she was next on the list . . .

He pulled a face. Now he was getting into the realm of soap opera. Before his imagination could run away with him he got out of the car and strolled down to the house. He pressed the bell, stood back and waited. Unsurprisingly there was no response. He tried again. When it was clear that no one was home, he had a quick look round, established that he was not being obviously watched, moved over to the front window and pressed his nose against the glass.

The living-room walls were papered in a bright swirly pattern. There was a sofa and two chairs, a coffee table and a large TV in a cabinet. What there wasn't was any sign of someone currently in occupation. No mugs on the table. No newspapers or magazines. No items of clothing left lying around. Nothing to suggest that someone might be back soon. But maybe they were just the tidy sort. Heather had suggested that mother and daughter had scarpered and if the property had been let out furnished this was entirely possible.

He stood back, not wanting to look like a burglar who was casing the joint. He glanced at the houses either side. Which one to try first? He retreated to the pavement, chose the one on the left, prepared his spiel and advanced up the path. There was no bell so he gave a couple of sharp raps on the door. Nobody answered. He looked at his watch – ten past five – wondering if it was too early. People who worked would still be travelling home. He'd try the house on the right and if that got no result he'd do one more either side and then go and wait in the car for a while.

Luckily, he had more joy this time. The door was answered by a middle-aged woman with a frizzy perm. She was holding a tea towel which she proceeded her wipe her wet hands on. 'Hello,' she said, her plump lips almost but not quite smiling, as though she hadn't made up her mind yet whether he was friend or foe.

'Hello,' he said. 'I'm sorry to disturb you, but I'm trying to get hold of Hazel. Next door? I've been ringing for the past few days but nobody answers the phone so I thought I'd come over and . . . '

'You a friend, love?'

'Her cousin,' he said. 'Tom. Tom Finch.' He was counting on the fact that if Hazel hadn't lived here for long, her neighbours might not be too familiar with the family tree. 'I've been working up in Glasgow and haven't seen her for a while so . . . She does still live here, doesn't she? She hasn't moved out or anything?'

'Heavens, no. Think I'd have noticed if she had. No, they're just away on holiday, love, having a bit of a break. We all need those every now and again.'

'You're not wrong there,' Nick said, glancing up at the sky. 'I wouldn't mind a bit of sunshine myself.'

'Oh, they've not gone anywhere fancy. Not abroad or anything. Only a caravan in Clacton but it's better than nothing.'

'I wouldn't turn my nose up,' he agreed. 'Still, it's a shame I missed them. I'm only back for a few days.'

She smiled, easy with him now. 'I wish I had a niece who'd whisk me away – even if it was only to Clacton.'

Nick took a gamble. 'Ah right, have they gone away with Heather?'

The woman looked blank.

'Short fair hair,' Nick said. 'Drives a red Mini.'

'That's the one,' she said. 'Turned up . . . when was it now? Over a week ago. It must have been. Hazel popped round to let me know, asked if I'd feed the cat while they're away.'

'I don't suppose you know when they're due back?'

'Monday, I think, or it could be the weekend. She didn't seem too sure.'

'Ah well, I'll give her a ring next week, see how the holiday went. Thanks for your help.'

'I'll tell her you called by.'

Nick nodded and waved and walked back to the car. He didn't hang about but started the engine straight away and set off back to London. He'd learned something that didn't altogether surprise him – Heather had lied about the Finches doing a disappearing act. She had spirited them away, presumably so that neither Esther nor anyone else could find out the truth. But what was she trying to hide? That Vicky was Kay Fury or that she wasn't? That small detail was still missing from the picture.

52

Thursday 22 September. Kellston

Lolly couldn't settle in the flat. Her feet pounded the carpet as she paced from one side of the living room to the other. She felt angry and frustrated, angry at what Tony Cecil had done to her, frustrated by her lack of progress with Laura Sandler. How was she supposed to help Vinnie when she couldn't even talk to the damn woman? Although she knew Nick was right, that she might do more harm than good if she confronted her, it went against her nature to just sit back and do nothing.

At half past five, unable to bear the confines of the flat any longer, she went out and dashed across the road to the phone box. It rang for a long while before a girl eventually answered.

'Yeah?'

'Is Stella there, please?'

'No, hon, she's not in.'

Lolly didn't recognise the voice – someone new, someone to replace Dana, perhaps. 'Is she at the Fox?'

'I dunno. She could be.'

Sensing that this was the best she was going to get, Lolly thanked her and rang off. She picked up the change from the slot, pushed open the door and stepped back out into the rain. Pulling up the hood on her raincoat, she began walking down the road towards the pub. She needed some company, someone to talk to, and a drink wouldn't go amiss either. Perhaps a few stiff voddies would silence the clamour in her head.

When she got to the Fox the first thing she did was check out the car park to see if Terry's motor was there. It wasn't. This was good news although she was still wary as she stepped inside the pub. Immediately her gaze flew over to his usual table but it was empty. Relief flooded through her. She didn't want to see Terry's accusing eyes tonight or listen to any more of his angry words. She'd done wrong, she knew that, but what choice had she had? Without the ring, Mal wouldn't have stood a chance.

The girls were seated near the back. Stella was there along with Jackie and Michelle and a few other faces she vaguely recognised but couldn't put a name to. She bought herself a vodka and tonic at the bar – she couldn't afford to fork out for a round – and then went over to the table.

'Hello, love,' Stella said, shuffling to the right so Lolly could squeeze onto the bench beside her. 'Come and sit beside me.'

'You okay?' Lolly asked, although the question was redundant. She could see that Stella was already drunk, her eyes glazed and unfocused, her hand struggling to light the cigarette hanging from her lips.

'Oh, I'm fine and dandy. You know me. Nothing gets me down for long.'

'Try telling your face that,' Jackie said.

'Oh, fuck off,' Stella muttered, although not with her usual spirit. 'How are *you* doing, hon?' she asked Lolly.

'I'm good, ta.'

'Glad to hear it.'

Stella gave no indication of knowing about Esther's murder, and Lolly decided not to enlighten her. No one needed another violent death to think about. She was aware of the atmosphere at the table. There was a brittle quality to the girls' voices, a false boldness and bluster as they tried to blank out the fear that what had happened to Dana could just as easily happen to them. They were joking and bantering, exchanging stories about punters – weird cocks, floppy cocks, the rough men and the quiet ones, the blokes who liked to pee on them.

Nothing the girls said shocked Lolly. She had heard it all before, and worse. The conversation flowed over and around her. There was a chance, she knew, that she could have ended up working the Albert Road if Mal hadn't taken her away from Kellston. Few of the women actually chose the occupation but slipped into it through poverty or abuse. Without a decent education, without support, when you were emotionally damaged, options were always limited.

Lolly's knowledge of sex, at least in a practical sense, was also limited. However, she was no longer a virgin and was pleased about that. It was a label she had worn around her neck for too long. Sometimes she had imagined she would stay intact for ever, that she would never meet anyone she would even want to share a bed with. Well, no one apart from Jude and that had always been a non-starter. Pascal, a French student, had been refreshingly different from the blokes she usually met: funny and gentle and smart, away from home for a year and as lonely as she was. It had not been a sweep-you-off-your-feet romance, but they had enjoyed each other's company and that, at the time, had been enough. He was back in Rouen now and although she had said she would visit she knew she never would.

'I'm sticking with my regulars,' a pale red-haired girl said. 'Least till they catch the bastard.'

Stella puffed on her cigarette and said softly, 'He probably *is* somebody's regular.'

There was a collective shudder as this thought sank in.

'I'll tell you something for nothing,' Jackie said. 'Joe Quinn wouldn't have stood for it, not on his patch. He'd have caught the shithead by now, cut off his balls and rammed them down his throat.'

Stella gave a snort. 'In the good old days, huh? Joe only ever got off his arse when there was something in it for him.'

Lolly wondered if Stella had made any progress in tracking down the mysterious Freddy but suspected not. It was like searching for a needle in a haystack. She decided not to mention her abortive visit to the library. There was still the *Gazette* to try but she didn't really fancy it. With everything else that was going on she was better off staying away from reporters.

'I spend the whole time looking sideways at them,' Michelle said. 'I'm always wondering, you know, if it could be *him*. You start imagining all sorts.'

'He'll do it again,' Jackie said. 'That type always do.'

Stella emptied her glass and rose unsteadily to her feet. 'I need a pee.'

'You'll need a fuckin' stomach pump if you go on knocking them back like that.'

Stella waved away the comment and stumbled towards the Ladies.

'She needs her head seeing to, that one,' Michelle said as soon as she was out of earshot. 'She's just looking for trouble.'

'What do you mean?' Lolly asked.

'She's been hanging round the arches, hasn't she? Reckons the bastard will come back at some point, have another go. She'll end up the same place as Dana if she carries on like this.'

Lolly shivered. 'Jesus, can't you stop her?'

'Think we haven't tried? She won't listen to no one.'

Horrified, Lolly jumped up and followed Stella to the toilets. She found her standing there, staring blankly into the mirror, her fingers gripping the edge of a sink. Her eyes were like deep hollows. She didn't ask if she was okay – she quite clearly wasn't – but instead laid a hand over hers.

'Are you going to be sick?'

Stella shook her head. 'I can't bear the thought of it, Lol. What he did to her. It tears me up, makes my guts ache. And he's still out there somewhere, walking around and breathing fresh air. It ain't right.'

'I know.'

'And the filth are doing fuck all about it. It's like she was nothing, nobody. Like she just didn't matter. As if she wasn't worth caring about.'

'*You* know she was worth it. *You* cared.'

Stella pulled her hand away and turned on the cold tap. She splashed some water on her face and stared at her reflection again. 'Look at the state of that,' she said, trying to smile. 'It's enough to scare the horses. Get us a paper towel will you, hon?'

Lolly fetched a couple of towels and passed them over. 'Is it true that you've been going down the arches?'

'That bloody Jackie been shooting her mouth off again?'

'It wasn't Jackie. It doesn't matter who it was. They're all worried about you. Why are you going there? I thought you were looking for this Freddy bloke.'

Stella wiped her face, taking off a layer of foundation at the same time. 'I am. That's where he's going to be, isn't it? He must have known about the place to take her there. I reckon he'll come back sooner or later and when he does I'll be waiting for him.'

'For fuck's sake,' Lolly said. 'For one, if he's got any sense he'll never go near the place again, and for two, what if some other bastard decides to have a go? You know what it's like down there. It's full of bloody psychos.'

'I can take care of myself.'

'You're ninety-nine per cent alcohol, and you can hardly stand up. How is that in any way taking care of yourself?'

'I didn't say I was going there tonight, did I?'

'I'm worried about you. Everyone is.'

'Yeah, you said.'

'So why aren't you listening?'

Stella crumpled up the paper towels and dropped them in the bin. She suddenly looked old, exhausted. 'Sometimes you don't have any choice,' she said. 'Sometimes you have to fight back.'

'Not this way,' Lolly said, frightened for her friend. 'Getting yourself killed isn't going to change anything.'

But Stella seemed beyond caring. She ran a comb through her hair and reapplied her lipstick. The red looked very bright against the grey paleness of her face. 'You know what we need, hon? Another bloody drink. I'm spitting feathers here.'

53

Thursday 22 September. Soho

It was still too early to see Candy and so instead Nick did a quick tour of the West End pubs that his colleague Mickey Ross frequented. He found him on the fourth attempt, perched on a stool at the Red Lion, nursing the last inch of a pint of Guinness.

'Ah, here you are. I've been looking all over for you.'

'And now you've found me. If you're after cover, you're out of luck. Anyway, I thought you were off for a few days.'

'I am. It's not that.' Nick sat down beside him and gestured towards his glass. 'You want another?'

'Depends what it's going to cost me.'

'Ten minutes of your time.'

Mickey shrugged. 'I reckon I can manage that.'

Nick beckoned the barman over and ordered a couple of pints. 'I need to talk to you about Brent Sandler.'

'How come you get all the fucking excitement?' Mickey grumbled. 'I follow the bloke around, and what? Nothing but hours of fuckin' tedium. The minute you take over ... bang! The bloke gets aced in broad daylight.'

'Yeah, I get all the fun. Next time I hear someone's going to be murdered on my watch, I'll be sure to give you a call. That way you can spend hours down the cop shop with the law shining a light in your eyes instead of mine.'

'That bad, was it?'

'Bad enough.'

The barman put the drinks down in front of them and Nick paid him.

'Cheers,' Mickey said, lifting his pint. 'So what are you after? What do you want to know?'

'What Sandler was doing on Monday.'

'All the paperwork's in the office.'

'Exactly. That's why I'm asking you.'

'What difference does it make now? The bloke's brown bread. Case closed.'

'Not for Vinnie Keane,' Nick said. 'He's looking at life for something he might not have done.'

'What's it to you? Let the law sort it out.'

'The law doesn't give a damn. Come on, Mickey, all I want to know is where he went, who he met, what his movements were that day.'

'You want to know what he ate for his lunch too?'

'The devil's in the detail.'

Mickey drank some more Guinness and licked the froth off his upper lip with his tongue. 'Monday,' he said. 'Let me think.'

'It's not that long ago.'

'I'm just trying to ... yeah, he was at his office most of Monday. Only went out once. Had a meet in Mayfair early afternoon, same pub as on the Friday, that flash joint on Mount Street. Came out looking pretty pleased with himself.'

'He always looked that way,' Nick said.

Mickey shrugged. 'More pleased than usual then. He was with Les Poole. The two of them spent over an hour together.'

'Was Terry Street there?'

'No, it was just Poole and Sandler.'

'You sure?'

'I've got eyes, mate. Just the two of them, not even Poole's head buster and those two are usually inseparable.'

'Rico,' Nick said.

'Yeah, that's the scumbag. I slipped into the pub to take a look, hung out at the bar for a while. Champagne, that's what they were drinking. All right for some. I reckon they were doing a bit of business. Poole gave him an envelope, a nice fat one.'

'Money?'

'Well, I haven't got X-ray vision so I couldn't swear to it, but it disappeared into Sandler's pocket pretty pronto.'

Nick mulled this over. Sandler was supposed to be Terry's man, not Les Poole's. You couldn't work for two masters. But maybe Sandler had been there on Terry's behalf, just collecting the dosh. He wondered how likely this was and decided not very. He couldn't see any reason for Poole to be paying Terry either. Even if, as was rumoured, a shaky peace had broken out between the two firms, it was still early days. Had any kind of deal been going down, Terry would have wanted to be there in person.

'You didn't think that was odd?' Nick asked.

'I'm not paid to think.'

Nick raised his eyebrows. 'Good thing or you wouldn't be collecting a wage packet at the end of every month.'

Mickey grinned, aware of his own shortcomings. 'You want my fuckin' help or not?'

'Okay, moving on. Did Sandler meet up with Terry Street after that?'

'Not that I know of. Certainly not on Monday.'

'Or on Tuesday. So maybe the payment wasn't for Terry.'

'You're thinking Sandler might have been double dealing, selling Terry up the river?'

'You see,' Nick said, 'this thinking business isn't beyond you after all.'

'Very funny. But if Terry got wind of what Sandler was doing, he'd want him dead. And who would he ask to do that? Maybe the law has got the right man after all.'

Nick sighed into his glass. For Lolly's sake, he hoped this wasn't true. If she couldn't find a way to clear Vinnie's name she'd be up the proverbial shit creek without a paddle. 'What about the wife, Laura Sandler?'

'What about her?'

'Got any opinions?'

Mickey leered over the rim of his glass. 'She's a looker, classy. I'd do her if that's what you're asking.'

'I wasn't.'

'What then?

'You ever see her with Vinnie Keane?'

'Nah, but I wouldn't, would I? We were only tailing Sandler. If Vinnie was doing the dirty, he wouldn't be around when the husband was.'

'I just meant out and about – here, there, anywhere. If they were seeing each other, they must have met up some place.'

'Sorry, mate, can't help you there. Be a bit risky to meet up in public though. Or her place come to that.'

'People do. It adds to the frisson.'

'The *frisson*?'

'The thrill of it all, the danger. That's what affairs are all about, isn't it? Sneaking around behind the spouse's back, playing with fire.'

'I wouldn't know. If the missus caught me at it, she'd slice my bloody bollocks off.'

'You'd better behave then.'

Mickey gazed morosely round the bar, as if temptation might suddenly present itself. 'Fat chance of doing much else.'

Nick, returning to the point, said, 'They probably met up at Vinnie's flat.'

'If he *was* shagging her, her prints are going to be all over the shop.'

'Unless she was very careful, and the only reason to be that careful was if a situation like this was likely to arise.' Nick wondered if the law had checked the flat for fingerprints. He couldn't imagine even the dimmest of cops would have taken Laura Sandler's denial of the affair at face value.

'You reckon she's fitted him up?'

'It's not impossible.'

Mickey drained his pint and put the glass down on the counter. 'Whichever way you view it he's screwed. Either he topped Sandler to get the wife or he topped him for double-crossing Terry. Christ, I wouldn't like to be in that bloke's shoes.'

Nick nodded, his expression grave. It wasn't looking good for Vinnie – or for Lolly.

54

Thursday 22 September. Soho

Nick found the record shop, now closed, without any bother. To the right was a chipped green door with the paint peeling off and beside that was a row of bells. He ran down the list of names, all female, until he came to the bell he wanted and then pressed it.

A crackly voice came over the intercom. 'Hi.'

'Hi. Is that Candy? I was just wondering if you're free. I'd like to—'

But Nick never got the chance to explain what he'd like to do. 'Second floor, love,' the voice said, and then the buzzer sounded, unlocking the door. He pushed it open and stepped inside.

There was a short narrow hallway leading to an uncarpeted flight of stairs. He tramped up two floors – the seedy décor would be enough to dampen anyone's ardour – until he came to a landing where one of the doors was ajar. He knocked lightly and waited.

'Come in, love.'

Nick went in.

The room was whitewashed, clean and tidy, dominated by a

king-size bed. Candy was in her early twenties, a long-legged peroxide blonde dressed in a shocking pink PVC dress and pink stilettoes. Her curves were what could only be described as generous. She smiled, showing a row of straight white teeth.

'And how are you?' she asked. 'What would you like today?' As though he'd just nipped into the corner shop for a few groceries.

'My name's Nick Trent,' he said. 'I'm a private investigator.'

Her smile faded. 'And what are you investigating, sweetheart?'

'I want to talk to you about Brent Sandler.'

'Never heard of him.'

'I've been told he was a regular of yours.'

'Then you've been told wrong.'

'Ah, come on, Candy. I'm trying to help Vinnie here. You don't want to see him go down for life, do you? Not for something he didn't do.'

Candy put her hand on her hip and stared at him. 'Look, hon, I'm running a business here, not a flaming charity. Don't even try appealing to my better nature 'cause I ain't got one.'

Nick took out his wallet. 'What are we saying then, a fiver?'

'A score,' she said.

'Ten and that's my final offer.'

Candy looked like she might hold out for the full twenty – her eyes were firm, determined – but then they softened a little and she seemed to have a change of heart. She held out her hand and he gave her the note. It quickly disappeared down the front of her dress. She sat down on the bed. 'Well then?'

As there was nowhere else to sit, Nick perched beside her. 'Sandler was at Marcie's last Thursday night, right?'

'He could have been.'

'He *was*. That was the night you covered for another girl, remember?'

'Yeah, I remember.' She paused as if in two minds how much to tell him, and then she continued. 'He was being his usual charming self. Trashed, of course. He was even worse when he was drunk and that's saying something. He wanted to come back here with me but I wasn't having any of it. I prefer my face the way it looks if you get my meaning.'

Nick nodded. 'I get it.'

'He used to be a regular but I stopped seeing him a few months ago. Some of the other girls were prepared to take their chances – he always paid well – but not me. What's the point of a purse full of cash when you're lying in a hospital bed?'

'Why didn't anyone report him?'

'For beating up a whore?' She gave an empty laugh. 'The law don't give a toss. And Sandler had half the Met in his pocket. They were more likely to charge the girl than him.' She laid her palms down on her smooth ivory thighs. 'I'm not going to say I'm sorry he's dead, because I'm not. He was one sick bastard and he's exactly where he deserves to be.'

'Got any ideas as to who might have done it?'

'I should think there was a long queue, hon.'

Nick was aware of the cedar smell of joss sticks mingling with Candy's perfume. The aroma of the burning sticks reminded him of church, of incense, which seemed curiously at odds with his current surroundings. 'Going back to Thursday. You spent some time with him, yeah?'

'A few hours, but only at the table. He didn't like sitting on his own or drinking on his own. And he enjoyed having someone to brag to.'

'What was he bragging about?'

'Oh, some deal or another. He didn't go into detail. But I got the impression it was big – and that he'd got the better part of it. He was like the cat that got the cream. He loved getting one over on people. It made him feel good. He was that type of bloke.'

'Never happy unless someone else wasn't.'

'You've got it, hon. That was him to a tee.' She stopped, looked at him and asked, 'Why does any of this matter? He was shot on Tuesday, wasn't he?'

'I'm just working my way back, trying to figure out why someone finally lost patience. Do you remember anything else about that night, anything unusual, anyone else he might have talked to?'

'No. Well, only Terry.'

'I don't suppose he mentioned Les Poole?'

'No.'

'Are you sure?'

'Yeah, I'm sure.'

'And what time did Sandler leave?'

'About midnight or thereabouts. He was too pissed to drive so Terry took him home.'

'Why didn't he just call him a cab?'

'I don't know, hon. You'd have to ask him that. Maybe he wanted to make sure he got home safely.'

Nick wondered if something had happened during that journey back to Primrose Hill. Had Sandler's mouth become loose? Had Terry decided he couldn't trust him? But then what was the point of asking Lolly to check out Laura Sandler? If Terry had done the deed there was nothing to be gained by it. Unless he wanted to know how much *she* knew.

'I've heard Vinnie was screwing Sandler's wife,' Candy said.

'News travels fast.'

'I've got a few cops like to come around. They're always a mine of information.'

'I thought you didn't do talking.'

Candy grinned. 'Depends on the circumstances, hon. When they're getting it for free, I like to get something in return.'

'You think he did it? Vinnie?'

'If he did, I'd shake his hand and buy him a drink. He's done every working woman in this city one big favour.'

Nick couldn't think of anywhere to go from here. He was no better off than when he'd arrived – and ten quid poorer. He stood up to go. 'Well, thanks for your time.'

'Always a pleasure.'

'Take care of yourself.'

'I will, babe. There's no one else to do it.'

'See you around.'

Nick was just opening the door when she said, 'I did hear something, a rumour. Can't say if it's true or not. About Laura Sandler.'

'Yeah?'

'About her and Les Poole.'

'What kind of something?'

She hesitated. 'You didn't hear this from me, right?'

'We've never even met.'

She gave him a cool look, but then nodded. 'Let's put it this way: from what I understand she and Poole have got history.'

'What kind of history?'

'The kind where *she* lies on her back, and *he* takes the money.'

Nick's eyebrows shot up in surprise. 'He was her pimp?'

'We're talking years ago here, nine or ten maybe, but apparently that's how Sandler met her. She was high-class, pricey, working out of one of the Mayfair hotels. He wanted her all to himself. She probably thought she'd hit the jackpot – rich solicitor, glamorous lifestyle – but I doubt it took too long before she realised it had been a big mistake.'

'But she stayed with him.'

Candy shrugged. 'Perhaps it was still better than what she'd had. Who knows? But everyone's got a breaking point and . . . '

'And maybe she reached hers.' He smiled. 'Thanks, Candy. That could be useful.'

She didn't smile back. 'Close the door on your way out.'

55

Thursday 22 September. Kellston and Primrose Hill

Lolly checked her watch as she left the Fox. Seven forty-five. Stella was on a binge, unstoppable and immoveable, refusing to go back to Albert Road while the pub was still dispensing alcohol. Seeing that she was beyond persuasion, Lolly had decided to call it a night and leave her in the care of the other girls. Stella was probably better off paralytic than down the arches where anything could happen.

It was dark now and still raining. She tramped through the puddles, the water seeping into her shoes as she headed for home. Nick would probably call by after he'd been to Marcie's. That's if he didn't get distracted by all that naked flesh. She felt a slight feeling of . . . she wasn't sure what it was exactly. Not jealousy, it couldn't be called that, but something faintly proprietorial lurked at the edges of her mind. She didn't like the idea of him ogling other women. Puzzled by this thought, she pushed it away, not wanting to investigate further.

Lolly took a few deep breaths, trying to clear her head. She wasn't drunk but she wasn't sober either. Drinking three voddies on an almost empty stomach hadn't been the best of ideas. All she'd had to eat today was that sandwich at Primrose Hill. A hollow rumbling came from the depths of her guts. Was there anything in the fridge? A few eggs, perhaps. She would make an omelette and eat it in front of the TV.

As she was crossing the road she noticed a bus waiting at the lights. 'Camden Town' it said on the front, and something clicked in her head. It seemed like a sign. She had just been thinking about Primrose Hill and now here was a bus going in that general direction. The fates were talking to her. And the lights were changing. With no time to weigh up the decision she jogged to the bus stop and put out her hand.

The journey passed in a blur. She was too preoccupied by what she would say to Laura Sandler to take any notice of the passing streets or her fellow passengers. She *had* to confront her whatever the consequences. She was sure she was doing the right thing. Either Laura had denied her relationship with Vinnie out of fear of becoming a murder suspect, or she'd deliberately set him up. The latter seemed more likely but it might not be the case. The truth was out there somewhere and the only way of getting it was face to face.

She got off the bus at Camden and strode purposefully along Parkway towards Regent's Park. While she walked she tried to construct the right questions, the ones that would matter, the ones that would force Laura into a confession. But the words kept dancing away from her. She'd get halfway through a sentence when something else jumped into her mind. And now she was thinking about Esther again, about her body lying on the ground by the lake, about Mal's desperate eyes.

She shook her head to try and clear it. Maybe she was drunker than she'd thought. The sound of the rain hitting the ground mingled with the noise of the cars and buses going by. At least her legs seemed to know where they were going. She was walking quickly, her feet hitting the pavement with a slap. Eventually, after a couple of right turns, she found herself on the street where Laura Sandler lived.

It was only when she reached the house – the lights were on, the curtains drawn – that she began to have second thoughts. Was this a crazy thing to do? What if Laura called the police and had her arrested? Her shoulders slumped. But she'd come this far, it seemed wrong to turn back. Yes or no? 'Don't be a coward', one voice whispered to her, while another murmured, 'Don't be a fool.' She decided to walk to the end of the street and back while she tried to decide which voice to listen to.

After leaving Candy, Nick had driven straight back to Kellston to share his information with Lolly. There had been no reply at her flat and he'd wondered if she was still with Jude Rule. But he'd dropped her off at the estate hours ago. Surely, she would be home by now. That's when he'd started to worry. Although she was convinced that Jude would never do her harm, her confidence could be misplaced. Jude's exact address was unknown to him. Somewhere in Haslow House, but the tower was vast with over a hundred flats.

He'd checked the takeaway and Connolly's but drawn a blank there too. His next port of call had been the Fox where he'd recognised some of the girls Lolly drank with and, to his relief, one of them had told him that she had left about fifteen minutes ago. He'd driven slowly back up the high street but there had been no sign of her. The flat had still been empty, the lights still off. He'd rechecked the takeaway and the caff. Where else could she have gone?

That's when he'd thought of Primrose Hill. Which was why he was here now, pulling up to the kerb a few doors down from the Sandler house and wondering if he was wasting his time. But he knew what Lolly was like. Once she got an idea in her head it was hard to shake it. He could see that the house was occupied but had no way of knowing whether she was inside or not. He prayed not. If what Candy had said was true, Laura Sandler was a dangerous woman.

He watched the rain fall against the windscreen, thinking about what Mickey and Candy had told him. A picture was starting to build. He'd got something, he was sure of it, even if all the details hadn't quite slotted into place. The Les Poole connection was an important one. Who else would Laura turn to if she was desperate? She knew the gangster wouldn't baulk at murder – not for the right price. And she'd have plenty of money once she was a merry widow.

He drummed out a beat on the steering wheel, unsure as to what to do next. For all he knew Lolly could be at home right now watching the telly with her feet up. Except she wasn't a feet up type of girl, not when something was bugging her. It was at that very moment, just as he was attempting to decide whether Lolly's drive was a virtue or a vice, that he noticed a figure strolling slowly down the street.

Nick smiled. Even with her hood up, he knew it was her. So he'd been right. She had come back. He watched her approach, ready to intervene if she turned into the Sandler place. There was a hesitancy about her, a nervousness, a sense of hanging back as though she was still undecided.

She stopped at the gateway and looked up at the house. Thirty seconds passed. Then, just when he thought she wasn't going to go through with it, whatever doubts she might have had seemed to suddenly evaporate. She pushed back her shoulders, took a visible breath and began to march towards the front door.

Nick leapt out of the car and sprinted the ten yards to the

house. 'Lolly!' he hissed as loudly as he dared, not wanting to alert Laura Sandler.

Startled, she turned. 'What are you doing here?'

'I need to talk to you.'

She didn't look keen on the idea. Having geared herself up for the big encounter, she clearly wanted to get on with it. She glanced from him to the front door and back again, irritation etched on her features. 'Go away. I have to do this.'

Nick nodded. Now wasn't the time for an argument. 'Okay, but just listen to what I have to say first. Two minutes, yeah, and then you can do what you like.'

Lolly stood and waited, as though he was about to explain right there and then.

'Not here,' he said, looking towards the lit window. 'Come and sit in the car.'

'Two minutes you said.'

'Two minutes I'd rather spend not getting soaked to the skin.' Before she could put up any further objections he took hold of her elbow and gently propelled her back down the drive. He could sense the frustration in her, the exasperation at being thwarted at the last moment.

They got into the Ford together. Lolly immediately folded her arms across her chest, like a defence against anything he might have to say. In the confines of the car he could smell wet clothes and alcohol. She'd obviously had a few drinks in the Fox before setting off. Dutch courage perhaps.

'Well?' she asked snappily. 'What is it?' And then before he could reply she added, 'I don't get what you're doing here. Have you been following me?'

Knowing that she wouldn't appreciate his concern for her welfare, no matter how well meant, he laughed and shook his head. 'Why the hell would I be doing that?'

'So it's just a coincidence then?'

'No, it's not a coincidence. You want to know what Laura Sandler's up to and so do I. I thought I'd drop by for half an hour and see what was happening.'

She considered this for a moment, staring at him, her eyes full of suspicion. Then she moved her head to gaze out through the windscreen at the rain. 'Yeah, right.'

Before she could start dwelling on his motives for being here, he quickly moved on. 'Look, I've found out something about Laura. I think you'll want to hear this.' And then he explained it all to her, everything Candy had told him about Les Poole. It wasn't a long story and she listened without interrupting. When he got to the end he said, 'I know it's not proof of anything but there is a connection between the two of them.'

'You sure she was telling the truth?'

'I think so. Candy strikes me as the type who knows what's going on. And it makes a twisted kind of sense. Laura wants rid of an abusive husband and Poole's happy to take the job on – for a price of course. But that's not a problem. She won't be short of money, not in the long term.'

'Why bother to involve Vinnie? Why not just arrange the hit?'

'Because it takes the heat off. She's going to be the number one suspect so she needs to convince the law that someone else had a better motive than she did. Enter Vinnie Keane: gangster, obsessive stalker, a man who just won't take no for an answer. I imagine he hasn't got an alibi either; she'll have made sure of that. The two of them needed a scapegoat and Vinnie fitted the bill perfectly.'

'Poor Vinnie.'

'You still want to go and have a chat with her?'

'Not so much,' she said.

'I think we should pay Terry a visit.'

'But we don't know anything for certain.'

'We know enough.'

Lolly wrinkled her nose, probably not relishing the thought of having to face Terry Street again. 'You think?'

'You want Terry off your back or not? We give him what we have and then it's down to him what he does with it.'

'What if he already knows about Poole being Laura's former pimp?'

'He might but I doubt it. It was before his time, years ago. He was just a cocky teenager with empty pockets and big ambitions when all that was going on.'

Lolly sighed and then nodded. 'Okay, let's go and look for him.'

56

Thursday 22 September. Kellston

The problem was that Terry could be in one of a number of places. Lolly wasn't even sure if she knew all the pubs and clubs he owned. But it was a weekday night and still relatively early so she suggested they try Kellston first. It turned out to be a good call. He wasn't in the Fox – and nor was Stella, she noticed – but they found him in the second place they visited.

Of all the pubs she'd ever been into, the Hope and Anchor was the worst. It was a small spit and sawdust dive, a throwback to another era, and had all the comfort of a prison cell. This was where local villains gathered to recruit for jobs, to make plans or just to chew the fat. Outsiders, especially women, were as welcome as a pork chop at a vegetarian supper.

Terry was sitting alone at the bar. She felt eight pairs of eyes follow them as they walked over to join him. Silence had fallen, a nasty kind of silence filled with menace. The effect of the booze, which had given Lolly courage earlier on, was rapidly wearing off. She had a headache and a dry mouth and that, combined with her uneasiness at seeing Terry again, was making her feel slightly sick.

'Can we talk?' she asked softly. 'It's about Vinnie. This is Nick Trent. He's a private investigator.'

Terry looked him up and down, said nothing.

'I work for Marshall and Marshall,' Nick explained.

That got Terry's attention. He rose to his feet, picked up his glass and gestured towards the rear of the pub. He then leaned over to the barman and ordered, 'Play some music.'

They took a seat to the dulcet tones of Fleetwood Mac singing 'Don't Stop'. Nick was the one who did the talking and Lolly was happy to leave him to it. He told Terry about how he'd been part of the team doing surveillance on Sandler. 'I've just spoken to one of the girls he visited on a regular basis and she reckons Laura Sandler used to be a tom, albeit a high-class one. The man she worked for was Les Poole.'

Lolly watched Terry to see his reaction, but he had his poker face on. It was impossible to know what he was thinking.

'And?' he said.

'Perhaps they've stayed in touch,' Nick said.

'You got any proof of that?'

'No. But he might be someone she'd turn to if she wanted help in getting rid of her old man.' Nick paused and then said, 'There's more. Sandler was observed meeting up with and receiving money from Poole on Monday. Do you know anything about that?'

This time there was a definite change in Terry's demeanour. 'What?'

'The Pear Tree in Mayfair. They had a cosy little chat, shared a bottle of champagne.'

Terry's eyes flashed. 'What are you claiming, mate? That Poole had Sandler in his pocket?'

'I'm not claiming anything. I'm just telling you what was observed. Do you have any reason to think Sandler might have been passing on information? Any good deals that went south recently?'

'Deals are always falling through.' But Terry had grown agitated and with that agitation came suspicion. 'Why are you telling me all this?'

'I wouldn't ordinarily. And I'm putting my job on the line just by being here. Let's call it a favour.'

'And what do you want in return?'

'Not a favour for you,' Nick said. 'For Lolly. You asked her for information on Laura and now you've got it, with something extra on Sandler thrown in. What you do with it is up to you.'

Terry sipped his whisky and studied them both. He didn't offer them a drink. After a while he said, 'If Poole *was* getting the lowdown from Sandler why would he agree to the hit? He'd be more useful to him alive than dead.'

'I don't know. Maybe he'd got all he wanted from him. Maybe he'd served his purpose and it was time to say goodbye before Sandler lost his nerve or let something slip and you found out what was going on. Maybe the money he was going to make from the hit was more important to him than the information he could get from Sandler. Or maybe he's the sentimental type and still has a soft spot for the lovely Laura.'

'For someone who knows jack shit, you've got a shitload of opinions.'

'They're only theories. Take your pick.'

Lolly could see the anger brewing in Terry, not at Nick but at Sandler's treachery. And at Les Poole's too, no doubt, although this would have come as less of a surprise. It all reflected badly on him, on his decisions and his judgement. If word got out it wouldn't do much for his reputation either.

She finally opened her mouth. 'Do you think any of this could help Vinnie?'

Terry looked at her, his expression dour. 'Yeah, I'm sure Les Poole's going to walk straight into the nick and confess everything.'

Before Lolly could respond to the sarcasm, Nick quickly asked, 'What about fingerprints at Vinnie's flat? Laura's dabs must be all over the place.'

Terry continued to stare at Lolly for a moment – a dark, unforgiving stare – before shifting his gaze to Nick. 'She's claiming she went there once, months ago, that Sandler had to pick up some documents and that they stayed for a brew. She's covered her arse in case she hasn't been as careful as she thought she was.'

'She'll have made a mistake somewhere along the line,' Nick said. 'They always do.'

'She made a fuckin' mistake the day she decided to screw over Vinnie Keane.'

Lolly didn't want to know what Terry planned on doing about it all. That was his business, not theirs. She caught Nick's eye and tried to telepathically convey that they should be leaving now. They'd done what they came to do and it was best to get out of there before Terry's rage exploded and they got caught in the fallout.

But Nick hadn't finished yet. 'One more thing,' he said. 'This has nothing to do with Sandler but . . . I'm wondering if you remember a man called Stanley Parrish? He was a private investigator too – and my uncle. I think he may have accidentally trodden on Joe Quinn's toes. Anyway, he was killed in a hit-and-run about six years ago.'

'Joe's dead too,' Terry said.

'I'm aware of that.'

'So what difference does it make?'

'It makes a difference to me. I'd just like to know. Call it closure if you like.'

Terry shook his head. 'I've never heard of him.'

Nick took out a pen and wrote his home phone number on the corner of a beer mat. 'Just in case anything comes back to you.' He pushed the mat across the table to Terry. Terry didn't touch it. Nick stood up and nodded. 'Thanks for your time.'

Lolly scrambled to her feet, relieved they were done.

Terry looked up at her. 'You still owe me for that diamond.'

'You'll get your money.'

'I'd better.'

With those ominous words ringing in her ears, Lolly turned and headed for the door with Nick. The eyes were on them again, hard glares, as if they were fair game now they'd left the circle of Terry's protection. She didn't look at any of them, not so much as a glance. She kept her gaze straight ahead and her chin up. Sometimes you had to pretend you were tougher than you were.

Once she was outside the breath seemed to leave her lungs in a rush. She was aware of her damp jeans clinging to her legs and the chill evening air. A shiver ran through her.

'I think our work here is done,' Nick said. 'You hungry?'

'Not very.'

'I could eat a horse. Blind fear always gives me an appetite.'

She was surprised by the admission. Most men liked to put on an act, to pretend they weren't afraid even when they were. 'I wouldn't have guessed,' she said. 'You were great in there.'

'Only a fool wouldn't be afraid of Terry Street, especially in the current circumstances. He didn't get to be boss by knitting scarves for the homeless.'

'Thanks for doing all this. I'm grateful, I really am.'

'Don't mention it. You're still not off the hook though.'

'Yeah, but at least it's a smaller hook.'

They got into the car and started the short journey back to

Lolly's. She didn't ask why he hadn't told her about the meeting between Sandler and Poole – she understood, when it came to his job, that some things were supposed to be kept confidential – and hoped he wouldn't live to regret telling Terry. He would lose his job if the Marshalls found out. While she was contemplating this, a question jumped into her head. 'Why would Poole bother to give Sandler money if he was going to shoot him the next day?'

'Why not?' Nick said. 'It lulled Sandler into a false sense of security, made him feel like he was in control. And it wasn't as if Poole would never see the money again. It would all go to Laura eventually.'

'I guess.'

They were quiet until they drew up outside Lolly's flat. Nick switched off the engine. 'You fancy sharing a takeaway? My treat.'

'It should be mine,' she said.

'Yeah, well, if you'd stop handing out diamond rings you might have some cash to spare.'

Lolly grinned. 'Okay, but I'm paying next time.' Then, on an impulse, she suddenly leaned across and kissed him quickly on the lips.

'What was that for?'

She wasn't sure how to answer. Perhaps she was still drunk. Except she didn't feel that drunk now. Because she was relieved to have cleared the air with Terry? Partly. But mainly because it had simply felt right. She shrugged. It could have been awkward but somehow it wasn't. 'Just for being here.'

As they got out of the car, Nick asked, 'Do you have any plans for tomorrow?'

'Nothing special.'

'How do you fancy a day out in Clacton?'

57

Friday 23 September. Kellston

Freddy woke with a start and stared into the darkness. A bad dream had brought him spiralling up from sleep and he could feel his heart thumping in his chest. The brown-haired girl, Lita, had been standing in front of him, her eyes accusing, her small pink mouth spitting out the words: 'You killed Dana! You killed Dana!' By the lifts it had been, down in the foyer, and other people had been gathered there, watching, listening, seeing him shamed in public.

Why had she done that? She should have been grateful – hadn't he saved her from the Cecil brothers? – but instead she was bent on trying to destroy him. That was women for you. Never happy, never satisfied, always looking to put the knife in. You could walk to the ends of the earth for them and they'd still find fault with the colour of your shoes or the route you took.

He was damp with sweat, anxious and agitated. What if she'd gone to the police already? That would mean a knock on the door sometime soon. They would snap the cuffs on his wrist and escort him from the flat with the maximum of fuss. Just so all the neighbours could see, just so they could all point the finger.

Pushing aside the bedclothes he turned his head to look at the alarm clock: it was only ten past twelve. He'd barely been asleep for an hour. He pressed the palm of his hand against his clammy chest, hoping he wasn't going to have a heart attack. He felt hot and cold and sweaty all at the same time. That wasn't a good sign. Lita's voice echoed in his head, as ominous as a death knell.

It was only a nightmare, he told himself. Calm down. Don't get in a stress. But dreams had meanings. They were thoughts and ideas locked inside your brain. She *knew* about Dana. She must. It was the only explanation. And a part of him, some subconscious part, had sensed it. She was playing a game with him, cat and mouse, trying to lure him into the open, to make him give up his secrets.

He couldn't go back to sleep now. He stared again at the luminous dial of the alarm clock. He stretched out one leg and then the other. Slowly he swung them over the side of the bed, his feet coming to rest on the roughness of the worn carpet. He stayed like that for a moment, listening to the rain smattering against the window before pulling himself upright.

He padded over to the chair, sorted through the clothes that were piled on it and got dressed. In the living room he stood listening to the snores of his mother. Once he was sure that she was fast asleep, he picked up his keys and left the flat, taking care to close the door quietly behind him.

The lift jerked down to the estate car park, a subterranean pit stinking of piss and dope and alcohol. It was ill lit and gloomy, full of shadows. He kept his eyes peeled for any lowlifes as he walked towards the car. You had to have your wits about you in a place like this. The old silver Vauxhall was exactly where it had been left – no one would bother to nick it, not even to go joyriding. It was old and battered, dented and scratched. That it still ran was a miracle.

He drove up to ground level, the dream revolving in his head. He couldn't shake it off. Resentment bubbled up inside him. What right did that girl have to accuse him? She was a bitch, a troublemaker, a fucking tart. She needed teaching a lesson.

It was quiet on the high street and even the takeaway was closed. He pulled in beside it and leaned over to peer up at Lita's windows. All dark. He considered getting out, ringing the bell, waking her up. Why should she sleep when he couldn't? He could confront her, right here, right now.

'I know your bloody game,' he would say. 'Stay away from me or you'll be sorry.'

Except, of course, that was exactly what she wanted. The words would be tantamount to a confession. She'd laugh in his face and then go and phone the cops. No, he had to bide his time until he thought of a better way to deal with her.

Driving on towards the station, his thoughts shifted to Dana. If she'd shown more respect, she'd still be alive today. He'd told her he needed more money to pay someone, a woman who could give them information about her mother. And what had she done? Turned up with nothing, sod all, claiming she'd had debts to pay. Well they both knew what sort of debts they were – for that fuckin' junk she couldn't stop taking. The girl hadn't known the meaning of priorities.

'A couple of days,' she'd said. 'I'll have it then, I swear. A couple of days won't make no difference, will it?'

And, of course, he'd seen red. Who wouldn't? He'd borrowed a tenner off his own mother and now he wouldn't be able to give it back and he'd be forced to put up with her moaning and groaning and saying what a shit son he was. That's when the idea had come to him.

'I've already set up the meet. I suppose I could pay her so long as you pay me back.'

'Oh, would you do that, Freddy?' she'd said. 'You're a real darlin''

And there'd been something about the way she said it, something that made him wonder if she was on to him, if that was why she wasn't paying out. Just taking the piss, laughing at him, letting *him* fork out for the info on *her* mother. Not that there was any info, or any woman, but she didn't know that. And everything had got confused in his head and all his hatred of the female sex had risen to the surface.

He'd only meant to scare her, but somehow it had got out of hand. 'We have to meet her at the arches.'

'That's a funny place to meet.'

'Not if you don't want anyone to see you. She's nervous, see, worried someone she knows might spot her.'

'Do you think she's for real?'

That doubt in her voice feeding his anger. As though his judgement couldn't be relied upon, as though he was the type of bloke who could be taken in by some lying bitch. 'I wouldn't be paying her otherwise.'

And Dana had trusted him so she'd let him lead her into that dark and dangerous place where the row of arches stood like gaping mouths. Only a thin light from the back of the station, barely enough to see by. Still, he'd had a good look round to make sure they were alone, that there wasn't some dosser curled up for the night or some tart turning a trick in the shadows.

'Over there. The one at the end.'

'It's a funny place to meet,' she'd said again.

It was the last thing she ever said to him.

58

Friday 23 September. Kellston

Stella wasn't sure what she felt. Not so much drunk as exposed, like her head had been cut open and a bright light shone into it. The Fox had closed over an hour ago and she'd come back to the house, gone upstairs and lain fully clothed across her bed. When sleep had eluded her, she'd headed down to the kitchen. There was no one else around.

She stood by the open back door, staring out into the night. Rain fell against the concrete of the yard. The air was heavy and humid like there was a storm brewing. In the distance she heard a rumble of thunder. When she turned she almost expected to see Dana sitting at the table, her fair hair falling around her face, her eyes as bright as a child's. For all her bravado, all her smart talk and lip, there had been something curiously vulnerable about the girl, something that had brought out Stella's maternal instincts.

What she felt was worse than just missing her. It was a physical pain that wouldn't go away, a wrenching at her heart. Anger and guilt and regret tumbled through her mind. For some people – and Dana had been one of them – there was no joy to be found in the world. From the moment she'd been dumped on that church doorstep, it was as though her future had been predestined, a short life of abandonment and despair.

She lit a cigarette and knew what she had to do.

The rain cooled her as she walked along the alley, following its curve until she emerged onto Albert Road. A couple of cars pulled up but she waved them away. The punters swore at her, hissing their displeasure but she didn't care. There was only one type of business she was interested in tonight.

She crossed at the lights and made her way round to the side of the station where a narrow road led down to the arches. The scene of crime police tape had already been pulled away. It lay coiled on the ground like a dead yellow snake. It was here, at the entrance, where she was clearly in view that she stopped and waited.

'Come and get me,' she murmured. 'I'm ready for you.'

The other girls said he wouldn't do it again, not so soon, wouldn't take the risk. Or that now his murderous desires had been sated it would be a while before they rose in him again. But they didn't know. Nobody did. The street girls were taking extra precautions, pairing up and writing down the registration number of every punter's car. Although this only worked if they agreed not to both be away at the same time. And it didn't stop you getting raped or beaten or strangled or stabbed; it just meant they might eventually catch the bastard who'd done it.

She sang softly under her breath while she waited, a song she remembered from long ago by the Everly Brothers: 'Bye bye love, bye bye happiness ... ' She paced a few yards to her left, turned and retraced her steps. The rain was coming down harder now but she barely noticed. Her mind was focused on one thing alone.

Time passed. Ten minutes, twenty. She didn't give up. She

remained on guard, patrolling her patch. And then she saw it, the light-coloured car slowing as it approached, the driver trying to make up his mind. He drove on past but then stopped and reversed, leaning across to wind down the window.

Stella walked over to the car and bent to talk to him. 'Hello, love.'

'You free?' he asked, as though there might be an invisible queue.

'Yeah.' She climbed inside. 'Where do you want to go?' Glancing at him, but not staring too hard – some punters didn't like your eyes on them – just enough to get a few impressions. Middle-aged, thin, brown-haired with a bland sort of face. Unmemorable. The type it would be hard to pick out in a line-up.

'Anywhere,' he said, but he was peering through the windscreen at the road leading down to the arches. 'Is it open down there?'

'It's always open, love.'

He seemed on edge, nervy, twitchy, his hands gripping the steering wheel. There was a thin sheen of sweat on his forehead. 'Okay,' he said.

She wanted to ask. 'What's your name?' but she didn't. It was pointless. Even if they told you, it was usually a lie. No ring on his finger but that didn't mean he wasn't married. Anxious because he didn't do this very often or for another reason?

The car bumped down the narrow road. Flanked by two high red brick walls, it had a claustrophobic quality, like a tall coffin. From where she was sitting she couldn't even see the sky. A piece of card in the shape of a Christmas tree hung from the rear-view mirror giving off a smell like disinfectant.

'Wasn't this where . . . erm, that girl?' he asked.

'It might have been.'

'I saw it on the news.'

His voice was tight, strained, London. His gaze flicked sideways, not at her face but her tits. That's all she was to him: tits and a cunt, a body to fuck. He wasn't interested in *her* name, her history, her grief. And after he'd fucked her what would he want then? Some kind of retribution, perhaps, for what she'd forced him to do.

They emerged into the dark expanse of the arches. He drove to the far end, pulled up and switched off the engine. He went to get out but she said coolly, 'That'll be a tenner.' She wasn't going anywhere without the cash. Always get it upfront in case they do a runner or decide, after they've shot their load, that you weren't worth the bloody money.

He looked for a moment like he was going to wrangle over the price, try and get a discount because of the wet and bedraggled state she was in. His mouth set in a thin, straight line. But then he got out his wallet and reluctantly passed over a couple of crumpled fivers. Stella shoved them down her bra and nodded. 'Ta.'

She opened the car door and stepped out into the rain. There was no one else around, at least no one she could see. The ground was wet, littered with rubbish, and she hoped he wasn't going to want to lie down. A thin streak of lightning flashed across the sky followed by a crack of thunder. The rain fell more heavily. He strode towards the mouth of the nearest archway as if he knew where he was going, as if he'd been here before. She had a bad feeling about him. It was instinct as much as anything else, a sense of something being off.

She wasn't afraid. She felt numb, disconnected. She wondered where Dana had died. There would have been markings, she thought, but it was too dark to see clearly. She walked beside the man, casting quick sideways glances, trying to read his expression. Inside the archway, black and smelly, he roughly pushed her up against the wall, his stale breath in her face, his hands all over her.

He fumbled for his flies, pulling out his cock like it was precious treasure. He pushed up her skirt and entered her with a groan. She looked over his shoulder at nothing. She listened to his heavy breathing, his grunts and growls, his whispered obscenities. His right hand, which had been gripping her breast, moved up towards her neck. She felt the fingers close around her windpipe. Her head, pinned against the wall, began to spin. She struggled but that was what he wanted, to feel that he was taking her by force, exerting his authority, proving his maleness.

There wasn't time to think twice. It was now or never. She reached into the pocket of her jacket, grabbed the knife and plunged it deep between his shoulder blades. He gave a gasp, stopped moving and then staggered back. She didn't look into his eyes. She stayed very still, watching as he silently revolved in a half circle, crumpled and then slumped to the ground.

Another flash of lightning lit up the sky. She stared down at him, his body unmoving, no breath coming from his lungs. His limp cock lay like a pale worm between his legs. She felt no pity, no guilt. She had done it quickly and painlessly, affording him a mercy he hadn't given Dana.

After a while she bent down beside him, pulled out the knife and returned it to her pocket. She walked over to the car – he hadn't locked it – opened the passenger door and cleaned the handles with the sleeve of her jacket, inside and out.

Then she walked away.

59

Friday 23 September. Clacton

Last night's storm had cleared the air. There was hazy sunshine and a light breeze, the perfect conditions for a day out by the sea. As Lolly climbed into Nick's car she flapped a piece of paper at him.

'Look what I got this morning.'

He grinned. 'I'm presuming that's an invitation from DI Latham, requesting the pleasure of your company tomorrow.'

'You got one too?'

'I got a phone call.'

Lolly put the piece of paper back in her bag and fastened her seatbelt. 'I don't understand why he wants to meet at the house. What's wrong with the police station?'

'Perhaps he wants to add a little drama to proceedings, bring us all together at the scene of the crime and hope one of us loses our nerve.'

'But you can't be a suspect. Why do they want to see you?'

'I'm as good a suspect as anyone else,' he said, with mock indignation. 'What's wrong with me?'

'You don't have any motive for wanting Esther dead.'

He started the car and set off along the high street. 'I might. Anyway, they're not looking for the murderer – Mal's firmly in the frame for the actual deed – they're looking for the person who *helped* the murderer.'

'Which puts me at the top of the list.'

'Yeah, it probably does, but they can't prove anything. Stick to your story and you'll be fine.'

Lolly sighed and nodded. She had gone over her story so many times in her head that a part of her was beginning to believe it was true. Mal hadn't been caught yet which was a relief, but he'd remain a fugitive until the real murderer was found. 'I wonder where he is,' she said, thinking aloud.

'Mal? You're better off not knowing.'

'Do you reckon Jude and Heather will be at West Henby too?'

'Can't think of any reason why they wouldn't be.'

Lolly watched the road go by for a while. Not wanting to dwell on Mal's fate, or Esther's come to that, she changed the subject. 'I've never been to Clacton before. What's it like?'

'Like most other seaside towns,' he replied. 'Sea, sand, pier, crazy golf, lots of candyfloss. You'll love it. We used to go there when I was a kid – well, to Frinton, which my dad thought was a cut above – and stay in a B and B on the sea front. I spent many a happy hour watching the rain hammering against the windows.'

Lolly, who had never been on holiday, envied him those childhood memories even if they had been sullied by the vagaries of the British weather. 'I bet you still had fun.'

'As much fun as you could have with a dad who disapproved of virtually everything.'

'Oh,' she said.

'Oh indeed.'

Lolly wished she'd had the chance to walk beside the sea with her mum. She'd have liked a memory like that, something special, something to store away and only take out now and again. Thinking of her mother made her sad so she tried to stop doing it. 'How many caravans do you think there are in Clacton?'

'Hundreds. Thousands maybe.'

'Are you planning on us checking out all of them?'

'Only the one that Hazel and Vicky are staying in.' He saw the look of surprise on her face and said, 'I did some ringing round this morning, all the main sites.'

'And you found out where they are?'

'Valley Park. It's near the centre.'

'Congratulations, Mr Trent. You really are a detective.'

'Thank you,' he said. 'It's always gratifying to have one's talents recognised.'

It was twenty past eleven by the time they arrived in Clacton. Nick parked as close as he could to the site. Valley Park had a sea view and was vast with caravans of all sizes lined up in rows. Finding Hazel would probably have been impossible without the information he'd managed to secure from the manager. Impersonating a police officer was getting to be a habit, a bad one, but it got results. It was surprising how much people would tell you if you claimed to be calling on behalf of the Met.

He examined the map at the entrance to the site, located the position and put his finger on it. 'Right there,' he said. 'On the left. Let's go find Hazel.'

As they walked Lolly said, 'You don't really think Vicky is Kay, do you?'

'It's unlikely.'

'So why are we here?'

'Because I don't like loose ends. Heather's spirited them away for a reason. She's lied about not knowing where they are which means she doesn't want anyone else talking to them. Doesn't that make you curious?'

'It makes me angry,' she said. 'If it wasn't for Heather raising Mal's hopes, he wouldn't be on the run right now. He wouldn't have gone AWOL and he wouldn't have gone back to West Henby. She made him think Vicky was his daughter, dangled the prospect in front of him so he'd do something reckless. And now look where we are.'

'She couldn't have known Esther was going to get murdered.'

'I don't think she cared about the consequences. All she's interested in is her stupid book.'

The caravan Heather had rented was on the smaller end of the scale but it looked newish and clean. He knocked on the door. There was no response. He moved to the side and peered in through the window; there were clothes neatly folded on a shelf, and a suitcase in the corner. A box of tea bags, sugar and a bottle of squash were lined up by the tiny stove. 'Someone's still in residence.'

'Out and about then.'

He stood back. 'Okay, let's have a wander and come back in an hour or so.'

They left the car where it was and walked down to the shore. Although the kids were back at school there were still plenty of people around, mostly of an older generation taking advantage of the off-season rates. The beach was lined with stripy deck-chairs. A few courageous souls were braving the sea, but on the whole the visitors were sticking to dry land.

He kept his eyes peeled, scanning the crowds. He had no idea what Hazel looked like but there was chance he might recognise Vicky from the photo he'd been shown. They walked up and down the pier, went into the penny arcades and ate hot dogs sitting on a bench. Lolly seemed entranced by it all, smiling and relaxed, and he thought about everything she'd missed out on as a kid. He was glad she was enjoying herself; tomorrow, he suspected, would be a far less pleasant day.

Neither of them mentioned the kiss she had given him last night. Something had changed between them though. From the moment he'd picked her up this morning, he'd sensed it, a shifting in the way they looked at each other, stolen glances, small smiles, an unspoken understanding that things had started to move on from mere friendship. It was, he admitted to himself, what he'd always wanted. That *she* wanted it too was more than he'd ever hoped for.

At one o'clock they returned to the site and made their way across the grass to Hazel's caravan. This time there were signs of life, an open window and the sound of a radio. He looked at Lolly, raised his eyebrows, and said, 'Here we go then.'

Nick knocked on the door. It was opened by a neat, middle-aged woman with carefully coiffed blonde hair and light blue eyes. She was wearing a sleeveless white summer dress adorned with a pattern of roses. She half smiled, the way people do when they don't know who you are but don't want to appear unfriendly.

'Hazel Finch?'

She nodded. 'Yes, that's me.'

'My name's Nick Trent,' he said. 'This is Lolly.' He held up his ID for her to see. 'I'm a private investigator working on the Kay Fury case.'

Hazel visibly paled. 'What?'

'I was wondering if—'

'I don't know anything about it,' she interrupted before he could explain what he was wondering about. 'I've got nothing to say. Please leave me alone.'

'I'm sorry, but I can't do that.'

'Who told you I was here?'

'Heather Grant,' he replied. It wasn't a complete lie. By telling him about Harlow, she had, in a roundabout way led him to this place. His answer, understandably, both surprised and confused Hazel.

'Why would she do that?'

'She thought you might not have heard the news.'

'What news?'

'About Esther Fury. She was murdered on Wednesday night.'

Hazel's eyes grew wide with shock. 'She's dead? What? Oh my God!' And then her self-preservation instincts kicked in. 'But that's got nothing to do with me. I don't even know the woman. I was here. I haven't . . . I don't understand.'

'If I could just have five minutes?' Nick asked. 'I'd like to clear up a few issues regarding Kay – and your daughter.'

'No,' she said emphatically. 'Leave me alone. You've got no right to harass me like this. I've already told you, I've got nothing to say.'

'All right,' Nick said. 'If you'd prefer to talk directly to the police . . . '

Hazel's mouth dropped open. Something flashed in her eyes – fear, anger? – and her body grew rigid. 'Why would they want to talk to *me*? I can't tell them anything. I've been here, haven't I? You can ask anyone.'

'No one's suggesting you're involved, of course not, but the murder could be connected to Kay's abduction. If you'll just give me five minutes, if we can go over what you told Heather Grant then there won't be a need to take it any further.'

Hazel thought about this for a few seconds. 'If you've already talked to Heather . . . '

'I'd like to hear it directly from you.'

Hazel looked from Nick to Lolly and back to Nick. She

clasped her hands together, unlinked them. Finally, she conceded. 'Five minutes then. You'd better come in.'

It was cramped inside the caravan, especially with three of them in there. He and Lolly sat down side by side on a cushioned bench that probably converted into a bed. 'Your daughter's not here with you?'

Hazel sat down opposite. 'She's meeting some girls in town. They're having lunch together.'

Nick was glad Vicky wasn't there. The mother might talk more openly in her absence. He launched straight into the questions before she could change her mind. 'So, Heather approached you after she discovered you'd had a relationship with Teddy Heath?'

Hazel flinched a little at the mention of Teddy. 'That's right. Said she was writing a book, that my name had come up and . . . But me and Teddy were over way before all that dreadful business. The bastard dumped me, didn't he, as soon as he found out I was pregnant. Didn't see him for dust and not a penny of maintenance.' She scowled, the betrayal still rankling after all these years. 'What kind of a man does that?'

The evil kind, Nick thought, the kind who'd murder, the kind who'd abduct someone else's baby. 'That must have been tough. You never saw him again?'

'No, never.'

'And you had no idea what he'd done?'

Hazel's scowl grew deeper. 'Of course not! You think I'd have stood by and let him get away with it? If I'd thought for one minute . . . Well, I'd have been straight down the police station. I wouldn't have thought twice.'

'How much does Vicky know about her dad?'

'Everything. *Now* she knows everything. She was always aware that he was a waste of space, that he didn't want anything to do with her, but then all that stuff came out at Mal Fury's trial, about how Teddy had snatched that poor baby and Mal Fury had found out and killed him.'

'Mal didn't kill him,' Lolly said, speaking for the first time. 'He died of a heart attack.'

Hazel glanced at her and gave a shrug, as if the details of his death were neither here nor there. 'Anyway, that all came as a shock as you can imagine, to both of us. We didn't even know he was dead. But it was worse for her. I mean, who wants a man like that for their dad? It's not something to be proud of. It's been hard for her coming to terms with it all. The only consolation was that no one else knew.'

'And then Heather Grant came knocking on your door,' Nick said.

Hazel's hands did a dance in her lap. 'I knew what she was thinking as soon as she showed up. It was written all over her face. She saw a photo of Vicky on the mantelpiece, saw she was about the same age as Kay Fury would have been, put two and two together and made five. She was mighty disappointed when I showed her the birth certificate. April tenth, 1958. That's when Vicky was born. It's all there in black and white.'

'I don't suppose you have it with you?' Nick asked.

'Of course I don't. Who brings a birth certificate on holiday with them? But I can show you, soon as we get home. Or you can go and look it up in that place? What's it called? You know, where all the births and deaths are registered.'

'Somerset House.'

'That's it. You go and take a look.'

Nick nodded. For a while, before the evidence was placed before her, Heather must have thought she'd solved a mystery nobody else had been able to. But Kay's birthday was on the first of June. The girls, although born within weeks of each other, were two entirely separate people. 'Okay, but there's one other thing I don't understand. Why did Heather bring you here? What was the point? If, as you say, Vicky is your daughter why are you hiding out in Clacton?'

'No one's hiding,' Hazel said indignantly. 'Who said anything about hiding? We're on holiday, that's all. Everyone's entitled to a break.'

'A break that Heather Grant is paying for.' He wasn't entirely sure of this, but thought it was a reasonable guess bearing in mind what the neighbour in Harlow had told him about a 'niece' whisking them away on holiday.

'Well, so what?' Hazel snapped back, confirming his hunch. 'She was the one who caused all this trouble in the first place.'

'Which particular piece of trouble are we talking about here?'

'With the journalist,' Hazel said. 'Heather said there'd been a leak from her publisher and some journalist had got wind of me and Teddy, one of those tabloid types looking to dig the dirt. She reckoned he might start hassling, trying to pressure me and Vicky into giving an interview.' Hazel's face grew tight. 'We're respectable people. What would the neighbours say? Anyway, she swore she could put a lid on it but it would take a week or so. She felt bad about the leak so she offered us this place for a fortnight, said by the time we got home it would all be sorted. Well, I wasn't going to say no, was I? A free holiday doesn't come along every day.'

Nick was pretty sure there wasn't any journalist and that Heather had only been making sure that nobody – particularly Esther – could discover that the Finch connection was a dead end. If Esther had employed someone to make enquiries, the only thing they'd have discovered was an empty house. Heather had wanted to keep hope alive and she'd succeeded, in Mal's case at least. He couldn't think of anything else to ask and so he rose to his feet. 'Well, thank you for your time. I appreciate it.'

Hazel looked up at him, worry back in her eyes. 'You won't be telling the newspapers any of this?'

'You've got my word.'

Lolly stood up too. 'I'm presuming Vicky would agree to a blood test just so we can draw a line under it all?'

'That's down to her. She's nineteen now. She's an adult. But you'll be wasting your time – and hers.'

Nick and Lolly said goodbye and stepped out of the caravan. Hazel closed the door firmly behind them. As they walked across the grass, Nick asked, 'What made you ask about the blood test?'

'I just wanted to see how she'd react.'

'And?'

Lolly shrugged. 'She didn't seem terrified at the prospect.'

'No,' he agreed.

They reached the car but didn't get in immediately. Lolly gazed over at the sea, lifted her face and sniffed the salty air. She looked downcast.

'You're disappointed,' he said.

'It's what I was expecting, but it's still sad. For Mal, I mean. He just wanted it so much. He'd made up his mind that Vicky was Kay and now . . . '

'Yeah, it's going to be a blow.'

They fell quiet, both lost in their own thoughts. A few minutes passed and neither of them moved. The world carried on around them, people coming and going. Three gulls wheeled overhead. Nick was the first to break the silence. He leaned his elbows on the roof of the car and looked at Lolly. 'I don't know. Maybe we've got it all wrong.'

'What do you mean?'

He shook his head, trying to grasp the thin wisps of whatever was hanging in his mind 'We're missing something. I just can't figure out what.'

60

Saturday 24 September. West Henby

DI Latham roamed the empty house getting his thoughts in order before the others arrived. It was a warm day, a nice start to the weekend and the sun streamed in through the windows. The rooms were full of beautiful items – Persian rugs, paintings, sculptures, clocks – and he took pleasure in them without feeling any envy. He wouldn't have wanted to change places with the owners of these treasures, not for all the porcelain in China. The Furys may have had money, even fame, but happiness had eluded them.

He settled eventually in the library where he sat down on the leather chair. Progress had been made over the last couple of days and he was starting to see a clearer picture. Mal Fury had gone to ground but he would surface eventually. It was the others he was more concerned with at the moment. They all knew more than they were saying.

He picked up the file from the side table, put it on his lap, opened it and read through the first few pages. It was the connections that interested him, the tangled threads that ran between these people. When he studied their statements, it was obvious than no one had a solid alibi for the time in question. That was the trouble with parties, with guests moving around, with snatched conversations, alcohol and distractions. Easy to slip away for ten minutes and for the absence not to be noticed.

The pathologist had confirmed that Esther Fury had drowned. She had still been alive when she'd gone into the lake – her lungs were full of water – and accidental death might have been a possibility if it hadn't been for those bruises at her throat. It was easy to get blinded by the obvious – and often the obvious was true – but he had the feeling darker forces were at work here. Darker forces? He raised his eyes to the ceiling. He was beginning to sound like a detective from some Victorian novel.

The front door opened and closed, followed by the tapping of heels on the marble floor. Mrs Gough back from doing the shopping in the village. He had given her money to buy provisions for lunch; starving his interviewees might loosen their tongues but would probably be frowned upon by HQ.

The housekeeper was currently staying on at the house until she could make other arrangements. He hadn't quite got to grips with her yet. She was a hard-faced, bitter, difficult woman who made no bones of the fact she resented their presence, and yet had volunteered to cook for everyone. Perhaps, in a final act of retribution, she would poison them all.

He raised his head and looked out of the window towards the row of trees and the lake beyond. What had taken place here was the stuff of nightmares. He thought of his own children, grown now, and shuddered. Dealing with the loss of a baby was bad enough but not knowing what had happened for so many years would be enough to send the sanest parent crazy.

The front door opened again and a sturdier set of footsteps made their way across the hall. DS Barry poked his head into the library.

'All set, guv?'

The sergeant didn't approve of the gathering here at the house; such manoeuvrings were outside his comfort zone. He liked everything to be done strictly by the rules, to be black and white with no shades of grey and had accordingly voiced his objections. Latham had duly noted them without changing any of his plans. Sometimes you had to take chances. Sometimes you had to shake things up a bit.

'All set.'

'Not long now.' Barry glanced at his watch and withdrew.

Latham closed his eyes and let his thoughts settle like dust. The motive for Esther's murder lay not in the recent past but in something more distant. He already had most of the answers but by the end of the day he hoped to have them all.

61

Saturday 24 September. West Henby

Lolly and Nick were the last to arrive in West Henby. Nick had been late picking her up, apologising, saying there was something he'd had to do. He hadn't elaborated. Something work related, she'd presumed. She felt her stomach tighten as they approached the house, knowing she was in for a grilling. Could they prove she'd helped Mal to escape – evidence, fingerprints, something left by mistake in the summerhouse? – because if they could she might not be going home tonight. DI Latham had not demanded her presence here today but merely requested it as an aid to their enquiries. Saying no hadn't really been an option. Saying no would have made it look like she had something to hide.

Nick had been distracted throughout the journey and she had given up trying to make conversation once they had passed through the Blackwall Tunnel. Instead she had sat quietly and listened to the radio, letting the music flow over and around her. Now as he parked between Heather's red Mini and a cream-coloured Bentley, he seemed to suddenly focus again.

'Well,' he said, gazing at the Bentley, 'either the police are getting paid way too much or we've got more company than we expected.'

'I think that's the Leightons' car,' Lolly said. 'Claud and Anna. They were at the party.'

'Any particular reason why they'd be here?'

'Claud had an affair – well, *another* affair – with Esther after Mal went to jail. He left Anna for her. They're back together now.'

'Ah, love, hate and revenge – always good motives.'

They got out of the car and walked up the steps. There was a police officer on the door who sent them to the sun room. Here they found Jude and Heather. Mrs Gough was sitting in the corner like a lurking black spider. The Leightons were in the garden, strolling back and forth on the lawn.

Jude looked at them and nodded.

Heather said, 'Hi.'

Mrs Gough didn't bother to acknowledge their presence. Her gaze rose briefly but then descended to the floor again.

Lolly and Nick sat down in the wicker chairs. There was an understandable tension in the room, a feeling of nerves pulled tight. The heady smell of lilies floated in the air. Lolly tried to clear her mind, to drive the fear from her thoughts. She didn't succeed.

'How much longer are we going to have to wait?' Jude asked of no one in particular.

And because nobody knew, nobody answered.

Claud had been grumbling before he arrived and was still grumbling now. 'Why are we even here? It's bloody ridiculous! If Latham wanted to talk to us he could have done it down the station.'

'No one forced you to come,' Anna said. 'It wasn't obligatory.'

'*You* said it would look bad if we didn't.'

'Since when did you ever listen to anything I said?'

If truth be told, Anna was enjoying herself. She liked to see her husband discomfited, his nose put out of joint. And she was fascinated by the gathering of suspects. That she too was a suspect didn't bother her in the slightest; it only added to the thrill. She rather liked the idea of being thought of as a femme fatale, a dangerous woman who was prepared to kill to get what she wanted.

'Go home if you want to,' she said. 'Go, stay, it's up to you, but just stop whining about it.'

Claud threw her a filthy look. 'You're enjoying every minute of this.'

'If you didn't murder Esther you've got nothing to worry about.'

'Balls,' he said. 'Mud sticks and you know it. Anyway, I've got better things to do than hang around here all day.'

Anna shielded her eyes against the sun and smiled. 'I hope you've got your story straight or the only place you'll be hanging around is prison.'

Jude was the first person to be called. He jumped up, hesitated and then strode out towards the library. While he was gone Nick made small talk with Heather. Lolly half listened but didn't join in. She would have liked to go outside – it was stuffy in the sun room even with the doors open – but feared she'd be instantly leapt upon by Anna and subjected to a cross-examination.

She poured herself some squash from a jug left on the coffee table, asked if anyone else would like some, but nobody did. The squash was warm but it was better than nothing. She sat and sipped from the glass, wondering if one of them would be arrested for murder today. Jude? Heather? Even Mrs Gough wasn't above suspicion. Her eyes fell on the Leightons again. They were still walking but there was distance between them now. Claud had a face like thunder. Anna looked pleased with herself.

'No sign of Hazel Finch yet?' Nick asked Heather.

Lolly quickly transferred her gaze.

Heather inclined her head, gave a faint smile and said, 'What, since yesterday?'

Nick smiled back. 'She called you then. I wondered if she would.'

'Yes, she called me. Did you find out what you wanted?'

'You could have saved me the bother of a trip to Clacton if you'd been straight from the start. You knew Vicky wasn't Kay, didn't you? Hazel had already proved that to you.'

'You're the detective,' she said. 'Didn't they teach you to always double-check your sources, to never take anyone's word for anything?'

'So what was the point of saying she'd disappeared?' Nick asked. 'You knew the truth was going to come out eventually. Or where you just playing for time, keeping Mal and Esther's hopes alive while you gathered as much information as you could for your book? Once they knew the Vicky angle was a dead end, they might have changed their minds about collaborating with you.'

Heather shrugged. 'What does it matter now?'

Nick, being provocative, said, 'Esther wouldn't have been too happy if she'd found out. Did she find out?'

But Heather was unfazed. 'Esther never believed it in the first place. She was only letting the book go ahead to spite Mal. It was just another chance to put the knife in.'

Mrs Gough glowered at her from across the room but kept silent.

Lolly was less taciturn. 'You made Mal believe Kay was still alive. If it hadn't been for you, for your lies, he'd never have absconded.'

'I didn't lie about anything. All I said was that there was a chance – and there still was when I told him that. It's not my fault if he took it as rock-solid evidence.'

Lolly knew Heather was twisting the truth, trying to put herself in a better light. In anger she almost blurted out what Mal had told her – about Esther being seen with Vicky, about his fear that his daughter would be snatched from him again – but managed to stop herself. Now wasn't the time to be making stupid slip-ups. Instead, trying to keep her voice steady, she said, 'I don't suppose you discouraged him from believing it though.'

Heather shook her head. 'That's not true.'

Lolly's lip curled but she kept her mouth shut. Better to say nothing more than to risk saying too much. One thing, however, was clear: for all her culpability when it came to Mal's situation, Heather really didn't have a motive for killing Esther. In fact, the opposite was true. Without Esther's input, the book might never get published.

The room fell silent and the exchange left in its wake a bad taste, a sense of something sour. She suspected that this was what the police wanted, for them to turn on each other, for the accusations to start flying, for loyalties to be tested. With Heather an unlikely suspect, her attention moved on to the others. Both Claud and Anna Leighton were capable, she thought, but Jude had to be up there at the top of the list. Her attempt at uncovering his possible guilt had been thwarted by the Cecil brothers. Could he have done it? Would he have done it? She had no choice now but to leave the questions to the law.

*

By the time Lolly was called everyone else had been interviewed. The term 'making her sweat' came to mind. She went into the library with her nerves jittering. Latham and Barry were seated on one side of the desk and she was directed to the chair opposite. From here she had a view of the garden and a glimpse of the lake, the latter a visual reminder – perhaps a deliberate one – of where Esther had died.

'Sorry to have kept you waiting,' Latham said.

Lolly sat down.

The next ten minutes followed more or less the same pattern as her original interview, going over the events of Wednesday night: where she had been, who she had seen, who she had talked to. She kept her answers short and concise, repeating what she'd told them before. Even though everything she said was truthful she felt herself starting to sweat. She knew they were trying to catch her out in a lie, to find some small discrepancy in her responses.

'Let's move on to Jude Rule,' Barry said. 'You've known him a while, I understand.'

'We used to live in the same tower block.'

'In Kellston?'

'That's right.'

'And you were close, the two of you?'

Lolly sensed some trickery in the question. 'We were mates, that's all.'

Barry gave a thin smile. 'Close enough for you to give him an alibi over Amy Wiltshire's murder.'

Although Lolly knew she shouldn't be surprised by the fact they knew about this, it still caught her off guard. 'Being close or not has nothing to do with it. I just told the truth. I was at his flat when it happened; we were watching a film together.'

Barry gave her a sceptical look. 'And would you have still given him an alibi if you hadn't been there?'

She glared at him. 'What sort of a question is that?'

'One you don't need to answer,' Latham said. 'I apologise. No one's suggesting that you gave a false alibi.'

Lolly guessed they were doing that good cop/bad cop thing again, with Barry asking the shitty questions and Latham pretending to be the nice one who was protecting her. 'Well, I didn't,' she stressed. 'I've never done anything like that.'

Latham smiled and nodded. 'Of course not.'

Barry sat back and folded his arms across his chest. 'But you were the one who introduced him to Esther?'

He posed the question as though it was an accusation.

'We lost touch for a while. I moved here and . . . ' She shrugged, thinking of the letters she'd written to Jude, the letters that had gone unanswered. 'Then, after about five years, we got back in touch again. He came to visit.'

'And started a relationship with Esther. Were you happy about that?'

Lolly was doing her best to maintain her cool, not easy when old hurts were being hurled in her face. 'I don't know anything about their relationship.'

'But you said you were mates. Don't mates talk to each other?'

'It was around then that all the stuff between Mal and Esther blew up. Mal was arrested, everything came out about Teddy Heath and . . . '

'You took Mr Fury's side.'

'Yes.'

'And Jude took Esther's.'

'I suppose so.'

'That must have been galling.'

'Not really. I had more important things to worry about.'

Did they believe her? She doubted it. Even to her own ears it sounded implausible.

Thankfully, the subject of Jude was dropped and they moved on to – for Lolly at least – the safer ground of Nick, Heather Grant and the Leightons. The book was discussed for a while. She was vague about it and vague about Claud and Anna too. 'I barely know them. We've only met a couple of times.'

They seemed to come to a natural halt in the interview and for a moment Lolly thought it was over. Papers were shuffled, glances exchanged. Neither appeared to have any more questions. She was trying not to look too relieved when Latham burst her bubble.

'I think we'll break for lunch now. After that, would you mind accompanying us to the lake? We'd like to go over the route you took that night.'

Lolly did mind but she could hardly say so.

62

Saturday 24 September. West Henby

Lunch was served by Mrs Gough – lemon sole, potatoes and peas – before she sat down to join them. There were nine in all gathered round the dining table. Lolly felt the weight of something ominous. The room was overly warm, the atmosphere tense and uncomfortable. Only Anna Leighton seemed at ease, always in her element when she spotted vulnerability. Spoilt for choice, the woman looked around with the hungry eyes of a fox in a henhouse.

'Poor Esther,' Anna said. 'Who'd have thought it would come to this?' She gazed at Jude, her face all mock sympathy. 'How are you bearing up, sweetheart?'

Jude glared back at her. 'How do you think?'

'Yes, it's all been a dreadful shock. I still can't believe what's happened. Such a terrible thing. And now we're all under suspicion . . . although I suppose some more than others.'

'We all know who did it,' Jude said. 'The one person who *isn't* here.'

'Not if he was in Argentina,' Lolly said drily.

'Argentina?' Latham enquired.

The inspector clearly hadn't been apprised of this fanciful titbit. 'Buenos Aires,' Lolly explained. 'Mal was seen there, apparently.'

Latham looked unconvinced.

'It was just a rumour,' Anna said. 'Probably nonsense.'

'Of course it's bloody nonsense,' Jude said. 'If there's one person who wanted her dead, it's him.'

Anna begged to differ. 'Oh, I suspect there's more than one. I mean, when you think about it, we *all* bore our grudges. Take Claud for example.' She glanced at her husband, a sly smile playing round her lips. 'Rejection doesn't sit well with some people.'

'Just shut up, can't you?' Claud snapped. 'No one wants to hear your half-arsed opinions.'

But Anna was enjoying herself too much. She looked at Jude again. 'She'd have done the same to you eventually, my dear. Got bored and cast you aside. Esther had a very low boredom threshold. She picked people up and threw them away; that's just the way she was.'

'And what about you?' Jude said. 'When it comes to motive, you're hardly out of the picture.'

'You're right,' Anna said, almost triumphantly. 'I can't argue with you there. Esther stole my husband, albeit temporarily. I suppose I *could* have killed her for that, but all things considered, I'd be more likely to kill Claud.'

'I'm sure you'll get around to it,' Claud said.

Anna ignored him. 'And what about you, Mrs Gough? I heard that Esther was going to the States and leaving you behind. Or was that just idle gossip? If it's true, I don't imagine you were too pleased about it.'

Mrs Gough paused in her eating, her fork halfway to her mouth. She put the fork down and stared at Anna. 'Mrs Fury is dead,' she said stiffly. 'Have some respect.'

Anna barked out a laugh. 'Respect. Esther didn't know the meaning of the word.' Her gaze flew round the table again, resting briefly on Heather before moving on to Lolly. 'And then there's you, Lita.'

Lolly sighed, already tired of Anna's game. 'What about me?'

'No one would have blamed you, darling, not after the way she treated you. I mean, all those years of contempt, of ridicule. And then just to throw you out like that. Not to mention ... ' She glanced pointedly at Jude. 'Well, if I'd been in your shoes, God knows what I'd have done. Everyone has a breaking point.'

'I never wanted her dead,' Lolly said calmly.

'Really?' Anna said. 'Not even in the darkest depths of your imagination?'

'Not even there,' Lolly said, although it wasn't true. Esther's cruelty, her utter disregard for the feelings of others, had indeed provoked the occasional murderous thought. There was a difference though between thinking it and doing it.

Heather took a sip of iced water – the only refreshment available – and put down her glass. 'I suppose I'm next on your list.'

Anna considered her, obviously trying to come up with a motive but struggling to do so. Eventually she flapped her hand. 'Maybe you fell out over that book you're writing, had an almighty row and ... '

'Ah, yes. We authors are known for our vicious tempers.'

Anna smiled and ate some fish.

Latham wasn't saying much, Barry nothing. Lolly was sure, however, that they were listening to every word. She would have liked to have been sitting beside Nick but had found herself on the other side of the table. There had been no chance to talk to him as her interview had followed directly on from his. She tried to catch his eye, just to make some contact, but he was chasing peas around his plate.

There was silence for a minute, broken only by the scrape of knives and forks.

'And what about Nick?' Heather asked. 'You're not going to leave him out, are you?'

Nick looked up. 'Fire away.'

'I'm afraid you're a minor character,' Anna said, 'in this little drama, I mean. A walk on-part rather than a starring role. I think you can be disregarded as a suspect.'

'I beg to differ.'

'Oh, have I missed something?'

'Stanley Parrish,' he said.

Anna looked blank. 'Should that mean something to me?'

'He was the private investigator Mal employed to try and track down Kay. I think it's fair to say that Esther hated his guts. He died in a hit-and-run, probably not an accident. Maybe I blamed her for his untimely death.'

'And why should it matter to you?'

'Because he was my uncle,' Nick said.

Anna's lips curled up at the corners. 'How interesting. Well, in that case I'll certainly add you to the list. Yes, I believe I recall Esther mentioning him now. Something along the lines of a user and a creep – her words, you understand, not mine. Still, I can't imagine her taking out a hit on him. What do you think, Inspector?'

Latham – who wouldn't talk with his mouth full – finished what he was chewing before replying. 'It's probably better if I keep my thoughts to myself.'

'Better for you, perhaps, but decidedly dull for the rest of us.'

'Speak for yourself,' Claud said. 'Personally, I'd prefer to eat my lunch in peace.'

'Peace,' Anna snorted. 'You won't find much of that in this house. Death and disaster, that's all there is here. Poor little

Kay snatched, Mal sent to prison, Esther murdered. Where's the peace in any of that?'

Latham spoke again. 'Not to mention the nanny. We shouldn't forget about her.'

Lolly saw Nick glance at the inspector, saw a look pass between them. In that moment she realised they both knew something she didn't. She tried to catch Nick's eye again but to no avail. Instead he turned his face towards Heather and said, 'Ah, yes, the nanny. That was tragic. Did you talk to Esther about her?'

'A little,' Heather said.

'It must have been terrible for her family. She got kind of overlooked with all the fuss about Kay.'

'For God's sake,' Jude said. 'Can't we talk about something else?'

Nick took no notice. 'Stanley went to see her parents but he didn't find out much – and not the most important thing. No, unfortunately that was kept hidden from him. Kept hidden from the world, in fact.'

Heather shook her head, her expression bemused. 'And what exactly was that?'

Latham joined the exchange, his face serious, his voice soft but firm. 'Come on, Heather. It's over. It's time to tell us who you really are.'

Everyone stopped eating. There was utter silence. Eight pairs of eyes focused on Heather Grant. Lolly held her breath, confused but riveted, aware that something momentous was about to be revealed.

For a moment it seemed that Heather would continue to play ignorant, but gradually her expression changed. Her face paled and her eyes flashed with anger. She pushed aside her plate and placed her elbows on the table. She glared at Latham. 'The *nanny*,' she spat out. 'Why does everyone call her that? She had a name, you know. She was more than just her job.'

'Yes,' Latham said. 'She had a name – Cathy Kershaw – and a mother and a father . . . and a daughter.'

Heather sucked in a breath and gazed around the table. 'A daughter she wasn't allowed to bring up as her own. No, Cathy had to be sent away, banished, because her parents couldn't bear the shame of her having a child out of wedlock. They preferred everyone to live a lie. Respectability was more important than the truth. I was two years old when she was murdered and I didn't even know she existed until six months ago.'

'How did you find out?' Nick asked softly.

'I found her letters after my mother died. Well, the woman I'd called my mother – Cathy's mother, my grandmother. My grandparents raised me as theirs, you see, moved away so the neighbours wouldn't ask any awkward questions.' Heather's face twisted. 'The letters Cathy wrote were pitiful, pathetic, begging for news about me. She should have been at home and instead she was here, taking care of someone else's baby.'

'So there was never any book,' Nick said. 'You just . . . what, used it as a means to get close to Mal and Esther? Why not tell them the truth, who you really were?'

'Because they'd have just fobbed me off, told me how sorry they were and sent me on my way. I wanted more than that. I wanted to see where Cathy had lived, where she'd died. I wanted to get to know the Furys. I wanted to understand what these people were like.'

'You were looking for someone to blame,' Latham said.

'Teddy Heath was to blame. But they played their part too. It was Esther who brought that man into their lives, and what did Mal do about it? A big fat nothing is what he did. He tolerated her affairs, let her get away with them. They had a toxic marriage and neither of them gave a damn about the consequences of their actions.'

'Too true,' Anna murmured.

Nick kept his eyes on Heather. 'So you used the book as a cover, did some research?'

Lolly couldn't understand why he was still banging on about the book. There were more important things, surely, to be concentrating on.

'I was a reporter, remember? All I had to do was find a plausible lead, a way in. A few months' hard work chasing down Teddy Heath's old friends and Hazel Finch's name turned up. She was the perfect candidate, an old girlfriend with a daughter around the same age as Kay. I knew Mal wouldn't agree to see me unless I had some hope to offer – and so I gave it to him. I wanted him to be here when I revealed who I was, to be here in the place my mother died. I wanted to confront them both, look into their eyes and make them realise what they'd done.'

'But Mal didn't show up,' Latham said.

'No.'

'How did you get Esther down to the lake?'

The question was a leading one and for a moment Heather said nothing. But then, knowing the game was up, she started talking again. 'I told her Hazel Finch was there, that she wanted to talk, that she wouldn't come to the house because of all the other guests. Even though Esther didn't really believe Vicky was her daughter, I knew she wouldn't be able to resist.'

Heather sipped more water, ran her tongue along her upper lip.

'But you were the one who did all the talking,' Latham said. 'You told her who you were, right?'

Heather's face grew dark. 'I knew she was going away soon,

that everything was rosy and going her way. She was going to make a big announcement about getting the starring role in some stupid bloody film, about going to Hollywood, and I couldn't stand that smug expression on her face. She was swanning around like the bloody queen and I was just so . . . I don't know, angry and frustrated, I suppose.'

'And what did she say when you told her who you were?'

Heather's smile was grim and there was venom in her voice. 'She accused me of trying to profit from my mother's death, said I was a greedy little bitch who'd never see a penny from the book. I told her it wasn't about that. It was about them caring, giving a damn about what had happened to Cathy. She'd died protecting *their* baby when she should have been at home with me.' Heather briefly closed her eyes, opened them again. 'She said if Cathy hadn't been so useless, Kay might still be alive today.'

There was a collective intake of breath, a murmuring that rolled into an edgy silence.

'I didn't mean to kill her.'

Lolly could feel the anger growing inside her. All the lies, all the deceit. And Mal left to take the rap for a murder he hadn't committed. She half rose from her seat, but DS Barry, sitting to her right, laid a restraining hand on her arm.

'What happened?' Latham asked softly.

'It was an accident, I swear. I only wanted her to shut up, to stop saying those things. I grabbed hold of her, put my hands around her throat, and there was a struggle. She . . . she staggered back, stumbled and kind of rolled into the water. I don't know, she might have hit her head on something on the bank. I tried to help, to get her out but the water was too deep. I just panicked and ran.'

Lolly stared at Heather along with the rest of them. A

dreadful quiet filled the room. Did anyone believe her? Did the police? She didn't have to wait long for an answer.

DI Latham pushed back and his chair and stood up, his expression grim. 'Heather Grant, I'm arresting you for the murder of Esther Fury . . . '

63

Saturday 24 September. West Henby

It was four o'clock in the afternoon. Lolly and Nick were sitting on the bench by the lake, their eyes fixed on the rippling water. They'd be leaving soon, going back to London, and Lolly had the feeling she would never see this place again. Latham and Barry had already gone, taking Heather Grant with them, and the others – apart from Mrs Gough – had departed soon after. Nick had offered Jude a lift back to Kellston but he'd preferred to take the train. Lolly sat very still, turning everything over in her head.

'You knew about Heather before we went into lunch, didn't you?'

'Latham told me.'

'Why would he do that?'

'Because we pooled our information this morning. I told him what I knew – I'll explain about that later – and he told me what he'd found out about Heather. They'd done a check on her, followed the paper trail and discovered exactly who she was.'

'So why not just arrest her?'

'Because being Cathy Kershaw's daughter isn't a crime.

Latham couldn't prove she'd killed Esther. He knew she'd be on her guard during the interview and so he kept that brief, acted like she wasn't under any kind of suspicion and waited to make his move over lunch. He reckoned the element of surprise might be enough to get a confession.'

'What will happen to her now?'

'If she's got any sense, she'll get herself a decent solicitor and plead manslaughter with diminished responsibility. She'll go to jail but with the mitigating circumstances . . . finding out about her mother like that . . . Who knows? Five, six years?'

Lolly stared hard at the water, feeling the weight of the past crowding in on her. She thought of Cathy Kershaw wheeling the pram beside the lake, looking down at someone else's baby, feeling the torment of being apart from her own.

'Cathy was sixteen when she got pregnant,' Nick continued. 'Unmarried and probably not a hope in hell of getting a ring on her finger. I imagine her parents gave her the choice, adoption or letting them raise the baby themselves. The latter having a condition of course, that she kept her distance and didn't live at home. After her murder they moved again, even changed their name to Grant, so Heather would never find out about her real mum or that she was illegitimate.'

'But the truth always comes out eventually.'

'Not always,' Nick said. 'Some things stay buried for ever. Still, Mal's in the clear now. Do you think he'll hand himself in when he hears that Heather's been arrested?'

'I hope so. They'll give him extra time but he's better off doing that than being on the run for the rest of his life.'

'Yes, he'll want to come back. What I was saying before about telling Latham something . . . well . . . '

Lolly didn't understand his hesitation. 'What? What is it?'

'You might want to prepare yourself.'

'Now you're starting to worry me. Just say it. Tell me.'

Nick left a short pause but finally started talking again. 'The reason I was late this morning was because I went to Somerset House. I wanted to check out Vicky's birth certificate, just to make sure that Hazel was being straight with us.'

'And was she?'

'Only partly.' He took a sheet of paper from his pocket, unfolded it and passed it to her. 'Here, this is it.'

Lolly quickly scanned the details and then looked at him, puzzled. 'I don't get it. It says here that Hazel's the mother and Teddy Heath's the father. Where's the problem? That's what she told us and there it is in black and white.'

'You know what else she told us? That Teddy scarpered as soon as he found out she was pregnant and that she never saw him again. Which put her in the clear as regards Kay's abduction. If she was no longer with Teddy, she couldn't have been a part of it.'

'Okay,' Lolly said, still nonplussed.

'Except . . . ' He put his forefinger on Teddy's name. 'There's a little detail Hazel Finch overlooked. The mother is only allowed to register the father's name in his absence if they're married.'

The penny finally dropped with Lolly. 'And they weren't. So he must have been there with her?'

'Exactly. Which rather belied her claim that she hadn't seen him since her baby's birth. Now why would she lie about a thing like that? That's what I wondered and so I did another search, this time through the deaths register, and came up with the answer.'

'Which is?'

'That Mal was right about Vicky. She *is* his daughter.'

Lolly's mouth dropped open. 'What?'

'Yeah, Hazel's daughter, Victoria, died when she was just a

few months old. Rheumatic fever. Teddy dumped the Fury baby on her after the kidnap went wrong, and did one of his disappearing acts before the law could catch up with him. Hazel's already been picked up by the police. She came clean as soon as she was presented with the evidence of Victoria's death.'

'But why did she keep Kay? I mean, she knew what it meant to lose a child. You don't just take someone else's.'

'You might. If you were disturbed, grieving or just too scared to hand her back. With Teddy gone, she'd be the one to take the rap. Who knows what was going on in her head.'

Lolly wasn't sure what was going on in hers either. She felt shocked, stunned, elated for Mal but scared for him at the same time. What if Vicky rejected him, refused to accept him as her father? How would the girl deal with Esther's death? And with what Hazel had done? What if Mal didn't hear the news about Heather and never came back? There were so many unknowns and they all swirled around her head, jostling for position, bumping and colliding until her temples started to ache.

'So Heather was right,' she murmured.

'That's the irony – she'd found Kay and didn't even realise it. She got so caught up in all her own lies, she couldn't see the truth when it was staring her in the face.'

They both fell quiet. Lolly was thinking about the morning Vinnie had pulled up by the gates, of the cries she'd heard, the cries of a baby. Even now she didn't know where they had come from – an echo from the past or just her mind playing tricks? She gazed at the willows, at their long silvery fronds brushing the surface of the water. Once, in a park long ago, she had asked her mother why they were called that, why they were *weeping* willows. 'Because they come from China and they're missing home.' She supposed it was time for her to go home and yet she couldn't quite bring herself to leave. Just another minute or two . . .

Nick stirred beside her. 'I'm here, you know, if you ever need someone to talk to.'

Lolly nodded and leaned against him, feeling the warmth of his shoulder against hers.

Epilogue

Three Months Later

Everything had changed and yet some things remained the same. Lolly was standing in a prison visitors' queue waiting for her number to be called. After handing himself in to the Garda, Mal had been returned to London where six months had been added to his sentence. He'd taken it philosophically. Once the time was done he'd be a free man again. He'd come back to a blaze of sympathetic publicity – the man who'd been wrongly accused, the man who'd been forced to run to prove his innocence – and now his reputation was restored. A villain one minute, a hero the next.

Naturally he'd said nothing about the help she'd given him at West Henby. Latham had his suspicions but could prove nothing. Perhaps he didn't even want to. Some cases were complicated enough without adding extra paperwork to them.

The day after Mal's return she'd received a letter in the mail, posted from Dublin. Inside was a cash cheque for a grand. She knew he must have sent it shortly before he'd handed himself him, money he'd got for the ring and the necklace. She had gone down to the Fox and given the cash to Terry.

'So are we quits now?'

'Sure,' he'd said. 'We're quits.'

But she knew she'd never work for him again. The trust was gone and it was never coming back. Still, perhaps it was for the best. You could only play with fire for so long before your fingers got burned. There were safer ways to make a living.

She glanced at the clock on the wall and tapped her foot impatiently against the floor. It felt like the bond between her and Mal had grown, been strengthened, after everything that had taken place. Things had changed but not in a bad way. A part of her had feared that she would lose his affection now that his real daughter had been found, that she would be surplus to requirements, but the very opposite had happened. They were closer now than they had ever been.

Vicky had come to see him for the first time last week. In addition, letters were being exchanged, thoughts written down, small connections gradually made. The girl had her own demons to face and nothing would be easy. It would take time but eventually a new family might be forged, unconventional and tinged with tragedy, but with the only thing that was really needed – hope.

Vinnie knew that he had dodged a bullet – and learned a painful lesson in the process. Never trust a bloody woman. He was lucky to be a free man, out on the street, breathing in the lovely London air. Les Poole had been shot through the head three months ago, murdered as he left a nightclub in Soho. The gun used to kill Sandler had later been found in his home. Ballistics had come to his rescue. Or maybe Terry had. To this day he didn't know the truth and doubted that he ever would. There were some questions it was better not to ask.

When he thought of Laura, something still shifted in his

chest, but it would pass. Had she conspired with Poole to have her husband murdered? He didn't think so. He preferred his own version of events where she had simply panicked after her husband's killing, looked for someone to blame and put him firmly in the frame. Well, either way she'd betrayed him and there was no going back.

There was something else niggling in the back of his mind. He had a sneaking suspicion that Terry had arranged for Sandler to be despatched, unaware of Vinnie's relationship with Laura and oblivious to the fact that the killing was going to land Vinnie in the shit. Had he killed Poole too and planted the gun at his house? It was not beyond the realms of possibility.

Anyway, whatever the truth, he was off the hook. He stopped outside the Fox and lit a cigarette. Laura was history, gone, a mistake he would never repeat. Well, not until the next time . . .

Gradually it was slipping from Stella's memory. She could go whole days and not think about it once. She'd read about him in the paper of course, just after it happened. The man stabbed to death at the arches. A travelling salesman called Henry Browning. A wife and three kids. A tiny seed of doubt had entered her mind. But he'd been Freddy, she was sure of it, and there'd been no murders since so she had to be right.

She was drinking less now, getting a grip on things. At the time the other girls had given her a few sideways looks but she'd soon put them straight. She'd been bladdered that night, hadn't she? Barely able to walk, never mind stab a bloke to death. She'd been in the house on Albert Road, passed out on the bed, snoring like a train, when he'd gone to meet his maker. Most of them believed her, and those that didn't – well, she didn't give a toss.

She did still think about Dana, though, still saw her occasionally when she stepped into the kitchen. Some ghosts stayed with you for ever.

Freddy's fears had subsided as the weeks passed. No knock on the door, no more nightmares. Lita seemed to have disappeared from his unconscious world and from the real one. He had gone by her flat a few times, loitered on the green, but hadn't set eyes on her. He decided that he'd been worrying unnecessarily; she wasn't a threat. The fuss about Dana had died down now. She was yesterday's news. Interest in her death had been superseded by the murder of the man at the arches – some loser who'd picked the wrong tart to shag – and even that was fading away.

He would be more careful in future. That was twice he'd got away with it and he wasn't going to risk a third. Kindness was his downfall, wanting to help other people. Dana had thrown it back at him and so too had Amy Wiltshire. He sighed as he thought about Amy. He had seen her arguing with the boy, seen him walk away, seen her face twist as though she was about to cry. All he had done was touch her arm and ask if she was okay.

'What's it to you?'

'I was just . . . '

'Yeah, I know what you were just doing, you bloody pervert.' Her eyes filling with contempt, her pretty mouth taunting him. 'Like young girls, do you? Is that what you get off on? You should be bloody reported. They should lock you up and throw away the key.'

He had taken to carrying the knife because the estate was a dangerous place. He'd felt safer with it in his pocket, the thin blade a protection against unspecified threats. He had seen where it was going with Amy and knew that she was going to scream. What choice had he had? She had brought it on herself.

His mother was grumbling about money again. He stared at her thick legs with their blue knotted veins. He sought out affection, he thought, because he had none in his life. That was *her* fault. She had made him what he was, moulded him, twisted him, crushed him to the point where he could barely breathe. Everything that he was, that he would be, was down to her.

Heather Grant was keeping herself busy behind bars. Her trial was due to start in six weeks and she was still working on her defence. If Mal Fury could get away with murder, why couldn't she? And anyway, it hadn't been murder, not really. She had only lured Esther to the lake with the intention of confronting her, not killing her. Manslaughter was nearer the mark. It wasn't her fault that Esther had drowned. If the bitch hadn't said those things, hadn't taunted her like that . . .

Now all she had to do was convince the jury. She was spending long periods practising her remorseful expression, eyes downcast, lips quivering. With her shoulders slumped, she would look every part the victim that she actually was. Hadn't she suffered too? Hadn't she been to hell and back? Sympathy was what she needed and she intended to get it. She would be prepared for the onslaught of the prosecution, for all their lurid accusations, and would meet them with reason and fact.

She was, however, realistic about her prospects. Getting off scot-free was hardly on the cards. There was, on balance, every chance she would be returning to jail but she refused to be downhearted. Whatever the outcome of the trial, whatever the sentence, there would be a damn good book at the end of it all.

*

In the dead of night, when other men's nightmares echoed through the prison, Mal would think about that moment on the ferry when he had looked down into the water and seen in its depths a chance of release. Death had beckoned to him then and he had almost answered the call. How close he had come to giving up. If it hadn't been for Lita, for her faith in him, her belief, he could not have found the strength to carry on.

He was still coming to terms with Esther's death. Their lives had been linked for so many years, bound by love and hate, by the agony of despair. He liked to remember her the way she had been when they'd first met, vibrant and beautiful, full of life and love and laughter. Perhaps, as a young woman, everything had come too easily to her, her beauty opening doors that were closed to other people, her expectations so high that nothing in the end could really satisfy them. The world had disappointed her, and so had he. By the time Kay was taken, her experience of loss and pain was too limited for her to find a path through. She had fallen back on bitterness, on anger and resentment. She had turned away from love.

Mal had happier things to think about though. Kay – Vicky – was back in his life. He replayed the scene in his head as she'd walked into the visiting room last week and sat down in front of him. What he'd expected to feel was awkwardness, difficulty, and there had been some of that, but there had also been elation. His heart had leapt at the sight of her. He had wanted to take her in his arms, to hold her close, to tell her everything would be okay. All those years and now . . . his child had been restored to him.

Vicky had swept back her long fair hair and gazed at him with eyes full of confusion, of caution. 'I don't know what to say.'

Mal had searched her face for signs of himself, of Esther, but apart from the colour of her hair had found little. It was as though the genes had come together, been shaken and stirred to produce someone quite new. Although there was, perhaps, something of his mother in the arch of her brows, the shape of her mouth . . .

'I know. It isn't easy, is it?'

'I always wanted a dad. When I was a kid, I used to dream about him turning up one day. Even an awful one like Teddy. Anyone would have been better than no one.' She had clasped her hands together, stared down at the table, glanced up again. 'You must hate her. Mum, I mean. What she did. Holding on to me like that, lying about it all.'

Mal did hate Hazel Finch, loathed and despised her, but knew, for his daughter's sake, that he must keep these feelings to himself. It would not be long until the trial and then Hazel would go to prison, but it wouldn't even begin to pay back the time that had been lost or the agony she'd inflicted. 'There's no point in looking back.'

'I hate her too,' she'd said, 'but I love her as well. That's what's so confusing. She's the only mother I've known. Do you understand?'

He'd nodded. 'Of course.'

'I knew you would.'

She had suddenly reached out and laid her hand over his. He had felt its warmth, felt love surge through him. Her lips had curled into a smile. 'I'm so glad you found me.'

These were early days, first steps. The joy he felt at finding his daughter was tempered by the reality of the long journey that lay ahead. Nothing could bring back the years that had been lost. Biology linked them, blood, but would that be enough? He feared rejection, feared losing her for a second time, but refused to relinquish hope. He would look forward and not back. He would take whatever she could give and be grateful for it.

It was not that long now until Christmas. The streets they had strolled through had a festive feel, the shop windows lit up by fairy lights and glistening with artificial snow. Lolly still had 'Silent Night' rolling harmoniously through her head, an echo from the Salvation Army band they had passed at Camden station.

The first-floor flat they had come to view was a reasonable size – not huge but not tiny either. Its position on the busy Camden Road meant that the rent was more affordable than in quieter spots. She didn't mind the noise from the traffic, the buses and cars going by almost constantly. That sense of movement, of change, was what she liked best. The country had its charms but she was a city girl at heart.

'What do you think?' Nick said, looking around the empty living room. 'It's not too bad, is it? We've seen worse. And there's a market here at Camden Lock. You'll be able to sell your stuff.'

'Stuff?'

He grinned. 'Sorry, let me rephrase that – your excellent restorations.'

'Better.'

They examined the kitchen, the bathroom and the bedroom, seeing nothing to put them off. Back in the living room they stood side by side and gazed out of the window. It was dark outside but the road flashed bright with the headlamps of cars. Across the road a group of strangers waited for a bus.

'I got a call from Terry,' Nick said.

She looked at him, surprised. 'What did *he* want?'

'He said he'd made some enquiries about Stanley, that he'd heard – although he couldn't swear to it – that it wasn't an accident. Joe Quinn probably was responsible for his death.'

'Did he say why?'

'Only that Stanley had been asking awkward questions. That's the way of it, unfortunately; you turn over too many stones and eventually the nasties slither out. He was only investigating the Fury case but Quinn thought he was interested in something or someone else. He saw Stanley as a threat and decided to get rid of him. Terry wasn't forthcoming over the details.'

'Does it help, knowing the truth? Or part of the truth?'

'I suppose it draws a line under it all.'

Lolly wondered why Terry had bothered to call. Some kind of return, possibly, for the information they had given him on Laura and Les Poole. Or a parting gift to the little girl who had once run errands for him. Maybe he had seen what she had until recently failed to see: that Nick's peace of mind, his happiness, was important to her.

She slid her hand into Nick's, thinking of everything that had happened. How would she have coped without him? He had stood by her throughout, solid as a rock, and she knew he would never let her down. But she valued more than his reliability. He got her in a way that no one else did, understood what made her tick. To him she was not defined by the struggles of Kellston or the debatable privilege of West Henby; she was just herself, a girl who was, apparently, worth loving.

'So what do you reckon?' he asked.

She had no doubts about Nick, about the flat, and only asked the question in case he still had. 'You don't think it's a bit soon for us to be moving in together?'

'Probably. You could have all sorts of bad habits I haven't found out about yet.'

'I don't have bad habits, only charming ones.'

He laughed and looked into her eyes. 'Shall we take a chance then?'

Lolly didn't hesitate. Life, she decided, was too short. 'Let's do that. Let's take a chance.'